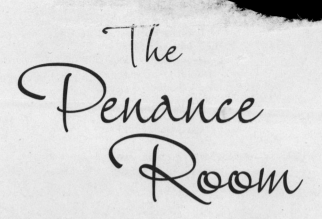

The Penance Room

WITHDRAWN FROM STOCK

LIMERICK
0068433 8
COUNTY LIBRARY

Carol Coffey

D0313500

POOLBEG

of fiction. The names,
portrayed in it are the work of the
Any resemblance to actual persons,
events or localities is entirely coincidental.

Published 2011
by Poolbeg Press Ltd
123 Grange Hill, Baldoyle
Dublin 13, Ireland
E-mail: poolbeg@poolbeg.com
www.poolbeg.com

© Carol Coffey 2010

Copyright for typesetting, layout, design
© Poolbeg Press Ltd

1

The moral right of the author has been asserted.

A catalogue record for this book is available from the British Library.

ISBN 978-1-84223-452-5

All rights reserved. No part of this publication may be reproduced or
transmitted in any form or by any means, electronic or mechanical,
including photography, recording, or any information storage or retrieval
system, without permission in writing from the publisher. The book is sold
subject to the condition that it shall not, by way of trade or otherwise, be
lent, resold or otherwise circulated without the publisher's prior consent in
any form of binding or cover other than that in which it is published and
without a similar condition, including this condition, being imposed on the
subsequent purchaser.

Typeset by Patricia Hope in Sabon 11.5/15.5
Printed by CPI Cox & Wyman,UK.

www.poolbeg.com

Note on the Author

Carol Coffey grew up in Dublin and now lives in County Wicklow. She has a degree in Special Education and is currently completing a Master's Degree in Social, Emotional and Behavioural Difficulties. Her first novel, *The Butterfly State*, was also published by Poolbeg.

ALSO BY CAROL COFFEY

The Butterfly State

Published by Poolbeg

Acknowledgements

Thanks to Paula Campbell of Poolbeg Press both for the opportunity to publish this book and for her on-going support and encouragement. Thanks also to all Poolbeg Press staff including David Prendergast, Sarah Ormston, and the Accounts and Warehouse staff for getting this book from my computer to the shelves. A special thanks to Gaye Shortland for her eagle-eyed editing and her endless patience.

WITHDRAWN FROM STOCK

For my brothers and sisters

Chapter 1

"Mum!" I scream as I jump from my bed and stare into the darkness. Sweat drips from my face and, as my breathing eases, I realise that I have dreamt the same dream once again and have woken as usual just in time to feel the vibrations of the 3 a.m. freight train to Sydney as it passes by the back of our house. I can never understand how its passing doesn't wake any of the residents in my mother's nursing home where I live. I am the only one who is woken by its passing and left to roam the hallways unable to return to sleep.

I slip quietly from my room past the nurses' station where Aishling is sitting writing her notes. She doesn't notice me and I am relieved about that. She doesn't like me creeping around at night but I can never sleep after that dream and feel a need to be near my mother. I walk downstairs. When I reach the hall I can see a sliver of light coming from under the door of the bathroom beneath the stairs and I wonder if my father is also awake. I move towards the front of the house where the vibrations of the trains are not so disturbing and where my parents' room is. I pass a large ward on my right whose residents are referred to as

1

"the babies": nine men and women who can no longer do anything for themselves and who lie in bed all day, looking at the ceiling or with eyes closed so tight you'd think they were afraid to open them. I pass the kitchen, the dining room and the large bay-windowed lounge room where the residents while away their days, and then I turn the handle of my parents' room across the hall. I look down at my mutilated foot from which I still feel pain, a punishment for my stupidity. It happened almost five years ago when I was eight years old. I was playing with my friends on the train line, something my parents didn't want me to do because of my hearing.

I can see the accident like a film reel whose middle is caught in the projector and you can only watch the first part of the movie over and over. I am throwing stones into the small waterhole on the opposite side of the track at the back of our house. It is almost lunch-time and I decide to walk along the tracks behind my friends. They don't want to play and I plead with them to spend more time outdoors. I try to entice them by trick-acting on the tracks but they ignore me and walk down the line towards their homes. My memory goes fuzzy then, and there are things about that day that I cannot remember or perhaps that I don't want to remember. Foolish things. But I do remember the rumble of a distant train, the vibrations running up my feet and moving through me like a bolt of electricity. I remember my friends' mouths opening and closing quickly. Simon, who used to be my best friend, is jumping wildly and waving his arms. I realise that he is trying to warn me and turn around just in time to see the train bearing down on me. I know the timetables by heart and think that it is earlier than normal, which I guess is a strange thing to think about when a train is coming at you. Everything seems to move in slow motion and it is like I am describing something that happened to someone else in another lifetime. Frame one: I try to run but my lace is caught. Frame two: I fall and try to get my shoe off as the rumble of the train increases. Then the reel snaps and my next memory is being carried by my mother towards the house. I want to close my eyes but her mouth says, "Stay awake, Christopher, stay with me," as I drift into a deep sleep. When I wake up I am in a different place. A tight bandage is tied around what is left of my foot. I can see my mother crying at the bottom of the bed. She looks faded and misty in the strange light. My father's big shoulders are drooped forward as though I have taken the very life out of him. I have never seen his face, usually scorched by the hot Australian sun, so ghostly pale. I can tell that all his hopes for me, his only child, are gone.

I don't think I have recovered from the shame and regret I felt that day and although I try, I worry that I can never make it up to them.

I limp closer to my mother's bed where she is sleeping soundly. My father is missing so I know it is him in the bathroom. She looks as though she is smiling and her long dark hair falls over the white pillow. She is beautiful and I have often seen my father say this. I think she senses me since she touches the locket around her neck in which she has a photo of me when I was younger. She half-opens her eyes. "Christopher?" she asks but I slink back into the darkness and leave the room. My mother doesn't get enough sleep and has to get up twice during the night to help Aishling turn some of the patients to prevent bedsores.

I am fully awake now and feel that it would be useless to return to bed. I decide to wander around the nursing home, which is a habit I have developed since my accident. The home used to be a boarding house for workers when the mine was busy in the 1940s. It is the last house on Menindee Road and lies at the bottom of a small hill that sweeps up steeply on either side of it – which is where the name "Broken Hill" comes from. There is rolling countryside to the right and the town is a short distance to the left.

3

I climb the stairs. There are five rooms on each side of the narrow upstairs corridor. Aishling's room and mine face each other at the back of the house and are divided by the narrow stairwell that leads to the lower floor. She is the only nurse who lives in and has worked for my mother almost since she arrived in Australia about fifteen years ago. Not everyone here needs nursing care. Some of the people are boarders but have no family to help them, so they live here on the upper floor.

Wilfred Richter sleeps in the room next to mine. He is from Germany and is in his fifties, younger than most of the residents. One of the nurses said he was a Nazi during the Second World War but I don't know if this is true. He knows I love history and used to tell me all about his life in Germany when he was a boy. But he doesn't talk much any more.

I pass his room and the bathroom and stand for a moment outside Jimmy Young's room. His door is slightly ajar and I can see him curled up in his bed. He is one of the few residents who was born in Australia and came to live here after he had a stroke and could no longer run his farm. His speech is hard to understand and the left side of his body doesn't work very well. I look at him as he sleeps and like how still he is. When he wakes, he bangs things around his room, looking for attention. I understand how he feels. It is hard when people ignore you because they cannot understand what you want. I have a voice but I don't use it, unless I am afraid or get a fright like when the train wakens me. When I was little and still had some hearing, I didn't like the sound my voice made. My words didn't sound like other people's. The staff ignore me like they do Jimmy but, unlike him, I don't bang things and I try to stay out of everyone's way.

Martin Kelly is next. He has a disease in his lungs which makes him cough up black phlegm and a clot on his brain that gives him headaches. My mother says that one or other of these conditions will kill him some day.

When I get to his room, I notice that Aishling is standing in his open doorway. He is out of his bed and flailing his thin arms around the room.

"Help! Help me! Someone, please!"

He looks straight at me and then turns to Aishling. He says something to her and I watch as the side of his mouth moves backward and forward. He has forgotten that I am deaf and I can only lip-read if he faces me. I wonder if he is dying. I see death a lot around here. I am used to it. My mother says death is simply another part of life and is nothing to be afraid of. I think she is right. I move around him to make sure I can follow his words.

"Can you see her? Can you?" he asks.

"Martin, there is no one here, now go to sleep. You're waking everyone up," Aishling tells him crossly.

"It's my wife. She's come for me. She's right behind you. The boy can see her." He looks at me. "Can't you?" he asks and I hang my head.

Aishling blesses herself quickly and takes a deep breath. "There is no one here. Your wife died fifteen years ago, Martin," she scolds him. "And if she were here, she'd probably be haunting you, you old scoundrel!" Locals in the town have told her that Martin was known to beat his wife throughout their marriage. "I'll leave your light on, all right?" She's feeling slightly sorry for the old man who is tormented day and night by imaginary attackers.

I follow Aishling out and watch while she returns to her small desk outside my room. I look out the window at the other end of the hallway which faces the front of the house. It is a beautiful night and a full moon shines directly on to our sign: "*Broken Hill Nursing Home and Day Care – Vacancies. Proprietors Emma & Andy Monroe.*" I look at the large gum tree, which is shining in the moonlight, and remember swinging from its branches when I was younger. I can see our cat, Paws, licking his lips and meowing on the fence although I cannot remember what this sounds like.

I walk along the other side of the hallway. Mr and Mrs Klein's room is first. They are the only married couple here and at the moment they are the people I am most interested in. Neither of them can remember our names any more or the fact that they were once prisoners in a concentration camp. Neither do they remember that their son Jacob died at the camp, which my mother says is a blessing. Despite being in his eighties, Aron is still a tall, broad man. His face is deeply lined and his eyes are a sad deep brown and always look far away, even if he is staring straight at you. Iren is a tiny woman who sits shrivelled up in a chair all day. She calls his name most of the time even though he is right beside her and rarely leaves her side. He pats her hand and hushes her when she cries and she settles if only for a while. I walk over to their bed and watch as he sleeps with his arms wrapped tightly around her tiny shoulders. My mother says he has cancer in his lungs and that she will soon have to move them downstairs. He coughs loudly and shifts. I am afraid that he will wake and I leave their room quickly.

I pass by Mina Jensen's room on my tiptoes. She never seems to sleep and if she hears me she will start shouting that the Japs are coming and Aishling will know that I have been creeping around. Mina was a prisoner of war in Indonesia during the Second World War. She boards here as she was afraid to live on her own when her husband died. She walks with a frame and has two long scars on her hips. She is not as confused as some of the other residents but sometimes it seems like she doesn't remember that the war is over. She hides food underneath her clothes and is afraid of Li, our cook, who is Chinese not Japanese but Mina doesn't seem to know the difference. Each night, when the staff help her to her bedroom, they take away the food that she has hidden in her clothes. She begs for it to be returned to her and my mother has to calm her down. She doesn't believe that there will be more food tomorrow and the day after that and my mother says it might have been better if she had died back then because her mind is still a prisoner and only her body is free. I worry that when she dies her soul will be trapped in the war and she will spend eternity searching for food. I am like that, an unusual child. I worry about things that most other kids probably don't even know about.

Next to Mina is Father Francis Hayes. He was a Catholic priest and is from the same part of Ireland as Aishling. He is senile now and often forgets how to speak English but my mother says that, long before he became confused, his mind broke and his Church sent him here. He often cries for no reason and sometimes Aishling is woken from her day-time sleep to comfort him in Gaelic. She hushes him and he smiles and calls her 'A stór' – which Aishling says means 'my darling'. My father, who is from the Hebrides in Scotland, can speak this language even though some of the words from his island are different. I see him speaking with Aishling sometimes and watch as their mouths move in a strange fast way. My mother doesn't like to see them speak together but I don't know why. Perhaps it is because like me, she doesn't know what they are saying and she feels left out of this part of my father's life.

Two sisters, Penelope and Victoria Miller, live in the room before Aishling's. Their father was a lieutenant in the British army and they spent their childhood in army camps all over the world. Despite being born in and eventually settling in Australia, they speak with upper-class English accents and the nurses sometimes mock them if they think my mother will not hear. The spinsters dress almost identically and live their lives by a strict routine. If a meal is late, or they cannot find a belonging, they become so distressed that my mother has to send them on top-secret government work around the nursing home which quietens them for a while.

I wander slowly back to my room and stare out my window

at the tracks that are visible even in the darkness. The train has long since passed and I feel a sense of relief even though I know that I will relive it all again tomorrow night. All day long trains pass here carrying goods and passengers to and from Sydney but, for some reason, only the 3 a.m. train frightens me. Perhaps that is because in three short hours the house will come alive with the movement of staff and residents and in the vibrations of life, or what is left of it, I will not notice the trains coming and going. As I ease myself back into my bed, I gaze around the room. As every other room is occupied by residents, the staff sometimes have to use my room for storage. Large boxes of medical supplies line the wall on the right making large, unusual shapes in the darkness. I lie down and turn on my side. As I enjoy the cool breeze from my open window, I stare at the ceiling and pray that I may drift off again into what will hopefully be a peaceful sleep.

Chapter 2

When I awake I find that I have slept in yet again. I stretch and wonder what time it is. My watch appears to have stopped during the night. I shake it but the second hand doesn't move. It has been doing that a lot lately. My room is hot with the morning sun but a welcome breeze starts to blow against my fly-screen, cooling my face. I limp over to my window and look out onto the back of our property. I can see Simon and Philip making their way down the train line towards school. I wave but their eyes are looking downwards, out of the glare of the sun. I have never been to school and would have liked to go with my friends, even for one day, but my father said they could not teach me there.

A train comes slowly down the track and I strain my neck, worried that my friends are still walking east, towards the town, but I cannot see them in the glaring light. I was on a train once when I was five. I still remember getting dressed up with my parents, my thick brown hair slicked back like my father's, my mother fussing, making sure Aishling remembered everything that needed to be done while she was away. The direct train to the hospital in Sydney took almost fourteen hours so we would have to stay two nights with a friend of my mother's there. My mother packed sandwiches and water into a basket and we set off. When the train pulled out of the station in Broken Hill, I watched as people waved and laughed, opening their mouths wide and closing them again. My father held me tightly by the hand as we walked down the wood-panelled hallway and sat in a carriage on our own. Someone was eating freshly made bread and I could feel my mouth watering from the smell. Even though it was still early morning, my mother was already sweating in her long patterned skirt and boots and dabbing her forehead with a white handkerchief. The seats in our carriage were deep red and had matching red-velvet curtains over a large window from which I could watch the towns speeding by. Towns I had never been to and have never got to since. Darnick, Condobolin, Katoomba and Parramatta. I could read these names even though I should have been starting school only that year. My father used to teach me in the evening when he got home from work and said that because I was partially deaf I needed always to be ahead of kids my age. I am well ahead by now.

For most of the journey, my father held a newspaper in front of his face while my mother looked at me with that frown on her forehead that told me she was worried. I smiled at her and her eyes watered. She looked away and my father suddenly held out his hand to her and squeezed hers. I remember it all so well.

I remember the sadness in my father's face the following morning when the doctor told him the last of my hearing was gone and there was nothing to be done for me. My mother cried and Father hushed her gently. He doesn't like to see her crying, even now. My father told the doctor that he was wrong, that I always knew what he was saying. The doctor insisted that I was already lip-reading. He told me he was going to ask me a question and turned me away from him. I waited but I didn't hear anything until I was turned around again into my father's arms. He hugged me so tightly that I knew it was bad news.

That afternoon, we got on another train to a special school in

Sydney that the doctor had asked my parents to visit before we returned home. I saw them arguing in the station. My father was saying "No. Never." My mother was standing firm. She looked cross, an expression she doesn't wear often.

When we arrived at the school, it was brightly lit and children walked down white-painted hallways. I saw my father say the silence was creepy. He didn't know what life was like in my world. Children were making shapes with their hands, moving them quickly and nodding to each other. Sign language. This is what the doctor wanted me to learn. My parents talked to a white-haired woman in her office and I was left outside watching the children talk with their hands, swinging my legs on the hard wooden bench.

Then the office door opened abruptly and my father walked out quickly, startling me, my mother behind him looking upset. His face was red but not because of the sun. He was angry.

He lifted me up into his arms and said to my mother, "No. I'll get a tutor to teach him this language but he is staying with us where he belongs."

And so he did. A tutor named Thomas Smithers came and lived in Martin's room. He taught sign language to me, my parents and even some of the staff. I have not had a tutor for a long time now.

I know that my father regrets not sending me to that school where I might have learnt all sorts of things. I know he thinks that I would not have had my accident because I would not have been here. And I know my mother thinks this too and that, although she blames him, they rarely talk about it. They are both too sad.

I sigh and pull my blind down to shield my room from the sun. We don't have air-conditioning and the house needs a lot of repairs but my mother cannot afford it. I walk slowly downstairs and make my way to the lounge room, a large room with deep bay windows that have long stained-glass panels running along the sides of the glass. There the residents sit around in a large circle, staring at each other or into space. My father calls it the Penance

Room because some of the residents, who were once at war with each other, now spend their days looking into each other's faces. But there is another reason for the name. My mother's father was a minister who came from England to work with the Aboriginal people when he was a young man. I don't remember him or my grandmother who helped him in his work. When bushfires burned the roof of the church, some of Grandfather's congregation helped him and my father to carry some of the smaller wooden pews to this house where they placed them along the bay window overlooking our garden. With the stained-glass panels behind, it does make the room look a little like a church.

I stand by the doorway and look into the room. Mina Jensen is hiding food from the dining room under her skirt. Wilfred is sitting on a side pew which faces into the room, a blank expression on his face. Facing him are Mr and Mrs Klein. As usual she is calling him: "Aron! Aron!" He smooths her arms and says something in Hungarian which is the language of the country they were born in. Penelope and Victoria are of course wearing matching dresses and brooches and are reading the romance books that the staff buy for them. When they arrived here, my mother tried very hard to get them to wear different clothes but it upset them so much that she wondered if sometimes it is too late to help.

Jimmy is staring at Martin. Kora said he hates Irish people and that he and Martin used to fight each other when they were younger. But Martin was born in Australia too and I wonder how long it takes before you get to be Australian. Kora is my aunt or a "kind of aunt" and she works here almost every day. Her mother was Aboriginal and Kora went to live with my grandfather when she was eight. Kora says that she doesn't remember her parents and that because her father was white, she was taken from her mother when she was three and sent to an outback orphanage run by the evangelists. She remembers being very happy there. My grandfather was the minister for the home and when my mother and Kora became friends, Grandfather "adopted" Kora and took her with him when the family left to open a ministry in Broken Hill. But it wasn't always a happy situation. I saw my mother telling Father that when Kora was a teenager, she became obsessed with finding out who she really was and she ran away lots of times. When my grandfather found her she would say that she was looking for her real family and that she hated him. Mother said Kora was very unhappy then and that she still resents my grandfather for taking her from the only place her real mother could find her. Kora told my mother that when she lived in the orphanage, she didn't think much about her family or how she came to be at the home but, when she left its security, she wondered if every Aboriginal woman she saw could be her mother. She wrote to the home she had been at and found out that her father had been a drifter named Hill. Her mother's name was not recorded and she didn't even know if Kora, which means "companion", had been the name her mother gave her. She told my mother that it was fitting that she had ended up in Broken Hill because that is exactly how she saw herself, Kora Hill, damaged beyond repair. Mother said that Kora wanted to know simple things like when her real birthday was and that until she found her family she could never get on with her life, that she could never be truly happy. With the help of my grandfather, she began her search but never found them. My mother likes to call Kora her sister and, even though they smile at each other and laugh together, I don't think Kora likes this. She stopped writing letters many years back but she never gave up hope that her family would find her one day.

I smile at Kora but she is busy with Mrs Soldo, one of the day patients whose families work and need someone to look after them during the day. Jana Soldo is from Yugoslavia and came to Australia as a war widow. She dresses in traditional Croatian clothes and has worn only black since her husband died almost thirty years ago. Her daughter is a teacher in the town and drops her mother off every morning. I often watch as Dora Soldo kisses her mother tenderly and sits her down in the Penance Room. It doesn't seem to me that Jana has any penance to do.

Usually, I sit in the room and watch the residents talking about their lives but today when an ambulance pulls up I remember that it is Tuesday and that Aron is due at the hospital for treatment. Iren is too weak to go with him and it would take two staff to accompany them both, which my mother cannot spare. I watch Tina, our part-time nurse, climb into the ambulance with Aron. He no longer understands why he has to go to the hospital and struggles for a moment with the ambulance driver. I think he is reliving memories of uniformed officers pushing him in the concentration camps. I often know what people are thinking. Like I said, I am an unusual child and I have seen some of the staff say this. One day, I was watching Tina from the doorway. She was talking to Rita, one of the other nurses. Tina picked up a photo of me as a little boy. When Rita, who was new, asked about me Tina put her finger to her head and made a "crazy" gesture. Even though she came to Australia from Italy as a teenager, she still speaks in a halting style. She said, "Very strange boy, always standing in doorways, always watching . . . crazy boy . . . but Emma and Andy, well, they never seem to notice," and she shook her head as she dusted my photo. I tried not to cry and hid in my room for hours reading the schoolbooks that I had already read from cover to cover.

As the ambulance driver pulls away, Iren starts to scream for her husband: "Aron! Aron!"

Wilfred, who was sitting quietly reading the newspaper, stands suddenly and leaves the room. He cannot stand to hear her calling out. It brings painful memories to him. Kora takes her by the hand and sits her beside Jana Soldo who is still smiling into space. Jana takes over from Aron and smooths Iren's hands and she settles, if only for a while.

Chapter 3

At five thirty I leave my room where I have spent the afternoon reading and wander into town, hoping to pass a couple of hours. Just outside our house a magpie is screeching from the gum tree where she has made her nest. I watch her mouth open and close over and over. My friend Simon said magpies make an awful sound, almost as bad as the screech of bats that live in the barn at his farmhouse. I think that just once I would like to know what that sounds like for I have little memory of the sounds my parents say I used to be able to hear.

When I reach the top of our road I turn left onto Crystal Lane where there are usually a few children playing in the late afternoon, but there is no one about so I venture further down side streets and laneways looking for company. I see a group of boys playing a game of rugby on some wasteland. They are older than me and I don't know any of them so I move on.

I remember my father taking a photo of the sunrise near here when I was about seven. I remember him putting his hands on my face and saying: "Look, son, a beautiful new sunrise in a beautiful new country. Fresh chances here, Christopher, fresh chances." But I was younger then and didn't know anything about fresh chances. My home and my mind were full of wars and disappointments.

I turn down Beryl Street and go into the park to read the inscription on the Titanic Memorial. It was built for the band on the ship that played to the very end even though they knew the ship was sinking and they were going to die. I used to dream that one day I would be known for my bravery and that my name would be on a memorial stone for helping others.

I leave the park and walk home via Sulphide Street where I will have to cross the tracks. I try to face my fear every now and then. On my way I see Maria Moretti standing on the street corner where she used to live before her house was torn down. Her grandfather's tailor's shop is just across the street but he is ill and doesn't sell much stuff now. I saw my mother say that Joe Moretti was thinking of closing the shop after almost forty years in Broken Hill. Maria is wearing her usual white dress and she stares at me as I pass. We are the same age though she looks much younger and if she was a boy I would like to be her friend. I wave at her and her sad brown eyes look back at me. Sometimes I think she is as lonely as me and that I should hang around with her even if she is a girl.

By the time I arrive back at my house, my father is returning home from work in his truck. It is spattered with orange mud from the mine where he works as an engineer, a profession he once hoped I would follow him into. My mother meets him at the gate and I watch as they kiss under the red sky. They both look tired as they lead each other by the hand into the house. I sit a while longer on the porch and take in the smell of the heat. The sky is a canvas of red and orange streaks and everywhere people and animals are looking forward to the cool evening.

When I eventually come inside, Aishling is awake and ready for her night shift. She is writing another letter to Ireland even though no one ever answers her. Kora is still here and is tending to Aron who has returned from his treatment and is feeling ill. Kora is an excellent nurse even though she didn't do her nurse training. My grandfather pleaded with her to travel to Sydney with my mother where he hoped they would both train as nurses, but she didn't want to leave Broken Hill and still lives in the tiny house they all shared when my grandparents were alive. I saw her say that she had moved so much already that her roots would never grow. I look at Aron and know that my mother will ask the hospital to stop his treatment. I know her every move. She will not put him through it any more.

In the evenings my father likes to liven up the atmosphere in the house and, though he is often tired, he doesn't show it. Some nights Wilfred agrees to play the violin for the others. He usually needs coaxing but he will do anything for my father as they share a love of music and history. My father plays the fiddle but sometimes when he plays he looks so sad that I cannot bear to watch him. He plays traditional Scottish and Irish tunes and Aishling loves to sit in the window and listen. She looks so far away that I know she is imagining herself in Ireland with its cool rain and soft sunshine but I know that she can never go back there. These evenings rarely turn out as my father hopes. Most of the residents stare into thin air with moist eyes and quivering chins and I know that this is not what my father has in mind. He wants to remind them that they must have known happy times. They must have some happy memories. So on Tuesdays and some Fridays, Bill comes in with his guitar. He is a friend of my father and can play the sorts of tunes that cheer everyone up, everyone except Wilfred who is a classically trained musician and doesn't like this sort of music. He says it is not pure. You cannot keep everyone happy. I often think it is my job to make people happier before they die even though I don't know how to go about it. I think this is why I am here, to figure it out.

Kora leaves just as my father brings around small glasses of whiskey for anyone who wants it. She doesn't like alcohol and believes it was the ruination of her people, but it could also be because her adoptive father brought her and my mother up to believe alcohol was sinful and made the devil's work easy. I know now that there is no devil. Just our own minds tormenting us for our failures.

Bill sits himself down on one of the softer seats and takes a large sup of whiskey. He asks for requests and doesn't seem to mind when only Jimmy and Martin answer him. As he breaks into song I can see some of the residents' toes tapping. Penelope and Victoria sway slightly to the rhythm but are careful to behave like ladies. Iren sits bolt upright and opens her eyes so wide that it looks as though she has just woken up after years of sleeping. Her husband smiles and asks her for a dance. She agrees and they sit smiling together, neither getting to their feet. There is a part of them that knows that they will fall. Father Hayes is also smiling and tries to sing along even though he doesn't know the words. I watch his mouth move differently to Martin's and Jimmy's who have both finished their whiskey and have beckoned to my father for more before my mother wakes up. Mina also looks happy and taps her tiny feet to the beat that I can feel in the far pew under the window, my favourite seat. My father asks her to dance and she laughs like a young girl. He lifts her to her feet and moves her slowly around in tiny circles, careful not to put pressure on her hip replacements. Aishling gets Father Hayes up and waltzes with him. His eyes are shining and he speaks to her in English. I see him say, "I've been looking all over Mount Tubber for you, Deirdre," and Aishling plays along and tells him she was looking for him too and is glad to have finally found him. Her kindness brings tears to my eyes. Bill moves into a faster tune and my father asks Aishling for a dance. As they swirl around the room everyone claps except Wilfred who walks out briskly. Everyone ignores him but I can see the look of disappointment on my father's face. He worries about Wilfred. Aishling leaves the room to check on the babies but returns quickly to enjoy the music. I wish that we could have the party in the babies' ward so everyone could join in. It would be nice if the music woke them from their endless sleeping. It gives me an idea to ask my mother to put on the radio that is perched high on a shelf in their room. It is wrong to live in silence if you don't have to.

As Bill starts another song my father leaves the room. I am hot on his heels as usual. The evening is almost over anyway so I will not miss much. My father climbs the stairs and goes to Wilfred's room. When we enter we find him kneeling at his bed crying. My father touches his shoulder to comfort him. I know that Wilfred is thinking of his family again. The war ended almost thirty years ago but he never gave up on finding them.

"Wilfred, come back to the party. Perhaps you'll play a tune for us?"

Wilfred shakes his head, which he has lowered to hide his tears. My father has seen him cry many times but Wilfred is still embarrassed by it.

"I'm sorry, Andy, but I don't feel like music tonight."

My father sits down on the bed and looks around the room, which is full of photos of Australian scenery. Wilfred has travelled a lot and my mother said he won awards for his photographs and that they were published in magazines.

"So much beauty!" he once said to me as we looked at the photographs together. "I need to see beauty."

Even though I cannot hear I know when words are said with sadness. My eyes see everything. My eyes hear things that other people miss.

My father doesn't speak but sits beside Wilfred with his arm around his shoulders. He knows there is nothing left to say.

"You know how I feel, Andy," Wilfred says flatly.

My father nods. "I do."

Slowly my father moves himself off Wilfred's bed and makes his way to the door.

19

"I'll see you tomorrow, Wilfred," he says sadly but Wilfred doesn't look up. He is already lost in thought as we slip quietly from his room.

On my way down the hallway I meet Aishling walking Aron shakily towards the stairs. He is very weak and walks bent forward. He stops abruptly and looks straight at me as though he has never seen me before.

"Jacob!" he says aloud even though he has had only one whiskey.

I nod and he breaks into a huge smile. He will not last the week.

Chapter 4

Martin is getting worse. I am probably the only one in the house who is glad about his night-time fears, which distract me from the dreaded vibrations of the train. Even though I hate to use my voice, I told him about my fear of the train last night as I stood in his room again after an exhausted Aishling gave up pleading with him to settle down and walked out of his room in one of her huffs. I hoped it would help him understand that he is not alone in his fears. I watched later as Aishling made a note to call the doctor about increasing his night-time sedation which no longer seems to have any effect on him.

When morning came and Doctor Alder arrived, he just nodded as Martin listed the many people who visit him at night to torment him, all of whom have two things in common. they are all dead and they are all people he has wronged even though he would not agree with that fact. I watched with interest as Alder wrote a new prescription for him and agreed with him that the people were real and that, yes, he could see them.

Aishling stood with pursed lips. She didn't think it was right to agree with Martin and couldn't see how this would help him

LIMERICK COUNTY LIBRARY
00684338

or help her get her work done at night. As she walked with Doctor Alder out of Martin's room she could not hold her fiery tongue any longer.

"I don't think it's right to agree with him. The man is tormented and he depends on us to tell him it's his imagination."

Alder smiled. He has worked in this town for over thirty years and his father was the local doctor before him. He knows many of the home's residents well, especially Martin who he has known since childhood.

"Miss, it is not his imagination. When he's calling you, these people are in his mind and he can hear them. It's his conscience and the conscience is as real as it gets."

I watched Aishling frown at him and knew she was thinking that this was rubbish but something about his words stung her. Something about them rang true.

"Then why? Why is he troubled now after all these years?"

"Ah," Alder said, "that's the sad fact about life. We are forced to face our regrets when we are least in a position to do anything about them."

Aishling could feel her heart quicken. I knew she had regrets of her own, regrets that she had no idea what to do about.

"Well, is there anything else we can do to help him?"

"Yes. When he sees them, agree with him. Tell him to say that he's sorry, that they'll forgive him. That they are just waiting to hear those words and then they will disappear and leave him in peace."

I watched Aishling nod and knew she was not convinced.

"Okay," she said. "I'll try it," she added doubtfully.

After Aishling goes to bed for the day, I wander into the living room where Victoria and Penelope are anxiously waiting for their nephew to visit. Henry Miller is the sisters' only relative and has recently returned from Vietnam. When he wrote to his aunts stating the day and the exact time he would visit, my mother thought he must know how important details are to his aunts. But it turns out this isn't so. When Henry marches into the lounge room in full uniform I can see my mother and Kora exchange glances and laugh discreetly at the how similar Henry is to the old ladies, but their smiles turn to worry as the women immediately start to shake at the sight of him. Penelope, being the older sister, puts her arms around Victoria and starts to sing to her as Victoria sinks her face under her sister's armpit. My mother frowns and moves over to the sisters as the young man halts with his mouth open, not knowing what to do or why his aunts are behaving this way. He has not seen much of them since his father died and in truth he hardly knows them but he stands to inherit some money when they die so he feels the least he can do is visit them from time to time. My mother puts her arm around Penelope.

"This is your nephew, Henry. Your brother's son. Remember?"

"Not Daddy?" Penelope asks.

"No, Penelope. It's your nephew."

My mother takes the young man by the arm and sits him in front of the sisters. Victoria doesn't move her face from Penelope's comforting body and refuses to look at him. I can see my mother's eyes moisten. The sisters are afraid of this man who I realise must look just like their father.

When no one speaks, my mother sits down and tries to act as an interpreter, much like she used to do for me when I was little on the rare occasion that a friend called to play with me.

"I think the ladies imagine you are their father. You must look like him."

"Em – yeah. So I'm told. I never met him."

I can see sweat bead on Henry's face and feel sorry for him even though I know he doesn't love his aunts and only wants their money. I saw Kora say this.

"But you've seen photos?"

"Yeah. I guess he did look like me," he replies.

"What was he like?" Mum asks.

I can see Victoria move her eye upward to view the visitor

who she thought was going to be a little boy, not a man in a uniform, not a man like Daddy.

"Dad said he was real hard on them. That he ran the house like a regiment."

Penelope looks at him. I can see her mouth moving but she isn't saying any words, just thinking about it.

"That would explain a lot," Mum says sadly, looking at the sister's.

Henry relaxes a little. People do that around my mother. She never judges anyone. She has seen too much suffering.

"What about your dad? What was he like? They speak fondly of their baby brother. Don't you, ladies?"

I watch as Henry's face darkens slowly like a dying light bulb.

"He was a good dad but a lousy officer. He hated the army. Said Granddad pushed him into it. He could paint though. He was an artist. I still have some of his paintings."

"What did he think about you joining up? The war in Vietnam isn't popular, as I'm sure you've found out since you've come home."

Henry sighs. It clearly feels strange talking about such personal stuff to this woman he hardly knows but it saves him from sitting in silence in front of his aunts.

"I think I joined to spite him. He was an unhappy man. We were close when I was little but when I got older nothing I did was good enough. You know, when Dad left the army Granddad wouldn't let my aunts see him. He said he was a disgrace. Mum said Dad never got over it. He loved his sisters."

I can see Henry's chin shake.

"Anyway," he says, pulling himself together, "that's how it was."

My mother knows she has asked enough questions to ease the sisters' nerves and excuses herself from the room.

"I'll leave you to catch up with your nephew, ladies," she says. "See what a fine young man he is now," she adds as she leaves, ensuring the sisters know it is not their angry father sitting in front of them.

I follow my mother into the office. Today is the day she normally does her paperwork and Tina comes to work with Kora. I know I should be studying but I have read all of my books already and even read some of them twice. The mail has arrived and I watch as she opens several bills, many of which I know she will find hard to pay. Halfway down the pile there is a letter with a Sydney postmark on it. It is from the university and is signed *Stéphane Laver*. My mother reads it quickly and puts it down to move on to other mail so I read it over her shoulder. She is used to me doing this. I am her right-hand man.

Dear Sir / Madam

I am currently undertaking a research Master's Degree which focuses on the life experiences of Australia's aging immigrant population. I am also interested in the experiences of first-generation Australians who might provide information on how the previous generation of immigrants settled into Australian life. I would appreciate it if some of the residents of your nursing home would be willing to tell me their personal stories. Confidentiality is assured and pseudonyms will be used if requested. I have attached an expression-of-interest form that should be returned to me in the stamped addressed envelope. Please also provide information if interpreters are required. If you would like further information, please don't hesitate to contact me on the number below.

Stéphane Laver

I read the letter again. I am unsure what "pseudonyms" means but decide it has something to do with hiding who you are. I realise that this is what I have been waiting for. I have been looking for someone with a voice so that the residents can tell their stories and, in doing so, be released from their regrets and mistakes so that when their time comes they can die in peace and I will not have to worry about them hanging around here.

I think about this as my mother works.

Some time later she is disturbed by voices outside her door and opens it quickly.

Henry Miller is about to leave and is smiling at his aunts who are waving from their chairs. My mother looks quickly into the Penance Room and relaxes when she sees that they are smiling back.

"That went well," he says. "I actually enjoyed talking to them. They were telling me about their time in Europe. They're pretty interesting."

My mother smiles. "You mean a lot to them. Eh, Henry, I hope you don't mind me saying this but, next time, could you come without the uniform? It upsets them . . . you . . ."

"No need to explain. I didn't think. It was thoughtless of me. I'll wear civvies next time, promise," he replies.

"Tell me. Did you ever make up with your dad?"

"He died while I was in 'Nam. Who would have thought one war would have lasted so long?"

My mother thinks about this for a moment. I can see the familiar crease on her brow.

"Some people's wars last a lifetime," she replies.

While my mother is talking to Mr Miller, I move the letter from Stéphane Laver to the top of the pile. She notices this as soon as she returns and takes a deep breath.

"Now what, Christopher?" she says as she lifts the letter and reads it again.

She is frowning and I know that the visit from Henry Miller has made her both sad and happy at the same time and that she is hopeful that he will come back and see his aunts. As she sits down she picks up a blank piece of paper so I know she is about to write to Mr Laver. I surge with excitement because I already know that when Stéphane Laver arrives, things are going to change around here.

Chapter 5

I wake long before the night train comes and instantly know that something is wrong. I leave my room quickly and make my way down the hallway.

Aishling and my mother are in the Kleins' room. I tiptoe in and stand over the bed with them. Aron's arms are clasped tightly around his wife and there is a faint smile on his lips. We wonder how long he has been dead. I see Aishling say that she checked him just before eleven and he was fine. It is now almost one. We leave the room and I watch as the women decide how best to deal with Iren. It is her that they are sad about as Aron was very ill. My mother knew he was in terrible pain and she felt he had suffered enough in this life, that they both had suffered enough.

They decide on a plan and my mother wakes Iren and takes her out into the hallway. She loves to eat and my mother takes her to the kitchen and sits her in front of a cup of steaming coffee and a slice of Li's cake. Iren eyes my mother suspiciously. She understands a little English but can only say a few words. My mother's eyes are filled with tears. Except for her friend David Berman and the staff at this home, Iren is all alone in the world now. My mother pats Iren's hand and tries to plan her words.

"Iren, your husband was very ill. Yes? You understand?"

Iren nods but finishes her coffee quickly and hands her cup to my mother with wide child-like eyes. She is hoping for another one. My mother rises from the table and reboils the kettle, glad of the delay. When it whistles, Iren covers her ears. She is always frightened by sudden noise.

My mother places another coffee in front of her and adds lots of milk. Iren gulps her food down quickly even if it is too hot and has burnt her mouth more than once. Like Mina Jensen, she thinks there is a food shortage but, unlike Mina, she doesn't think to hide any for later.

"Iren. Aron was very ill. He had lots of pain. Lots of hospital. Yes?"

My mother has now got Iren's attention and she pushes her empty cup away and stares at my mother across the red wooden table. Her mouth starts to quiver and she looks more lucid than I have ever seen her.

My mother reaches across the table and squeezes her hand. At first she thinks my mother is going to hurt her and she pulls back and pushes her tiny shoulders up towards her ears. But my mother perseveres and grabs her hand. She wants Iren to have someone to touch. Tears are rolling down my mother's face. She doesn't want to have to do this.

"Aron died, Iren. I'm sorry. Do you understand me?"

Iren looks at my mother and then to the door. She tries to stand but her legs have been weak for some years now. My mother stands quickly. She knows Iren wants to go to him. She reaches out for Iren but the old woman has returned to her confused state as quickly as she left it.

"Please," she says, "I give gold. Please have husband."

My mother realises that she thinks we have taken Aron away.

"No, Iren. He is gone. He has died, sweetheart. I am so

sorry." She tries to hug Iren who is trying to get away from her and makes for the kitchen door.

Aishling comes into the room and tries to prevent Iren from leaving. She has woken my father who will help her take Aron into the lounge room until the funeral directors come. Iren runs straight into my father and starts screaming.

"Aron! Aron! What you do? Aron!"

My father pulls her close to him and smooths her hair like her husband used to do. She collapses against him and starts hitting him until she weakens and cries like none of us have ever heard her cry before. We know she understands now, if only for a while. Her frail body looks tiny as she leans into my father's strong frame and my mother and Aishling are now crying freely in the kitchen. I try not to cry. I am thirteen now and I try to follow my father's lead. I look down and focus on my stump which is bare on the linoleum floor. When she settles, my father thinks it is better to bring her to see Aron in their bedroom. My father is not convinced that she will remember he is dead but she lies down beside Aron and cries openly. She starts speaking Hungarian and kisses his face over and over, trying to bring him back to life. We leave the room and give her some time with her husband.

My father knows that Aron would have wanted a Jewish funeral but the synagogue closed almost ten years ago. Instead he has phoned Mr Berman. He is Iren and Aron's solicitor and acts as their advocate when they have to make important decisions. He is also the Kleins' long-term friend and will know what to do.

Ten minutes later my mother goes in, takes Iren by the hand and leads her back to the kitchen while my father prepares the body, following the directions Mr Berman has given him. I stay in the room and watch with interest. This is our second Jewish funeral and I wasn't there for the first one for Mrs Levi, which was before I was born.

When my father is finished we sit in the room in silence as we are not to leave the body alone. He has forgotten some of Mr Berman's directions and even though he remembered to cover the mirror, he is worried that he was supposed to do this earlier.

"Religion!" he says.

My father was raised as a Presbyterian and met my mother at her father's church service but I know that he considers himself a man of science and doesn't completely believe in the afterlife.

When Mr Berman arrives he helps my father dress Aron in a long white shroud. He cuts all of the fringes off Aron's prayer shawl which hung in the wardrobe and puts it over the shroud. It is dusty and smells of mothballs and I have never seen Aron wear it. I watch Mr Berman place a tiny white hat on the top of Aron's head. James and Robert, the funeral directors, arrive. They are brothers and we know them well. They have brought the simple pine coffin Mr Berman requested. When he is ready Iren is taken back into the room and she starts to cry again. Aishling has given her a strong whiskey and I worry for a moment that Mr Berman will be angry but he says nothing and goes about his business. He is saying words in a different language but it doesn't look like Hungarian which is the language I have seen Aron use. I have never seen these words before. When they eventually take Aron away I go to my room. I am exhausted and very sad that Aron didn't get to tell his story. I pray that he is in a peaceful place with his son where no one can harm him. I pray that he will not hang around here waiting on his wife to join him. I sit on my bed and look through my window into the darkness. I am alone now and feel that it is safe to cry. I notice that my watch is working again and that it is 3.30 a.m. I am amazed that I have missed the night train and didn't feel its vibrations from the Kleins' room. I ease myself into bed and drift into a fitful sleep where I can hear Aron and Iren calling each other through the night.

The following morning Aron is brought to the Jewish section of the cemetery on Rakow Street for burial. Mr Berman, who sat with the body all night, is at the top of our small group with my father and they help James and Robert carry the coffin with two other men I don't know. I cover my eyes as we pass my grandparents' grave on the main pathway and notice my mother stiffen and pause for a moment as she passes. Kora notices this too and squeezes my mother's hand as they walk slowly with Iren who has not said one word since last night. Doctor Alder is there and looks sombre in his dark suit and black armband. I see Mr Berman mouth words to a special prayer that I have never seen before. I suspect that my mother has given Iren some medication because she is looking vacantly ahead and doesn't look into the grave as her husband is slowly lowered into it. She is not crying and when she asks Mr Berman a question in Hungarian, he doesn't answer her. Mr Berman is from Germany and he doesn't speak Hungarian.

When the ceremony is over, we take the large black car back to the nursing home where Rita has been trying to manage on her own. I see her tell my mother that she had to wake Aishling up once but that otherwise everything went well.

When I enter the Penance Room, everyone is quiet. Wilfred looks at Iren and I can see that he is wondering if he should sympathise with her for her loss but I know that he feels this would be a strange thing for someone like him to do so he moves to the other side of the room as Kora sits her on a pew and fetches her a drink. Mina moves forward on unsteady legs, hugs Iren and tells her in English that she is sorry for her loss. Martin stands and shakes her hand. He doesn't speak as he doesn't know what to say. Jimmy waves his good arm toward her and tries to speak but his words are garbled and she doesn't understand him. He drops his arm, frustrated, and looks away. Penelope and Victoria are in their room. They don't like Rita as she teases them and will only come out when my mother or Kora have returned. Father Hayes is sitting in the corner, probably dreaming of Ireland. My father has taken the day off work and wishes secretly that it was an Irish Catholic funeral where there would be a loud and cheerful celebration of the person's life. Li, our cook, has planned a special lunch and even sought out recipes from her elderly Hungarian neighbour. It was the first time they had spoken to one another.

Even though everyone gets to work there is an air of sadness about the place. Everyone is concerned for Iren, even Wilfred.

Aishling gets up even though she has had only a few hours' sleep. As usual she checks the mail first to see if any of her family have written but there is nothing for her. There has never been a letter for her even since before I was born but still she checks every day and has not given up hope. I like Aishling best of all the nurses and find myself looking at her long red hair when she brushes it. Sometimes I blush when she is near me. Like my father, she has very pale skin. I wish that just once there would be a letter from Ireland and that Aishling would be happy. The rest of the evening goes slowly. Everyone looks sad and I am tempted to go roaming the streets but I don't want to be rude. Aron was very nice to me and by now I have very good funeral manners. I have been to a lot of them. Li's meal was lovely and my mother congratulated her on it. Li asked Iren if the meal was how she remembered it in Hungary but she didn't answer. Twice before bedtime she shouts for her husband and I watch my parents look at each other with worried faces. Already she has forgotten what has happened. My mother gives her a sleeping tablet and leads her to her room but she will not go inside without her husband so Kora and Aishling set up a cot in the babies' room for her. Slowly the others drift off to bed. Penelope and Victoria thank my father for a wonderful party and he bursts out laughing. It has been a long day and everyone is tired. Martin has had more than enough whiskey and I saw my father slip him more than he should have but I will not tell my mother. I know that he doesn't have much time left.

Later that night as I am sitting with Aishling, she rushes to his room and I follow her. At first we cannot see him but find him hiding underneath his bed. Aishling lifts up the blankets that hang over the side of the bed and kneels down to look in at him. She has decided to be calmer with him following her talk with Dr Alder.

"Martin, why don't you come out now and talk to me?"

Martin is shivering with fear. There are tears running down his face and I wonder if my father gave him too much to drink.

"Make them go away, please!"

"Okay, Martin. I'll do that."

Aishling turns and looks into the empty room.

"All right. Everybody out!" she orders. "Martin here has a right to his sleep and I have a right to get my work done so, please, everyone go back to wherever you came from."

I watch Martin peek out and look around the room. He stares at Aishling and then at me as his face shrivels and grimaces.

"Don't trick me. I can see them. They're going to get me. They said it. It wasn't my fault. Everyone was against me."

Aishling puts her hand under the bed and tries to locate Martin's hand.

"Martin, just take my hand and come out. If you like, you can sit with me at the desk and we can have a chat, all right?"

My mother enters the room. It is time to turn the babies and she has come looking for Aishling to help her. Between them they coax Martin from his hiding place but he is afraid and is scanning the room for ghosts. I move outside and watch them coax him from the doorway.

"Martin, there is nothing to be afraid of, I promise you," my mother says gently.

"But we understand. Everybody has fears," Aishling says. "Me, I'm afraid of water. Couldn't swim one stroke. What about you, Emma?"

My mother thinks about this. I doubt she is afraid of much. I watch her wrinkle her freckled nose.

"Burglars. I'm – I'm not really sure why," she finally replies.

Martin seems to relax and his breathing settles a little. His tears have dried and I can see that he is enjoying their company.

"Your son told me that he is afraid of the night train," he says. "The one that shoots through at 3 a.m."

My mother, who has been smiling, puts her hand to her mouth and stares at him. Her eyes open wide and I blush with embarrassment. When she runs from the room, crying, I watch Aishling stiffen. Her face is full of questions that she doesn't know how to ask. As she turns to leave the room to check on my mother, I slink further into the darkened hallway, embarrassed that people now know about my fear. She stops and looks back at him.

"You heard Christopher say that?"

"Yes."

She frowns and thinks for a moment. "Martin?"

"Yes?"

"There is no night train."

Chapter 6

Jimmy Young's son is visiting and is standing just inside his bedroom door with his head bowed and his akubra held firmly in his sunburnt hands. He twirls the hat around, anxious to distract himself from his father's weekly interrogation. Like some of the staff, Jeff understands everything his father says but probably wishes he didn't. Each Sunday he stands patiently as his father asks questions about the farm and about how his bachelor son is running it. Jimmy also has three daughters who are all married with children of their own. My mother said this bothers Jimmy who wants his son to marry and have grandsons to carry on the family name but she has known Jeff a long time and said he was always a nice, quiet man who was shy of people. Jeff is only about forty but he looks older from years working in the sun. His eyes are narrow and slanted and have long lines running towards his hairline making him look like he is always smiling. I have seen my mother say he is sweet on Kora who blushes when he is around. Mother said that when they were younger Jeff and Kora went on a few dates but that when Jimmy found out about his son courting an Aboriginal, he was so angry that Jeff finished with Kora but that neither of them ever dated anyone else since. My mother says it is fate that Jimmy ended up here with Kora looking after him. She also says that even though Kora is embarrassed when she sees Jeff, secretly she likes to be here when he comes and refuses when my mother suggests she take the day off.

When he leaves his father's room, Jeff comes looking for my mother who is busy planning a birthday party for my father. She has written to my father's three older sisters in Scotland, thanking them for the gifts and asking if they would visit sometime. She knows how much this would mean to my father who misses his home and sometimes becomes lonesome for it but they always write back saying the flight would be too long, or that there are too many dangerous insects here. Each year they send my father thick knitted jumpers with fancy stitches that he would never be able to wear in the Australian heat, not even in winter which my father doesn't think is cold at all, even if my mother and I are shivering.

My mother smiles when she sees Jeff. She has not given up on him being Kora's boyfriend again.

"Well, how was he today?"

"Same as ever," he replies, laughing. "He wants to come out and inspect the stock. Can you imagine how I'd get him on a horse?" he laughs.

My mother smiles sadly. She is good at seeing everybody's point of view.

"Must be hard for him, sitting here all day. Maybe you could take him for a drive around the farm?"

Jeff nods. "Yeah. I could do that. It's hard to listen to him sometimes though. As soon as he sees the farm, he gets frustrated about not being able to work any more."

My mother agrees.

"You busy next Saturday night?" she asks.

Jeff shakes his head. He never does anything except work and sit alone in the farmhouse.

"I'm having a birthday party for Andy. I'd be delighted if you'd come."

Jeff hesitates and my mother moves in quickly. She doesn't want to give him time to refuse.

"Kora would love you to come," she lies.

I watch him raise his thick eyebrows upwards.

"She would?"

"Sure. She'd love it."

"Em . . ."

I can see that Jeff does not believe my mother but he is too polite to say so.

She isn't going to give up easily but I have watched her try to get them together before and it always ends in disaster.

"Come on. It'll be fun. What have you got to lose?"

Jeff nods. I can see that he is feeling uncomfortable. My mother is very good at getting people to agree to things they don't want to do. If only she could have got my father to send me to that school. Then I wouldn't have to hang around here all the time.

I leave my mother to do her work and wander into the kitchen to watch Li making lunch. She makes sure that each of the residents gets a chance to eat their national food and today she is making a roast beef dinner to suit Penelope and Victoria. I watch as she roasts potatoes in the oven and slices carrots and broccoli. It looks like boring food and I am much more interested when she cooks fancy food like the Dutch cheese sausages she made for Mina's birthday.

I leave the kitchen and poke my head into the lounge room. Kora has helped Jimmy downstairs from his room. He snaps at her as she helps him into a more comfortable chair.

"Mind! Bloody blackfellas! Damn rough."

Even I know what words he is saying now. I have become used to his sideways mouth. Kora ignores him. Like my mother, she follows Jesus and tries to turn the other cheek. Most of the time she is successful.

37

Penelope and Victoria are sitting under the window reading romance novels that they have both read several times before. They usually forget the story line and are happy to read the books again. I wish I could forget that I have already read the books I own. I wish I could forget a lot of things.

Iren is asleep in the chair and everybody is relieved about that. It has been a week since Aron died and while she will now sleep in her own bedroom, she spends her waking moments shouting out his name over and over until one of the staff takes her outside to the garden or to the kitchen. My mother says we need a second lounge room but we are short on space and she cannot afford to have any fewer residents. The home is not doing as well as she'd like and I know that my parents are worried about its future.

I wander into the babies' room and stand on a chair to face the old radio that no one ever turns on. It is full of dust so I blow at it and cough. I reach forward and turn it on. Catherine opens her eyes immediately. She looks surprised by the sudden sound and pulls a face which disappoints me. I was hoping she would feel less lonely with the noise from the radio. Catherine used to be a real circus performer when she was young and did a trapeze act with her husband until he ran off with a clown. New staff think that this story is made up but it is true and Catherine used to be able to tell it until she had another stroke and now spends most of her time sleeping.

Kora comes into the room. She is frowning.

"What on earth is that noise?" she asks but she is not talking to me.

She sees the radio and walks over to it. I think for a moment that she is going to turn it off and perhaps even take it away but she turns the dial on the left around and around until I see Catherine's eyes open wide and smile.

"That's better, Catherine, my love," she says. "Tuned in for you properly now. It's a good idea. Bit of music no harm, eh? Pass some time, love."

I relax and sit a while with Catherine. I miss her stories and wish that she could still talk. She is very thin now and sits with long bony legs shrivelled up in the bed. Each day either my mother or Kora comes in and stretch out her limbs with cream. I don't like to watch as she pulls faces and I know that they are hurting her even though they don't mean to. She no longer wants to sit in a chair and used to cry with pain when they tried. She doesn't come to the Penance Room any more. As I recall her stories in my mind, she stares off into space. I wonder if she is picturing herself flying through the air, enjoying the feeling of freedom, the hot air of the circus tent blowing against her face. I wish I knew what that felt like. I went to a circus once with my father. It set up outside town and there was so much traffic that it was quicker for us to walk there. I remember being disappointed as it didn't have any exotic animals except three old camels. I got to ride a small horse and ate salty popcorn and sat with my mouth open as clowns and fire-blowers ran around in a circle. Other kids around me were laughing and slapping their knees and jumping up and down. After a while I didn't want to watch any more and sat quietly with tears falling down my face.

My father looked at me. "What's wrong, Christopher?" he said.

I asked him if I could go home, that I didn't want to see any more clowns.

"Is it because you cannot hear the clowns?" he asked.

I nodded.

He picked me up and sat me on his lap. "Christopher, you will never be able to hear clowns but you can see more than anyone will ever be able to hear."

We didn't leave and I understand now what my father was saying. He was saying, "Get used to this. Use your eyes, son, because this is all you have."

I use them very well.

I sit with Catherine for a while longer and watch as her toes tap beneath the white cotton sheet. I get up and walk along the row of beds, five women on the right, four men on the left. It is a large room and is even bigger than the Penance Room. All of the windows are open and the fly-screens tap gently with the welcome breeze. I look out onto the garden and notice my father and Wilfred talking on a wooden bench. I can smell Li's lunch cooking and know that it will be a while before it is ready. I walk out to sit with my father and Wilfred, hoping to learn something new.

Chapter 7

It is Tuesday and Martin's two younger daughters are visiting him in his room. The door is open and I peek in. I am always interested in their visits. Martin has four daughters who always visit him in pairs and two sons who only visit occasionally and always with their wives who Martin doesn't like and speaks rudely to.

Una Kelly is the youngest and is able to handle her father well but his other daughters are afraid of him. He says awful things to them and they usually leave in tears. I don't know why but they come back every week, probably hoping that he'll have changed.

The air in the room is tense as always and I see Ellen twiddling her thumbs around and around until he shouts, "Stop that, you silly girl!"

I can see the vibrations of his voice in the glass of water on his locker and I know that he has shouted very loud at her. Ellen's lip trembles and tears briefly well in her eyes. She pulls her baby onto her lap and cuddles him close.

Una clears her throat. "Don't shout at Ellen. She's good to come all this way."

Ellen married a man from Wilcannia and went to live there. He doesn't have Irish roots, which Martin is not happy about.

"Shouldn't have had to go there. What's wrong with a man from around here? Living in the middle of bloody nowhere!" he shouts.

Una ignores him and Ellen looks at her shoes. Her son reaches out to go to Martin and I watch him calm. He holds out his arms and takes the baby. Una and Ellen look at each other as their father coos into the child's face. It is the only time they ever see him soften.

"You know, he's the image of my father," he says, looking closely at the child. I know there is sadness in his voice. I can see it in his eyes.

Una and Ellen shift uneasily in their seats. They know he is going to launch into another long tale about Ireland, a place he has never even been to.

"My father came here with nothing except the clothes on his back, hoping for a new life. He never saw his family again. Never even heard from them. Can you imagine that? The poor bastard."

Una and Ellen both know that their father's relationship with his father was not good and that he was an outcast from the family when he was only seventeen. Sometimes they feel he is talking about himself when he recalls their grandfather's story and that their pasts have merged into one story with almost identical endings.

"Did you know that if a pommy was in charge of a job, they wouldn't give him a start because he was Irish? Bloody awful," he says. He wipes his eyes quickly. He is having one of his sad days. They are happening more often now. "When he finally got work on the mine, he worked hard, all hours. Got me in there when I was only fifteen. He had nine children. Only six survived. My poor mother, she worked hard too. No bloody fancy electric machines in the house in those days. She did everything by hand.

It took him almost fifteen years to save to buy a small patch of land out of town. He kept working though. Land didn't pay enough. He loved that land, loved to be out in the open. He hated every single day he spent underground . . ." Martin's voice trails off and his daughters know that this is as far as the story ever goes. They know what happened between their father and his family from listening to cousins but Martin can never bring himself to talk about it. He is too ashamed but I watch as the memories eat into him every day and whittle him down into a small old man with big regrets. Una always tries to get him to talk. She knows that if he can only admit what he has done, he may finally know some peace of mind. Una has even tried to get the priest to talk to her father but Martin doesn't like priests any more than he likes his family so she knows there is no point.

"What happened next? Why did you fall out with your family?" she asks.

Martin ignores her and stares off into space. He notices me lurking in the doorway and shifts in his seat.

"It's a bit early for you, boy!" he shouts so I move from the door quickly.

Una and Ellen look up in surprise but they don't see me and look quizzically at their father. Silence fills the room again as I leave Una and Ellen to watch the clock over Martin's bed tick slowly. They will only stay an hour.

As I pass by Penelope and Victoria's room, I can see Rita standing by their window looking through their photographs. They are standing to attention at the foot of their twin beds.

"Who is this?" Rita asks as she lifts a photo of the women as small girls standing with a stern-looking woman dressed in black. Even though it is an old black-and-white photo I notice that they are not dressed in the same clothes and I wonder when they started to do this and why.

"That's our sweet Nanny Betty," Penelope replies. Penelope usually does the talking for the two.

"Oh your nanny, is it? Aren't we the fancy pants?" Rita sneers.

I know she is mocking them by the way she is pulling faces and waving her hand around. Penelope looks worried and Victoria is moving nervously from foot to foot.

I know that my mother has had enough of Rita's behaviour. I move downstairs quickly and open the door to my mother's office. I have seen my father say that sound travels well in this old house. I don't want to be a tell-tale so I am hoping she will hear Rita annoying the sisters. When she appears on the stairwell, I relax and watch with interest as my mother stands behind Rita and listens to her annoying the ladies.

"That's enough!" she says angrily.

Rita spins around and I hide my face to conceal my laughter. I don't like her. Her face is red and she is spluttering. She tries to explain but only half-words come out and I am shamelessly enjoying her discomfort.

"I want you out of here now! You don't have to finish the day. I'll send your wages on."

Rita is trying to decide whether or not to try to explain herself but she decides there is no point and storms off.

"Will there be a court martial?" Penelope asks excitedly while Victoria stands nervously behind her.

"That was it, Penelope. I am judge and jury on this base," my mother jokes but I can see that she is upset by this. She would have liked to have got rid of Rita long before but it is hard to get part-time staff who will fill in at a moment's notice. It will take her a long time to get someone new and until then she will have to work even longer hours.

I am still smiling to myself when I look into the lounge room. I notice that Mr Berman is visiting Iren. He has been very good to her since Aron died and tries to visit as often as he can. Even though he is rubbing Iren's hand his eyes are on Wilfred who is trying his best to look away. Like me, Wilfred has noticed the line of numbers on Iren's forearm, her identification during her time in the concentration camp.

Some months ago, while standing in the Penance Room, Rita asked Mr Berman where he was from. When he said he was from Germany, Rita excitedly introduced him to Wilfred, telling him he was a fellow countryman. Mr Berman turned his back on Wilfred and said, "We have nothing in common."

I learn a lot from watching and although I am upset about how Mr Berman has suffered, I also feel sorry for Wilfred. He doesn't fit in anywhere and is alone in the world. Sometimes I feel the same way.

When Iren suddenly opens her eyes, she starts shouting "Aron, Aron!" She is starting to annoy the other residents and is even annoying Mr Berman. Kora goes to her side and tries to distract her with talk of food but she will have none of it.

"Aron! Aron!" she repeats.

Finally Wilfred jumps from his seat under the window where he has been trying to read music sheets that came in the mail and begins to shout. I can feel his voice vibrating off the wooden pews or at least I imagine I can. I have never seen him lose his temper before. He moves swiftly and stands over Iren. Wilfred is over six foot tall and she looks tiny as he bends forward and moves his face menacingly close to hers. She cringes and wraps her arms around herself in fear. I imagine a thousand memories flashing before her confused brain.

"Shut up! Shut up! He is dead. They are all dead!" he shouts before running from the room.

My mother comes quickly from her office and follows him but he has shut his door. She puts her ear up against the thin wooden frame. She must hear something. Perhaps he is crying again or listening to sad music on his record player.

"Wilfred. It's Emma. Let me in!"

He doesn't open the door. My mother's shoulders droop and her mouth makes a downward shape. I know that she is blowing out air. She doesn't know what to do to make Wilfred feel better. As she passes the lounge room, Kora is still trying to console Iren who is shouting for Aron.

I decide I have had enough sadness for one day and walk to the front of the house and watch the heat of the sun rise off the pavement in shimmering rays. I open the fly-screen and look out onto the scorched earth. The lawn is brown and every day my mother listens to the forecast, hoping for rain.

I slam the screen door as I always do and walk out onto the road. There is no one about. It is almost midday and most people are staying indoors until the hottest part of the day passes but the sun does not bother me. I walk the long way around to avoid the railway tracks and make my way across town.

I see Maria Moretti coming out of her grandfather's shop. There is a *For Sale* sign in the window that was not there the last time I passed and I wonder where Mr Moretti is moving to. Maria crosses the road and stands on the street corner. We are like two gunslingers weighing each other up as she stares at me with huge distrustful brown eyes. I decide that any company is better than none and that I will talk to her even if she is a girl. I cross the road and notice that she is wearing the same white dress and I think that she must like that dress very much. For a moment neither of us speaks. I am not used to talking to girls and I don't get to mix with other children much. She looks shy and has her head down. She has lovely black shiny hair that has been put into ringlets, some of which have fallen straight and are hanging in her eyes. I can feel my hands begin to sweat as it dawns on me that she might reject me which would be embarrassing. Maria doesn't seem to have any friends and, if she won't spend time with me, then I know that I am the least popular boy in the entire town.

Eventually she points to the spot where her house, which has now been torn down, used to be.

"I used to live there," she says simply as if I didn't know this.

I know she is almost the same age as me and wonder if there is something wrong with her.

I nod and wonder when I will tell her that I am deaf. I decide now is as good a time as any. I use my horrible voice and am glad that I cannot hear it. She leans forward trying to hear me. I try to make my voice louder even though I have no way of knowing if I have succeeded.

"Where do you live now?" I ask.

She points to her grandfather's house which is old and looks like it too should be torn down.

She starts walking and I follow her. I move quickly in front of her in case she is speaking and I cannot read her lips.

"I am deaf," I say bravely but she shrugs like this means nothing to her, like she doesn't mind.

"You'll have to look at me when you speak," I add, feeling even braver.

"Okay," she replies as we walk slowly together towards the park.

Chapter 8

On Friday morning, a letter from Stéphane Laver falls onto the front mat and shines like a flare in a pitch-black ocean. I stand behind my mother and almost use my voice in excitement when I read that he will arrive on Tuesday afternoon to start interviewing the residents. My mother smiles and nods thoughtfully. She agrees that it is a good idea to give the residents a chance to tell each other what happened to them before they came to live here. I know a little about the residents' lives already but I think that if they listen to each other's stories they will realise how alike their lives have been and that they have a lot in common no matter where they came from or what God they believe in.

Late that afternoon, Maria comes with me to the house and we sit in my room overlooking the train tracks. We have walked together every day and even though she doesn't say much, I feel we are becoming good friends. My mother has gone to town to place an advert for a new nurse in the paper. She would be glad to know that I am having a friend over as I have not had anyone here since my accident. I didn't tell Maria the story about my foot. It seemed enough to tell her about my hearing. Like me, she is unusual and she didn't ask any questions about what happened to me.

Yesterday, as we paddled in the pond in the park, I saw her briefly look at my stump and then look away. I could feel small tears of gratitude well in my eyes. I am tired of being different. I am tired of people shouting loudly in my face as if the volume of their voice will make any difference. Maria never shouts at me.

Tonight is my father's party and his friend Bill has invited him to his house after work so that Kora and Tina, our part-time nurse, can decorate the Penance Room in peace. I know he will love the idea of the party but that he will act all shocked and bashful when he comes back later and everyone jumps out to surprise him. I ask Maria to stay for the celebration but she says she has to get back to her grandfather as she doesn't like to leave him alone for too long. She told me that her parents live in Sydney but that she preferred to stay with her pop. They visit every few months but she will never leave Broken Hill to live with them. I am glad to hear this as I don't plan on leaving here ever and dream that Maria and I may marry when we are fully grown but I would never tell her or anyone else this as there is a part of me that knows it is just a dream, just wishful thinking.

Aishling is up early and as usual looks briefly through the mail. She has perfected the art of pretending not to care that there is no letter for her. I watch as she shuffles through the bundle like a deck of cards before putting them down quickly. She glances around to check if any of the staff are watching and then looks sadly at the mail and bites her lower lip for a second before going about her work. I once thought of writing to her family and telling them off. I would tell them that she is sorry and that there is nothing else she can do to make it better but I was afraid that I would get into trouble with her. I find that I am not blushing as much around her now that I am friends with Maria but she is still my favourite nurse.

When the decorations are finished, Kora accidentally bursts a balloon with her nail. Everyone except me jumps with fright, even Maria who, like Mina, doesn't like loud noises. Kora fusses with her dress and Aishling and Tina give each other a look I don't understand. My Aunt Kora seems nervous. I have noticed her looking in the mirror twice and smoothing down her curly dark hair which is perfect and doesn't need fixing.

When Bill finally arrives with my father, everyone shouts "Surprise!" and he pretends to look shocked. They both smell heavily of beer and I notice Kora frowning at my mother who is not complaining. She knows my father deserves a little enjoyment.

When Jeff arrives, he stands shyly in the doorway and doesn't know where to put himself. He sits beside his father who is already grumbling at him. My mother offers him a drink but he reminds her he doesn't drink and, despite the heat, asks for a coffee.

"Sissy," his father says and my mother glares at him with angry green eyes.

Wilfred has got dressed up for the occasion. He has not adjusted to the casualness of Australian life and sits sweating in a heavy suit and tie at the far side of the room. He is wearing black leather shoes and is swinging his leg slowly to music that would not normally be to his taste. I have noticed that he always sits alone and I know that if anyone except my father were to come and sit close to him, he would stand and find a seat at the other side of the room.

Mina is wearing a blue floral dress that suits her bright blue eyes and silver hair. She loves parties and although the music sometimes makes her sad, she likes reminiscing about her dancing days.

Li has finished cooking all of the food and jokes with my father that she has cooked haggis for him which he hates. She goes upstairs to get dressed in Aishling's room. Her husband, Jin, has already arrived and she has warned him not to sit beside

Jimmy who thinks that Asians have come to take Australian jobs or Mina who will think that he is a Japanese soldier. Jin looks around the room and chooses to sit beside Aishling who his wife has told him is nice and will not think he is anything except Li's husband. Father Hayes is seated on the other side of Aishling. He leans forward and asks her a question and I notice her eyes brighten. He doesn't speak often.

"Andy?" says Aishling.

My father looks over and nods.

"Father Francis just asked if the nice Scottish man would play a Gaelic tune for him."

My father's eyes widen. It is unusual for Father Hayes to refer to other people or to take notice of where they are from.

"I certainly will, Father," he replies.

Nobody except Aishling and Kora call Mr Hayes "Father" and I know my father is showing the priest respect by doing so.

Martin has seated himself as close to the whiskey as he can and I am already worried that he will see a lot of ghosts and keep everyone awake later. Iren is sitting beside Jana who is the only person who will not get annoyed with her. I feel my eyes light up when Tina wheels Catherine up from the babies' room to listen to the music.

"She wanted to come up. The radio has given her a new lease of life," Tina says.

Bill picks up his guitar and starts strumming. He is a policeman in town. He loves to tell jokes and loves beer even more and, though my mother likes him, she says she'd hate to rely on him to save her from anything. I find myself a wooden chair in the corner of the room and place my bare feet on the ground, feeling the vibrations moving up through me. Penelope and Victoria get up and dance together in the space my father had cleared in the centre of the Penance Room. We all clap to encourage them; it is unusual to see them so carefree. I think of Maria and wish she had waited for even one dance with me. I have never danced with a girl except my mother and Aishling when I was younger and not liable to blush so easily. I picture Maria sitting in silence with her grandfather at the back of the small shop that is now for sale and briefly wonder where in Broken Hill they are moving to. I hope it will not be so far that I cannot walk. When my father takes his fiddle out, I see Bill put whiskey in the punch that the women are drinking. It is no wonder that Penelope and Victoria are dancing. They are drunk. Bill is in his usual funny mood and winks jokingly at Penelope who puts her hand to her cameo brooch and says "Oh my!", sending him into fits of laughter.

My father asks Father Hayes for requests and immediately launches into the "The Mountains of Mourne" followed by "I'll Take You Home Again, Kathleen" but my father replaces "Kathleen" with "Deirdre" who we realise was someone Father Hayes loved before he became a priest and who he still thinks of. Aishling sings "Will You Go, Lassie, Go?" which I think is a song about dogs. I don't like dogs but my father, who joins in the chorus, seems to enjoy it. At the end of the song, Penelope says loudly, "The Irish make really good servants, you know" to Martin who is sitting beside her. Martin glares at her and my mother swiftly sits herself between them. It is too early for fighting.

When the noise settles, I watch as everyone turns around to face the back of the room. I wonder what they are looking at. I follow their eyes and find they are listening to a tiny voice singing in the background. Iren is singing a song in her native language. She has never sung at any of the parties before and no one understands why she would suddenly start singing now. Everybody sits completely still as they listen to the song which I assume by their eyes is sad and mournful. I hope it will not ruin the party. I need as much happiness as I can get and it is in short supply here. When she finishes singing, Iren opens her eyes and appears surprised by the clapping. It is as though she doesn't realise she was singing.

My father, who was spellbound by her voice, asks what the name of the song is.

She understands and leans forward. "'*Szomorú Vasárnap – á Sercss'*," she says.

My father looks at Wilfred to see if he learnt this piece during his musical training.

He nods but seems reluctant to say anything more. He is looking at his shoes and I can see his throat move quickly.

Father pushes him until he looks up and quickly says, "It was a poem, then song. 'Gloomy Sunday' or also called 'The Hungarian Suicide Song'. For lost love. For grief."

Father looks worriedly at Iren as she sits back into her soft chair. He exchanges a look with my mother. Iren's eyes glaze over once again as though she had woken only temporarily and is now returning to her sleep.

Wilfred has brought his violin to the party and as he lifts his bow I dread another slow, depressing song.

"Andy. You and your wife have given me a good home. Been good friends to me," he says. "So, I practise and learn a tune from Scotland to thank you for all you do. To thank you for being my friend. For your birthday."

My father nods and I can see this means a lot to him. Wilfred rarely speaks more than one or two sentences any more. He starts to play and I am surprised to feel a fast beat running across the floorboards under my feet. Everybody is clapping along and stamping their feet to the music that I wish I could hear. Martin is tapping his toes as is Father Hayes. My dad and Aishling are also enjoying it as they nod along with smiles on their pale faces.

Kora gets a drink for herself and Jeff and I watch Jimmy frowning at them. When Jeff returns to his seat I see his father say, "Don't you get any ideas about asking that blackfella out."

I hang my head. I am ashamed of Jimmy. I know that he is a sad man but I am angry that he thinks my aunt is not good enough because of her skin colour. I watch Jeff's sunburnt face redden even more and think he will back down but he turns in towards his father and I watch the side of his mouth move. I cannot see his words but Jimmy looks angry so I know Jeff has told him off and I am pleased.

Wilfred finishes his tune and everyone claps, including Iren. He smiles and returns to his shy ways. My father shakes his hand and hugs him and Wilfred looks both pleased and embarrassed at the same time. Bill picks up his guitar again to play some rock 'n' roll songs which my father also loves. My mother asks my father for a dance and I am happy to watch them twirl around the room. Aishling asks Jeff up and I watch Kora look enviously at them. When the song is finished Aishling hands Jeff over to Kora. I knew she was up to something. Like my mother, she is trying to encourage the couple along. Jeff, whose head is already light from the punch, reddens and stammers. He glances briefly at his father who glares back. Jeff smiles and I know he is wondering what is coming over him. He has no idea that Bill put whiskey in the punch. Nobody has. Nobody except Bill and me. I watch my mother fan herself from the heat and fill herself a large glass and I cannot help but giggle. If her father could see her, he would be preaching fire and brimstone for weeks to come.

The night wears on and everyone seems to be enjoying themselves, even Jin and Li who I hear telling Tina that they never get asked to non-Chinese parties. Martin is talking to Jeff even though there is no love lost between their families. When my father starts to play a tune on his fiddle, Mina gets up to dance with Bill. My mother whispers into his ear to go easy on her hips and he nods. He later dances with Penelope and Victoria. He asks Iren to dance but she refuses. Father Hayes, as usual, dances with Aishling and has that faraway look in his eye. Catherine is seated in her special wheelchair and is smiling out into the room. It is hard to tell by her expression but I think she is happy to be here. I watch my father ask my mother to dance again, a slow dance this time and he has the look in his eye, the look that tells me not to go into their room later even if I am afraid of the train. I am getting too big for that anyway.

Jeff has to leave and Kora, who has to help my mother and Tina get everyone to bed, goes to the front door with him to say goodnight. She is embarrassed that everyone is watching her as she leaves the room. She is now thirty-eight years old and feels foolish standing on the doorstep with a man she should have married almost twenty years before. I look through the crack in the door at the awkward couple.

"There's a dance. Next week," he says flatly. "Will you come?" He waits for the refusal and puts his hat too far forward on his head, concealing his eyes.

"I'll see," Kora says, quickly closing the door to ease her embarrassment. When she turns, she finds an audience gathered just behind the doorway: Aishling, my mother and me.

"Haven't you fellas got anything better to do?" she asks sharply as we break into laughter.

"You said yes!" my mother says, following her into the Penance Room.

"I said maybe," Kora replies sharply.

In the corner of the room Martin is arguing with Tina for another whiskey and she is trying unsuccessfully to cajole him to his room.

My father is sitting peacefully, smiling at my mother. Kora looks at him and smiles. She hates drink but she loves her brother-in-law.

"Emma, you best get this one to bed," she says, nodding at my father. "We'll look after the rest."

My mother puts her arm around my father's back and leads him to their room. He stops in the doorway and kisses her.

"It's my birthday!" he says and she laughs.

She throws her head back, her long golden neck shining with sweat. "I know," she laughs as she closes the door gently, leaving me on the other side.

Chapter 9

"Mum!" I scream as I sit up in my bed and shake the sweat from my forehead. It is the same dream. I look at my watch. It is 3 a.m. Same time as always. I rise and look out the window at the train track and notice that there is no train passing. I realise that I have known this all along and that for some reason, at exactly this time almost every night, my fear wakes me and leaves me to face a night of roaming around the hallways. I leave my bedroom and notice that Aishling is dozing at her desk, something my mother doesn't like her to do.

I think the party must have made her tired. I walk down to Martin's room and find him once again under his bed. I wonder if he has been calling out and worry that he needed help and Aishling didn't hear him. I see his shadow move under his bed in the dimly lit room and crawl under with him, scaring him half to death.

"Don't you ever sleep?" he asks me.

I nod.

"Sorry for telling your mother about the train. I suppose you didn't want me to say anything."

I nod again.

"If you stay quiet, you'll see them," he tells me, putting his fingers to his lips. He forgets that I am as silent as his ghosts. I am beginning to get frightened. I don't want to see angry spirits but I am even more afraid to crawl out from our hiding place. We wait a while. Neither of us moves. I can smell Martin's whiskey breath on the side of my head. In his hand he is rolling something in paper. I look at him.

"Oh. It's just my tablets. They think I don't know that they are trying to poison me. I figured it out. See these ones?" he asks, shoving a large collection of small red tablets towards me. "They're the nasty ones. They're the ones that send me to sleep. Can't afford that. Have to be on my guard all the time. Too dangerous to sleep with them around."

He looks up suddenly and puts his hand over my mouth. He keeps forgetting that I don't speak, or at least rarely speak. He hears something and I can feel my heart quicken. I can feel every muscle in his body tense up. His face is white and his chin is quivering. Even though I am terrified I look out from underneath the blankets but I cannot see anyone. Martin cowers back as though he can see someone looking in at us. He starts thrashing about and kicks me accidentally. He is trying to get out from under the bed but his foot catches in the blanket hanging over the side, causing him to fall.

"Get out!" he screams. "Get out of my room!" He is flailing his arms and legs but cannot get up. I can see the fear on his face as he tries desperately to get to his feet. He starts to cry. I forget my own fear and come out from my hiding place and put my arms around him.

"Can you see them?" he asks.

I nod.

"My brothers? You can see them?"

I nod again.

"I knew they were there and I knew that you of all people would see them. I am not mad."

He has a tight hold of me and is wiping his eyes in my pyjamas. I struggle to prise his grip off me and, signing to him that I'll be back, I go to my room to get my notebook. I return and write him a note.

"Tell them that you are sorry."

I am taking Dr Alder's advice.

He looks at me and looks into space where he thinks his brothers are standing.

"No!" he says, sending spit flying onto my pyjamas. "They blame me for my brother's death and for my father's but it wasn't my fault."

I shove the note closer to his face. Even now, when he is scared, he thinks that he was not to blame. He looks out into the room and swallows but then looks angrily back at me.

"I won't say it. I won't."

I write him another note.

"What about your wife? Will you say sorry to her?"

"She's not here. I thought you could see them?" His face turns red and he begins to cough.

Now it is my turn to be afraid. I don't want to make him angry. I don't want him to know I cannot see anyone.

"She was here when you were under the bed," I write, already feeling guilty. It is not like me to lie.

He looks around the room and checks again.

"She's gone," he says.

I nod.

I help him up and sit him on the bed. He gets under the blankets but doesn't lie down. I can tell that he is afraid to fall asleep as he breathes deeply and continues to shake.

"Will you stay with me for a while? At least until I fall asleep?" he asks.

I nod and I am amazed that within minutes he is sleeping soundly.

I take the tablets from his hiding place underneath the bed

and leave them on Aishling's desk outside my room. She is still sleeping soundly. I open my door as quietly as I can but my father says it creaks and no one has bothered to fix it. She raises her head sleepily.

"Christopher?" she asks as I move quickly into the doorway.

I close the door gently, hoping she will not remember that I was around.

In the morning, I wake early. I am tired and turn over to face the wall, trying to block out the sun that is glaring into my hot room. It is Saturday and the house is usually quieter on Saturdays when the day patients are at home with their families.

I pass quickly by Martin's room. Tina is helping him to the Penance Room and is scolding him for not taking his tablets. His arms are moving quickly and I know he is shouting. I pass quickly as I don't want to face him. He will know it was me who told.

I make my way to my mother's office. The door is open and there is a woman there that I don't know. I go in and sit down to listen. She has bright blue eyes and black hair tied tightly in a bun on top of her head.

"So, Greta, you're from London?" my mother asks.

The woman nods and smiles, revealing two gold teeth. I have never seen anyone with gold in their mouth before. I limp closer to her to see them and she doesn't move away from me. She has a happy way about her that I like.

"I nursed there for oh, about ten years. I came to Australia recently. Fancied a change of scenery. A bit of adventure. I got a few months' work at the hospital but that dried up. I know I'd get full-time work in a city but I prefer a smaller place. I want to see the real Australia."

"Well, you're the first to answer the advert. I only put it up yesterday," my mother says. "It's only part-time and there would be some shift covers if someone is sick. Do you think you could work at short notice?"

"Yeah. That'd be no problem."

"How do you feel about the elderly?"

My mother always asks this question.

Greta frowns and shrugs. "They are just people who are older."

My mother seems happy with this although I am never really sure what the wrong answer would be. She offers to show Greta around and they walk across the hallway to the Penance Room. My mother likes to introduce interviewees to the residents. She thinks they are good judges of character and she watches closely as Greta shakes their hands and smiles at them with her shiny teeth. Greta seems to pick up on Penelope and Victoria's nervousness and puts them at ease. She also knows not to try to shake hands with Wilfred who doesn't like to be touched. She kneels down to face Iren in her special chair. She has a gentle look in her eye and Iren smiles back. I swallow hard as she approaches Martin and Jimmy. They are in foul humour today, probably from drinking too much whiskey at the party last night. Instantly, and as though they planned it, they say in unison: "Fuckin' pommy!" Both men quickly turn to stare at each other, their eyes opened wide in amazement. It's the first time they have ever expressed the same point of view and this unnerves them both.

Greta, unperturbed, smiles at them. "Well, boys, no one knows for sure if the term 'pommy' refers to convicts transported here from the UK but, if it does, I came here of my own free will. Now, some of your ancestors might have travelled here free as 'Prisoners Of Mother England' but my fare cost me an arm and a leg!"

With that, Greta bursts out laughing and neither Jimmy nor Martin have any choice but to laugh along with her. Otherwise, it would look like she had got the better of them and they weren't having that.

Greta extends her hand to them and they both shake it. My mother is enjoying the scene and I notice her stifle a laugh.

She then takes Greta to the babies' room and introduces every resident there to her, even though most of them are asleep. She takes her into Father Hayes' room but he is kneeling down saying his rosary. Greta apologises for interrupting his prayers and moves quickly from the room. I can see the delight on my mother's face. Rita had upset Father Hayes more than once by taking the beads from his hands to look at them while he is praying. When they return to the Penance Room, Mina has come down and is sitting in her chair. She has obviously been stealing food from the kitchen again and a piece of toast is sticking out from under her. I see Greta look at it but she takes my mother's lead and doesn't say anything.

As they turn to leave the room they almost run into Kora who still has her hair tied up the way it was last night.

"Sorry!" Greta says jovially.

Kora frowns.

"This is my sister, Kora," my mother says.

I can see the look on Greta's face. I always enjoy it when my mother introduces Kora to people. There are always those few moments of awkwardness where people don't know what to say.

But Greta is not like most people and without malice or offence replies almost instantly, "Blimey, your dad got around!"

My mother and Kora look at each other and burst into laughter.

I can tell Mother is pleased. Everyone seems to like Greta and she has even got the better of Martin and Jimmy.

"When can you start?"

Greta smiles. "Whenever suits you."

I walk away and leave Greta and my mother to sort things out.

I usually follow my father around on Saturdays but he is still asleep. I go out to our side garden which is shaded by tall palm trees. Even though the back yard is much larger, you can see trains passing and though I am not afraid of them during the day, I still turn my eyes away as they pass and would prefer not to see them at all. I like the side garden better anyway because it feels like an oasis in a desert. My father has put a small water fountain to the side and a round wooden bench encircles a large gum tree in the centre.

Wilfred is sitting there alone. Like me, he is waiting for my father to wake up. I sit on the far side of the bench, anxious not to make him nervous. I can see the breeze blow the trees gently but it is not enough to cool us. Most of the garden is shaded at this time of the morning so it is a good time to sit here and think.

Maria said her parents are visiting this weekend but she has not invited me over to see them and I am unsure whether or not I should just visit anyway. I take off my shoes and love the feel of the hot sand beneath my feet. I stare at the hundreds of bull ants that are crawling over the bench and on the sand beneath us. I watch Wilfred scratch as the ants bite at him. They don't bother me now although I remember crying from the pain of a bite when I was little. My mother was asleep so Aishling put ice on it and gave me lollies to quieten me.

I sit in silence with Wilfred until my father comes out. He waves cheerfully as he enters the garden and sits down to settle into a conversation. As usual, I sit and watch. There is always something new to learn.

Chapter 10

It is Tuesday morning and I am sitting waiting patiently for Stéphane Laver to arrive. Not much happened over the weekend and I am anxious for some entertainment. Kora didn't go with Jeff to the dance but on Sunday, when he came to visit his father, she walked with him towards his car where they stood and talked for a few minutes. They stood sideways, leaning against the muddy truck and, no matter where I stood in the window, I could not see what they were saying. I wanted to creep outside and watch them from a closer position but I knew the screech of the fly-screen door would give me away so I seethed in the Penance Room, annoyed to be missing out on the news.

I give up on our visitor coming and walk towards the stairs. I am bored so decide to return to my room and read my history book. In the hallway I meet Mrs Bianchi who used to live in Jimmy's room before she was moved downstairs. She usually becomes confused at night and it is unusual to see her roaming in the daytime. I instantly know what she is looking for and go on a pretend search with her. Mrs Bianchi's husband died in an accident at the mine when she was only thirty-two and had four young children to feed. A few weeks after Mr Bianchi died, she pawned her wedding ring for cash but when she returned to retrieve it, someone had bought it and my mother said she never got over the shock. Mother said that Mrs Bianchi carried that shame with her for years and occasionally now I meet her in the hallway searching for her most prized possession. Together we look on the landing and in the dining room where Li is busy setting up for lunch. After a reasonable amount of time I pretend to pick up the ring and show it to her. Even though there is nothing in my hand she takes it from me and slips it back on her bony finger. She smiles and disappears, contented once more for at least a little while. I am bored and have a feeling of restlessness that is unusual for me. I go to my parents' room and look through my father's books but there is nothing new that interests me. Even though I am only thirteen, I have surpassed the school books for my age. That is what happens when you have no friends and nothing else to do. I go to Penelope and Victoria's room. They are downstairs so it is safe to lie on Victoria's pink-sheeted bed and stare at the sun moving across the ceiling. When they came here first my mother went to great lengths to decorate their room the way they wanted it. The whole room is covered in faded pink-flowered wallpaper with pink carpet and a matching pink wardrobe and dressing-table. There is a smell of musty perfume in the air and their matching floral dressing-gowns hang neatly on the wardrobe door.

There are several photos of the women on the dressing table and I pick them up, one at a time, and stare at their faces which change and look more fearful as the years advance. There is only one photo where they look happy. It is the photo that Rita made fun of. The sisters look to be about five and seven and behind them stands a large woman wearing a black servant's dress and starched white apron. There are big trees in the background and the girls seem to be standing in a large green field. In the far left-hand corner I can see the faint outline of cattle grazing. As

Penelope is older I decide she must be the taller of the two. She is wearing a white dress and there is an awkward-looking ribbon tied around her bobbed fair hair. Two of her front teeth are missing and she is smiling happily into the camera. Victoria is the cuter of the two and has long blonde ringlets and a confident dimpled smile. She has a frilly dress and what looks like ballerina shoes on her feet. What strikes me most is how different the girls looked from one another back then and how it is sometimes hard to tell them apart now.

I pick up the second photo in which the sisters are in their late teens or maybe early twenties. Gone are the ringlets and both sisters, dressed in tight corseted dresses, stare sombrely into the camera. I can see the outline of their white knuckles as they tightly hold each other's hands but their eyes give nothing away. It looks like a studio photo with no background and it is impossible to tell if they are happy or sad. I look closer into their faces and notice that their eyes look lifeless as if they were both gazing away to a far-off place of their dreams. I put the photo down and look at the next one. In this photo both women have become thin and gaunt. They are now much older and are standing outside a large building under a heavy grey sky. They have large dark circles under their pale eyes and only the third woman in the photo is smiling. I look closer at her and see that she is the nanny from the photo of the girls when they were small. I realise that I would love to know the stories behind these photos and hope that the women can remember all of these places. The other two photos are similar in that the women look sadder and much older, possibly taken shortly before they came here. There are no photos of their brother or their father, which I think is odd. I lie back on Victoria's bed and imagine their life. I used to think that it must have been exciting living on army bases all over the world and having so much money that you could afford nannies and house servants, but the sisters were not happy despite all that they had and I realise that money doesn't make anyone happy, that kind people make other people happy and Penelope and Victoria's father was not kind. I sigh and drag myself off Victoria's bed and cross the hall to my room. It is getting very hot and I decide to lie down for a while. As I pull down my blind, I look out onto the train line and see that it is clear.

As I drift off to sleep I imagine Stéphane Laver walking towards me. I don't know what he looks like but imagine him as having bright blue eyes and blond hair which is shining under the sun as he makes his way down what seems to be a never-ending road to our house. He keeps on walking though and doesn't seem to tire of the journey. Occasionally I say to him "Keep walking, you're almost there," and he smiles straight at me.

When I awake I look at my watch which is working again and find that it is almost five thirty in the afternoon. I feel the vibration of the fly-screen door slamming and jump out of bed, falling over a box of supplies that are in my way. I run downstairs and find my mother standing in the hallway with a blond man and I am amazed that Stéphane Laver looks just as I imagined him. He is carrying a large back-pack and looks more like a traveller than a university researcher. He has curly blond hair that reaches his collar and even from this distance I see can that he has the brightest blue eyes I have ever seen. There is something special about him and I find I cannot look away. He steps further into the hallway. He looks in my direction and smiles as if he knows me, as if he knows this house and all its worries and my heart quickens. I don't get much attention.

He introduces himself to my mother and apologises for being late. He tells her he had car trouble.

"You drove from Sydney?"

"Nah, I'm travelling from town to town. I flew to Bourke where I had some people to interview. Hired a car from there. Sorry I'm late. Left myself a bit short of time."

"No problem," said my mother and she laughs, "I thought you were going to be French!"

"Yeah. My parents are French. Guess they wanted me to have a French name."

"Oh. Were you born in France, Stéphane?"

"Call me Steve. Nah, right here in Australia. Sydney."

My mother smiles. "Right, well, how do you want to do this? I think it might be a bit late to start today. I've got consent from most of the residents. Some are not interested of course but I think you'll get some of the information you are looking for." She is looking through copies of the consent forms and laughs as she glances at Mina Jensen's form. She wants her pseudonym to be Marlene Dietrich. "Perhaps you should start with Mina. She seems most enthusiastic!"

Steve looks at his watch.

"Okay. Well, how 'bout ten tomorrow morning. That suit?"

"That's fine, Steve."

"Em – do you know if there's a good hotel in town? I didn't get around to making all my bookings."

"Well, yes, there are quite a few. I'll get Aishling to show you."

My mother calls Aishling who is up from her day-time sleep.

When she comes to the front of the house, she stares at Steve and he stares back at her. He is looking at Aishling the same way that he looked at me, as if he can see right through her. She blushes and I am embarrassed for her. I know how that feels. I follow them out of the house and watch as Aishling drives in front of Steve, leading him towards the nearest hotel. The sky has turned red with the descending sun and the last of the rays are shining on the gum trees, making them look as though they are on fire. I feel a sudden surge of energy. Tomorrow all my hopes of salvation will begin to unfold, freeing me and the people who live here.

Chapter 11

When Steve arrives on time the following morning, my mother takes him into the Penance Room and introduces him to Mina. I notice that Mina is dressed in her Sunday dress and she is wearing too much make-up. She seems anxious and I watch her throat move up and down quickly as though she is trying to swallow something hard.

"Mina, do you mind the others remaining in the room? There is nowhere else for them to go. But if you prefer, Steve could interview you in your room?"

Mina shakes her head. "No. It's fine."

Even though Mina wants to tell her story, she is nervous and prefers the security and company of the others in the lounge room.

Steve sits down and takes out a tape recorder. He is staring at the pews from my grandfather's church. My mother follows his eyes and laughs.

"My father was a minister. His church burned and, well, I like having the pews here. Feels like he's always near me."

Steve smiles. There is a calmness about him that I have not

seen in any other person. Mina looks around the room and takes stock of her surroundings. She looks at Jimmy and Martin who are looking coldly back at her. Wilfred is sitting on the farthest pew, reading or at least pretending to read. Iren is sedated and is smiling vacantly into space. Father Hayes is snoozing on the pew in the bay window. He is hunched over, his large nose creating a long awkward shape across his face and making him look like a sleeping koala. Penelope and Victoria are sitting upright as though a sermon is about to begin. Greta, our new nurse, is sitting beside them. She has taken a special interest in the sisters and already she has gained their trust which is very hard to do. Li is sitting by the door. She got through her work as quickly as she could and has asked my mother if it would be all right to listen to Mina's story. Even Aishling, tired from her night's work, is here.

Kora stands and whispers something to Mina who is wringing her hands. Small beads of sweat have formed on her forehead.

"No, I'm fine," she replies to whatever Kora asked her.

My mother nods to Steve to start.

He has a list of questions he wants to ask her but Mina doesn't want to follow a set interview. She leans towards the tape recorder and clears her throat to speak.

"My name is Mina Jensen and I was born in Rotterdam in 1903. I was Mina Van Buren then and I had a very happy childhood."

Everybody in the room is engrossed in Mina's words and nobody moves. She looks so happy telling this part of her life. Her blue eyes are shining and her smile seems to fill out the heavy lines in her thin face. My mother says that Mina speaks with a heavy Dutch accent. I have no idea what this sounds like but I can see that Steve is finding it hard to understand her as he leans closer and turns his ear towards her.

"Both of my parents were teachers and it was expected that my brother and I should go to university. We had a very happy home. But I never got to university although everybody said this was a shame because I was a bright girl who learnt easily, even easier than my brother Pieter who had finished his degree and who went to work in Indonesia as an engineer. His friend, Dirk Halse, went to college with him and often Dirk would come to our house for the weekend or perhaps for holidays. He didn't have parents alive and had an uncle who paid for his education. When Pieter went away, of course, my parents were broken-hearted. Dirk still came to visit and after a while we fell in love. One year later, he wanted to go to Indonesia where Pieter said he could get him a good job with a good salary. It was called the Dutch East Indies at that time. Dirk didn't want to go without me but I didn't want to leave my parents alone. My parents said it was better if we were all together in one place and they would come too. So in 1922 I married Dirk and took the long ship journey to Java. I was nineteen years old. My parents followed us one year later after they sold their house. I had to say goodbye to my grandmother and I never saw her again. She was too old to come with us and she didn't wish for a new life.

"In Java, life was good but I missed my home. This got better when my parents came to stay. We lived just outside Jakarta and it was the most beautiful place I ever saw. It was hot and always I hate the European winter. Always I hate snow. The people were friendly and nice to us. Mother and Father lived with us and Pieter lived in the town but stayed with us on weekends. Dirk had a good job and we could afford servants. I didn't speak any English then and could not speak Javanese. But I knew a lot of people there who were Dutch or who could speak Dutch so it was not too bad. After a few years I could speak the local language and also a little English. By then I had become used to the rich lifestyle and depended on the servants to do everything around the home. I could not cook then so it was better.

"My mother said one day, 'Mina, you are becoming useless and God has no use for idle people.'"

Mina stops talking and I can see that she is reflecting on this.

She shakes her head and takes a deep breath in, blowing it out with force and licking her dry lips.

"My mother was right."

She looks around and moves her hand across her body, as if she is turning the page of a book, a new chapter in her life.

"Dirk and I were very happy but sometimes he wanted to return to Holland. His uncle wrote often, begging him to return. But how could I go to Holland and leave my parents once again? We often argued about it. Pieter had not married and my mother was feeble with arthritis. She needed a woman's help and I stopped being useless and spent all my time looking after my mother. No matter what choice I made, I would have let somebody down."

Mina's eyes fill with tears. Steve asks if she wants to stop but she shakes her head.

"There was another problem also. I could not keep a child inside and lots of times I lost pregnancies and Dirk was angry with me. He would say, 'You are working too hard. You should not let your mother lean on you. Let the servants take care of her.' But my mother didn't want the servants to help her bathe or dress. My mother knew something that we in our ignorance and selfishness didn't. She often said to me 'Mina, one day there will be trouble.' The trouble that my mother spoke of came when I was thirty-nine years of age and five months pregnant – it was the longest I had ever held onto a pregnancy and Dirk and I hoped that we would finally have a family. The Japanese invaded Indonesia in 1942 and we, the Dutch, were enraged at their insolence. We didn't think that we were also invaders.

"My mother had died and my father spent most of his time at Pieter's house. He said there were too many memories at my house, that he could see my mother in every corner of every room. I missed him greatly but I was looking forward to being a mother and took very great care of myself. When I think of those times I think that we lived in a bubble. My husband and I had a life of luxury that we thought would never change.

"One day, we heard news that the Japanese were taking men to camps. Our servant, Ramalan, told me that he saw my father and brother in a truck driven by Japanese soldiers. I didn't believe it so I drove to Pieter's house but there was no one there. I ran to his friend Albert's house but his wife, who was an Indonesian lady, said that they had taken all the men away. She was crying and was holding her baby son in her arms. He was only a few weeks old. She said that they were taking them to a camp so I went there to look for them. At the gates, trucks were coming in and out and there were wounded European men lying on the ground inside the gate. I shouted to them. I asked for my brother and father but no one knew them so I thought that everything would be all right, that they were hiding somewhere, possibly even at my house. So I returned home. Dirk had come home as soon as he heard the news. He was worried for me and shook me when I arrived, saying I had put myself and our baby in danger.

"I waited for news all evening but no one came. I sent messages to people whom I thought Pieter and my father might go to but no one had seen them so we could do nothing but remain in the house with the servants all weekend. On Monday, Dirk went to work as normal. His employer, Mr Costar, said they were only collecting up some foreigners but that people working for him would be okay. Dirk never came home and a servant of Mr Costar's came to the house in the darkness and said that his boss and Dirk had been taken to the camp with the other employees. I never saw my husband again and I . . ."

Mina's lips begin to quiver and tears fall quickly and silently down her cheeks.

Steve takes a deep breath and looks around the room. He is amazed that he got so much history from one old lady but he feels he has put her through enough and stops the tape recorder.

"I'm not finished, young man," she says.

"Thought you might want a break, Mina."

"No, thank you. The rest is burning up inside my throat. I never told anyone this story, not even my second husband. Of course I met him there in that awful camp so what was there to talk about? He knew what I knew."

Steve turns his tape recorder back on and Mina continues.

"Every day I went to that camp looking for my father, my brother and my husband. Each day I would stand at the camp gates asking for them. One day a man, Lars Jensen, saw me and took pity on me. My pregnancy was visible and standing in the heat all day waiting for news was having its effect on my health. Lars was a baker in town and I had known him a little beforehand. He was overweight and not at all handsome. He called me over and asked if I had a cigarette. I snapped at him and asked if that was all he was worried about. He looked upset and I felt bad. He was locked up and I was free although I had heard that women were beginning to be taken to camps. I didn't believe this was true. What would they want to put women and children in camps for? Lars told me that Dirk was inside but that Pieter and my father had been taken to another camp. He said that Dirk was injured, that a Japanese soldier had beaten him on the head and stuck a knife in his leg. He said the wound was infected and that Dirk could not walk. He agreed to give him a message and I left that day with my heart soaring. I was still worried for my brother and father but my husband was alive and he could help me find them when he got out. I began to realise how useless I had become and that my mother had seen all this coming while I was enjoying parties and becoming more useless as each year of my life passed. I made a promise to myself that I would never be useless again, that I would always be strong – and here I am with two shattered hips and no courage to live in my home any more. I didn't even keep my promise to myself." She pauses and adds, "I think that if I had left Indonesia when my husband asked me to, he might have lived."

73

Mina falls silent and this time agrees to a break. Li brings cake and coffee in and everybody eats in silence. I watch as she moves towards Mina as if she is going to hug her but Mina looks up at her and as usual glares at her, an expression of suspicion spreading across her face. Li returns to the kitchen and I know I am the only one who sees her wipe a tear for Mina Jensen.

When everyone finishes eating, Steve turns his microphone on again and Mina sits up straight to continue her story.

"For weeks that was all I did – stand at those gates and speak with Lars and other people I knew. It was overcrowded and the men looked filthy. They were all losing weight, even Lars who had been a fat man. Sometimes Lars would have a note from Dirk and my heart would beat fast with joy. Some of the Japanese soldiers were nice but still they would not let me in to see him. At night I would sleep with Dirk's notes under my pillow. I would keep saying, 'You will get out of this and we will return to Holland together with our baby.' But of course, this never happened. I never saw a doctor during this time because the Dutch doctor we used to visit had disappeared and no one knew where he was gone. One day, I got to the gates and Lars looked upset when he saw me but he didn't tell me what he knew. He was afraid for my baby. For two more weeks I went there and each day I realised a little more what was wrong. My husband had died and Lars would not tell me. A red angry infection had crawled up his leg from his wound and poisoned his blood. Even now I think of my – my lovely man lying dying on a filthy bed only needing a doctor but no one helped him. The Japanese didn't care if he lived or died. Every day, I think it was my fault. But then I think that Holland was occupied by the Germans so perhaps we would have escaped Jakarta and died in Holland anyway."

Mina looks over at Wilfred but he looks quickly away. I feel that he wants to leave the room but is too afraid to move. He doesn't want to draw attention to himself. He spends his life trying to avoid people's eyes.

"I remember Lars' eyes as he stood holding the bars of those gates. I never saw a man cry before but he was crying for me. I said: 'Lars, please tell me. I know, I know, so please tell me.'

"When he said those words I screamed so loud that I frightened myself. Lars put out his strong arms and pulled me closer to him. He held me so tightly that I could feel the hard metal of the gates crushing into my body. His eyes were imploring me to quieten. He said 'Stop, stop crying!' in Dutch. I didn't know that a soldier was walking down to see what this noise was. Then I remember someone pulling me away. A short Japanese man was staring at my face. He ordered me to do something. I didn't speak Japanese but I understood his tone. In one moment I thought how ridiculous this was. I was bigger than him and I think at that time I must have gone a little mad. I started slapping his chest and screaming for Dirk. He stood there and stared at me with his narrow brown eyes that had no look of life in them and then raised his rifle and hit me in the face."

Mina raises her hand to her forehead and massages the long white line that runs across her brow. She stops for a moment and turns her head to the right, as if she is again turning a page to a new chapter in her life. The room is completely silent and nobody moves. Even Iren seems to be listening.

"I fell down but stood up quickly. I could see it all happening as if I was watching myself from far away. Blood was pouring down my face but I didn't feel any pain and in my memory I have an expression on my face that was very strange. I said 'Murderer' over and over to him. I could hear Lars pleading with me to stop and I could hear Mr Perkins, an Englishman we knew, shout out in English but they seemed very far away. The soldier shouted something to me that I didn't understand but no doubt he was ordering me to stop, giving me one last chance to back down. I moved closer to him and did something I have never done before. I spit in his face and even now, even with what he did, I am horrified that I did this. My parents would have been so ashamed. The soldier raised his rifle. His face and neck were bright red with anger. I thought he was going to shoot me and in that moment I didn't care. I wanted to be with Dirk. But he didn't shoot me. He hit me in the stomach and I fell forward onto the ground where I knelt in pain on the hot sand. Someone tried to stand me up. My eyes were closed tight from the pain but I could hear the soldier shout out and I was put back on the ground. It seemed to me that I was left there for a long time, perhaps as a lesson to others. I could feel myself drift off and wake again. I thought I heard Dirk's voice and that he was trying to lift me but it was two soldiers raising me roughly to my feet and dragging me away. I looked back at Lars who was holding on so tight to those bars that they should have snapped in his big hands. I will never forget the look on his face yet I cannot describe it. On the ground was a long red streak of blood, my baby pouring from me. I never saw Dirk's body so I realise that on that very spot I left my husband and my baby and also in reality, myself. Nothing that happened after that mattered much to me."

Mina stops talking and Steve reaches forward and stops the recorder. He takes a deep breath. I can tell by his face that he hadn't planned on obtaining this type of story and what he really wanted was stories of poverty-stricken Europeans leaving their homeland and settling happily in Australia, the land of plenty. He wanted stories about how they managed to adjust to a new country and keep their own culture at the same time. Steve takes a large gulp of water and offers Mina a drink. I search her face and even though her eyes are watery she looks determined to finish her story. I realise that she needs to finish it today and that nothing will dissuade her from this.

Steve turns the machine back on and she continues.

"I woke up in the hospital and a nurse told me that my baby was gone, as if I didn't already know this. She said it was a boy and I cried for the rest of that day and the day after. Someone sent word to my household that I was there and Merpati, my maid, came to see me at the hospital. She was crying but I could tell that she was afraid when I grabbed her tight and held onto her while I cried. I had never touched her before, not even to shake her hand for all she did for me. There is a lot for an old woman to be ashamed of. Merpati brought me photos of my family, my jewellery and as many clothes as she could carry. She knew that I would not be returning to my home but I didn't know this then. Three days later I was brought with two other European women in my ward to a truck which was already full of other white women. One of the women from the hospital was English and had a new baby girl that she had named Hope. Her husband was missing and she had heard nothing from him for weeks but she was glad to find her younger sister on the truck. I watched them embrace and thought about my brother and my father. I no longer believed that they were alive and, even if they were, I wondered how they would ever find me. I watched as the woman tried to feed her child but she had not much milk and the baby cried almost all of the time. Each time the baby cried I felt a deep pain in my stomach. As darkness fell I could not stand to listen to any more crying. I grabbed the baby from her mother and put her to my breast. It was the hardest thing I have ever done in my life. The baby started to suck but I could not look at her. I looked away and cried silently as the truck drove further and further away from my home. The child's mother moved across and sat beside me. She said 'I am Mary' and held my hand as we both cried silently.

"It was dark when the truck stopped and we had not been given anything to eat or drink all day. One by one we were unloaded into several buildings. I could see nothing around except palm trees and jungle. I had no idea where we were or which direction we had taken from Jakarta. Mary and her sister Jane were in my building with two other women and a younger girl of about fifteen. One of the women, Scyler, was Dutch and I had known her socially. She was wealthier than Dirk and me and I was shocked to see how dirty she looked. She could not face me and at first she pretended not to know me. We were given dirty mattresses to sleep on and all night we scratched our skin because of fleas. The following morning we were made to work carrying stones a long way and building walls that seemed to have no purpose. We settled into a routine and ate whatever little food was given to us. I kept feeding little Hope even though she didn't seem to gain much weight. One day when there was no one else around Scyler said to me, 'You need to stop feeding that English baby. To survive, you need all your weight for yourself.' I couldn't forget her saying that and I wondered what was becoming of us. Of course, I kept feeding the child and despite myself I had a bond with her. When her mother died of malaria, she called me Mama. It hurt my heart. I didn't want anyone to call me Mama except my own son. We lived there for more than one year and every day was the same, working hard in the hot sun and lying on dirty mattresses at night. Sometimes at night it was cold and we struggled to stay warm. But we didn't know how lucky we were there. The soldiers sometimes beat us for breaking rules but it was not all that bad.

"One day we were rounded up and taken by truck a very long way and then we boarded a train. We were brought to another camp, much bigger. It was overcrowded and people there were really sick. I thought to myself, 'This is where I will die.' At the first camp I had recovered from malaria and even though I had become very thin, I was stronger than most of the women but I knew that my strength would not last forever. Within two months of our time there, Scyler died and her words warning me to look after myself rang in my ears and haunted my dreams. Hope was now fourteen months old but she still needed nursing so I continued to feed her even though I was turning to skin and bone. I encouraged her to call her Aunt Jane 'Mama'. If she reached for me, unless it was time to feed her, I would shove her away. Everything she did I knew my son would be doing now – every new tooth, her first step – he should have been doing too. But she had lost her mother as I had lost my son so, in a way, I loved her. I realise this now. You come to realise a lot when you are old. Before they took Scyler's body away, I took the jewellery that I knew she had hidden in her underclothes. I used it to get things for Hope: medicine, extra food and clothes. Some soldiers were happy to take gold for such things. I felt guilty then for stealing but Scyler was gone, she no longer needed it, and I had to keep Hope alive.

"Some nights the Japanese soldiers would come inside our dorms and take one of the younger women away. I was almost forty-one then and glad that they were not interested in me. I would lie on my mattress and think of Dirk and our son. I was in a dorm with many women and things were not good between us. People were desperate for clothes and you had to sleep on your belongings to keep them. Food was scarce and the Japanese didn't give us enough to live on. If you didn't eat quickly, someone would take your food. Lots of people had dysentery and, if you were ill, you had to hide your food in your clothes and eat it when you felt better. The only one I gave some of my food to was Hope. She remained a skinny child with hardly any hair. I figured that if she died, my hope would die with her and I would die also so I made sure she had everything she needed to survive. I was caught trading jewellery for which I was beaten but I no longer cared about such things. I had changed. Life was not worth much and my only reason to keep going was to see if my papa and brother were alive and waiting for me in Holland.

"Sometimes news leaked around the camp and other women said that the war was coming to an end and that the Japanese were sending prisoners back to Holland by ship. Some of the women worked outside the camp and one time two of them were caught smuggling things inside. For punishment, the soldiers left us without food for three days. When they finally brought food to us, I didn't eat ravenously as the other women did but ate only a small amount of what they brought. I promised myself that I would never go hungry again so I portioned out my food and hid it in my clothes. For some reason I always felt hungry, even when I had just eaten and I hated this feeling so much. It was as if I could not satisfy something inside myself . . . but I survived . . ."

Mina smiles a self-satisfied smile to herself. I see Li whisper to Tina that she now understands why Mina hides food and Tina responds by saying that she knows why Mina becomes angry when she tries to take her clothes away for washing. Everyone else remains quiet and even Jimmy looks like he is affected by Mina's story.

"What happened to the little English baby?" he asks with sad eyes.

"She lived," Mina replies, smiling. "She writes to me," she adds with a proud face.

Steve stops the tape. My mother looks at her watch and cannot believe that it is lunch-time. Li runs to the kitchen to cook a quick meal for everyone. Steve stands and stretches.

"Would it be all right if we started again tomorrow, Mina?"

Mina nods. I suspect that the worst part of her story is over and that she is glad to have got it off her chest.

My mother walks Steve to the door and agrees for him to come again tomorrow morning at ten. When the meal is ready, Li calls everyone to the dining room but Mina remains in the lounge room looking out the window. She moves her walking frame forward and makes her way to the stairs. My mother follows her.

"Aren't you coming to eat, Mina?"

Mina shakes her head. "I'm not hungry, Emma, thank you."

My mother stands for a few minutes looking after Mina before lowering her head and coming in to join the others.

When she sits down to eat, I see her say to Kora, "I hope this isn't a mistake."

I think, "No, Mother, this is not a mistake."

80

Chapter 12

When I awake it is already half past nine and I realise that I did not dream of the train and had slept soundly. Instead I had dreamt of Mina as a young girl running through fields of sugar cane with her brother. There were no lines on her face and she was smiling. I wonder what she dreamt last night and hope they were nice dreams of when she was happy. I get out of bed and look briefly at my foot and notice that it is not as sore as it usually is. I raise it towards me and prod the unevenly stitched flesh but it does not hurt. I wonder if it is finally getting better and smile to myself as I dress quickly before racing down to the Penance Room for the rest of Mina's story. Steve is already there and I notice that Aishling has waited up again and is smiling strangely at him. Something about her face makes me redden and I feel a little angry towards Steve although I don't understand why.

Mina coughs and prepares to continue with her story. She is wearing the same blue dress and again has too much make-up on. There are dark circles under her pale blue eyes that already look filled with tears. I am worried now that she spent her night going over all the bad things that happened to her and I worry that my mother is right. This is not what I want. I want everyone to put their bad stories behind them and think about the times that were happy.

Steve plays back the last few minutes of Mina's recording but she pulls at her brooch impatiently and doesn't look as if she needs to be reminded where she stopped. She puts her hand to her neck and closes her eyes. I can see her throat moving up and down and know that she is nervous.

"We stayed at the new camp for more than another year and around me everyone was dying of disease. Those that lived were getting angry and no one wanted to share anything, even to share for children who were dying faster than adults I noticed. There were no boys. They came and took them all away except the little ones who were still not much more than babies. No one told us where they went and it suddenly came to my mind that it was better that my son didn't see any of this. It was best that he died and didn't live a life of feeling afraid."

I look quickly over at my mother who swallows hard. I know she is thinking of me.

"Twice I nursed Jane, Hope's aunt, back to health. I told her, 'You cannot die. Hope needs you.' Once she asked me, in a fever, 'Will you look after Hope?' and I said, 'No, I will not – you must live, Jane. I cannot look after anyone.' I think this is why she lived. Once when she wrote to me from Canada, she asked if I was telling the truth all those years ago and I think of course I would have looked after Hope because I would have had no choice. I could not let her die. As I have said, if she died I would also have died. There would have been no reason to live.

"For many months I had sores on my feet and even then I still had to work. At night I would cut them and let the liquid pour out from them. I remember it smelt very bad and used to burn. I still hold onto food and keep it safe. I was always afraid that there would be no more and I would die. I stayed out of the soldiers' way and worked hard. I never looked them in the eye.

They didn't like you to do that. I kept thinking that it was possible that my brother and papa were alive so I didn't allow myself to think of them dead even though I had dreamt this very often. It is hard to control your dreams.

"After one more year we heard that the war was over but the Japanese didn't tell us at first. We saw that there were fewer soldiers and one day an important soldier came and we had to line up and tell them where we came from. Again I thought, this is it, they are separating us and will only kill the races they don't like. But we were all sent to another camp, this time not so far on the truck. The soldiers said it was for our safety. They told us that the Indonesians wanted to kill us but I didn't believe this was true.

"When we arrived I could see lots of people in the town moving around and I could see the ocean but I had no idea where this place was. We were put into different buildings and for the first time I was separated from Hope and Jane. All of the women in my room were Dutch and I knew something was about to happen. I saw Jane in an exercise yard and I told her where I was from in Holland. She gave me her parents' address in England. We had nothing to write on and I spent the day trying to memorise the strange-sounding English words in her address. We realised that we didn't know each other's last names and smiled as each of us spelt them out like we were being introduced for the first time. We both laughed as we realised how silly all of this was because we both thought that we were soon going to die. For the first time I hugged Hope and ran my hand over her blonde head. I smelt her and I cried like a baby until she pulled away, afraid. A soldier shouted and I walked away quickly.

"The next morning we woke to the sound of big noise. There was shouting and I could hear people crying. I know the sound of fear. I have never forgotten it. All of the women in my group were put on the truck but no one told us where we were going. One woman said we were being taken a long way and put on boats to be set free . . ."

Wilfred gasps and everyone looks his way. No one knows why he has reacted this way. Mina continues.

"I strained my neck looking into the large yard for Hope but there were too many people and everyone was in panic. When the truck pulled away I thought 'Why do they not just shoot us here?' But when we arrived at the water there was a big ship there and already I could see people on this ship, European men who were staring down at us and my heart jumped. I realised that we were being set free."

Mina's thoughts are broken by something on the other side of the room. It is Wilfred. His face has gone bright red and he looks as though he cannot breathe. No one knows why the mention of the ship has frightened him but I feel that when Wilfred gets to tell his story, we will understand. Mina looks at him for a moment and continues.

"Then the soldiers just walked away from us. One said 'Goodbye to colonialists!' in English and I understood. We climbed onto the ship which was already crowded. A woman there told me we would not leave until the next day because we were waiting on more people. No one seemed to be in charge so I found a bunk and lay there. Everywhere people were talking about going home but this was my home. I had been in Jakarta for more years than I had lived in Holland and, also, there was no one there now. My family had all died here and Holland didn't seem home without them. I wondered what I would do there. I had no money and no place to stay. It will seem silly to say that a part of me wanted to return to the camp and work for my food. I was suddenly very afraid.

"That evening, I stood and watched the sun setting over the ocean when three trucks screeched up, letting more men off to board the ship. Some of them were injured and I watched them help each other on board with pity and joy in my heart. The sun was still bright and I put my hand over my eyes. A man walking with crutches looked familiar to me and I squinted at him, trying to get a closer look. My mouth dropped open and I let out a scream. *'Pieter! Pieter!'* My brother looked up at me and dropped to his knees. Someone helped him up and handed him his crutch. 'Mina!' he shouted as he climbed the stairs. I ran to meet my crippled brother halfway and when we finally reached each other we stopped more than two metres from each other and stared at our lovely faces on the crowded hallway. We both looked so different but I knew him. I knew my brother. I could see tears falling down his face at the very sight of me. I then ran to him and hugged him so tight because I was afraid he would soon disappear. He stood back from me.

"'Papa?' I asked but he shook his head.

"'Dirk?' he asked but he didn't wait for an answer and hugged me again as I cried into his chest.

"Neither of us were ready to find out how the people we loved had died. There were no bunks left so I brought my brother to my bunk which another Dutchwoman was holding for me. I helped my brother lie down on it and sat on the floor beside him. I looked at his damaged leg and worried that he was permanently crippled. I remember him looking sadly at me.

"'My leg will heal,' he said to me in Dutch, 'but, sister, I don't think our hearts will.'"

Mina's lips begin to tremble and her eyes fill with tears. Penelope gives her a hankie and pats her back. Steve stops the tape and Li goes to organise coffee. Everybody looks sad and I can see Jimmy staring at Mina like he has never seen her before.

While everyone has coffee, I sit by the window and notice Jeff Young pulling up in his truck. He has a cage on the back and comes smiling up the pathway with his hat as usual covering his narrow eyes.

Kora is in the garden and I watch as she follows him to the back of the vehicle. She is smiling at something. It is rare to see Kora smile like that so I decide to follow them out and investigate. In a large cage, two black and white sheepdog pups are panting in the heat. Kora lifts one up and hugs it closely. My heart pounds a little. I don't like dogs because I was bitten once when I was five.

"Oh he's gorgeous, mate!" Kora says to Jeff and she smiles at him the same way I saw Aishling smiling at Steve earlier.

"Ya want him? Bitch had a large litter and these two are left. They're good work dogs."

I gulp. Please say no, Kora, I am thinking.

"Not sure I've much use for a sheep dog but might make a good pet. Gets lonely at my place at night. There's been a few break-ins, ya know. Might be good protection."

I see Jeff move his lips as if he is going to say something but he decides not to and leans against the truck as he smiles shyly at Kora.

"Maybe Emma would like the other one?" he says.

I sigh heavily. I was afraid he would say that.

"She'd love it, mate. She had a dog just like this once. I remember she was heart-broken when it died. She didn't speak to me for weeks after . . . don't know why . . . hmm . . ." Kora stops talking as if a painful memory has made its way to the front of her mind. She frowns and shrugs, as if unsure what exactly it was. "I'll bring her in."

"Him, they're both male," he says, laughing.

Everyone has returned from the garden and has taken refuge from the heat in the cool Penance Room. When Kora puts the dogs on the floor, I tense. Even though they are only pups I am afraid of being bitten. The dogs sense it and I hide behind Martin as they snarl at me which makes everyone in the room laugh.

"I don't think they like you, Martin," Kora laughs but he doesn't say anything.

Only my mother and I notice that Mina has not eaten any cake or biscuits and has barely touched her coffee. She sits stony-faced waiting on the others to listen to the rest of her story. I see Penelope lean towards her but I can't see what she is saying. Mina smiles and Penelope touches her face gently while Victoria touches Mina's knee as she passes. I have never seen them interact with each other before.

Steve returns from the front porch where he has been talking and laughing with Aishling. I didn't go out to watch their conversation. I didn't want to know what he was saying to her. Aishling, exhausted from her night's work, goes to bed and Mina clears her throat once again and begins to speak.

"We found out that our ship was sailing first to Sri Lanka and then on to Rotterdam. We all wondered what Europe would be like after the war but everyone agreed that it could not be much worse than where we had been. Each night Pieter would talk with the men on the deck while the women gathered in the sleeping areas to chat while they put the children to sleep. I remember feeling strange during these evenings and it was the first time I realised that I didn't really belong anywhere.

"Many of the women had lost children but most had at least one surviving child with them. On our first night together as a group I noticed the women being quiet when a woman who lost all three of her children came into the dorm. Her husband had also died and the women felt sorry for her as she would face old age childless. I could not stand for them to pity me so I decided not to mention my son to them. I have never been able to cope with pity. It was something I had no use for. I think that they must have thought me to be cold but I didn't care about this. Some nights I would sit and stare at the bunk above me and wonder if Hope had survived and if so, where she was. I hoped she was all right and found myself praying that I would only hear news that she survived. If she died, I never wanted to know this.

"One night Pieter came to my bunk very excited. He was able to walk a little better and had moved in with the men where he met Lars. When he brought me to meet him, it was strange. We had shared such personal moments at those gates where he watched me for weeks waiting to see my husband and watched me lose my child but our reunion was shy and awkward as if we were both embarrassed by the memory and wished to erase it. Over some weeks, we would walk the ship at night and talk only about the future. Lars wanted to open a bakery in Rotterdam where he still had family. The day before we arrived in Holland he asked me to marry him and I said yes. I saw no reason not to. It was suitable that we should marry. He knew I was now too old to have another child but he didn't care. We had endured such an awful thing and I think we could only face a future with someone who understood this – although, you know, you may not believe it but we never spoke of it. But it was always there. The memory of Indonesia was always around us even if we didn't give it words.

"When we arrived in Rotterdam, things were not as we expected. All over Europe, damage from bombs could be seen. People were tired and angry. Some Dutch people didn't welcome us as we thought they would. They called us colonialists. The only happy event was that almost two years after we arrived, a letter came in the local post office for me. I almost didn't get it as it was addressed to Mina Halse but I was now Mina Jensen. Luckily, someone remembered my parents and remembered I had been married to Dirk Halse. It was from Jane and she had married a man from England and moved to Toronto. I could understand English but not to read it so much so I had to get some help. In the envelope there was a photo of Hope and it made me cry with happiness. She was a beautiful little girl with lots of curly hair and she was sitting on a not-real horse in a photograph studio. I remember thinking that she looked like Shirley Temple. I wrote back and we stayed in touch.

"In the winter of 1947, two years after we arrived in Holland, Lars closed his bakery and we moved to another colony, to Australia. Pieter came with us and Lars' brother who was also a baker and his wife Bertha. Together we took another long ship journey and I was glad to start in a new place. Pieter got work as an engineer with the mine so Lars and I came with him here to Broken Hill. His brother and wife stayed in Sydney where we had first arrived. Bertha had a sister there who could get them both work.

"Lars and I opened a bakery and each day he would teach me how to bake. After a short time I was able to bake anything you wanted. I was no longer useless. My mother would have been proud. Pieter died almost twelve years after we first came here. He was only fifty-eight years old but I was thankful to God for giving my brother back to me for that time and they had been happy years where we ate and laughed together. It was like we returned to our childhood. Life seemed finally to be peaceful and we were thankful for everything that we had. You know, our lives in Holland had been rich and higher class and yet here I was up to my elbows in flour but we were happy. I am glad that Pieter had some happy years before he di–"

Mina stops talking and touches the scar on her forehead. I can see her eyes fill with tears again.

"You have to be thankful. That's what I have learnt. Everywhere, people have hard times but you need to be happy where you can. Lars and I were never in love like Dirk and I. It was a different marriage. Not so passionate but love just the same. Every few months I got a letter from Jane and I watched Hope getting bigger and bigger. Something I had nurtured was growing in this world so it was not all for nothing. Something good came from something very bad. Lars died peacefully in his sleep which I am also glad about. He was not ill. We closed the shop one evening and we sat together listening to the radio. He said he was tired and so we went to bed early. When I woke up the next morning, he was cold but it looked as though he was just sleeping. I kissed him and covered up his cold arms. I sat there for a long time thinking of him, sending him off with good thoughts. This is important, you know. I never reopened the shop. I could not face it without him.

"One year later I had to have my hip operated on and the

next year an operation on my other hip. I had been lonely after Lars died but something else had changed. I became afraid to be alone and I started . . . I started hiding food in the house in case there was another war. I began to think about Jakarta but not about the happy years when I was young and rich. I thought about the war and everything that had happened. I had time to think of only bad memories and this was not good. I became afraid of – of Orientals and began to dream of them breaking into my house and stealing my food. In the morning after those dreams, I would worry that I was going mad. In the end I decided that I didn't want to spend any more time alone and even though I am not yet seventy, I moved in here where there would always be someone to help. And here I am . . ."

Mina stops talking and everyone looks up when she doesn't go on, amazed at how abruptly her story ended. She senses that her audience are not entirely satisfied. She reddens slightly and knows there is something else they want to know.

"I know that I still get afraid. I still think perhaps there will be no more food. Things change quickly. You have to be prepared but at least I am no longer alone."

When no one says anything, my mother who is tearful, stands up and hugs Mina.

"Well done, Mina. That must have been so hard for you. I think I can speak for everyone here by saying that you are great to have come through everything. We are proud to call you a friend."

Mina smiles as Kora and Greta clap. Slowly everyone joins in – everyone except Wilfred who I know has heavy things on his mind. Jimmy stands awkwardly on his stick and wobbles slightly. As he passes Kora she offers to help him but he pulls abruptly away from her. As he passes Mina he puts his hand on her shoulder.

"You're all right, Mina," he says.

Martin nods in agreement and Iren stares at Mina with a

strange look on her face. She stands and painfully walks over to her and we watch as she puts her hand into her pocket and takes out a sweet biscuit that she must have kept since morning tea. She hands it to Mina and mutters something in Hungarian before hobbling away, causing my mother to burst into tears.

I have a sudden urge to get some air. I walk out of the house and make my way to Maria's house. I have not seen her in a couple of days and am missing her company. The air is still hot and the sky is beginning to show long streaks of red that tells me tomorrow will be another hot day. When I reach Maria's grandfather's house there is a strange car outside. Maria is, as usual, sitting on the corner. I sit down beside her.

"Who owns the car?" I write.

"It's my parents'. They've come to help Pop find a new home," she replies.

She looks sad so I know not to ask any more questions.

"You look tired," she says and I nod as we sit together and watch traffic pass. She leans towards me and puts her tiny hand in mine and together we sit watching the sun set in a blaze of red on the horizon.

Chapter 13

The following morning I stand in the shadows and watch Greta talking with Victoria while Penelope is in the shower. She is helping Victoria sort out her wardrobe.

"What's your favourite colour, Victoria?"

"Penelope likes blue," she replies.

Greta smiles sadly at her and moves a bit closer. "Blue is nice but what is *your* favourite colour?"

Victoria puts her hand to her throat as though she is being strangled. Greta pretends not to notice her nervousness and smooths down her blue striped uniform which complements her striking blue eyes.

"My sister loves green but, me, I am a red sort of girl. I even have red pjs!" she informs Victoria who laughs nervously and keeps her hand over her throat.

"Do you like red?" Greta asks her.

Victoria lowers her eyes to the ground. "I don't know."

Greta looks closer at Victoria.

"Yes," Victoria says shyly. She looks around the room quickly as though someone might be listening. "I like red."

Greta smiles at her and opens the wardrobe door wider.

"Well, then," she says peering into the collection of floral dresses, "we'll have to get you some red clothes."

I leave them and walk to Martin's room. He is talking with my mother about Steve. He looks at me the same way he does every time he sees me, an expression of suspicion and nervousness in one. You'd have thought he'd have got used to me by now.

"I don't know, Emma. I'll think about it. Thought he only wanted to speak with foreigners. I was born here, ya know?"

"Yeah, I know, but I think you'd have a good story to tell, and Jimmy too. You know, the experiences of first-generation Australians in comparison to their parents'?"

"I wasn't that popular with my parents," he says and I watch my mother sigh.

"Well, think about it, eh?" she says.

Martin nods and looks at me. I sign "Yes" and he throws his eyes up to heaven.

"I said I'd think about it," he repeats.

My mother frowns at him and walks quickly out of the room. "I heard you first time," she says as she goes.

"Satisfied?" he asks me and I nod and smile before following my mother downstairs to her office. My father is off work today and he is waiting for her.

"What can I do to help?" he asks.

My mother takes the seat facing him. She is biting the side of her mouth which I know is something she does when she is worried.

"Do you think the residents telling their life stories to a stranger is a good idea?"

My father shrugs and looks out the window. "What have they got to lose? I think it might help, even if they are upset at first. It's sort of like counselling, isn't it? The mine sometimes hires in a bloke when there's an accident. He talks to the men about how they feel. I think it helps. Might even be able to help them put their lives in perspective.

Li knocks and comes into the office. I can tell she has something on her mind. She sits down and looks at my mother.

"Emma, I was thinking, perhaps we could offer Mina a job in the kitchen? She can bake and I could use the help. It might make her feel useful and have less time to think about the past."

My mother's eyes brighten and she nods enthusiastically. "She'll have to know it's a real job offer. You heard her, she hates pity. I could lower her boarding rate or give her a small wage. I couldn't afford much but I think it's a great idea, Li. There's just one thing . . ."

"I know what you're going to say. I'm hoping that spending time with me will show her that she has nothing to fear from Asians. It's worth a try . . ."

"That's very charitable of you, Li," my mother says, touching her forearm.

"No. Not charitable. I love cake!" Li laughs.

I am so happy that I feel my heart quicken and feel goose bumps moving up my arms. This is even better than I had hoped. I walk back to the lounge room and my mood darkens as I see Aishling agreeing to a date with Steve. I am hoping that it is just as a friend although I know this is silly and selfish. Aishling doesn't go out much and I know that Steve is a nice man who might take her mind off looking for letters from home.

I open the door and kick some sand around the porch, trying to think of what I can do with myself until dinner-time. I walk out to the road and walk slowly towards Maria's house, glad to have some happy stories for her. As I walk to the end of our lot, I see Wilfred sitting alone in the garden. I try not to look at him as I don't want to be sad. I think to myself, Wilfred, you are next.

Saturday comes around sooner than I would have liked and I sulk as Aishling prepares for her date with Steve. Before they leave, they have a beer on the porch as they watch the sun setting. There is a light breeze blowing around the yard and I sit on my swing watching them talk. From time to time Steve looks over and smiles in my direction. He is an unusual man and seems to look right through me. He seems to know everything that I know and I wonder if he too was an unusual child. Aishling looks happy and I squirm as she flashes her bright eyes into Steve's face and laughs at his words. I decide I have seen enough and as darkness falls I go inside the house and follow my mother around. Kora is still there and together they put the less able residents to bed.

The only good news is that Mina was delighted with the offer of a part-time job in the kitchen and has even refused payment. The bad news is that Mina thinks she is in charge and that Li is her assistant but I have enjoyed watching Li slowly enforce her authority and Mina slowly back down. What Li really wants is for them to be equals and I know that she will achieve this in time. I wander upstairs where my mother is once again having trouble with Martin. She looks tired and not in any form to argue with him.

"Martin, you and I both know that if you don't take this medication, you will imagine all sorts of things later and have half the house up with your fears."

Martin shakes his head. "It's the damn tablets that are causing it. I'm not taking them and that's final."

My mother sighs. "Fine, Martin. Suit yourself," she replies, walking out of the room.

She looks angry and I can see large red veins bulging in her neck. I know that she cannot afford for Martin to cause trouble on a night that she is working alone so I decide that I will return to his room later to quieten him down when his fears begin.

I follow my mother to Iren's room. She is already in bed and Kora has given her a sleeping tablet. We all know that she is getting worse and that she is missing Aron more as each week passes. Even Mr Berman's visits no longer seem to quieten her down. When she sees my mother, Iren sits bolt upright in the bed. She understands that my mother is in charge.

"Please . . . husband?"

My mother sits on her bed and smooths her hair. "Iren, Aron died. Remember?"

Iren closes her eyes tight and shakes her head.

My mother gently lays her back onto the pillow and sighs. Like me, the sadness here sometimes overwhelms her. As we leave Iren's room my mother starts to cry but wipes her tears quickly when Kora calls her to assist with Jimmy who is refusing her help. When we get to his room, Kora is standing at the door. I can see that they have been arguing.

"I can do it myself. I don't want the likes of you touching my stuff. Probably creep back later and steal it," he snarls at Kora who is standing red-faced in the doorway.

I once saw my mother say that Jimmy never gave his wife enough money to run the house and that she had to steal money from his pockets when he was asleep. When he had the stroke she signed him in here because she didn't want to look after him. She rarely visited him but her peace did not last long as she died suddenly two years later. My mother said he is still bitter about this and never understood why she would not take care of him. Usually my mother is very understanding of Jimmy but I know that she gets annoyed when he is unkind to her sister.

"Jimmy, if you are going to be rude to Kora, you'll have to find another home to go to," she says. I can see her mouth ending in a tight line and she is staring at him with tired red eyes.

Kora folds her arms and smiles smugly at him from the doorway.

"She's got you and that son of mine wrapped around her finger," he spits. "Don't be taken in by her. You can't trust blackfellas. I know all about them!"

My mother and Kora decide to ignore him and leave, but as Kora is closing the door he says something which causes her to freeze. My mother tries to hold her but she flings his door wide open and marches in.

"It was your son that asked me to marry him all those years ago, not the other way around. Do ya want to know why I said no? Because of *you*. And I loved him but you told him I wasn't good enough. It is because of you that Jeff sits alone out on that farm with no one to talk to. It is your fault. He didn't want anyone else. He wanted *me*."

My mother moves Kora from the doorway and pulls Jimmy's door shut so quickly that I don't get a chance to see his reaction. She hugs Kora tightly.

"I'm sorry," Kora says but my mother hugs her even tighter and then leads her to the kitchen where they sit in silence at the old wooden table that once belonged to their parents.

I walk out to the porch and wonder where Aishling has gone with Steve although I don't want to think about this too much. Kora leaves for the night and my mother slowly goes from room to room turning lights off. She knocks on Wilfred's door. He is still reading and she smiles and waves at him from the doorway, wishing him a good night's sleep. She opens her room where my father is sleeping soundly. She turns off his bedside light and kisses him gently before going out to sit down at Aishling's desk outside my room with a book. I smile when I see what she is reading. It is an English-Gaelic dictionary. I go to my room to collect my paper and pens and when I return to her desk her eyes are already half closed with tiredness.

I open Martin's door and sit quietly on the chair by his window. He is asleep but I know that after midnight he will wake and face his demons. But at three it is me who is afraid as I wake and feel the familiar vibrations of the train beneath my feet. I jump up from the chair in Martin's room and for a moment I forget what I am doing there. He sits up suddenly, awoken from his sleep and stares wildly at me. His thick grey hair is standing on his head and his glassy blue eyes are trying to focus on me in the darkened room.

"Well, if it's not my brothers it's you!" he shouts but I put my fingers to my lips and plead with him to be quiet. I don't want my mother to know that I am in here nor do I want her to know that the imaginary train has woken me once again.

"There is no train!" he shouts but I see his face soften quickly and he suddenly looks sad, "There's no train, son," he says again but this time I know he is speaking quietly as I don't feel his words vibrating off the bare floorboards of his room.

He pats the bed for me to sit with him but I hesitate and sit back on the chair.

He lets out a long groan and looks about the room.

"There are no brothers either, are there?" he asks but I know he is not asking me this question but that he is talking to himself. His eyes water and he slowly swings his legs out of bed and sits at the side, looking at the pale coloured wall before him. He rubs his wrinkled hands together and coughs loudly.

"I haven't smoked for twenty years. Still got the cough though."

I understand what he means. He is still suffering for his past.

Minutes pass and he continues to rub his hands together as if he is trying to wash them clean. Eventually he coughs again, a hard cough that racks his body and turns his pale face red and purple.

I feel the vibration of the front door slam and I know that Aishling is only coming home now. I look at the clock above Martin's bed. It is almost three fifteen. I walk toward him and touch his arm. He feels cold even though the room is hot and stuffy. He shifts slightly and looks directly at me.

"I had three brothers and two sisters. There was more than that but only six of us survived, typical Catholic family. We lived in town for years, renting two rooms in a rundown boarding house. Called all sorts of names because we were Irish. My father was proud, always getting into fights. Couldn't walk away if people called him names. He used to say that he came here to be free so no one was going to get away with treating him bad. My mother, now she was a tough one. I saw her lying in the bed, screaming with a new baby coming and afterwards she got up and cooked a meal. She was something, you know. I was afraid of her. Took me a long time to understand that."

Martin quietens and I am afraid that that is all he is going to say but he licks his lips, takes a drink of water from his locker and continues. His eyes are facing the wall and I have to strain my head to read his lips. It is as if he is not talking to me at all but is reliving his story to himself. I wonder how often he does this or if this is the first time he has done it out loud.

"The father, he worked in the mine. There wasn't much else to do around here. Whole town almost ran on the mine. He was lucky to get in. Not many Catholics got steady work. It was the pommies. They said we weren't to be trusted, that we were lazy and stupid. You should have seen the things used to be printed in newspapers. You wouldn't have believed it. Anyway, my father worked hard and for a while until he saw sense, he drank hard. I think he drank heavy back then because he found it hard to be accepted. He used to come home and take it out on my mother. He said to her one day that he would not be happy until he had a small patch of land to call his own. So he saved and took any extra work going at the mine. Sometimes he worked double shifts and came home long after we were asleep. He would fall into bed and be gone again the next morning before we were up. When I was just fifteen he got me and my brother a job in the mine but Tom's chest was weak and my father took him out even though we needed the money. We were twins but I was always bigger and stronger than him

"When my father finally saved enough he bought a few acres out of town and started to grow his own vegetables and keep a few sheep. Tom looked after it mostly. He wasn't much good for anything else with his coughing and wheezing. But I loved it and I wanted more than anything to get out of the darkness of the mine and into the fresh air. It was in my blood. Both my parents had come from farms in Ireland but they favoured Tom and his uselessness and kept me in the dark where I sometimes worked twelve hours a day. Danny, my younger brother, had no interest in farming and was delighted to go to work in Sydney with my mother's brother so it was just me, my younger sisters and Liam, who was the baby of the family.

"One night when I was about seventeen, I listened to my father and mother talking in the kitchen late at night. I heard my father say the land would eventually be left to Tom. I could feel my heart beat fast as I tried to pretend I was asleep in the next room but I was so angry that I thought my heart would jump out of my chest. They never cared about what I wanted. It wasn't my fault that he was frail. I didn't make him ill but yet I was paying for it. I got out of the window and walked the whole way to town. I went into the pub and spent a huge chunk of my savings. A few shillings would get you drunk in those days and I didn't have much anyway, gave most of it to the mother to run the house. I stayed there until I was rotten drunk but it didn't ease my anger and I walked home in an awful temper."

Martin stops talking and licks his dry lips twice. His head lowers slightly and I know that he is finding it hard to tell me what he did next. I touch his arm to reassure him but he pulls back quickly as though my touch has burned him.

"*What happened next?*" I write.

His mood changes. His eyes darken and I almost feel afraid of him.

"Why don't you mind your own bloody business? Daft bloody kid!"

I move a few steps back but remain in the room.

"You're just like the bloody rest of them. Why doesn't anyone ever believe me? Eh?"

I put the notebook that I had hoped to communicate with him through back into my pocket and move toward the door. He moves forward suddenly and I can see that he doesn't want me to leave.

"When I got back . . . a fire . . . started in the barn. My mother blamed me. I could hear our nag moving at the back but it was too late to save her."

Martin hangs his head lower and starts to cry.

"My father worked long hard hours to save for that horse, useless that she was. When the blaze took hold I tried to get her out but it was too late. She was trapped and I could not get to her. I can still hear the awful sound she made as she burned. I . . . Tom heard her too and came running. He was naked from the waist up and I shouted at him to get away. He pushed past me and tried to get the horse out. Without her, the work was too hard for him. He ran into the barn. He was coughing with the smoke and I called to him. I shouted, 'Tom, come out for Christ sake! It's too late!' but he mustn't have heard me. My father was fast behind him. He shouted at me to get a bucket but I stood frozen to the spot. Tom came around the side and tried to pump water as fast as he could. He was wheezing so bad that my mother had the get the little ones to pump water while Tom and my father tried desperately to save what was left of the barn. In all that time I just stood there and watched my family try to save our livelihood. The smoke was throwing black clouds into the air and neighbours started coming from around with buckets and sacks. Tom fell to the ground and my mother tried to sit him up but he could not breathe. The smoke was in his damaged lungs. Even in the noise and shouting, I heard my mother say to my father 'He's gone!' I heard my father scream as my mother cried quietly for Tom. I had never seen her cry before. He was her favourite. I watched my father grip his chest and fall into my mother's arms. Two neighbours carried him inside while another put sacks over Tom so the little ones wouldn't see him. Someone went for Doctor Alder. It's his youngest son that is the doctor round here now.

"When there was nothing else to be done, I slipped inside and hid in my room and lay in my bed. I just lay there. I couldn't think of anything else to do. I was sort of numb. The doctor gave my father medicine and put him asleep. He helped the women lay Tom out in the room he shared with me and I sat and looked at my brother's corpse as the sun rose. When the flames had died a neighbour called my mother outside. I saw her talking to him as he handed her something. I couldn't see what it was. Suddenly she was standing at the doorway with it in her hand: a broken bottle of whiskey. She threw it at me and I remember the sound of it smashing against the wall so clearly. It seemed like I was asleep until I heard that sound. She knew I'd been drinking. She knew I'd been in town.

"She said 'You – you –' but she could not finish her sentence. She could not say what I knew she was thinking but I knew it. I could see it in her eyes. 'Get out,' she said coldly, 'and don't you ever set foot back near here.' I stood up and walked past her. She followed me into the yard and threw the few clothes I had after me onto the wet ground. I didn't pick them up and I didn't try to explain. I walked from the farm and walked the whole way to town with only the clothes on my back.

"My father never recovered from his heart attack and could not return to work. Danny had to leave his life in Sydney and replace my father in the mine. He was only fifteen. I worked with him for forty years in the mine, side by side, and he never ever spoke to me. I didn't blame him. Liam was taken from school and tried to work the land with my mother. He was only a little boy, around ten I think. She never got over Tom. I saw her in town from time to time and it saddened me to see her lovely dark hair turned snow white. My father died three years later. I left town for a while but I came back here. Even though I knew that everyone blamed me, I didn't want to be anywhere else. In time, my sisters married and moved away. Most of them are dead now. Danny married and had three boys of his own. He called the eldest one Tom. I'm sure that made my mother happy. I never went to either of my parents' funerals. I thought I wouldn't be welcome. Danny's on his own now and lives out at the farm. Liam was killed in the war. He never had a chance. The whole family, ruined because of that fire . . ."

Martin looks up at me and then looks around the room as though he has been dreaming. I move towards him and hug him.

"I see them at night: Tom, wheezing and black from the fire pointing at me and Liam, a teenager, staring back at me as if he would rather be anywhere else than marching with a rifle to his death."

I take my notebook back out of my pocket and write him a note. *"Did you start that fire?"*

He doesn't answer.

"If you did, they forgive you," I write but he turns his face away and lies back down on his bed to face the wall. I can see his back tremble and I know that he is crying.

Chapter 14

The following morning, Jeff arrives early to take his father to the farm as my mother suggested. Kora is working early with Greta while my mother sleeps and, as she opens the door, she moves closer to Jeff and turns her body sideways to avoid anyone overhearing. She has to be sure that Jeff will give her the answer she wants.

"That dance you asked me to, it running next weekend?"

Jeff flushes with embarrassment. He was not expecting this. I watch his lips and know he is stammering.

"Y– y–yes."

"Fine, then I'll expect you to pick me up Saturday at eight. That is, if you still want to ask me?"

Jeff nods and looks around him quickly. Kora has taken him completely by surprise.

"Y–yes. I do."

Kora winks at him and walks quickly away. Jimmy is already dressed and waiting for his son inside the Penance Room. Kora knows he has been watching them and I can see that familiar smug smile on her lips. She has had enough of people making decisions for her.

Penelope and Victoria's nephew Henry is coming later with his fiancée and the sisters have been looking forward to his visit all week. Victoria is already sitting in the lounge room and is wearing a new dress that she bought when Greta took her shopping. It is mostly white with small red flowers all over it. I climb the stairs and see that Greta is trying to work her magic on Penelope which is no easy task.

"What about some curls?" she asks as she brandishes an unusual electric rod at Penelope who jumps back slightly. She is always frightened by anything new.

"Oh no, Daddy doesn't like silliness," she says nervously.

Greta is not deterred easily and moves closer to whisper into Penelope's ear.

"But Daddy's not 'ere, is he?" she smiles mischievously.

"Not yet," Penelope says in her army voice, "but he's coming today and we need to be shipshape."

Greta looks sadly at Penelope and touches her arm. "It's Henry who's coming today, Penelope – your nephew – and I'm sure he'd love to see your hair done nicely."

Penelope starts talking to herself and Greta admits defeat.

"Okay, love, not to worry. Maybe next time?"

Penelope nods and checks her appearance in the mirror. She is wearing her usual blue floral dress that makes her look older than her years, and her hair which is almost grey is cut in an awkward bob. A long string of worn pearls hang loosely over her thin frame. She straightens her dress out and Greta looks at her long thin fingers.

"You'd have made a good piano player."

"I played the piano in the evening for Daddy," she says flatly.

"Did you enjoy it?" Greta asks. "I'd love to be able to play."

"I wanted to play different music," she says with dull eyes.

"What kind of music?"

Penelope flushes and looks around her as if her father is listening. She giggles suddenly like a young girl and puts her hand over her mouth. Greta instantly reaches forward and gently moves Penelope's hand down.

"There's no need to be afraid. You can say anything to me."

I watch Penelope look closely at Greta as though she is deciding if she can trust her.

"You won't tell Daddy or the other servants? They do tell on me, you know."

"I won't tell," Greta promises.

"Jazz," she giggles.

Greta laughs loudly. "I can think of worse. I don't like to consider myself out of touch but you should hear the stuff the kids listen to these days. You know, we could get you some jazz music."

Penelope shakes her head. She has been in trouble for this before. "My brother brought me some music sheets from London but Daddy found them and made Henry take them back. He threw poor Henry out even though it was raining and he wouldn't let our driver take him to the station."

Greta smiles sadly. "That was a long time ago, Penelope, when you were a girl. You are a woman now and you make your own decisions."

Penelope doesn't answer.

"Have you ever played Emma's old piano in the dining room?"

Penelope shakes her head.

"Well, we shall have to see to that," Greta says. "Now, let's go downstairs. Your handsome nephew will be here soon."

I follow the women downstairs and I can see my father talking with Wilfred in the garden. My mother's new dog is sitting beside them and it has taken a dislike to me. My mother once said that dogs sense your fear so you have to show them that you are not afraid, but even thinking about this makes me scared so, while I decide to follow them out, I sit on my swing at the side of the garden and watch them talk. Today is my father's day off and I know he wishes my mother didn't have to

work last night and could spend the day with him. When I read
their lips I realise that they are talking about Steve.

Wilfred is shaking his head and my father is leaning in
towards him.

"I never tell anyone what happened, Andy. Never. No one
would want to hear my story, believe me."

"I know you, Wilfred, and I have no doubt that you were as
much a victim as Mina. I know you lost as much as she did."

Wilfred shakes his head. "Her country didn't start the war."

"I know, but you said you never wanted to be a soldier so this
will give you a chance to tell people what happened."

Wilfred looks at the ground and I am afraid I will not be able
to read his reply. He is the person I most want to save. He is the
person who needs to tell his story most. But he raises his head
suddenly and looks my father in the eye.

"Andy, you are my friend and I always thank you but you
don't know who I am or what I have done. I cannot say it."

My father nods and looks toward the sky. He knows it is best
to change the subject.

"Looks like another hot one. Fancy a beer?"

Wilfred nods. "Your wife, she must be sleeping!" he jokes.

"Yes, but my sister-in-law is here and she's worse. I'll have to
sneak in," my father replies laughing.

The dog takes an interest in me and starts to growl as my father
passes so I slink back and follow him inside. Iren's sedative has not
worked and she is shouting so loud that Henry Miller, who has
just arrived, cannot hear his aunts talking to him. Greta
approaches her and gently raises her to her feet and coaxes her to
the kitchen. Mina is seated at the large wooden table and is
reading through the pastry books that Li uses and is tut-tutting.
Greta looks at Li who raises her eyes briefly up to heaven but
smiles anyway. She is determined to get on with Mina.

"Just getting Iren a coffee," Greta explains to Li but Mina
thinks she is talking to her.

"Yes, that's fine. I'm not busy right now," she replies.

Iren sits and the coffee and cake in front of her quietens her for a while. Mr Berman will visit tomorrow but today she will have no visitors so the staff know that it will be a long day for both themselves and her.

"What's for lunch today, ladies?" Greta asks but the two begin to speak together and Li stops to give Mina the floor.

"I decided on chicken with roast vegetables followed by my own recipe for chocolate cake and ice cream."

"Delicious!" Greta replies, looking at Li who is not sure how to handle the situation.

"Are you making it all yourself?" Greta asks her.

Mina purses her lips for a moment. "No. I am the baker but the other cook is better at the food," she acknowledges.

"The other cook?" Greta asks mischievously.

"Yes," Mina replies. "This is Li and she says she is not from Japan."

Greta smiles broadly at Li who is pretending to look for something in the cupboard. I can see a smile in the corner of her mouth and know that she feels things are moving in the right direction.

"And even if she were Japanese, it wouldn't be a bad thing," Greta says but Mina ignores her and flips over a page, peering closely at a picture of a cake.

When I leave the kitchen, I notice that Aishling is up and although she is not working today, she is sitting in the Penance Room looking at Father Hayes who is smiling back at her.

"Kora?" she says to my aunt who is staring out the window, watching my father and Wilfred drinking beer. "I was just thinking, poor Father Hayes wouldn't be able to tell Steve his life story. You know, how he came to be here. But I wrote recently to the family of this Deirdre that he talks about to see if they can tell us what happened. It would be great if they replied now. She might be still alive."

"How did you know how to find her family?" Kora asks.

"I know the village he's from. She seems to have been from the same place. Her last name was McGonigle I think though I couldn't get him to confirm that. I hope its right."

Aishling stands up and moves closer to Father Hayes until she is only inches away from his face. His eyesight is poor and his hearing is not good.

"Father Hayes. Was it Deirdre McGonigle from Mount Tubber?"

A huge smile spreads across the priest's face and he nods.

"*Deirdre, a stór*," he says, smiling at Aishling.

Aishling kisses him on the cheek and he grins like a sheepish schoolboy. I wonder if this is what I looked like to her when she kissed me one day after I fell off the swing. I was only five then so if I did smile like that, she wouldn't hold it against me now.

As Aishling returns to her seat, Kora decides to ask her about her date. I want to leave the room but I am stuck to the chair.

"Well, how was it?"

Aishling smiles and raises her thick eyebrows. "He's different, you know, not like other men. It's hard to put words to it but it's like . . . it's like he sees right through you and accepts you as you are . . . you know?"

Kora nods and is showing her white teeth through one of her rare smiles. I decide I have heard enough and jump off my chair, making it bang hard off the wall and startling the love-struck women who are old enough to know better. I open the screen door and peer around to make sure the dog is not around. I look down the street. It is twelve o'clock and not the right time of day to go outside but I am bored and lunch will not be ready for ages.

I walk down the street and make my way to Maria's house. I want to cross the tracks to build up my courage but at the last minute I walk straight across the highway junction and take the long way there. There is no one around and everywhere blinds and shutters are pulled to block out the midday sun. I look at my arms and notice that they are unusually pale. I was lucky to inherit my mother's skin which tans easily and not my dad's Scottish skin which burns and peels even on a sunny winter's day. I squint at the heat rising up off the tarmac and push forward towards my only friend's house.

When I get there Maria is not sitting on the corner but is seated at the back of her house in the shade of the garden. There are two smaller children playing in a sandpit with a green awning protecting them from the sun.

"Who are they?" I ask her.

"My brothers," she says without looking up.

I sit down beside her and wipe the sweat off my forehead. I decide not to take my shoes off as I don't want Maria's family looking at my half foot.

"I didn't know you had any brothers. Why don't you want to live with them?" I ask.

Maria has her usual sad expression and I wonder if she ever really smiles.

"I wanted to stay here with my pop," she says.

I don't need to hear the tone of her voice to know that she doesn't want me to ask any more questions.

I also decide not to ask where her grandfather will be moving to. I can see people moving in the kitchen, a tall dark-haired man and woman speaking fast and waving their hands around much like Tina who is also Italian. I can smell food being cooked and my mouth waters. The screen door opens and Mrs Moretti storms out of the back door with two small ice lollies for her two younger children. She leaves them on a plate and walks back inside. Maria's head lowers and she scowls. I wonder if she doesn't like her mother but I am afraid to ask.

We walk together to the park where we will find shade in the bandstand. I tell Maria about my conversation with Martin last night but not using my voice as I don't like to do that for very long. I have taught her to understand a few signs but mostly I write her notes. I tell her how I think I am saving Martin from becoming an unhappy ghost when he dies but Maria crosses her arms and says she doesn't want to talk about ghosts, so I change the subject and tell her about Steve and the good he is doing in the nursing home. I leave out the part about him asking Aishling out on a date as I know my face will blush and I don't want this. When the heat gets the better of us we take off our shoes and paddle in the pond. There is no one around so I am free to bare my stump and enjoy the feel of the cool water moving back and forward over my swollen feet. I notice that Maria's feet are tiny and that she has pretty nail varnish on her tanned toes. I think about kissing her and although I know my face is red, I lean in and move my lips towards hers. I don't close my eyes because I depend on my sight to tell me what is going on. She folds her arms again and frowns at me.

"I'll kiss you if you never mention ghosts to me again," she says with a tight mouth.

I agree and wonder if she is worried about what will happen to her when her grandfather dies or if it's because she is a Catholic. I know that they are not supposed to believe in such things. I lean towards her again and she closes her eyes. I can see her long dark eyelashes fluttering on her olive skin and think she is even more beautiful than Aishling right now. When our lips meet she moves away quickly so my first real kiss is over before I have a chance to remember what it was like. She stands up and pats her feet dry on the grass. I follow her through the park and think of asking about her parents. I take out my writing pad.

"*You look like your mother,*" I write, trying to introduce the subject but she shrugs and keeps walking.

"*She's pretty – I mean, for an old woman I guess,*" I write. I know I am not doing a good job of this and consider changing the subject. I start a new page and begin to scribble when she touches my arm to make me look at her.

"She's not old. She might be having another baby. I heard them talking," she says. She turns away from me quickly but I can see tears in her eyes.

"Don't you want another brother or sister?" I write.

"I don't want a sister. I am here and they might forget me if they have a girl."

"They won't forget you. They still come here, don't they? And, you could always go and stay with them even though I wouldn't like it. I wouldn't like to be so far from you . . ."

"I want them to come back here and build a house where our old house used to be. They – they're trying to talk Pop into going to Sydney so they can care for him . . . they were fighting about it."

"What did he say?"

"He said no. He said he couldn't leave Broken Hill. He said since he left his village in Italy, he never lived anywhere except here."

"Why can't they come back here?"

Maria kicks some sand and shrugs her shoulders. "My dad said there are too many bad memories here."

"Like what?" I write quickly.

"Do you have to ask so many questions with that stupid notebook?" she says. She moves towards me and rips the sheet of paper from my hand, tearing it into tiny shreds and throwing it on the grass beneath us.

I have never seen her angry before and I can feel tears in my eyes. Maria is my only friend now and I cannot afford to lose her.

"I'm sorry," I sign and for the first time she signs back. She doesn't look directly at me but her large brown eyes sneak a quick, guilty glance my way.

"It's okay. I'm sorry for shouting and, Christopher, you don't need your notebook. I understand everything you say."

"You can understand sign?" I ask and she nods.

I want to ask her how, and why she hadn't told me before, but it suddenly doesn't seem to matter.

"Come on," she says. "My grandfather will be worried about me."

I follow her and by the time we arrive at her house, her parents' car is gone and her grandfather is sitting outside the closed shop alone, peering into the distance. She stops and looks at me. I can see the disappointment in her face.

"They'll be back in a few weeks when the shop sells," she says as she walks away.

When I finally move down her street, I see her standing beside her grandfather, patting his arm. He doesn't look at her but instead gazes at the empty space across the road, lost in his thoughts. I know she is speaking Italian because I cannot read what her lips are saying. I walk towards home and hope that I am not too late for lunch.

Chapter 15

The following morning, Steve arrives early and I can see that he is disappointed that Aishling has already gone to bed. I feel a little satisfied by this but instantly feel guilty. My mother has tried to teach me what her father taught her but I fear that most of it is wasted on me. I have not read much of the Bible and prefer books on history, which my mother said only teaches me about the world's mistakes.

We are all surprised when Jimmy insists that he is next to tell his story and shouts that his story is as good as any foreigner's. I can see Kora sitting on the other side of the room with pursed lips. She is close to Iren who spent the whole night shouting for her husband. I am a little disappointed as I was hoping that Wilfred would tell his story, which might release him from the awful memories he lives with, memories that I know often keep him from his dreams. Jana Soldo is here as her daughter is back at work and will collect her mother after four o'clock. We will not be hearing Jana's story as her daughter has refused her consent. Dora believes that it will do no good to raise a past that her mother tried hard to leave behind. Martin asks to return to his room. He doesn't want to listen to Jimmy but my mother pleads with him to stay and gives him the newspaper to read in the corner.

Steve turns the tape recorder on and Jimmy starts to speak. Like Mina, he has never done this before and thinks he has to lean forward so that the machine can record his voice. I know that he is worried about his slurred speech and that he hopes Steve will understand him.

"My name's James Young and I was born in the outback in 1902. That would make me . . . em . . . I'm seventy years old now and I've lived longer than I ever expected to."

Jimmy looks expectantly up at Steve. He is unsure what to say next. He doesn't have any stories of long journeys to this land but I am sure his story will surprise us. Everybody's story does. Steve nods at him to continue.

"My family originally came from England. My great-great-grandfather, Thomas Chapman, was sent out here from Liverpool on a convict ship for stealing food to feed his widowed mother and sisters."

I look at Martin who is suddenly interested. He puts his newspaper down and looks in Jimmy's direction. While Martin's direct ancestors came to Australia as free labour, I once saw him talk about a great-uncle who was also transported to Australia for stealing food. I can see Steve look at my mother and I know that he doesn't understand much of what Jimmy is saying. My mother gives him a look and somehow he understands that he should not mention this. My mother can listen to the tape later and help Steve write down Jimmy's words. However, when Jimmy speaks again he is making a big effort not to slur his words.

"So my family were part of the first Australians. We were first here. Before any of the wogs or Chinese got here, we were already here."

I can see the other residents shifting uncomfortably in their seats, even those whose English is not good. Everyone understands the word "wog".

Steve, unfamiliar with Jimmy's personality, says "Well, the first Australians were actually the Aboriginals, Jimmy."

Jimmy scowls at him but continues. "Bloody Abbos. I'll tell you a thing or two about them here and now."

Kora stands and leaves the room, ignoring my mother's looks as she moves quickly past her and out the door. Jimmy hardly notices and keeps talking.

"My great-great-grandfather earned his freedom and worked on farms all over New South Wales. He was an odd sort, had no regard for tradition, for keeping things right. Weren't anyone else in the family like him before and I hope never after. When he was old enough, my great-grandfather, also named Thomas, tried to save for some land. He loved it. He bought a small station long way out east. Never got to see it myself although I always wanted to but he was too fond of the drink and lost it all. My great-grandmother moved into town with him but he was in bad health and he died before his son was old enough to remember him. That'd be my grandfather James Chapman. I was named after him. He drifted around and took work where he could. When he was twenty-five, he got work on a big station. Big place, lots of workers coming and going. He married my grandmother, June Hadley. She was an orphan. Her folks came out from England as free settlers but both died when she was only fifteen. She was sixteen when she married my grandfather who was a lot older than her and had my father when she was not yet eighteen. They lived a simple life but they had only one son, Nathan, my father. Even though my grandfather was getting on in years, he got work also keeping the peace in town. The Abbos would come in at night and get pissed and start fights."

My mother looks down at the ground and I know she is glad that Kora is not in the room. Steve stiffens but tries not to show his discomfort. Jimmy doesn't notice the effect his words are having on people in the room, or perhaps he doesn't care.

"When my father was old enough, he took him with him to help out. Years later, when I was twelve, they went out one night to break up some fighting. There had been a lot of trouble from the natives and the police were trying to keep them calm. They were making complaints against the whites. Said we were harassing them and that sort of thing. Anyway, Grandfather wasn't popular among the natives and some of the other settlers didn't think it was a good idea that he went near them at all. Said he only stirred up trouble. My mother told me that she had a bad feeling that night. She said she begged him not to go. Some people are like that. They know things before they happen. She told me that as he went out the door she said: 'Nathan, don't go. Something bad is going to happen.'

"Anyway, this Abbo came at him with a knife. My father was only trying to get them to get out of town, trying to send them packing back to the reserve. He tried to defend himself but got cut. He grabbed the knife and stabbed the Abbo and killed him. My mother said that the police took my father away and none of the other men would stand in his corner. They said my father started it. My father was arrested and locked up for trial.

"Someone told my mother that my grandfather had been riling my father to do it, not to back down from the Abbo so she blamed my grandfather. She went to his house and told him she was leaving and that he'd never see his grandson again. She was bitter against my father as well because she was now without a man to provide for her. She only went to see him once in jail and that was only to tell him that she was leaving town. When she got there he told her that he heard the Abbo had the same name as himself 'cept it was spelt differently – 'Natan' – and he said, 'I've killed myself.' She said her goodbyes and 'cause she had no other kin she took to the road. That was around 1915. She had no money and she told me . . . she said she had to do whatever she could to get by.

"She came to Broken Hill to work in a . . . guest house. I used to wait outside till she finished work . . . not a great start in life. I knew what she had to do. I understood and it sickened me.

"She met her second husband then, Sam Young. She divorced my father or at least I think she did and she changed my name. Young was a widower, years older than her. He had no kids but a widowed female cousin lived with him at that time. Well, Young never took to me and everyone in the town knew I wasn't his and he never let me forget it. When my mother bore no more children, he reluctantly left the farm to me but on the condition that I marry his cousin's daughter. I was still so young but I had no choice but to do it. Young threatened to throw me off the land if I didn't – said he'd leave it to a stranger first. My mother pleaded with me to do as he said or else she'd be on the street with me and she was not in good health so I did it for her. She was a tough woman. I was relieved when I was drafted because I got away from my wife and from Young for a while. Only time I felt free in my whole life and that was when bombs were being blown up all around me so that should tell you what a miserable excuse for a life I've had. So you see that Abbo, that Natan, ruined my father's life and my mother's and my life. Like I said, they're no good."

Young looks at Steve and clasps his hands together. He looks pleased with himself and feels that he has explained his dislike of Aborigines and therefore of Kora. He doesn't understand the look on Steve's face, a look of disbelief.

"Jimmy, do you really think that your problems were caused by that Aboriginal? Have you ever thought that your father should not have killed this man? Or even thought about the effect that man's death had on his family?"

Jimmy raises his eyebrows at Steve. "Haven't you been listening? He attacked my father. He ruined our lives."

Steve sits back and clasps his hands together as though in prayer.

I can see he has no idea where to start with Jimmy.

"Did you not think that it was your own father's actions that ruined your lives?" said Steve. "That you should instead be ashamed of your father and grandfather?"

Jimmy's tongue moves from his mouth and for a few seconds it looks as though he is sticking it out at Steve. His eyes bulge and his face reddens. He puts his hand to his mouth and leans forward as a cough racks his body. He tries to answer Steve and splutters "No – now – you – you listen here!" but the cough overcomes him and he looks as though he cannot breathe.

My mother jumps up and tries to help him but he falls sideways off his chair onto the floor, gasping. She shouts for Kora as Greta runs to phone Doctor Alder and Jeff. As he is lifted up, drool pours out of the side of his mouth.

"He's had another stroke," my mother says quietly.

An ambulance arrives and while they are lifting Jimmy into the back, Jeff pulls up quickly and jumps into the ambulance. He asks Kora to ride with him but she moves a few steps back and shakes her head. Even though she didn't stay for Jimmy's story, his rude remarks earlier have made her doubt that they will ever get along.

My mother looks upset and says to Greta, "Just when they were getting along again."

When we all go back inside, Kora takes up her bag up and walks to the door.

"You going to sit with Jeff?" my mother asks and she nods.

"I just didn't want to ride with them. Doubt the old man would have wanted me there."

My mother nods and sits down exhausted in her office chair. Her face is pale and there are dark lines under her eyes. Li brings her a coffee and she takes it in both hands, warming herself despite the heat of the day. I stand in the doorway half-watching my mother's conversation with Li while looking out for Steve who is still in the Penance Room.

"Thanks, Li," my mother says. "I hope we didn't cause Jimmy's stroke. I had reservations about all of this storytelling but Christopher seemed to want it so I thought . . ."

Li looks closely at my mother. "Emma, are you all right?"

"Yes – yes – I'm fine. It's just . . . I'm afraid this reminiscing is doing the residents harm."

Li stands for a moment and moves her lips back and forth, translating her next sentence from Mandarin to English.

"It is never too late for change and for accepting things," she replies as she leaves the office, frowning.

My mother watches her leave and looks confused by Li's words. She shakes her head and curves her back into the chair, looking out of the window. The sun is beaming in and she squints at a large cobweb in the corner of the window-pane. A fly is trapped in the middle of the web and is struggling to get out.

"I know how you feel," she says as she takes another sip of her drink.

A sudden knock on the half-open door makes my mother sit upright and brings her back from her daydream.

It is Steve.

"Guess I'll push off."

"Oh Steve, em . . . yes . . ." she replies sighing. "Come in."

Steve sits down in what is normally my chair and once again I feel uncomfortable. I am sitting on the window sill enjoying the heat. He looks at me and smiles with those brilliant blue eyes. He leans back and makes himself comfortable, waiting on my mother to gather her thoughts.

"Steve . . . I'm not sure this is such a good idea. I . . . well, it's worked out for Mina . . . but some of the others, they've led dark lives. Some of them have a lot of regrets and well, you saw the effect it had on Jimmy. I'm – I'm worried about it. I'm thinking of . . . cancelling the others telling their stories."

I jump from my seat and feel the panic rising in my chest. I am thinking, no, Mother, please! She doesn't understand that their salvation might also be mine. There are things I have kept to myself. Things even my mother doesn't know. Steve decides to put words to my fear. Almost word for word, he speaks my thoughts and leaves me open-mouthed.

"Emma, is everyone not entitled to their salvation? Is the salvation of the residents not connected to the salvation of everyone here?"

He gives me a little look and takes pleasure in my eyes appealing to him to keep going. My mother puts her hand to her locket as she always does when she is anxious.

"You sound like my father. I thought you were a historian, not a preacher," she says.

I cannot read her face. She is wearing an expression I have not seen before. I decide her look is one of unease.

Steve beams one of his bright smiles that Aishling seems to like. "Yes. I am a historian but I'm also a sociologist. I have an interest in people's pasts and how they've dealt with life. I have my own secrets, as do we all," he laughs.

I can see he has my mother's attention. She leans forward.

"Steve, how many other nursing homes are you visiting?"

Steve shrugs and stretches his arms out above his head. "Oh about thirty, give or take. I plan to be out of here by next week. Next stop, back to Bourke, then down to Dubbo, Orange and then up again to Tamworth." He is still smiling. "You know, sometimes I get to a place and I get a sense of . . ." Steve looks at me and I know his words are directed more at me than at my mother. "A deep sense of loss. I get a sense that there is work I can do to help the people I meet, to reach out to them. All most people are looking for is a bit of understanding and a lot of forgiveness. It wouldn't be right for you or me to stand in the way of that."

"Catholic?" my mothers asks, smiling. Steve now has her eating out of his hands.

"Shows that bad, eh?"

My mother laughs. "I'm a preacher's daughter," she smiles.

121

"Yes, that's right. Evangelical?"

"Yes."

Steve stands. He senses that he has won this battle. He can see my mother is a woman of intuition and that for now she will let him carry on.

"So I can come back tomorrow?" he asks. I can see a deep furrow in his forehead.

My mother nods. "Yes. But only if it doesn't cause distress. Who's up next?"

"Em, your Iren."

"Iren?" my mother asks, surprised.

"Yes, her friend Mr Berman is coming to help her but she speaks fluent French so I can translate for her."

"Iren speaks French? I never knew that!"

"Yeah. I was in the lounge room teaching Aishling a few words and all of a sudden Iren sits up in her chair and starts speaking to me in fluent French. Seems that she spoke French before she ever learned English."

My mother is shaking her head. "I never knew . . ."

When Steve leaves, my mother flops back into the chair and places her hand under her chin. I know what is on her mind. She is thinking that she will have to open her eyes more around here. But she doesn't have to worry. That's what she has me for.

I leave my mother to her thoughts and take the twenty-minute walk down to the mine's entrance. Sometimes I like to wait for my father to finish work and to ride home with him. I like to see him full of red dust and dirt although I don't like to think of him underneath the ground. He told my mother she doesn't need to worry. As an engineer, he doesn't spend too much time below ground and mostly he just sees that the work is going to schedule. When he finally comes out I am already sitting in his open truck on the site.

My father jumps in and lets out a breath of air. "What a day!" he says.

He turns the radio on and immediately launches into song. I like seeing my father here because he seems happy. But something happens as he approaches our house. Little by little, his shoulders drop forward and a sad expression moves over his sunburnt face. Sometimes he rubs his hands through his hair as if he is trying to find an answer to his problems. I know that the nursing home needs more money but it would be foolish of me to think that this is why my father looks so sad. My father is sad because of me. Sometimes I spend the entire journey home looking sideways at him and trying to mouth the words of the song he is singing, even if I am a few seconds behind in the words or perhaps I have got them wrong altogether. My father knows that I will never sing the songs he loves so much, nor will I play the fiddle like he does. One of the wishes that I make in the park is for my parents to have another baby, a son or daughter who can hear and who can sing songs and play musical instruments but there is a part of me that doesn't think that this wish will ever come true.

When we walk together up the garden path, my mother comes out and tells my father about Jimmy. I can see his shoulders drop even further forward and notice how much smaller he looks as we enter the house. It is as if this house and all its problems is eating him up. He hugs my mother and they stand there in the fading light. He smooths out her hair and whispers something to her. She smiles sadly and opens the screen door for him. He follows his usual ritual and has a shower before walking down to Wilfred's room for a chat while my mother heats up his dinner. I climb the stairs to my room and as I gaze out at the railway line I hate it for changing everything, for making my father and mother unhappy but most of all I hate myself for my stupidity. I open my mouth and say words out loud, something I rarely do.

I say: "I will make it up to you. I promise."

Chapter 16

The following morning Jeff and Kora arrive home exhausted and make their way to the kitchen to tell my mother the news. They have sat at Jimmy's bedside all night but he has not regained consciousness. Breakfast is over but my mother makes them some scrambled eggs and sits down to hear about Jimmy. After Jeff tells her about his father's condition, my mother asks the question that kept us both awake last night.

"Did anyone tell you what your father told Steve yesterday? About his past?"

Jeff shakes his head. "No, but I heard it all before. I know how he feels about Aboriginals and it doesn't matter what he believes. He's an old man. Times have moved on." He looks at Kora but she continues to stare at the kitchen wall with a sad expression on her face.

"They haven't changed that much," Kora says. She looks down and wraps her fingers around the coffee cup.

"Maybe to some," Jeff said quickly. "But to most, to the people that matter, it's not important what colour a person's skin is."

Kora doesn't answer but my mother smiles. It is the most we have ever heard Jeff say in one sitting. Kora sighs and looks away from Jeff. I know that she is thinking that their relationship will never work, that neither of them will be strong enough to put up with Jimmy's prejudice.

When Mina wheels her walking frame into the kitchen, Jeff and Kora leave but I stay with my mother who wants to wait until Li clears up the dining room before leaving Mina in the kitchen alone. Mina immediately opens the pantry door and starts counting the bags of flour and other dry goods. She looks back to ensure that my mother is busy and puts a packet of cookies into her skirt pocket. My mother notices this and points discreetly at the thief when Li enters the kitchen to plan lunch with Mina. Li raises her eyes up to heaven but smiles at the same time. She has decided to ignore Mina's stealing in the hope that a few more weeks in the kitchen will reassure her that the food will not run out.

I feel the familiar rush of air as the front door bangs and run to see if Steve has arrived, but it is Mr Berman who has come to help Iren with her story. As her advocate he has signed Steve's consent form on her behalf. Steve arrives soon after and Aishling comes downstairs to greet him. I watch Aishling for a moment and stare at her long white legs below her uniform skirt. I know Steve is watching me so I turn away and try to remember Maria's kiss instead but I cannot. It seems that when I am apart from her, her memory fades and only returns when I walk to her street and see her standing on her favourite corner, looking for what I will never know and probably will never have the courage to ask.

Aishling asks Steve if he'd like to go out on Friday night. He is due to leave soon and I wonder briefly if she will be sad. Everyone assembles in the lounge room and I take my usual spot on the pew under the window. Steve speaks to Iren in French and she nods at him. She looks more awake that I have ever seen her and I wonder if her language problems have made her seem more confused than she is. I understand what it is like when nobody can communicate with you and how people think you are odd or stupid. I watch my mother look at Iren's face lighting up and know she is thinking about this too. Mr Berman starts first and speaks clearly into the microphone. Kora once said that he speaks exactly like Wilfred and I wish that I knew what this meant. I wish I had a chance to hear all these wonderful voices around me.

"My name is David Berman and I am a long-time friend of Aron and Iren Klein. I am here today to help explain Aron and Iren's early life with the assistance of a French interpreter. I met Aron and Iren in Broken Hill in 1950. I was then twenty-six years old. My uncle was friends with the Kleins and he sent me every day after work to help them because they had no family in Australia. Aron Klein was then about, well, coming to sixty I think and Iren, of course, some years younger. We spoke many times of their life and Aron was like a father to me. My own parents were German and I was born there. After the – after the war – we came – my uncle and I – to Australia. Both my parents had died in the camp and my uncle worked long hours here. Aron told me that he was born in Budapest in –"

Iren interrupted, the mention of a familiar place causing a huge smile to erupt on her tiny face.

"*Budapest!*" she shouts. Her eyes light up for a moment and then darken. "*Apa, Anya,*" she says and she quietens again.

Mr Berman pats her hand and smiles at her before returning to the story.

"Aron was born in 1890. His family were well off. Aron's father was a doctor and he wanted Aron to also become a physician. Aron's older brother had already graduated from university in Italy but his heart was in physics so in – I think 1908, he travelled to France and began to study at the University of Paris. In Hungary, only a small percentage of Jews could enter university so he thought it was best not to hope to be among their numbers and to travel for his qualifications. It was there that he met Iren."

Steve turns his attention on Iren who is smiling and nodding at Mr Berman but we have no idea how much English she understands. He explains that he will speak in French first before translating into English to ensure that Mr Berman is in agreement with his questions.

"Don't change it to English," Greta laughs. "I love listening to Froggies. It's so romantic!"

I am glad that Aishling was too tired to hear Steve speaking French. I am afraid that she will fall in love with him and leave here.

"Iren, you met Aron in Paris. Can you tell me how you met?" he asks.

She sits forward and stares into Steve's face.

As she answers him, he translates her words into English. We are amazed at the clarity of her mind and if we were not sitting here watching her mouth open and close quickly, I would think Steve was making it up.

"My father ran a jewellery store in Paris. I was born in Budapest where both my parents were from but, when I was two, my parents left for a new life in France. My father was a brilliant goldsmith and rich French people came from afar for his pieces. My father knew friends of the Kleins in Budapest and they asked if he could put a young student up in the loft during his studies. My father said yes, of course. I was eight then and Aron came and stayed with my parents and me. I instantly fell in love but I was only a little girl with a handsome tall boy in my house. I had no brothers or sisters and Aron gave me extra lessons in written Hungarian. I could speak Hungarian but not write it very well and so he taught me. Aron also spoke German but I didn't. He was very clever. When he comes home from work at the university, I will have cooked for him his favourite meal."

Everybody looks at each other and no one knows for sure how to handle Iren's sudden departure from reality. Even Martin seems to be enjoying the story and only Wilfred is sitting with his back to the group, staring at the pup chasing flies in the garden. Steve decides to play along with Iren. Like the rest of us, he doesn't want to break the spell.

"Yes, of course, a fine meal will be lovely but in the meantime, could you tell me a little about your life with Aron when you were younger?"

Iren nods and puts imaginary long hair back behind her ears and giggles at Steve as though she is still a young girl.

"In the evenings, my father with no son would teach Aron how to make fine jewellery and this boy who loved only books liked helping in the shop. I was a little jealous for I too helped and I was also becoming good at making things. We were not as well off as Aron's family but he took to our life and soon he and my father were good friends. When he finished his studies I was almost twelve and I cried when he left although he came back when I was sixteen and he worked as a research assistant in Paris. I was a silly girl at that time and didn't yet know what physics meant. My mother had died and it was just me and Papa running the shop.

"After I left school, I worked all the time in the shop and my father said it was a pity he didn't have the time or means to make me a lady. Sometimes Aron honoured us and came for meals at our house. He now lived in an apartment and had fancy friends who he told me had breeding but no money. I was in love with him but to him I was just a little girl. And for many years that was how we met. He would come to my house and I would cook Hungarian food for him rather badly. My papa said: 'Daughter, you are more French than like us and we shall have to find you soon a Hungarian husband.'"

Li looks at my mother and whispers, "No wonder she didn't think much of the Hungarian meal I made for Aron's funeral. She didn't know what it was!"

Iren goes quiet for a moment and looks like she is reliving a memory.

"Once he said this in front of Aron and my face went so red that I left the table and refused to return. My papa didn't realise that I was in love with Aron and looked on him like an older brother for me. Then, when Papa got sick, it was too late for us to return to Hungary which had been his plan and I tried to run the shop myself and look after Papa. I was in my early thirties then, an old maid, and from time to time Aron would call and check that I was all right. I had given up on him seeing me as a woman and I was not so unladylike as to ask him if he had an interest in me.

"When Papa died, Aron came and stayed for a few days even though his apartment was only about one hour away. When he was leaving, he kissed me and I asked him why he did not try to kiss me before. He said he owed a great debt to my father and that he didn't want to offend his generosity. I realised then that perhaps my father was right, perhaps I didn't understand Hungarian ways and that I was a French girl. Aron said he wanted to see me and asked if I wanted this too. I could not believe it. All those years and he didn't ask. I think my father would have been pleased. I think Aron was wrong to wait. So when I was almost thirty-three and Aron forty-three we married and two years later our son was born."

Iren stops talking suddenly and sits up straight. She looks around the room and stares vacantly at everyone. It is as if her mind has shut down and is unwilling or unable to recall the rest of the story. Steve looks at Mr Berman who decides to fill in the gaps.

"Aron kept his job at the university. He was becoming recognised for his research in the field and although it was unusual for the time, Iren kept the shop open and still made jewellery. I think it reminded her of her father and kept his memory alive. In the evenings Aron and Iren worked together and the shop did so well that Aron could have given up his job if he'd wanted to. They were quite well off. Their son, Jacob, was named for Iren's father and he too learnt the craft from an early age just as Iren had. By the time Jacob started school, there were rumblings of war. People were talking about it and while Aron and Iren heard the talk, they didn't believe it would ever come to anything."

Wilfred gives an involuntary cough and my mother crosses the room to check on him. He still has his back to everyone and I can only see him putting his right hand to his mouth as he waves her away with his left hand. He doesn't want any attention on him and I know that he feels more trapped now than he felt during the war.

Iren starts humming to herself and looks away from Mr Berman. She focuses on a tiny ray of light that has entered the room and she watches it dance and jump across the white painted wall. I follow its source and realise it is coming from Wilfred's gold watch as he dabs sweat from his brow. He knows that he could get up and leave but somehow he decides to stay. He is forcing himself to listen to Iren's story. It is as if his very soul depends on it.

"On Iren's forty-first birthday, May 14th, 1941, many Jews were arrested in Paris. By August, these Jews were detained in Drancy, north of Paris. Aron told me that at first the French police controlled the camp and that Iren was outraged that her own people were handing her over to Nazis because she was a Jew. Many French people helped their Jewish neighbours though and there were organisations that hid Jewish children and got them safely to Sweden and Britain. But Jacob was not so lucky. The police were walking up and down the street where they lived, shouting and taking people from their homes. Iren and Aron knew what was happening and they prepared themselves for the worst. When the police stormed the shop, Aron, Iren and Jacob were sitting together having a meal. It was the last meal they had together."

Steve looks at Iren and I know he feels a sense of guilt for the part his people played in the death of their native and foreign Jews. I can see that he fears Mr Berman's words will upset her. She is humming louder now and I am acutely aware of Wilfred's shoulders rising up towards his neck. He knows how the story ends. We all do.

Mr Berman senses Steve's discomfort and shakes his head. "She doesn't understand what I have been saying. She only understands a few English words. She never really learnt the language."

Steve looks sadly at her and starts the tape recorder again.

"I don't know everything that happened to the Kleins after that but I too was in a concentration camp. Not at Auschwitz, which is where the Kleins ended up eventually. At first, they were taken to Drancy in occupied France which was just a holding place while they awaited transport to Auschwitz. I do know that the following March, in 1942, the Kleins and thousands of others were taken from France to Auschwitz by train. There they were separated, Jacob who was by then not yet seven years old being taken away with the other young children.

"Aron was put to work sorting gold. For many months, it was not known that he was a highly educated man, a physicist with a brilliant future and he was recorded as a goldsmith. One time, a high-ranking soldier spoke to Aron and was impressed with his intelligence. He too was an educated man and he grew to enjoy Aron's company. They often spoke about subjects only they understood. As a consequence Aron received special treatment and of course begged for Iren and Jacob to be with him but he was told Jacob was no longer in the camp and he feared the worst. As for Iren, moving her was too much for the soldier to achieve, Aron's request was refused and she continued to endure a life of slave labour. I think Aron spent the rest of his life carrying a lot of guilt because he had received better treatment than Iren and he was very protective of her during the years I knew them in

131

Broken Hill. She did get certain privileges though and that solider had someone look out for her in the women's camp. Of course she didn't escape every cruelty and many things happened to Iren there that she never wanted to talk about. But she did talk to my aunt who spoke Hungarian and I know that one time an operation was done to make sure she would not have more children. Some of the women were raped. It also happened at my camp. I don't know if that ever happened to Iren but I know from my aunt that she kept many things from Aron to protect his sanity. Her son Jacob was –"

Steve looks at Iren and interrupts Mr Berman with a wave of his hand. I know he is worried that she will be upset by the conversation but I have been watching her and each time the word Auschwitz, Jacob or Aron is mentioned she looks up but loses interest when she can no longer follow the conversation. He makes another signal to Mr Berman.

"Perhaps we should call the boy 'J'?" Mr Berman asks. Steve nods and Mr Berman continues. "J was not so lucky and was sent to the gas chamber as soon as he arrived at the camp but Iren did not know this.

"In 1944 many people arrived in the camp from Hungary. Aron knew some of them but he never found out what happened to his parents or his brother. It was in January 1945, more than three and a half years after they were first captured, that the Soviets liberated Auschwitz. The Kleins were reunited and when Iren learnt of J's death, she had a complete breakdown and spent many months in a hospital in Switzerland. She was very frail and thin and the years of starvation had taken their toll on her physical and mental health. When I was younger and our community got together, Aron would always be at her side. She seemed always to be nervous and would cling to him when loud noises occurred.

"When the war was over, they didn't wish to return to Budapest and for Iren it was not home anyway. Neither did she wish to return to France where she felt her people had betrayed her. The Kleins were a people without a country. Even though modern Israel was not founded as a country until about 1948, many Jewish people went to live there after the war where they felt they would be safe, but the Kleins wanted a new start and in 1947 they came to Australia.

"I remember the goldsmith shop they owned and ran and, of course, it was not without problems because even in Australia Jews were mistrusted. Business was not too good. Not many people had money for such luxuries. I don't know why the Kleins decided to come to Broken Hill. For me, this is where my uncle had a job to come to. There were more Jews here then than there are now and we looked after each other. The Kleins started to make jewellery that they sent to Sydney and their work became popular. They became well off again but there was always a sadness about them.

"They were quiet, simple people and you would never know that they were so rich. They paid for me and my cousin and a few of the other young Jewish children to go to university in Sydney. But they were not only kind to Jews. They were generous to the whole community, helping to raise money quietly for charity and equipment for the hospital. They bought an old house outside of town and gave money for it to be turned into a local community centre for disadvantaged children. It is still there today and the council runs it for children's activities. They loved Australia and the home it had offered them and they wanted to repay this kindness. They never boasted about this or spoke of their charitable work. When you visited them, they focused on you, on your life, on your achievements and asked nothing but your company in return.

"Aron never returned to his research in physics and I think this saddened him but he never spoke much of it. He kept up reading about it and learnt to read and speak good English. I tried to be the son that they lost. I tried to give them some normality, some sort of life they would have had if Jacob had lived. I brought my wife to see them, and my children. Everything they missed out on because of the war, I tried to make right."

Mr Berman stops talking and dabs his eyes with a white cotton handkerchief. I know that as well as feeling the losses the Kleins endured because of the war, he is also reliving his own.

"In all of those years of friendship though, I gained more than I gave in return. I was just a child when war broke out and spent my boyhood in a camp outside Berlin where my parents and sisters died. I was angry when I came here and my uncle, he often felt angry that he lived where his brother, my father, didn't and he was bitter about the war until he took his last breath. It made me bitter as well. But when I visited the Kleins, I saw that it didn't have to be this way. They showed me that there is a way to be at peace with what has happened, a way for you to live on. If not for them, I would not have the happy life I have now. I know I was meant to find them and if you are a believer in God, you will think as I do that the Kleins were my saviours and God, in his wisdom, sent me to be the son that was taken from them."

Mr Berman dries his eyes again. I look around the room and tears are flowing freely down all of the women's faces. Even Martin looks upset. Suddenly everyone begins to look in Wilfred's direction. I know they are listening to something. I follow their eyes and watch as he sobs into his open palms, his watch continuing to make pretty colours on the ceiling of the Penance Room.

Chapter 17

"Wow!" Steve says as he follows my mother into her office. "That was some story."

My mother nods. She looks tired. She sent Greta after Wilfred to ensure that he was all right and already Iren has started to call out for Aron. My mother closes the door and Steve sits automatically.

"Who's next?" she says wearily.

"I was thinking of the sisters the day after tomorrow. Greta said their nephew would come and help."

"Well, I'm not sure that you'll get much out of them. One mention of their father and they go doolally."

"I love that saying – 'doolally'."

My mother ignores Steve's attempts to lighten the conversation. "You're not seeing anyone tomorrow?"

"Em . . . no. Aishling said she'd take me around a few of the sights. Is that okay?"

My mother frowns. "Of course but . . . you're going back to Sydney and Aishling . . . well, let's just say that she's easily hurt."

"You really do look out for everyone here, don't you, Emma?"

My mother frowns. "That's my job," she replies and I can see that she is slightly annoyed with how familiar Steve is with her.

"And who looks after you?" he goes on. "Can you speak to Andy about the things on your mind?"

I know his game. He is waiting for her to talk about me. To tell him what happened to me. But I don't want Steve's pity. Although I need his voice and his hearing, I am the one trying to save souls here.

"I am fine, thank you, Steve," she says and I can tell by her lips that her words were said sternly.

He smiles at her and nods. "Sorry, occupational hazard," he says.

My mother doesn't answer. She knows that she and Steve are a little alike.

Steve stands up and fixes his shirt. He looks at my mother and his expression changes from his usual smile to an intense gaze.

"Don't worry. I won't hurt Aishling," he says before opening the door quietly and slipping away.

I ease myself gently into the chair beside my mother. She wipes a runaway tear and stares out the window. Steve has exposed the secret she keeps from herself. He knows that she is as lost as some of the residents here and that the knowledge of this weighs heavily on her.

Later that night, I lie in my bed and wait for movement outside my door which will tell me that Martin is awake and frightened. When I feel the feet of Aishling's old chair scrape on the wooden floor, I rise and follow her down the hallway. I check my watch and it is two o'clock, later than normal for Martin to face his night-time fears and earlier than normal for me. I ease my way into the doorway past her and stand by the window. Sometimes I feel that there are two Martins, one who sits in the Penance Room and antagonises most of the people around him and the other who cowers in fear at night when there are no distractions from his conscience.

Aishling is wearing an angry expression on her face. I know she wanted to get some sleep during the night so that she is fresh for her date tomorrow with Steve.

"Martin, will you please take your sleeping tablet? You can't expect to have any peace without it," she says.

He looks up and when he sees me, he decides to co-operate. He knows I will sit with him until he falls asleep.

"I won't ring no more," he says.

"And you'll take your tablet?" Aishling asks hopefully.

"No, God damn it! You deaf or something?" He looks sheepishly at me. "Sorry," he says.

But Aishling rejects his apology and storms off, leaving the two of us staring at each other.

"My mother was the same. Hot-tempered Irish!" he says smiling.

I move from the window and sit on his bed while I take out my notebook.

"Did you see your brothers again?"

Martin nods and sighs.

"Did you talk to them?"

"Don't make any difference. Maybe Aishling's right, but they're so real that when I see them I can't accept that I'm imagining it, that they're not really there. I've been thinking about it . . . maybe it is my mind playing tricks on me and, if it is, doesn't seem much I can do about it now. I think I'll spend the rest of my life seeing them and what kind of a life is that? I'd rather be dead."

"No, you wouldn't," I write. *"It's much harder to put things right when you are dead."*

Martin laughs loudly and we both tense in case Aishling returns and tells us off.

He pats my head and laughs. "You're a strange little bloke," he says and laughs again.

I think that this is better than crying in fear, even if he is laughing at me.

"You want to sit here till the train goes by?" he asks and I wonder at this. We are both afraid of things that don't exist.

I nod and he smiles.

"Good boy."

"What did your brothers say tonight?" I write.

"They said: 'Go see Danny.'"

"Your brother on the farm?"

"Yeah. Haven't seen him since I retired off the mine. Never spoke to him then either."

"Will you go?" I sign. I have been teaching Martin basic sign and he is learning.

He throws back his head and laughs at this outrageous notion.

"And give them another chance to send me packing?" he says, shaking his head.

"There's just you and Danny left now. Maybe he needs to hear from you. Maybe he needs you to apologise so that he can move on too?" I write.

Martin looks at me with his bloodshot eyes. I can see tiny burst veins all around his face. For a moment I think he is going to hit me as the veins in his neck bulge. I can see a small vein jumping on his leathery neck and I move back a little.

"What have I got to apologise for?" he shouts. Spit flies out of his mouth and I become very afraid of him. He looks into my face and calms suddenly. Perhaps he is tired of looking at fearful faces, the faces of people he should have been kinder to. He reaches forward and I jump off the bed but he opens his locker and takes out a bottle of whiskey and an old tin box. He opens both and laughs again.

"Got the girl to bring this in to me. Ssh!" he says, smirking.

I know he is referring to his daughter Ellen who is frightened of him. She will do almost anything he asks, even if it is bad for his health. He opens the box and inside are several old photos.

"My mother got these done. Must have cost her a fortune. I

didn't see some of these photos since I was a boy. When Una visited Danny, he gave these to her. If I know Una, she outright asked for them. She got copies done and brought them back to him. She said he was nice when she visited and made her tea."

Martin runs his wrinkled hands through the photos and finds the one he is searching for. In the photo are four boys, one smaller than the other. Martin points himself out first, the tallest boy to the left of the black and white photo.

"That's me, and the boy beside me, that was Tom. See, we looked nothing alike for twins."

I look at Tom and can almost see his barrel-shaped chest, the shape of a boy who gasped for breath each day of his life in this dusty country. Martin on the other hand stands tall in the photo with a mop of dark hair and a defiant expression on his thin face.

"That was Liam" he says, pointing at the smallest child who is seated in front of his older brothers on a tall wooden stool. He is dressed in what looks like a little sailor's outfit, so many miles from the sea. He is a cute boy with bright coloured hair that curls up at the bottom as he stares into the camera with a serious expression.

"And this," he says, pointing at a tall dark-haired, serious-looking boy, "is Danny."

I look into the photo and look closely at the boy whose dreams of a life in Sydney ended when his father died and he had to work in the mine.

"He looks like you," I write.

"Yeah, some said that all right," he says, still looking at the photo.

He puts the photo on his locker and starts rummaging through the rest of the photos. He picks out a photo of his mother and tells me that it was taken long after they had fallen out and I look at the photo with interest. Bridie Kelly is tall and lean with a mass of white hair tied in a bun. She has bright, piercing eyes, even brighter than Steve's and there is something about her that unnerves me, as if the anger she felt at life is burning through the photo itself.

As I try to think of something nice to say about the intense woman, I feel the sudden vibrations of the train passing beneath my feet. It takes me by such surprise that I let out a roar. Martin leans forward and holds onto me as I sway. I can see the sudden fear in his face. I look down and can see my shoelace caught in the bolt that joined the tracks. I kick to free myself and panic.

"It's okay, Christopher," he says as he pulls me closer to him. "It's not real, son."

I grab onto his nightshirt and bury my head shamelessly in his chest where I cry until the fear passes. I look up at the clock above Martin's bed. 3.05 a.m. He releases me and I look away, embarrassed.

He puts his hand forward and lifts my chin.

"I'll think about it," he says.

I frown. I am lost in my own problems and am unsure what he means.

"I'll think about going to see my brother."

I open his door and creep by Aishling who is fast asleep at her desk.

I lower myself into my bed, my heart continuing to beat fast and as it slows I fall into a deep sleep where I dream of Martin and his brother, laughing about the past and all its foolishness.

When I awake the following morning, I get out of bed and dress slowly. I don't look at my foot and pull my sock over it quickly. There are some mornings that I don't want to be reminded of it. As I pass Penelope and Victoria's room I notice that Greta is there and that she is talking to Victoria alone. I wonder how she has managed to separate them and find myself admiring her persistence.

"Looks lovely!" she says to Victoria who is spinning in front of a tall mirror in the bedroom. I stand by the doorway and think that Victoria looks very different when she smiles and is not wringing her hands in fear. She is wearing a modern red dress that Greta must have bought for her.

"Do you like it?" Greta asks.

"Yes. But Penelope will never approve," she says sadly.

Greta puts her hands on Victoria's narrow shoulders and looks into her face.

"Victoria, you can make your own decisions."

Victoria nods and smiles nervously and starts wringing her hands again. She is wearing the same expression as Bill's son who sometimes comes here and gets told off for breaking the flowers in my mother's garden. Her head is lowered and all I can see are her two huge blue eyes that appear to be looking upwards at Greta even though the women are roughly the same height.

Greta decides on a different tactic. I know it is her final strategy as she doesn't want to manipulate Victoria but wants to try freeing her gradually from Penelope's authority.

"You know, it'd mean a lot to me if you wore this dress tomorrow when your nephew arrives."

Victoria looks away and says, "I . . . em . . . maybe."

Greta nods and moves over to the window. She opens it and takes a deep breath of fresh air.

"So, Victoria, are you looking forward to telling your story tomorrow?"

Victoria resumes looking like Bill's naughty son and starts to bite her lower lip.

"Yes. Penelope says it's a wonderful idea," she says but her eyes don't reflect her words.

I think she is nervous about tomorrow and that if it wasn't for Penelope's bossy ways, Victoria would have refused to talk to Steve.

"But she says I have not to speak."

Greta spins around. "Not speak? What's the point in that? How can you tell your story if you don't speak?"

"No. Penelope will tell our story. Penelope says it is best if I stay quiet. I'm . . . I'm not to be trusted," she says shyly.

Greta moves forward from the window. She opens her mouth to say something but thinks the better of it. I know what she is thinking. One step at a time.

I wander down to Jimmy's room and wonder if he is going to be all right. Jeff spent the previous evening at the hospital and I saw Kora say that Jimmy opened his eyes and smiled at his son. I hope he recovers and comes back. He has more work to do.

When I go back downstairs I see Aishling looking through the mail. She is dressed for her outing with Steve and is wearing short denim cut-offs and a cheesecloth striped blouse. I can see suntan lotion glisten on her legs and I think she is wasting her time. Her Irish skin will never be brown. I have seen my mother tell her this many times but she doesn't listen. I watch her pick a letter up. It is posted to her and my heart jumps when I see her tear it open but it is not from her parents. It is a reply from the McGonigle family, the family of Father Hayes' lost love, Deirdre. Aishling takes a breath. I can see the disappointment on her face but she is happy for Father Hayes. I stand behind her and read even faster than she does. It is written in English and is signed by Nóirin McGonigle, a niece of Deirdre.

Dear Aishling

Thank you for your letter telling us all about Father Francis. The letter came to my father, Pádraig, and he asked me to write back to you. His hands are bad with arthritis and he finds it hard to write. He was sorry to hear about Father Francis' ill health and asks that you give him his regards. You will be interested to know that his name is not actually Francis but Aiden. I know you asked about his life before he left Ireland and this is what my father told me.

Aiden lived with his mother and father on a small farm about three miles from our own here. There were only two boys in the family, Aiden and his older brother, Francis. Francis was almost ten years older than Aiden and he joined the priesthood when Aiden was just a little boy. I hear that poor Aiden grew up in the shadow of his older brother. It was a great honour to have a priest in the family and his mother was very proud. Anyway, Aiden was a great hurler here and a scholar but he knew that he'd be the only one to run the farm. He wanted to be a teacher though. My father, who was a few years behind Aiden in school, remembers him well. When he was about fifteen, he started walking out with my Aunt Deirdre. They were an item from such a young age but it was all very harmless and innocent back then. But she came home and told my grandmother that they had agreed to marry as soon as they were both eighteen. Of course, no one took them seriously. Deirdre was a bit of a wild one. She was a fine-looking girl and I've enclosed a photo of her when she was around sixteen or seventeen that I thought Aiden would like.

Aishling stopped reading and looked at the photo. It was wrapped in soft paper and when she opened it, a black and white photo of a smiling girl stared back at us. Deirdre had long curly hair and bright eyes. She was smiling confidently into the camera like a movie star. Aishling nodded at the photo and could see why Father Francis confused herself with Deirdre. She returned to the letter.

You can't tell in a sepia photo but she had long dark-red hair and green eyes. She was quite a beauty. My grandmother wanted her to become a nurse in Dublin. She had an uncle living there then that she could have stayed with but she refused and said that she never wanted to leave. She knew Aiden would be tied to the farm and she was happy to marry at eighteen and live out her life in the village. When Aiden asked my grandfather for Deirdre's hand, he agreed but the condition was that she do her nursing training in Dublin and they could marry when she finished it. He was a quiet man who was fond of Aiden and knew he'd be good to his daughter. She came home on the train once a fortnight and Aiden would be waiting for her outside the station. He didn't care when the other lads made fun of him. He was an unusual sort, gentle and thoughtful, a real gentleman, my father said.

But it wasn't to be. Aiden's brother Francis was killed in Africa. He was part of the Missions there and he was murdered. My father never found out exactly what happened but Aiden's mother was devastated. She fell into a deep depression and poor Aiden didn't know what to do. All her hopes had been pinned on her religious son. He was her reason for living. Little by little she started praying that Aiden would receive a calling to join the priesthood and finish off his brother's work in Africa. She thought Francis' work trying to save the souls of Africans would remain unfinished unless she offered up her only remaining son to God's work. You have to remember it was a different time. Day by day she worked on him. My father said he lost a lot of weight and so did Aiden's father who was against him becoming a priest. But slowly over months she wore him down. I know that this is our own opinion here and you'd have to ask Aiden for his side but that was how it seemed to the people in the village.

When he broke his engagement with Deirdre, the whole village knew that Anne Hayes got her wish and that soon Aiden would be off to the seminary. My father said that Aiden wrote to Deirdre in Dublin explaining his actions and that she wrote back asking him to wait until she came home on Friday's train to talk about it. People didn't have phones then and it must have been an awful time for the couple. When she got off the train the following Friday, Aiden was not there to meet her. It was the end of summer. My grandmother sent my father who was just a teenager to wait for her. He remembers her looking around for Aiden as she got off the train in her blue summer dress. When he told her she cried in his arms and he was embarrassed that one of his friends would see him.

The next time my father saw Aiden, he had taken the name Father Francis, in honour of his dead brother, and it was like he never existed. He had taken his brother's name and his brother's vocation and few believed that Aiden had ever had a calling, not when he was so in love with Deirdre. She took it hard and when she finished out her training she went straight to New York. She told my father that she couldn't bear to live in the place where she had hoped she would spend her life with Aiden, that everywhere she looked she would be reminded of him. Aiden's father was never the same. He became ill and back then the doctors didn't know what was wrong with him. He only lived for eight months after Aiden was ordained. Looking back it at, my father thinks it was cancer he had, that the shock of losing two sons in such a short time finished him off.

Mrs Hayes stayed in the old farmhouse but the land was sold off and someone else runs it now. She used to bring photos of Aiden in his cassock everywhere and show them off without a care that she had ruined his life. Any time he did come home, he was the same gentle Aiden but he had lost that spark. He wasn't allowed to play hurling or any sports. My father said it would have been better if he'd never been born. My grandmother, who had been so against her daughter's early engagement, never forgave Mrs Hayes for ruining Deirdre's happiness. She felt Deirdre never got over losing Aiden.

The family would hear bits of news about Aiden over the years. He'd been in Africa mostly and South America. When Mrs Hayes died, my father never saw Aiden again and never knew that he'd been in Australia all those years. He asked me to tell you that even though it broke his sister's heart, he never held it against Aiden and he felt they were both victims of the times they lived in. He said he wishes him well.

I posted your letter on to Deirdre. Sorry, I should have mentioned that she is alive and well. She never came home from New York. After many years nursing there, she married a policeman, Joe. He was Irish. He died a few years back. She had a daughter and a son and, as odd as it seems, she called the boy Aiden. He lives in Sydney. Small world. He's married to an Australian girl. I've included Deirdre's address as I am sure that she would love to hear from Aiden.

I'm delighted to be part of such a love story. I knew a little about their story when I was a teenager and thought it was romantic and sad. The train doesn't come through here any more and the station is now overgrown with weeds, but I think about them any time I pass it. Perhaps they will finally have a chance to make peace with each other and with those that separated them? Thanks again for writing and please give our regards to Aiden.

Kind regards
Nóirin McGonigle

Aishling puts the letter down and wipes the tears that have been falling down her face.

"Poor Father Francis," she says quietly.

She walks into the Penance Room and sits beside him. She smooths a large tuft of grey hair from his eyes. He smiles at her. Aishling takes his glasses off and cleans them.

"Aiden?"

Father Francis looks up and smiles.

"Yes?" he says brightly.

"I have something for you," she says to him as she puts the photo into his hands.

He looks at it and a huge smile spreads across his face.

"Deirdre is in America," she says, smiling.

"In America?" he asks.

"Yes, Aiden. In New York. Deirdre is alive in New York!" She hugs him and rocks him slowly.

Aishling moves back from him and wipes the new tears that have fallen down her face. She stands a while longer and together we watch him talking to himself as he stares at the picture.

"*A stór!*" he says.

Steve arrives and Aishling returns to the kitchen to collect the picnic basket that she had packed earlier. When she gets there she notices that Mina has taken some of the food back out of the basket and has put it back into the pantry. Aishling just laughs and throws her eyes up at Li.

Li draws Aishling aside and says, "I was thinking . . . Mina missed out on teaching her son how to run the bakery. My son, Kai, wants to be a confectioner. I cannot help him. I am not so good at sweet things. Maybe I ask Emma if Kai can come here to learn from Mina?"

Aishling nods. "Sounds like a great idea. Hope she doesn't give him a hard time though."

"Will toughen him up, I think," Li replies. "Young ones too soft now."

As Steve leaves with Aishling I feel that surge of jealousy returning. I don't like feeling this way. I wander down to Wilfred's room. He is listening to music. I stand inside the door watching the turntable move around and around in a hypnotic motion. I look at the record sleeve which reads "*Mozart Symphonies No 40 and 41*". His eyes are closed and he looks like Mina does when she has had too much to eat: satisfied yet wanting, a look that I am still trying to find a better description for. He is facing the wall and is lost in thought. He moves his hand around in swirling motions, conducting the music. I follow his hand and find my upper body swaying slightly and wish I could hear the sounds he is so obviously enjoying. As the record is less than halfway through I leave him and wander down to Jimmy's room. Jeff is there and Tina is helping him to pack up some more of his father's pyjamas.

"How's he doing then?" she asks.

Tina always wears a kind smile on her face and I know my

mother wishes she could work more hours, but she looks after both her elderly parents who came to Australia from Italy. I wonder briefly if she knows Maria and her grandfather but cringe at the thought. I saw Aishling say that Australians think that Ireland is so small that everyone knows each other and it must be the same for other Europeans. When she'd go into town people would ask her of she knew Mick O'Brien from Galway or Mary Murphy from Dublin and it always annoyed her. She told me once that although Ireland is much smaller than Australia, it is not so small an island that everyone knows each other.

Jeff looks exhausted. His shoulders drop forward and he rubs his hands over his lined brow. "Not as bad as they expected. I mean, first night there they were telling me he's a goner. But he's pulling through. He's a strong old codger. Can't move his right arm at all. His left arm was affected by the first stroke so he's pretty helpless. His speech is much harder to understand. He's really frustrated."

Tina expresses her sympathy and puts her hand on Jeff's arm. "My dad had a stroke few years back but there's hope with the right care."

Jeff nods. "Be great if he'd accept the care," he said and I know that he is referring to Kora who has spent hours at the hospital when Jeff had to leave to feed his stock. Jimmy's daughters live far away and have only been able to visit him on weekends.

Tina nods. "He'll come round. He'll see how you two are meant for each other. He'll see how Kora's the woman for you."

Jeff blushes a little and makes his excuses to leave.

"Get some rest!" she shouts after him, "You look exhausted. Not safe to be driving like that."

Jeff waves back and I am once again left to wander the house alone.

I take a brief look into the Penance Room but leave quickly as Iren is continually shouting for Aron and the other residents, including Martin, are finding it hard to cope with her. Martin looks over at Jimmy's chair. I know he is missing his grumpy nemesis more than he'd admit. I know that right now he is thinking how alike he and Jimmy are. Both full of anger and regret. Brothers in arms.

I leave the room and sit on the front step to watch passers-by. It is not yet eleven and I am wondering about Aishling and whether or not she is enjoying herself. I look up into the sky and remember something my mother once said to me. "Look for happy things in your day," she said but all I see in front of me are dried-out trees and people, hoping for rain.

Chapter 18

Later that evening, Greta takes Penelope out of the Penance Room and brings her into the dining room. I follow the pair to see what is happening.

"'Ere. Look what I've brought you," Greta says, taking a crumpled booklet from her bag and handing it to Penelope who immediately begins to work out the creases in the paper without looking at it.

Greta waits for some recognition but when it doesn't come she asks, "Don't you like it? Thought that's what you wanted."

Penelope looks closer at the paper and begins shuffling through its pages. A rush of blood goes to her face and she reddens from her neck to her forehead. My mother once said I should not pass remark on this as it is normal for this to happen to older women.

"What is it?" she finally asks.

"It's a book of music sheets. Old time jazz," Greta says, smiling. "I got it for you in the bookshop. It's second-hand but I thought it'd do till we get you some new sheets."

"But it's not allowed!" Penelope says, looking behind her and wiping small beads of sweat from her forehead.

"Says who?"

Penelope takes out her handkerchief and dabs the rest of her face. She doesn't answer Greta but continues to look like a trapped hare. Her eyes dart from left to right and she begins to sway from foot to foot as though she needs to use the bathroom.

"Penelope, your father's not here. He died years ago. You don't have to be afraid any more."

"Henry got into trouble," she says finally, ignoring Greta's comments about her father being dead.

"Look, how about you leave it in your room? You don't have to play it. Not unless you want to."

Penelope nods and without as much as a thank-you races off upstairs to hide the sheets among her clothes. I follow her and stand in the doorway as she runs from drawer to drawer saying, "Oh my!" over and over until she finds the perfect hiding place. I watch while she opens Victoria's bedside locker and hides the music among her sister's underwear.

"There!" she says. "He'll never look in there."

Penelope looks into the mirror and dabs some powder on her face before returning to the Penance Room. On her way down the hallway I grin as she opens the dining-room door and looks briefly at the piano. I watch as a broad smile washes over her face and in that moment she looks like a naughty child, planning mischief. My mother once said that that is what Penelope and Victoria both are. Naughty children who were so hurt when they were little, they never really grew up. I return to the Penance Room and sit in my usual seat, watching the sun through the stained-glass window. Streams of coloured light make odd patterns on the floor and look like spotlights shining down from the heavens. I watch the light dance slowly across the wooden floor and illuminate the pews. I look up and notice that Iren is staring straight at me and smiling an odd smile. She gets up and painfully makes her way across the room. Victoria and Mina are sitting together quietly and they watch with interest as Iren stops at my pew and touches my face lovingly. They look at each other and back at Iren who looks quite beautiful and young in the sunlight.

"Jacob," she says quietly and as the light changes and moves away she returns to her chair and closes her eyes tightly.

Mina leans in closer to Victoria and says, "I think this poor lady has lost her mind." Victoria nods even though she probably doesn't know what is going on. I am overcome by sadness and I rise quickly, wiping my tears in my shirt.

A sudden blast of hot air tells me that someone has come in the front door and I wipe my tears quickly. I come out onto the hallway and see Aishling with sunburnt legs walking down the hallway with Steve. They are both smiling and I think my day cannot get any worse.

"Fancy a beer?" she says, looking back and shaking her long curls in his direction.

"Sure," he says in his easygoing manner that has begun to annoy me.

I have never been light-hearted. I wouldn't know how.

Aishling opens the screen door and directs Steve to the back garden where they sit on the bench at the back of the house. I race upstairs and go into my room to watch their conversation. I blush as I see her midriff showing and I can see Steve looking at her the way my father sometimes looks at my mother. I have a sudden urge to use my voice, to shout out my window for him to go away. I only wanted Steve to come here and help me. I didn't plan on him taking over. But I lose courage and simply watch their words. Aishling is tearing the label off the beer bottle and smiling at Steve. I can tell that this is not her first beer today and that she and Steve had probably been drinking before they came home. She starts to tell him about Father Francis and the letter she received that morning. Her expression changes and she looks sad.

When she finishes the story Steve, who has been listening carefully, says, "So, you feel sorry for his lost opportunities?"

Aishling takes a deep breath in. "I suppose, but it's more than that. Someone else made a decision for him that ruined his life and he sits in there now day in and day out. He doesn't really know what's going on. He had a breakdown years ago and he's been in care ever since. It's just . . . it just seems unfair that none of what happened was his fault, that someone else made decisions that affected the rest of his life."

Steve moves in closer and moves a long bang of hair from Aishling's eyes. He knows that Aishling's reaction to Father Francis' situation has something to do with her own reasons for being here. I can see him thinking about his response, waiting for the right moment.

"You know, I was once a priest," he says seriously and watches while Aishling's mouth opens in shock.

But she suddenly starts to laugh. She leans forward and places her head in her hands, concealing her face. I can see her shoulders rise and fall quickly and know that she is laughing hysterically. Steve starts chuckle too although he doesn't know why Aishling has reacted the way she has. I do because I have read her letters. She sits up and looks at him. There are tears in her eyes and her face has changed to a look of half amusement and half despair.

She looks up towards the sky and says, "God, what is it with me and priests?"

Steve is interested and motions for her to continue and so for the first time I see her tell the story of how she came to be here. A story my mother knows a little about and I know because of my snooping.

Aishling takes another swig of her bottle and looks cautiously at Steve. She is not drunk enough to make a fool of herself.

"So this is like a confession?" she jokes but I know what is worrying her. She is worried that her story will get out. Steve makes a mock Sign of the Cross and I see her stiffen on the hard wooden bench.

There is a pause and then she begins.

"When I was sixteen I was involved in the local parish folk group. You know, guitar-playing Holy Marys and that sort of thing."

Steve didn't know but he beckoned for her to go on.

"Well, most of the girls in the parish met their husbands that way. It was all so civilised and I only joined because my mother signed me up for it. I was a bit wild. Not doing well at school, hanging around the football pitch with my brothers and their friends. I only joined because if I didn't sort myself out, my parents were going to send me to an all-girl's boarding school."

Aishling's expression becomes more serious and she looks down at the beer bottle and sighs. I can see her eyes water and her long throat swallow, trying perhaps to push back painful memories.

"My parents had it all worked out for me. Nursing training after leaving school. My mother was a nurse. Marriage to a policeman or if I got lucky, a doctor. I was suffocating. It was such a double standard. They encouraged my brothers to travel after university, to see the world. There was no mention of marriage for them. They were free to see what the world had to offer them but for me, well, it was safer to see me married off to a nice man with a good salary who would look after me. The nursing training was for insurance if I couldn't manage that. There were such rows at home and all over me. If I'd had a sister maybe there would have been someone to share the pressure with but with three brothers who could do no wrong, well, I rebelled any chance I got. But the threat of the boarding school quietened me for a while anyway. I couldn't have coped with that. Despite my behaviour I was – well, I was a sensitive girl really – deep down anyway. So I went to the folk group and sang at Mass. After a few months a new curate came to our town."

Aishling blushes a little and Steve smiles. He is trying to make it easier for her.

"He was good-looking – an awful waste, some of my friends said. He was nice to me. He was nine years older and of course I fell in love with someone I could not have. I started going to confession and if I got the parish priest I would wait in line again in the hope that I could be alone with the curate."

Aishling reddens again. She tries to stand up but Steve grabs her arm and prevents her from fleeing.

"I just need another beer," she says but he gives her that intense gaze of his and smiles so sweetly at her that I can almost see her knees weaken as she sits back down.

"What happened next?" he asks.

"I – I chased after him. I spent as much of my time as possible at the church. I even helped my mother with the flowers for Mass on Sunday, something I wouldn't have been caught dead doing beforehand. I knew he was attracted to me and sometimes I'd think he was trying to avoid being alone with me. He'd seem nervous when I approached him with a question after Sodality Group. Oh, I joined that too, a bible study group that met each Wednesday evening. His stand-offish ways only made me want him more. I was stupid and reckless and sitting here now, so many years later, I cannot understand what made me the way I was. I thought it was a game. I'd chase him and he'd finally succumb to my charms." She sighed. "You know, I've never told anyone the whole story. You have . . . a strange effect on me."

Steve doesn't answer and she continues.

"Well, it went on that way until he'd break out in a sweat at the sight of me."

"That could have been your beauty. Perhaps he was struggling with his vocation?"

Aishling looks down at her empty bottle and an expression of guilt spreads over her face. "No. I – I think he was afraid of me. Anyway, during the summer, there was a retreat for some of the town's disadvantaged children. I put my name forward as a volunteer. Not because I wanted to see these kids get away for a few days but because I wanted a chance to be alone with him. There were four other volunteers, one lad and three girls who I knew at school. The girls and I shared a large dorm room in an old convent with the twelve little girls on retreat while Neil, the male volunteer, slept in with the boys. There were about six boys, all rough young lads who were hard to manage. Peter, Father Kearns, slept in a room on his own. In the day, we were supposed to teach the kids prayers and also to bring them out on walks through the countryside. I hated every minute of the day and spent my time day dreaming of – well – you know."

Steve tries to stop himself from smiling. "It's all right. I won't judge you."

Aishling doesn't respond and continues to look at the brown bottle in her hand.

"What happened next?"

"On the last night we had a barbeque or at least we tried to. It rained heavily so we had to abandon it and run inside. We were all soaked. We put the kids to bed and sat around talking about life. One by one the others drifted off to bed. Peter was quiet all night. He kept clearing his throat and looking at me with my wet hair and blouse. I knew that this would be the only chance I got so when he excused himself and went to bed I followed him into his room and sat on the end of his bed. I can still remember my heart beating so loudly. He sat up and asked me what I wanted. I . . . I told him that I loved him and wanted to be with him. I leant forward and kissed him quickly. Then he looked at me with . . . with such disgust . . . I . . . anyway, he jumped up and asked me to leave. I was so embarrassed. I said, 'You led me on . . . you made me think you liked me.' He denied it. He said yes, I was a beautiful girl and that as a man of course he had noticed me but that he had devoted his life to God. He asked me to leave the room. I don't think I've ever been so angry in my life. I ran from the room and cried my eyes out in the dorm. Margaret, one of the volunteers, asked me what was wrong but I couldn't tell her what I'd done, what a fool I'd made of myself so I said I had a bad stomach ache.

"The next day, we travelled back by bus and there was a terrible atmosphere. I could see Neil looking at me strangely and I began to panic that Peter had told him what I'd said. When we stopped for lunch, I saw Neil and Margaret talking and looking over at me. I began to imagine the parish priest sitting in my parents' parlour telling them what I'd done. I think my face must have been red all the way home and I spent most of the journey looking out of the window trying to find a way out of the trouble I was sure I was in.

"As soon as I got home I ran to my room and cried my eyes out. Finn, my eldest brother, came in and asked me what was wrong and in that moment, without thinking, I said . . . I said that Father Peter had taken advantage of me in his room . . . that I had gone there to ask him for some advice on one of the kids. I don't know why I said that. I was so . . . humiliated. Finn went mad. He ran downstairs and I could hear my brothers and my father shouting. Above it all I could hear my mother's tears. I had never heard her cry like that before.

"My father phoned the police and it all suddenly got out of hand. They took a statement from me and . . . I heard later that Father Peter was taken down to the station for interview. They interviewed the other volunteers and as none of them actually saw anything, it was my word against his. I think they believed me because Margaret had told the police that I had returned to the dorm that night very upset. I knew then that Father Peter hadn't told anyone about what I had done but it was too late, it was too late to tell the truth. He was released and the police asked my parents if they wanted to file charges. I begged them not to – I even – God forgive me – I asked them to be Christian about it and to forgive him. They relented even though my brothers were angry about this. They wanted to see him go to jail. Finn went up to the parish house and when Father Peter answered, he punched him in the face. He could have got a police record but Father Peter didn't make a complaint. Finn saw this as a terrible sign of guilt while I remained quiet and drowned in shame.

"Father Peter was sent to work in Columbia and I tried to get on with my life. But I couldn't get it out of my head and knowing what I'd done gnawed away at me so much so that I actually asked my parents to send me to boarding school for that last year of my education. I said I had to get away from the town and they agreed. It cost them a fortune. Two of my brothers were at college then and it was money they couldn't afford. I went straight from there to nursing training in Dublin. It was what my mother wanted and I felt I had no right to say no, not after what I had done. I went out with one or two men in Dublin but nothing ever lasted. It was as if I could not allow myself happiness. I could not allow myself a life because I had ruined Peter's life.

"When I was twenty-one, I graduated from nurse training. I realised I hated nursing but I felt I had no say in anything any more. It was like I was dead and only going through the motions of life. My parents and two of my brothers came to Dublin to celebrate. Finn was in New York at that stage so he couldn't come. My mother was so proud and my father, who I know felt he had not protected me, hugged me throughout the entire ceremony. I could see the tears in his eyes.

"We went to lunch and I spent the entire meal feeling like every bite I took was choking me. I had two glasses of wine and because I hadn't been drinking in months, it went straight to my head or should I say, to my tongue. I felt that my sentence should be over. I had done everything my parents wanted me to do. I was now a qualified nurse and had a job in a Dublin hospital for life if I wanted it, but the memory of Peter sat on my chest and I needed to get it off. I needed to feel like I could breathe. I decided to tell them the truth about what happened, right there and then in a busy Dublin restaurant with my two brothers staring open-mouthed across the table. My father's face went white as snow while my mother stood up and started to shout at me. It was over in a matter of minutes. Together they rose and left me sitting there alone. There was no penance given, no forgiveness. I spent the next few days calling them. Most of the time, the phone would ring out. Twice, I spoke to my second eldest brother, Darragh, who said my mother asked that I never contact them again. I started to write, one letter every day, trying to explain what a stupid thing I had done and how I was sorry, but I never received a reply. I spent the rest of that summer in Dublin trying to think of ways that I could make amends to my family. I called Finn in his office in New York and he ranted and raved at me about how he had assaulted a priest, an innocent man, for me. He told me that he never wanted to hear from me again, that I had broken Mammy and Daddy's heart and that they would never be able to hold their heads high in the town again.

"By September I had given up on ever finding peace. I tried to find where Father Peter had been transferred to. I wrote letters to the bishop in Columbia, hoping they would get to him, but I never heard anything.

"I decided to leave, to get away. I felt lost and alone in Dublin. I didn't meet many people and I had not made any friends in the hospital. I could not sleep and began drinking heavily, spending my time off work in the local pub. Before I left I had . . . a brief affair with a married man. I know that doesn't add up. I know that is not the action of a remorseful person but it happened. He didn't tell me he was married at the time although, if I am to be truthful, deep down I knew. It seemed like I didn't want to reach for anything permanent, anything that could make me happy. I think I wanted to punish myself, that I hated myself. I never went back to Donegal and I left Dublin for Australia where no one knew me, where I could start afresh."

"But you didn't start afresh?"

Aishling shakes her head. "No. As soon as I got this job I started writing letters home. I hoped my parents would see that I was trying to make a life for myself. I even told them that I had tried to track Father Peter down but still I received no reply. I started working nights here. My insomnia hadn't improved. I could sleep during the day, no problem, but could only get a few hours at night if I was really tired. I've been here now for about fifteen years and it seems like nothing has changed. It seems like I am still sitting in that restaurant waiting for my family to sit down and tell me they forgive me, still waiting for their letter to say it's okay, you can come home."

Aishling lowers her head and allows the tears that have been building to fall. Steve moves forward and wipes them with his tanned hands.

"Can you forgive yourself?"

Aishling shakes her head. "Part of me thinks it was all such a stupid, adolescent thing to happen, that it could have happened to any teenager but yet it ruined my life, Peter's life and my family's. I want to – I really want to put it behind me but I am stuck and I can't see . . ."

Aishling sobs again and puts her hand over her mouth. Steve holds her and I can see him patting her back as though she is a child.

"Continue," he says.

"I'm sorry. I can't believe I'm telling you this. W–without my parents' forgiveness, I can't see a way out."

"Aishling, you cannot control what other people do. You should understand that. Look at what happened to Mina, to Iren. People do things that hurt others. Can I ask you something?"

Aishling nods.

"Do you forgive your parents for turning their backs on you?"

Aishling's eyes open wide, spilling large tears. From my bedroom

160

window I can see her struggling to answer a question she has never before considered.

"Let them go," Steve finally says. "Forgive them. There is nothing more you can do."

Aishling turns to him and wraps her arms around herself. She leans forward and I can see that she regrets opening herself up to him. Steve puts his arms out and draws her in and she relents. I watch for a few moments as she cries in his arms, my emotions torn between relief for her and jealousy towards Steve for the feelings I fear Aishling has for him. I pull my blind down roughly and lie down on my bed. Darkness is falling and even though I am fully dressed, I drift off to sleep. I know Martin will need me later and I want to be ready.

Chapter 19

At two o'clock I wake abruptly even though I have not felt any movement from Aishling's chair outside my room. I rise quickly and make my way out of my room. Aishling is not at her desk but I decide not to check on her whereabouts. I open Martin's door and find him awake, sitting up talking to someone. I glance at his locker and notice the empty bottle of whiskey which had been almost full the night before. I stand just inside the door and watch him speak with an imaginary visitor. He suddenly notices me and beckons for me to come in and sit on his bed. I don't want to show any fear but he is looking at his window with such sincerity that I am afraid there really is a ghost, an angry ghost, the type I am afraid of.

"I'm sorry, Liam," he said. "I'm sorry you got killed in the war."

Martin waits for an answer and I can see him nodding. I prefer to believe the amount of whiskey he has consumed is causing him to hallucinate and conjure up the memory of the people he has offended. Like Dr Alder says, his conscience and not people, is haunting him.

"This is my friend Christopher," he says as if introducing me to a visitor in his room, a live visitor that is.

"Liam knows you," he says and I gulp.

"He says he has seen you walking the hallways, checking on people."

I am suddenly frozen with fear and feel the need to pee. I don't like it when ghosts are walking around here without my knowledge. I want to run and suddenly I know how Wilfred feels, sitting in the Penance Room, listening to others tell terrible tales and being too afraid to leave.

"Weren't my fault, Liam," he says but his face looks calm and he is nodding as if Liam is speaking to him.

"She's here?" he says, an expression of fear spreading across his lined face.

I feel a sudden draught and the curtain in Martin's room rises from the floor and blows towards us. He screams and I can see his mouth open wide, his few yellow teeth sticking out from his receding gums. His window is open wide and a sudden breeze has howled up from the side of the house.

Aishling comes running in. Her hair is hanging loose and her make-up is smeared. It looks like she has not stopped crying since her confession to Steve hours earlier.

"What is it, Martin?" she says. Her face looks panicked.

"My mother! She's just put her face in through my window. My brother – he brought her here to punish me. Jesus, they're going to get me! I know it! She pulled that curtain up straight off the floor. She's here. Please believe me. I'm not mad. The boy saw it. Ask him!"

Aishling walks to the window and pulls it shut. "It's the breeze, Martin. There's a storm coming. We might even get some rain. Look, no one is here, love. Go to sleep." She looks at the empty bottle of whiskey and sighs. "Martin, look, I can appreciate you liking a drop but it doesn't go so well with your medication, okay? No wonder you're seeing ghosts."

Martin looks at me and opens his mouth to argue but I don't want him upsetting Aishling tonight. I raise my fingers to my lips and signal for him to say nothing.

"Okay," he says.

Aishling sighs. "Look, I'm outside if you need me so don't be afraid to call, okay?"

Martin nods but his lips remain in their pursed, unhappy shape.

I leave Martin and follow Aishling into the hallway. She hears something on the lower floor and makes her way downstairs. I notice that her bedroom door is open and her small reading light is on. I walk over her dressing-table and see a letter she has written to her parents. I pick it up and read it shamelessly.

Dear Mam and Dad

I have promised myself that this is the last letter you will ever receive from me. I hope that this is one promise I can keep. I know now that you will never forgive me for the awful mistake I made and I accept this. I am trying to forgive myself and, for that, I will need all my energy, energy that I have wasted trying to explain my actions to you. I forgive you for feeling the way you do. I let you down and I am truly sorry. I wish you both well and I will always love you.

Goodbye

Your daughter, Aishling

Underneath I see another letter that she has written to Deirdre in New York. She knows that she cannot put her wrongs right but she is going to try to help Father Francis.

I feel her thundering back up the stairs and return swiftly to the darkened corridor. Aishling goes into her room and fixes her hair into a bun. I watch as she gasps and grimaces as she smooths cream onto her sunburnt arms and legs. In the dim light her face looks lined and there is a harshness about her that I have not seen before. A familiar sadness overpowers me and I leave her and walk downstairs where I stand outside my parents' room for a moment. It is five to three and I am tempted to climb in beside them until my night fear passes but I resist and try to tough it out on my own. I go into the Penance Room and notice how different it looks in the darkness. It seems lost without the tortured souls that sit here every day, as though the room needs them as much as I do. I sit on my window-seat and look out at the streetlight streaming over our garden and making strange shapes as our trees lash about in the wind that is still blowing. As my train passes, I dig my nails into the wooden pew and count numbers in my head. It will not last long. I have to be brave.

When it is over I rub my foot which always throbs at this time of night and hobble back upstairs to my room. Aishling is not at her desk and I ease my door open and climb into bed, hoping that the morning will come soon. But I don't sleep and spend what is left of the night thinking of Aishling and of Martin.

When the sun finally rises, I welcome it and make my way downstairs where I sit alone until the crowd shuffle in from the dining room. There is a teenage Chinese boy standing awkwardly in the hallway outside my mother's office. She opens her office door and brings him in. Tired as I am I follow and sit on the side of her armchair. The boy is seated facing her and I remember that he is Li's son and that she wants Mina to teach him to bake. He is a tall, thin boy of about sixteen or seventeen with coarse black roughly cut hair and dark brown eyes. He is lightly tanned and is wearing worn runners and faded jeans. I notice how nervous he looks as his eyes shoot around the small room.

"So, Kai, you want to learn to bake?" my mother asks.

Kai nods and looks at his feet. "Yes, Ma'am," he says.

"I suppose your mother has told you about Mina. She might be a little hard to get along with."

"Yes, Ma'am. My mother said that Mina has suffered a lot."

I follow Kai's words and notice that he speaks perfect English because he was born here and didn't have to learn a new language like his parents did. He is polite and respectful and I can see my mother warming to him.

"It won't be a proper job but you are free to come in a couple of times a week to learn from Mina."

Kai thanks my mother for the opportunity. I can see by her face that she doesn't think this will work.

"Kai, if Mina gives you a hard time, you let me know and I'll speak to her, okay?"

"Yes, Ma'am," he says again and my mother leads him to the door. My mother brings Kai down to the kitchen where she explains to Mina that she would like her to teach him the confectionary trade. Kora is standing by the sink with Li and all four of us take a deep breath, waiting for her reaction. She peers closely at Kai and looks back at my mother. It seems like an eternity before she answers.

"Why?" she asks, gripping onto the worktop and steadying herself from the sight in front of her.

I know she thinks Kai is a Japanese boy standing in her kitchen, near her precious food.

"Mina, Kai is Li's son and he would like to learn to bake. You know Li's not much of a baker so I thought you'd like an apprentice," my mother explains quickly.

"Li is not Japanese. She's Chinese," she says firmly and my mother nods.

"That's right," she says, "and Kai is an Australian boy."

Mina looks around her and for some reason darts a sharp glance at Kora who almost spits out her water. I think she feels defeated with so many people around and agrees to take on her apprentice.

"Okay, Emma. I will try but he better not be a stupid pupil."

Kai doesn't react to the insult but stands still in the kitchen waiting for his orders.

"Come back tomorrow," she finally says. "You know how to make cheesecake?"

Kai shakes his head. "No, Ma'am."

I am starting to think that this is all he will ever say – yes Ma'am, no Ma'am.

"Well, we'll start with this."

Kai leaves and everyone shoots quick glances at each other.

Li thanks Mina and she shrugs it off.

"I hope he doesn't eat much," she responds gruffly. "There's not enough to go around."

Everyone goes into the Penance Room where we wait to hear Penelope and Victoria's story. The sisters are already there and are seated side by side at the far end of the room. Victoria is wearing the red dress that Greta took her shopping for and it looks like she has been crying. Kora walks over to her and asks her what is wrong and she says, "This is a nice dress" through sobs. I watch Penelope stiffen and know that she has given her younger sister a telling-off about her choice of clothing. I suddenly wish that Greta was here because Kora doesn't understand what has happened. She doesn't know the ladies as well as Greta has got to know them in the short time she has been here.

"Yes, it's a lovely dress, Victoria. There's no need to cry, mate," Kora says as she walks away and takes a seat beside Iren. She has brought a packet of crackers to feed to Iren. Apart from medication, food is the only thing that will keep her quiet.

Greta arrives unexpectedly. It is her day off but she wants to hear the ladies' story. I feel relieved and watch as she walks over to Victoria and speaks quietly to her. She has her back to me so I don't know what she has said but when she walks away Victoria is smiling and sitting upright in her chair. I see Greta slipping Penelope another envelope which the elder sister opens quickly before hiding it under the cushion beneath her.

"Came in post this morning," Greta said, "Ordered it special."

I assume it is more music sheets and return to my seat under the window. The sisters' nephew Henry is here and, true to his word, he is once again dressed in civilian clothes. He kisses his aunts gently and takes a seat beside them. Steve turns the tape recorder on and begins. He starts with Penelope.

"Penelope, can you tell me about your early life and what brought you to Broken Hill?"

Everyone leans forward. The sisters are quiet and usually keep to themselves and we realise that we know very little about them.

"I was born in 1905 in Sydney where my father was an important man."

Penelope stops and looks expectantly at Steve, seeking his approval. He smiles at her and nods for her to continue.

"My father was in the army and we had to travel with him after my mother died. That was when Henry, my brother, was five, Victoria was seven and I was nine. My father said that travel broadens the mind."

Steve stops the tape and leans towards his nervous interviewee.

"Penelope . . . may I call you by your first name?" he asks.

Penelope nods. She looks down towards her shoes and pretends there is some dirt on them. She doesn't look up until Steve leans further forward. She moves away from him. He doesn't know that Penelope doesn't like anyone getting too close to her.

"Penelope, you don't have to take part in this research. I can interview Victoria or one of the other residents."

Penelope shoots a glance at her sister who has torn a paper tissue into pieces on her lap. "No. She won't get it right."

Victoria half-opens her mouth but shuts it quickly and lowers her eyes to the ground. She starts to tap her foot off the wooden floor and bites her lip.

Henry coughs to gain Steve's attention.

"It's all a bit public, isn't it? I think it would be better to interview my aunts on their own."

Penelope's eyes widen and Victoria starts to mutter something to her sister.

"No!" Penelope said. "Please not on my own. Please don't separate us."

No one understands Penelope's sudden fear. Henry shrugs and Steve pats Penelope on the shoulder.

"You sure you want me to ask you questions?"

"Quite sure," Penelope says.

"If there's anything you don't want to answer, that's fine, okay? And . . . I'm interested in *your* story, Penelope, not your father's so tell me about yourself, about your life, okay? Your sister will get her chance next."

Penelope nods and speaks clearly into the microphone. "Where was I?"

"You were born in Sydney in 1905."

"Oh yes, em . . . my father was . . ."

Steve looks at her with raised eyebrows.

"There is not much to tell about me. I was quiet. I tried to stay out of the way."

Steve flashes a smile to put her at ease. "Go on."

"When my sister was old enough to play with me I was happy. There were no other children around and we lived in a rather large house in Sydney. There were always lots of people coming and going, mostly people who worked with my father and there were lovely parties, at least when my mother was alive. My mother was so beautiful and all of the men loved her. It used to make my father angry. Women would wear such beautiful dresses and dance in our hall. Ladylike dresses," she says, glancing swiftly at Victoria. "My father wanted a boy and until our brother was born, he had our servant make sailor suits for us and other clothes that looked like they were for boys. Even though we are British our family have a long history in

Australia. Our great-grandfather Henry Miller the Third served with the British Army and in 1868 he was part of the last fleet to bring convicts to Australia for punishment."

I watch my mother look briefly at Martin who snorts and turns his back on the group. If Jimmy were here he would have done the same thing. The men have more in common than they think. Martin picks up a newspaper and starts to read, flicking it to drown out the sound of Penelope's voice.

"Our father was born in England and he served the Queen all over the world. He came here to serve her colony and he loved Australia but he said you would never want to be anything except British because we are the most important race in the world."

I look at Wilfred but his face is covered by a book. I wish I knew what he was thinking. I wonder if he still believes that the Germans are the supreme race or if he ever really thought this.

"And what race do you consider yourself to be?" Steve asks.

Penelope and Victoria look at each other and like identical twins they answer exactly the same rehearsed answer that their father must have taught them.

"We're British" they say in unison as they wring their hands anxiously.

My mother is looking on with interest. She has a half smile on her face and I know she doesn't think that Steve will get very far. She has tried many times herself and it has always ended in tears.

"So tell me about your lives when you were little girls."

Penelope lowers her shoulders and takes on a deflated posture.

"When my mother was ill, my father was in Africa fighting nasty savages who were trying to keep land for themselves. Someone from the camp sent word that Mother was dying. She was very hot and her face was quite red. There were sores on her hands and sometimes she didn't know who we were and we had to remind her. Daddy sent word back and a soldier came to the house to say that he was at war and had no intention of coming home but mother had died by then anyway and we had only servants to look after us. Daddy was wounded in Sandfontein almost a year later and he had to come home on a walking cane. Henry was very sad without Mother, and Victoria and I tried to make him happy but we could not. When Daddy settled in and we were allowed to see him, he asked what nonsense Henry was going on with. He said, 'Henry, you are six years old and you'd better sharpen up and be a man about this.' But Henry wasn't like Daddy. Henry was sweet and . . .'"

I could see the younger Henry stiffen and swallow. This was probably the first time he had heard details of what a terrible childhood his father had endured. Penelope straightens herself up again while Victoria never takes her eyes off the floor and swings her legs back and forth like a little girl with nothing to do.

"Henry never became happy. He cried at night and wet the bed and Daddy said he had had enough of this foolishness and sent Henry to a school very far from where we lived. When he was older he ran away from the school and Victoria and I tried to explain to him that it was better to stay quiet and be agreeable but Henry . . . Henry didn't like Daddy and even though he got caned, he still shouted at him and said he . . . that he hated him. We only saw our brother then on holidays but soon he was better behaved and Daddy said he could come home now that he was presentable. After that he took his lessons with us and we had to learn so much – Latin and French and ancient history. Then Daddy was sent to handle the troublesome Irish where there was another war with more savages trying to keep land. He took us with him and we had a house in the countryside. Daddy came to see us from time to time but we never got to see any savages. We met lots of nice people who looked after us and were very kind because we had no mother. Daddy's leg was better from his injury in Africa but he had a limp that you were never allowed to ask about. We loved Ireland and had a very nice nanny and servants who cooked nice food but it was very cold there with lots of rain."

Penelope quietens and looks as though she is trying to stifle a cough. She shrugs her shoulders as though she has nothing more to say.

Steve looks at her and is about to ask her to continue when she says,

"Then we went back to Australia."

"No, we didn't," Victoria, who hadn't appeared to be listening, says suddenly. "Remember, we went to India for more wars. You were seventeen and Daddy made you wear Mother's clothes."

Penelope jumps up and puts her fingers in her ears. "Shut up, Victoria! You're lying!"

Everyone looks at each other. Even though people had been used to Penelope bullying Victoria, they had never before heard the sisters shout at each other.

"It's true!" says Victoria. "The doctors advised Daddy to move to a warmer climate than Ireland. His old wound hurt and he needed a warm place to live so we moved again. In India, Daddy made Penelope wear our mother's corset and dresses that were too tight. It made Penelope very unhappy. He made her –"

"Stop it!" Penelope screams.

She jumps forward and slaps her younger sister hard on the face. Greta moves forward quickly and stands between the two. Henry's mouth drops open and he looks as confused as the rest of us. It is clear that he has no idea what is upsetting Penelope.

Steve looks at Henry for direction but the young man looks nailed to his chair. Then the realisation of what Victoria said seems to dawn on him. His face flushes and large veins jump on his forehead. Greta sits Penelope down and holds her hand. Penelope's lower lip trembles and she looks close to tears.

"I'm sorry, Victoria," she says but her sister ignores her.

"Victoria, let's forget about India. When did you come to Australia?" Steve asks.

Victoria, enjoying the attention that is now on her, rubs her face and leans forward to speak into the microphone.

"We came to Sydney in 1924. Henry was ill in India and Daddy decided that he would send us children back with an escort. He was worried that Henry would die because he was his only son and he didn't have plans to marry again."

Victoria looks nervously at Penelope but her sister is lost in thoughts that don't look happy.

"Penelope and Henry were glad to be going without him but I said I would miss him. But he got wounded again so we waited until he left the hospital and we all came back together. Daddy was sent to Broken Hill and we took a train here without him while he sorted out our things. I was seventeen by then. We moved into a large house near the base and there were no other people our age around. We had a new tutor but Daddy said Penelope was now too old for lessons and I was only allowed to attend language lessons and lessons appropriate for a lady. The tutor was not allowed to speak to Penelope alone and spent most of the time with our brother. Henry used to pretend to be stupid by failing exams. He was hoping that Daddy would not enlist him. Instead he wanted to paint and he was rather good at it. He didn't like fighting. Daddy gave him a good caning once because another boy punched him and he didn't fight back. We were terribly bored and we didn't see as many people here as we were used to. Daddy didn't let us mix with other young people but when we went to town Penelope and I would notice their modern clothes that we would have loved to have. Sometimes I begged Daddy for a new dress but he would have our servants make a new one and it was never what I wanted. Penelope did everything he asked but he left me alone."

Victoria looks at her sister and reaches out her hand to her.

Penelope grasps it and their eyes lock. The sisters nod as though they are communicating without words.

"When Henry was seventeen, Daddy enlisted him in the Royal Australian Air Force. He wanted Henry to join the army but felt that dropping bombs from a plane rather than face-to-face combat was more suited to our brother's sensitive nature. He was stationed at Point Cook but after three months on the base, Henry went AWOL. Daddy said they should have shot him but when they found him he was imprisoned on the base. A doctor examined him and said he wasn't . . . he wasn't . . . stable. The Air Force released Henry into Daddy's care until he was better. But when he got here, Daddy refused to see him and poor Henry stayed in his room all day. Sometimes Penelope and I would sit in there with him, especially when Daddy was on the base and not watching. He would talk to himself sometimes. Before summer, Daddy sent Henry to a hospital in Sydney where they were used to dealing with frightened servicemen but when he got better he left for England where he stayed for over two years. He didn't come back until I was twenty-two and a lot had happened in that time. He looked better and he was earning money as an artist. His paintings were beautiful and he had become less nervous. He wasn't afraid of Daddy any more and he wanted to help Penelope and me to – to get away. He brought perfume for us but of course we were not permitted to have it. He also brought music sheets for Penelope and when Daddy found them, there was an awful argument. Daddy threw Henry out for trying to poison our minds with evil music."

Victoria goes quiet and looks downward to try to hide the tears that have formed in her eyes.

"It was nearly twenty years before we saw him again."

"What happened to him?" Steve asks but both sisters become tearful and seem oblivious to his question.

Henry sits forward.

"I think I know the rest," he says.

"My father returned to London where his career as an artist took off. He wrote often to Penelope and Victoria but he knew they never got his letters. He kept the few letters that Victoria sent. My mother said he read them over and over and that he used to cry. He worried about them and wanted to take them away. He – he never told me how bad things really were for him. Today is the first time I've heard about his young life in such detail. Granddad had such tight control over his daughters and my father knew that his sisters were far removed from normal life and the excitement of growing up in the twenties. He said that they should have been enjoying life instead of being cooped up in that old house. They never went anywhere without an escort, usually a servant who would not disobey my grandfather's orders. All they had was each other.

"My mother said that Dad was scared of getting married, that he didn't think he had anything to offer family life so even though they met in 1940, they didn't marry until after the war. Despite my father's long hatred and fear of war and his desertion at Point Cook, he could not avoid conscription into the British forces. He was wounded at Normandy and when he returned home, my mother said he was a different man. I don't think he ever got over what he experienced there. He saw no glory in war and often painted war scenes to try to tell the world just how bad it was. I was born a year after my parents' marriage and they left Britain for Australia. Granddad died that same year so I never met him.

"When we got here, my mother said that things weren't good for Penelope and Victoria but I'll let them decide if they want to talk about that part of their life. The war had taken its toll on my father and while his paintings still fetched good prices, he was drinking money faster than he earned it. We were close when I was younger but in the few years before he died, we didn't get along at all. He stopped listening to me and became domineering. He wanted me to promise that I would never join the forces but from a young age I was fascinated by the army and I wanted to join as soon as I was old enough. It drove a wedge between us. It's ironic, isn't it? His father forced him to join and a generation later I joined up even though he begged me not to. Anyway, he was reunited with Penelope and Victoria but we lived in Sydney and didn't see that much of them because of the distance . . . and there were some other problems but I'll let them decide if they want to talk about that. Now that my mother is dead, I've decided to base myself in this town. They are the only family I have. I'm the last of the line."

"Your aunts never married?" Steve asks.

Henry sighs. "Well now, that's another story."

Steve looks at his watch. It is way past one o'clock and Li has been waiting to serve the residents their lunch.

Kora leaves the room unexpectedly. "Phone! I'll get it," she says.

I don't follow her as I am waiting to hear the rest of the sisters' story but, when my mother suddenly jumps up and runs from the room, I follow and Greta is fast behind me. Kora is standing in the hallway crying. My mother takes her by the shoulders.

"What's happened?"

We all think that Jimmy is dead and that Kora is taking it harder than we thought she would but her lips tremble and she crumples into my mother's arms.

"It's Jeff. He's been hurt real bad on the farm. They've taken him to hospital."

Kora starts to cry again. My mother runs upstairs and knocks on Aishling's door.

"Aishling, can you cover me for a couple of hours?"

Aishling opens the door. She hasn't gone to bed yet and is standing fully dressed in the doorway.

"What's wrong?"

"Jeff's hurt. An accident on the farm. I have to drive Kora to the hospital."

Aishling comes downstairs just as my mother disappears out the front door. I watch her look briefly at the pile of mail and for the first time she walks past it and goes directly to the kitchen. She makes herself a coffee and brings it to the Penance Room where she sits nursing the steaming cup with both hands. I see an exchange between her and Steve and wonder what it means. It is not like his previous looks. Not romantic.

As the residents slowly file into the dining room for their lunch, Steve stands and shakes hands with Henry.

"Maybe we better continue this tomorrow. Would you be free?" he asks.

Henry nods. "Seems like a lot happened to them that even my dad didn't know about."

Steve nods. "Yeah. Especially to Penelope."

Henry grimaces. He doesn't want to verbalise what we are all thinking, that his grandfather was abusing Penelope.

He says his goodbyes and quietly lets himself out, leaving only Aishling and Steve in the Penance Room. I stand in the hallway and watch him smile at her.

"You must be tired," he says.

She smiles a broad smile, revealing a neat row of white teeth that make the lines under her eyes look darker.

"You never told me why you left the Church," she says, running her finger around the edge of her coffee cup.

Steve turns to face her and leans his head to one side. "I woke up one morning and realised I didn't believe any more."

"In God?" Aishling asks with raised eyebrows.

"No. I believe in God but I saw more than I understood. I knew that I was beginning to believe in things I shouldn't."

"Like what?"

Steve looks suddenly serious and I know he is wondering if he should continue.

"Come on," Aishling says. "I told you all about myself. I told you things hardly anyone else knows about me."

Steve nods his head and looks directly at her. "There were many things that I began to question. I believe that there is no hell, that purgatory is life and if we don't make amends for our sins, we become trapped here."

Aishling lets out a loud laugh. "Are you telling me that you believe in ghosts? Now you're trying to wind me up!"

Steve laughs and shrugs his shoulders as he walks out the door. "There are many things we don't understand. Just because you can't see something doesn't mean it doesn't exist."

Aishling shrugs and smiles a half smile at him. "You need to speak with Martin so. His room is so crowded at night there's hardly room for me."

Steve moves out into the hallway and as he passes me he winks and I smile.

"I might just do that."

Chapter 20

At twelve thirty that night, my mother and Kora arrive back and collapse into chairs in the Penance Room. Aishling is waiting up. She has worked all day with Greta and Tina has come in to cover the night shift.

"How is Jeff?" she enquires.

"He's out of surgery. We waited until we knew he was stable before we left," my mother replies.

Kora looks exhausted and doesn't speak.

"What happened?"

My mother looks at Kora and when she doesn't offer information, she decides to fill Aishling in on the story.

"Ben D'Arcy said Jeff felt dizzy. He was helping him brand cattle in the pen. Thank God there was a neighbour there to raise the alarm. I can't bear to think what would have happened otherwise. He was sitting on the side of the pen when he felt light-headed and fell in. I'm not surprised. He's been overdoing it lately, working all day and sitting with his father every evening. He got a real going over. Horn went right through his leg and his arm's broken. They put two pins in it. His cheekbone is broken too and they had to stitch an open gash on his forehead. He looks a state but they think he'll be fine." She squeezes Kora's arm.

Aishling looks sympathetically at Kora. "Does Jimmy know?"

My mother nods. "We went and sat with him. Kora told him and it'd break your heart. He started crying and Kora – Kora hugged him." My mother smiles at her sister through her tears. "Dad would have been proud of you, Kora."

Kora's mouth gave a small smile but her eyes didn't change their sad expression. She got up to leave.

"Is Andy asleep?" my mother asks.

Aishling nods.

"Kora, stay the night, please. I don't want you on your own."

"You can share my room," Aishling offers.

Kora relents and, after ensuring that Tina will call her if the hospital phones, she drags her tired body up the stairs.

"What a day! Between the sisters' story and poor Jeff, I'm worn out," my mother says.

One by one the group go to bed. I decide not to sit with Tina and go to my room where I try unsuccessfully to sleep. An hour later I go to Martin's room and I am disappointed to find him sound asleep with a smile on his face. I return to my room and look out the window. I can see the streetlights shining on the far end of the train line. There is no one about except our cat, staring up at me and hissing. I pull my blind down and decide that I will cope on my own when my imaginary train passes. I try to focus on Penelope and Victoria and all the awful things that happened to them. I try to imagine the life they would have had if their mother hadn't died or if their father had been a nice man but I cannot. Some things are just too hard to imagine, like the life I could have had if my foot hadn't got stuck on that train line, or if I had never been deaf. Sometimes when I sleep I dream of walking with my parents and listening to their words but a feeling chokes me and I wake up waving my arms about as though I am drowning. I know what this is. It is the same thing that wakes Martin and makes Wilfred sit alone in his room listening to sad music. It is guilt. As I drift off to sleep, all I can hope for is that the sisters and everybody else here, including me, finally find peace.

In the morning, my mother and Greta have agreed that Penelope should be taken out of the room while Victoria is telling her story. Mother wants Victoria to feel that she can say whatever she wants to and we know that she will not speak freely if Penelope is in the room. Greta takes a reluctant Penelope to town to look around the shops. As she is leaving she looks into the Penance Room at her sister and gives her a look that turns my blood cold.

When she is gone, we all sit down to listen to the quietly spoken Victoria tell her story. Henry is here, sitting next to Victoria, and he has brought his fiancée with him, a tall Australian girl with a booming voice that bounces off the floorboards and travels up through my feet. She is deeply tanned with large brown eyes and is smiling confidently at everyone. She is the opposite of the ladies and the meaning of this is not lost on my mother and Kora who I see smiling at each other through the corners of their mouths.

"So, Victoria, we know that you returned to Australia and that your father was based in Broken Hill. What was life like then?"

Victoria looks like she is on the stand in a courtroom. She doesn't look directly at Steve but looks across the room at the stained-glass window and begins to speak.

"Daddy was becoming stricter. We saw more of him as he rarely got sent away. There were no wars to fight and he was getting older. Daddy loved a good war. He said it kept him alive but I remember thinking this was a strange thing to say as people

LIMERICK
COUNTY LIBRARY

die in wars but I didn't say anything. It wasn't polite to answer Daddy except to say 'Yes, sir'."

"You called your father 'sir'?" Steve asks. We could see the surprise on his face.

Victoria nods, unsure why Steve thinks this unusual.

"Everybody called Daddy 'sir'," she replies flatly.

Steve shakes his head and his expression is serious. He seems disturbed by what the sisters went through. Victoria doesn't seem to notice and continues.

"Penelope and I were bored at the house. Henry was gone and we had nothing to do all day except sit and read. We were not allowed to read any rubbish and Daddy usually chose our books."

"So no romance novels, the ones I see you reading here?" Steve says..

"No," Victoria answers, slightly embarrassed.

"Did you get a chance to experience any real romance?" Steve asks. He does not know the can of worms he just opened.

Tears spring to Victoria's eyes and she looks downward. I move forward, anxious to see her lips move. I don't want to miss one word she says.

"James was an officer at my father's base and he would often call to our house with messages for father. He was nice to me and once when father was in hospital with his bad leg, he brought me flowers. Penelope was afraid for me. She became really angry and . . ."

Victoria stops speaking.

"Please go on, Victoria," says Steve.

"I began to slip out of the house. We had large grounds. Penelope used to play piano every evening for Daddy so I'd meet James at the boundary wall of our property. No one ever went that far so we were safe. We were in love and James wanted to marry me. He was going to ask my father for permission."

Victoria looks up. "Maybe we should talk about Penelope. Maybe we should talk about India?"

"Penelope should tell her own story, Victoria."

"But it's important. It'll explain why she – it's important."

Steve relents. He knows as much as we do how intertwined the sisters' lives are, how much of their life they lived as one.

"When we arrived in India, Penelope turned seventeen. Daddy said she looked just like Mother and he'd take her out of our bedroom some nights and she would not come back for a long time. She would tell me to lock the door when she'd leave so . . . to make me safe. She'd cry when she'd come back and we'd sleep in the same bed. I'd try to comfort her. I asked her what was wrong but for a long time I didn't understand what was happening. He tried to put us in separate rooms and Penelope said she'd tell the servants so he didn't separate us. She said we could only stay safe if we were together. Penelope tried to make herself look ugly and she was happy to wear old-fashioned dresses and she'd only wear a little powder. She said it was important not to draw attention to yourself. She didn't want me to wear anything pretty as she was afraid Daddy would start to take me out of the room at night also."

I see my mother nod to herself, finally understanding Penelope's constant need to control her sister's clothes.

"Penelope changed. She was nervous and she started to make me nervous. I was always afraid at night of the door handle turning. I thought Daddy was beating her but there were no marks and there were always marks on poor Henry's back. Even when we returned to Australia it didn't stop but it started in India which is why Penelope never talks about our life there. That's why I kept James a secret from her. She didn't understand why I wanted to be with him and she was afraid of what Daddy would do when he found out. James was so good to me. So very kind. He even posted my letters to Henry although I never received a reply."

Henry squeezes his aunt's hand. He hadn't expected her to be so lucid. Even though Victoria is the younger of the two,

Penelope always seems stronger and more coherent. I know that my mother and the other staff present are wondering if they have misjudged Victoria, if all the time her confusion was really fear of upsetting Penelope.

"He treasured those letters," Henry says even though there is a look on his face, a look that tells me that his father was so lost in alcoholism that he couldn't help himself, never mind his tortured sisters.

"Did James ask for your hand?" asks Steve.

"He tried but . . ."

"So how come you didn't marry?"

"One day James arrived at the house. Daddy was in his study and he asked to speak with him. There was already someone speaking with Daddy so James stood in the hallway and paced up and down. He looked so nervous, standing there in full uniform. He looked . . . it is my most precious memory of him."

Victoria moves her hand towards a small cameo brooch neatly pinned to her collar. Tears form in her bright blue eyes and her lips tremble.

"He gave me this. In the garden one evening. I've never taken it off."

Kora and my mother look at each other. My mother moves her hand towards her sister and I watch as they hold hands for a moment. Steve moves his head slightly to bring Victoria back from her memories. She looks confused for a moment as though she is struggling with the next sentence, trying to make sense of a moment that changed her life forever.

"Penelope hid on the stairwell and listened to us speaking. I asked her to be polite and to come down. James told me that he was going to defend India from Afghanistan. He wanted to live in India permanently and that it was his hope that we could marry soon so I could join him there when the war was over. I heard Penelope running down the stairs and, for a split second, I felt as afraid of her as she was of Daddy, and in that moment I

184

wrongly believed that it was Penelope and not Daddy who would never let me leave that house. I don't know whether it was the mention of India that made her angry but she charged down the hall and grabbed at James. She begged him not to ask Daddy for my hand, that it would only bring trouble on me. She even suggested we run away together. James managed to prise her hands from him and stood back. He didn't know what to do. Penelope looked insane and he was afraid of her. Daddy opened the study door at that exact moment and shouted at us to go away. I think poor James almost died of fright. Daddy gave Penelope and me a look and we crept to our room. We never heard James leave and all I could think about was Daddy's answer to his request to marry me. My heart pounded wondering if I was going to get out of the madness of that house. Penelope kept saying that it was too late, over and over, and I had no idea what she was talking about. She understood Daddy better than I ever did.

"That night as we got ready for bed, Penelope went to the kitchen and brought up a knife. She put it on her beside locker and said that whatever happened, I was not to leave the bedroom if Daddy asked. I was so afraid that I could not sleep. We were both awake when Daddy turned the handle. Penelope stood immediately in the dark room and moved toward the door. He pulled her outside and even in the darkness I could see his eyes glinting at me. He knew I was awake and came towards me. I could hear Penelope crying but I could not see her. He leant towards me and said, "You are a filthy who–" Victoria can not finish the sentence but she doesn't have to. We can imagine how the sentence finished.

"I cowered in the bed and pulled my knees towards my chest. He said, 'You made a fool of me, Victoria. I thought you were the good one but you were showing yourself to him, weren't you?'

"I didn't answer at first but I began to cry and Daddy didn't like tears.

"'Weren't you?' he screamed.

"I said, 'No, Daddy. I didn't do anything. James is a gentleman.'

"He leant towards me and I could not stop crying even though I knew it made him angrier.

"'Well, you'll never see him ever again, ever. I've made sure of that.'

"Then I let out a huge roar. I think I screamed 'No!' and Daddy hit me so hard that I am not sure what happened next. There were noises and something fell – I think it must have been the photographs on Penelope's beside table. I heard Penelope scream. I jumped up and could see shapes moving, Penelope pulling at him from behind, trying to move him away from me. So brave, my sister. Much braver than me."

"What happened?" Steve asks, unable to bear the suspense.

"He turned and lifted her right off her feet by her throat. Even though she was gasping and fighting to breathe, I heard her say 'I'll tell.' I thought he was going to kill her."

Victoria's lips start to tremble and one heavy tear falls down her face, leaving a long furrow in her make-up. Her hands move up towards her throat as if she is reliving her sister's pain.

"I started to scream, hoping one of the servants would come but no one came to help us. The servants' quarters were in the basement at the other end of the house so Daddy knew no one would hear us. Then suddenly he let Penelope drop to the floor. She lay completely still and I was sure she was dead. I was terrified. I thought that the one person who could protect me was lying dead at my feet in the darkness. He came toward me and suddenly I saw no reason to go on. I saw the knife glinting in the floor. It had fallen when Daddy pushed into the table. I lifted it and – I – had no choice. I raised it to him and my hands shook – he – he knew I couldn't do it and he laughed, right there, in my face with my sister at his feet. I knew I was beaten. I could not win.

"There was no way out. I moved the knife and slashed the blade across my left wrist. I heard him shout and he grabbed the knife before I could cut my other wrist. I fainted and – and when I woke up my wrist was bandaged and the doctor was standing over me. The sun was rising and my head hurt from something he had given me. Penelope was sitting in a chair looking at me and there were bruise marks on her neck. She was crying. Daddy was in the room, standing over me. When I opened my eyes he gave me one of his warning looks. He said, 'Thank God you're okay. I've told Doctor Scott all about Penelope and you fighting. He has suggested I get you both the right help, away from here, that you need hospitalisation to sort out your nerves.'

"I opened my mouth to speak but he ran his hand over my face and pressed down hard, hurting me. Doctor Scott didn't realise what was going on. When Daddy left, Penelope looked at me. I had never seen her look so frightened before. She stood and grabbed Doctor Scott's hand. She told him all about Daddy and what he was doing to her but he didn't believe us. He said that he'd had no idea how ill we were. He said Daddy had told him all about our imaginings and that the poor man had kept it to himself for fear of losing us but now that we had attacked each other with such violence, Daddy had no choice but to send us to a psychiatric hospital where we would get the help we needed. We were locked in that room for the rest of that day with servants bringing us food and emptying our nightjar.

"The following morning we were taken a long way to a hospital in Sydney even though there was nothing wrong with us. We asked if we could go to London, to our brother who would take care of us. We didn't realise that no one believed us, that they thought we were insane. Each week a doctor would ask us questions about the delusions we had but we never changed our story. When we were there quite a few years they tried a new treatment on us. They put electricity on our heads and jolted us and oh my, it was frightful. Then they would ask us those same questions but we said no, we didn't hurt each other, Daddy hurt us. But you see Daddy was an important man and no one would believe us. After a while they said we were incurable and we just walked around a large locked ward all day with other people. They gave us medication to keep us calm and other tablets to cure our violent thoughts even though we didn't have any. At night we were locked in a long room with lots of other women and Penelope and I had beds beside each other. We used to hold hands in the dark. Some of the women screamed when the lights went out and even though we were afraid, we didn't have to worry any more about Daddy turning the door handle at night.

"The whole time we were there, Daddy never came to see us. We didn't want him to. Sometimes, our nanny Betty came to see us in Sydney. She had been our nanny when we were younger but Daddy kept her on as our companion and if we went to town, she had to go with us and make sure we didn't speak to anyone. Daddy had thrown her out when he realised that I had been meeting James in the garden. I remember her sitting facing us in the visitors' room and staring at us. She was tearful. I knew she felt guilty that no one had punished Daddy for what he did to Penelope and that we were locked away for no good reason, but even if she had told the police what she knew, no one would believe her word against my father. We asked her to write to Henry, to tell him where we were but she was too afraid.

"We were there for almost nineteen years and by then we were unwell. Penelope had a breakdown even though we were in a place which should help you with these matters. She began to imagine that Daddy was coming for us and she even woke at night and cried about it. Even though the medicine made her shake, they gave her more tablets. We would sit together in the room and I would wipe the drool that came from her mouth and it was all my fault. If I hadn't met James, Daddy would never have turned on us. Penelope knew what he would do. Penelope knew that what he really wanted was to control us and when he realised that someone wanted to take me away, he was enraged.

"Sometimes I would shake Penelope and beg her to wake up and take charge again. I was never sure what to do without her. I was afraid. New people would come into our ward and some of them were dangerous. I pushed our beds together and we slept beside one another. We kept hoping that somehow Henry would find out where we were but he never did. Then one day the doctor received a letter from my father saying that he had had a stroke and that he was very ill. He said he wanted to give us another chance and that he would take responsibility for our welfare. The doctor told us and we pleaded with him not to send us. We begged him to write to our brother but he refused. He wrote to our father and told him that we were too unstable to be released into society but Daddy wrote back and said he was our guardian and that he was taking us anyway."

I look around the room and notice that everyone is sitting forward, anxious to hear what happened and hoping that the women were not forced to return home.

"No one would listen to us. I told them that if they sent us back there that he would kill us but we were unmarried and Daddy had complete control over us. When we arrived back at the house, there were only two servants, a cook and a maid. We had never seen them before. Daddy had got rid of the all the servants who knew us and the new ones were instructed not to speak to us. A doctor came to see us regularly. He'd say 'How are your thoughts today? Anything unusual?' and Penelope and I would say 'No doctor, nothing unusual.' For almost a year Daddy didn't – didn't come to our room at night. His speech was difficult to understand and his left arm was paralysed. He looked very old to us. All day he sat in his room and wrote notes. One night he slipped a note under our door telling us he was sorry for what he did and that he wanted us to live in the house after he was gone. But as soon as we read it we heard his cane moving closer and closer to our door. He came in and tore the note from Penelope's hand and started calling us names, terrible words. He said it was his job to cleanse us. He said that he would always be watching us. Even after death, he would be in this house watching the vile women we had turned into.

"At night he would come to our bedroom door and we would hear him crying outside. He would touch the handle and turn it slightly. Sometimes we knew he was beating himself with his walking stick. We became afraid. We told the doctor. We said that we thought Daddy was mad but he told the servants to increase our night-time medication. Sometimes Daddy would come to our room during the day and look through Penelope's underwear drawer but he never touched mine. We knew then that soon he would start to come into our room again and that no one would believe us. He had complete control over us. We realised that there was no way out for us. We started saving up our medication and hiding it under my underwear. We made a pact that we would die together and we would go to a place where he could no longer hurt us.

"We had saved almost two weeks' medication when he became ill. He asked the servant to bring us to see him and we stood at the foot of his bed, afraid even though he could hardly breathe. The doctor listened to his heart and shook his head. He told Daddy to make sure he had his affairs in order and, you know, sick as he was, he smiled so strangely at us that we were more afraid of him than when he was able-bodied. He started to laugh and began to cough up green phlegm than ran down his nightshirt. The doctor left and Daddy waved for us to stay. I was glad he was dying. We were finally going to be free. Henry could come home and we would be a family again. He waved the maid away so it was just Penelope and I standing there, trembling but knowing that soon we would be released from the terror he had made us endure our whole lives. He tried to speak again and spit flew out onto the bedclothes. We squirmed and he noticed. He tried to sit up and we cowered. I can still see him. I can still see the dim light in the room. His face was crumpled into a red ball of anger. He seemed to know what I was thinking, what we were both thinking. His speech was slurred but we understood every word he said. 'My will!' he laughed. 'Henry can never come back here. If one of you marries, my estate will transfer to my second cousins and you will be penniless. You will not be able to sell this house and you will only receive a small weekly allowance to live on. You see, you will never be free of me. I will be here watching over you both for the rest of your days.'

"We were so angry. We had waited so long. All we wanted was for Henry to return and we would finally be happy."

"What did you do?" Steve asks.

No one notices the hot rush of air that has blown into the room except me. They are all engrossed in Victoria's story and don't notice Penelope and Greta return from their shopping trip. I can see Penelope standing in the doorway with an open mouth and teary eyes. She is shaking her head at her sister. Her face is saying: "No, don't, don't say it."

Victoria's face is expressionless, like she is reading the lines from a book.

"So we killed him."

Steve's mouth drops open and he stares wide-eyed at Victoria. A few moments pass before he can speak. He didn't see this coming and neither did I.

"You killed him? How?"

I can tell he does not believe her.

"I was so angry. I could see myself moving but it was like it wasn't really me, as if I had snapped in half and a part of me was still standing at the foot of his bed, trembling. I went to my room and took our angry tablets from the bureau and returned to his room. One by one I started to shove them down his throat. He struggled and Penelope held his mouth open for me until we made him swallow every single angry tablet we had left. He started to choke and his face turned red and then purple. When we were finished we stood over him and looked into his open eyes, hoping he could still see us."

An air of tension settles in the room. No one speaks, not even Steve who is wearing a strange expression that I cannot read.

"Penelope, would you like to tell us the rest?" Steve asks, without turning around.

Penelope walks slowly into the room and takes the seat on the far side of her sister. She suddenly looks smaller as though the secret she had made Victoria keep for all these years has taken the air from her. Her mouth is trembling and tears are falling down her powdered face.

"It was all because of me, you see. It started with me and ended with Victoria and I doing – what we – did. When we were in India, William, a second cousin of my mother's, took an interest in me. I saw him at garden parties from time to time. I was seventeen and he was an officer and although he was quite a few years older than me, he was very handsome and well educated. One day he asked if he might have permission to call on me. I asked him not to speak to Daddy just yet. I wanted to try to make peace first before William approached him formally. Daddy didn't care for Mother's family even though they were quite well off. I waited until the following evening. I played all of his favourite pieces on the piano but when I raised the subject he went insane. We moved abruptly and I was no longer allowed out unescorted. I never saw William again and I never knew what happened to him. That's when Daddy started to . . ."

Steve leans forward to touch Penelope's arm. He knows she cannot finish the sentence but she pulls back, afraid, lost in that terrible time of her life.

"I didn't tell Victoria about William or about Daddy. She was too young to understand at the time and I wanted to protect her but now I know I should have told her. I should have warned her not to fall in love, that he would never allow it. But I didn't and so we found ourselves all those years later standing over his body, neither of us feeling any remorse for what we had done. He ruined all that was good about us. When we were sure he was dead, we called the cook in and told her to fetch the doctor back. When he arrived, he told us he was sorry for our loss. Daddy had told him that when he died, he didn't want us to be returned to the hospital. The doctor thought this was a sign of his devotion to us but we knew what it meant. He wanted us where his evil spirit could watch and control us."

My mother looks very concerned. I know she is thinking that the women are mentally ill, even if they don't realise it themselves.

Steve doesn't react.

"After the funeral, we wrote to Henry and when the war was over he came to Australia with his wife. Needless to say, we ignored Daddy's insistence that Henry not return to the house. But nothing was going to be as we had dreamt. Henry was drinking heavily and when he did spend time with us, he argued with us for money that we didn't have. Sometimes . . . we were very afraid of him. He didn't like being at the house and rarely stayed for long. It frightened him the same as it did us. It was big and dark and we could feel Daddy in every corner. Sometimes we would hear our door handle turning in the middle of the night. We changed rooms but still it was there. We knew we were not imagining it. Two people cannot imagine the same thing, can they?

"The servants eventually left and Penelope and I tried to look after the house, something we had no skills for. We were always afraid. Daddy was right. We would never be free. Despite his death, nothing really changed. He was still there, watching us, controlling us. We didn't dress as we – or at least Victoria didn't dress as she had always wanted. I didn't play the music that I loved. In fact I stopped playing piano altogether. It brought too many bad memories back. We didn't go anywhere that he would have disapproved of. We had never lived on our own before. Henry called less and less and eventually he moved to Sydney with his wife and little Henry. When Henry died, a part of us died with him. Our hope died. That's what it was.

The house fell into disrepair. We lived alone at that house for many years because we had nowhere else to go. We didn't know how to fend for ourselves. The doctor, worried about our health, sent a social worker to check on us. She was a nice lady and the second time she called she had a doctor with her, a psychiatrist. He was shocked at how unwell we were. We – really did imagine all sorts of things or so they told us. Mostly I think they were real things – caused by the ghost of our father. The psychiatrist met with a team of people to decide what was best for us. Some of those doctors had been at the hospital. They decided that we should come here to live and things have been better for us but still, it is not the life we had been waiting for and hoping for. It seems that we will never have that life."

"What happened to James?" Mina, who had been sitting quietly under the window suddenly asks, taking the words out of all of our mouths. I know she is hoping that he and Victoria were reunited, a happier ending than her own.

Victoria puts her hand to her neck and runs her thin fingers over the brooch.

"He died there . . . in India," Victoria says sadly. "I never saw him again and I never knew . . . I'll never know what might have been. I don't know if he ever found out what happened to us."

Steve touches her wrinkled hand and smiles sadly at her. He stops the recorder and I think I am the only one who sees him erasing the tape. No one speaks.

"Ladies, do you still think that your father is watching you? Even here, in this nursing home?" he asks.

Victoria looks to her sister but the years spent in the psychiatric hospital have taught the women not to answer such questions. Both women look into their laps. Their refusal to answer tells me that the sisters believe their father's ghost is watching them but I know they are wrong because I have never seen him and I see everything. Like Martin, the ladies' conscience and not their dead father is haunting them. My mother beckons for Steve to come over to her. As he approaches, Greta and Tina also join them. Henry follows and within seconds all five people are standing outside the Penance Room looking in at the sisters who are now sitting staring into each other's faces, perhaps wondering where they will go from here.

My mother speaks first.

"Oh, I didn't realise the extent of their delusions."

Nobody speaks and for a few seconds I wonder if no one is going to take my mother's point of view, that there was no point in reporting the sister's confession to the police, that they have suffered enough.

Greta is the first to speak. "Oh yeah, imagine the poor souls believing all this time that they killed him. Blimey!"

Tina chews on her lip. "What did your grandfather die of, Henry?" she asks with a look of fear in her eyes.

Henry moves his eyes around the group and wets his lips. "He died of pneumonia. I'm – I'm sure – yes – that's what it says on his death certificate," he says with a worried expression. "Perhaps they're imagining that they poisoned him. I don't think they could do such a thing. I really don't."

No one knows what to say. I can see their eyes dart from one to the other.

"Well, are they delusional?" Kora asks. "Do they want to think they finally took revenge but he actually did die of pneumonia?"

"We'll never know," Greta says. "And does it really matter now anyway? Look at them! If they did do it, they've paid the price."

"So we're agreed then?" my mother asks. "That due to the women's mental illness, they are imagining that they took revenge on the man that tormented them their entire lives?"

One by one people start nodding, even Steve who I know is

wondering about the women's salvation. I look at my mother and I am proud of her.

When Steve returns to the room he walks over to the sisters and sits beside them. He is considering the women's penance.

"Could you do something for me?" he asks with those brilliant eyes.

They nod simultaneously.

"You said you learnt to speak French. Do you still remember it?"

Penelope and Victoria look at each other.

"We think so," they say in unison.

"Every day, I want you to speak with Iren. Talk to her, ask her how she is. Will do you that?"

"We will," Victoria replies through watery eyes.

Steve smiles and grips both their hands tightly. Then he gets up and walks slowly out the door.

Out of the corner of his eye he spots Wilfred looking at him. He has been watching the scene with the sisters and I cannot read the expression on his face. Steve looks directly at him and the two stare at each other. I understand Wilfred's look now. He is afraid. He has seen Steve get the sisters to give details of a crime they committed a long time ago, something that they could have taken with them to the grave. He looks away and stares out of the window at the setting sun, then returns to his seat and faces away from the group. It is his time and he knows it is long overdue.

I slip out of the house and make my way to Maria's, anxious to tell her about the sisters' story but when I get there I can see that she has been crying. I sit down beside her on her street corner and blow out some air. I know her well by now and she doesn't want me to ask her what's wrong. Nor will she want to hear my stories of happy endings. She is still waiting for hers. Together we sit and watch a real estate agent talk to her grandfather outside the rundown shop. He is waving his hands around, pointing at the bright yellow and red sign and smiling in an exaggerated way.

She sighs and I slip my hand inside hers. She squeezes it and together we sit in silence watching a scene that will change her life once again.

Chapter 21

When Kora arrives back from visiting Jeff at the hospital, my mother is waiting to fill her in on the news. My father is home from working late at the mine. They are sitting quietly on the porch and Father is drinking a beer and listening to the sound of the cicadas, something he says he loves to do. I move to the side of the house and watch them speak from a safe distance. Kora gets herself lemonade and together they talk about Victoria and Penelope and what a dreadful life they have had. My father starts to joke with Kora about Jeff. Father says Scottish people love joking around but Kora doesn't and my mother knows that Father's comments will annoy her sister.

"Well, how is the nurse–patient romance coming along, Kora? I hope you're not giving that bloke bed baths?"

Kora frowns and ignores him. She directs her conversation to my mother.

"He's having another test tomorrow. His headache hasn't gone and they're worried about concussion."

"Did you see Jimmy Young?"

"Yeah, mate. Would you believe the old sod's looking better?

Said a few words today. He even thanked me for bringing stuff in to him. His daughter arrived when I was there. Remember Lorna?"

My mother nods. "Yes – she lives a good distance away now."

"Married some bloke out the way. She's got three small ones. Anyway, she thought I was there because he was one of our residents but he introduced me as . . ." tears spring to Kora's eyes and I can see her swallow, "as . . . Jeff's girlfriend . . ."

My mother reaches forward and touches her shoulder. "I'm so pleased, Kora. I knew he'd come around. He's been impressed with how good you have been to Jeff and to him since the accident."

My father knows how to spoil the moment but only because he doesn't enjoy sentimental talk and always tries to lighten the atmosphere. The only time I see my father sad is when he is drunk. It is the time he thinks most about me and about what might have been.

"Too right he's impressed. He'd be lucky to have you. Mind you, Kora, Jeff will have to ask me for your hand, seeing as I'm your only male relative."

Kora is in no mood for jokes and stands up. She checks with my mother that she doesn't need her tomorrow and walks down the pathway.

"Don't forget what I said, Kora! He'll need my permission!" my father laughs after her but she doesn't look back.

"Andy, can't you see how that'd annoy her?" my mother asks.

"What?" my father asks with a mock-innocent expression on his face.

My mother frowns. "She doesn't really see us as her family. Don't think she ever really will," she sighs, looking out onto the road.

I watch my father move my mother's hair back.

"You look tired. Aishling up?"

"Yeah. She's not sleeping much. I've noticed that she seems smitten with Steve. I hope she's not going to get hurt. She's even stopped looking through the mail each morning."

"Well, that's good, isn't it? Time she gave up on ever hearing from her family again. I can't understand it. After all these years, you'd think they'd forgive her."

My mother sighs. "That's families for you. I suppose some things are too big to be forgiven."

My father looks surprised and turns to look at her. "Is that the reverend's daughter talking? If it is, I don't recognise her."

Mother smiles a strange smile. "Oh, it's just hearing all these awful things that happened to people here. It's really opened my eyes. Mina losing her baby and her husband in Indonesia and then coming here for a new life but ending up alone and frightened. You should have seen her face when Li's son came into the kitchen. She almost fell over. She was convinced that he was a Japanese boy. Jimmy holding onto a grudge against Aboriginals when all along he should have been ashamed of his father's behaviour. Father Hayes living his brother's life and leaving behind his fiancée because his mother wanted a priest in the family – and of course poor Iren, as alone as Mina with only her memories of Aron and her son to comfort her. And we haven't even got to Martin or Wilfred yet. God knows what happened to them!"

"Or what they did to others. There is another way to look at it, Emma. I mean, if Mina's country hadn't colonised Indonesia, she wouldn't have been there when the Japanese invaded."

My mother frowns and turns towards my father. "What? Are you saying it was Mina's fault?"

Dad shakes his head. "No! . . . I'm just saying that sometimes tragedy can befall us as a consequence of our own choices."

My mother thinks about what he says. I can see her tongue moving in her mouth.

"But Mina didn't do anything wrong!" Mother retorts.

My father puts his hands to his head. He hadn't intended to

argue with my mother and I know he feels she is taking him up the wrong way.

"Emma . . . I didn't mean, of course Mina didn't . . ."

"What about Wilfred?" she interrupts.

My father can see where Mother is going with this and I can see him becoming tense.

"The same goes for Wilfred. If you do wrong, own up to it. There's a lot of forgiveness in the world but people need to be honest about what they've done and, more importantly, they need to be sorry."

My mother stiffens and I can see a row brewing. She looks into the garden and I duck further around the side of the house. I know it will be about me. It is always about me.

"Oh, and you'd know where you went wrong? What about Christopher? If you had let him go to the school, he wouldn't have been on the train line that day!"

My father's mouth drops open. Even though my mother has hinted at this before, this is the first time she has said exactly what she thinks.

"Emma," he says as he tries to reach for her but she stands quickly and walks into the house, banging the screen door behind her.

He follows her so I move back onto the porch and look in. I can see her crying in his arms through the window of her office.

I watch them as my father kisses her on the forehead and they settle once again into the happy couple that I know they are.

"You look tired, love. You need more rest," he says. I know he is avoiding the conversation they need to have about me and that, like the dead heat, it will continue to stifle the air until the rain comes.

I am disappointed as I want to hear what my father has to say about my accident and whether or not he feels sorry that he didn't send me away where I would be safe from trains that I could not hear.

My mother looks out into the night. "I know but we can't afford more staff, Andy. We'll look at the books next month. See what we can do."

Father nods. I know Father is working his magic on my mother and changing the subject but he is not insincere. He just finds it too difficult to talk about me.

"I know it's hard seeing the residents recalling the awful things that happened to them but don't you think it has done them some good? If you hadn't heard Mina's story, you'd never have thought to ask her to help in the kitchen – and look how she's blossomed."

Mother smiles but has that distant expression on her face that tells me she knows father is trying to appease her but she is tired and will go along with it for now.

"Yeah but she's still stealing food. But – I know what you mean – it is getting better – she's happier. She feels like she is more in control of her life when she can see the food. Oh, war! Look what it does to people!"

Father doesn't answer and together they look out into the night, both lost in thought . . . both thinking about me.

The following morning, Greta arrives early for her shift and goes to the sisters' bedroom first. She has dark lines under her eyes and I know she has been thinking of the sisters all night. They are already up and their door is slightly ajar. When she knocks, both sisters jump with fright and, for the first time, Greta understands why. She smiles sadly at the two, who are once again wearing matching dresses.

"Sorry, ladies. Just me. Tell you what? What if I was to have a secret knock so that you'd know it was me?"

Both sisters nod nervously.

"What if I did three quick knocks or a nice musical knock?"

Greta demonstrates on the door and the ladies smile like children.

"Yes!" they say happily and they choose their preferred knock.

I feel sorry for Penelope and Victoria. I know that I should not have been in the room when some of the things that happened to them were discussed but I am thirteen now and I understand more than people realise.

"Good," Greta says.

I can see her looking at the ladies' identical dresses but she chooses her battles and decides to tackle this another day.

"Penelope, can you do me a favour? It's Wilfred's birthday next week and you know how he loves the piano?"

Penelope shakes her head. She doesn't know anything about Wilfred because he doesn't speak to anyone.

"He plays the violin," was all she could think of to say.

"I was wondering if you'd play for him. We'd all love to hear you play, wouldn't we?"

Victoria starts to bite her lip and lowers her head quickly. She knows how Penelope will react.

Penelope jumps up from the bed and begins to shake. "I can't. I can't do it."

Greta moves forward and places her hands firmly on Penelope's shoulders, trying to steady her. "It's all right. Don't worry, Penelope. No one will force you to do anything you don't want, okay?"

Penelope doesn't seem to hear Greta and starts talking to herself. She is moving from foot to foot and she seems to be saying the same few words over and over again. "I'm not a dirty girl. I'm not a dirty girl."

Greta moves back and sighs. "You coming down for breakfast, ladies?"

Penelope rushes from the room, glad to get away from her source of discomfort, and runs to the stairs. Victoria lingers and I can see that familiar look of mischief in her eyes.

"Greta, I like my red dress."

"I know, Victoria. It looks good on you."

"Could you ask Penelope if it's okay if I wear it?"

"Victoria, how old are you?"

"Em – it's 1972 so I'm – sixty-four – no – sixty-five. Gosh, I don't feel sixty-five!" Her expression changes from anxious to sad in an instant.

"So, who do you think should choose what you wear?"

Victoria swallows. "Me?" she asks, unsure if this is the correct response.

"Yes. You! You don't ask anyone what you should wear – ever. *You* decide."

"Yes but . . ."

Greta puts her hand up and stops Victoria from saying any more. She knows how to handle the women and knows that they each require a completely different approach.

"No buts, Victoria. You just put it on and pay no attention to what anyone says."

Victoria nods but I can see that she is not convinced and badly wants someone to intervene for her. Greta beckons for her to come downstairs for breakfast.

When I follow, I find Kai in the kitchen with Mina learning how to make pancakes. She is bossing him around and once again, he is saying yes Ma'am, no Ma'am. For a moment I think that she is treating him as if he is a servant, but I am puzzled when she leans towards him and says, "You are too skinny. I know where we can get extra food," and winks at him. I begin to laugh and hold my hand over my mouth. I am not sure who she thinks Kai is but I am glad to see that she is warming to him.

I make my way to the Penance Room where my mother is talking to Steve. There is no one to tell their story today as Wilfred will not come out of his room and Martin is still asleep.

A little later Steve makes himself a coffee and takes it out to the back yard. I know Aishling is there trying to catch some sun before it gets too hot to stay outside. I run up to my room and slyly watch them through my blinds. I cringe when Aishling smiles at Steve and moves over on the bench. He sits so close that his leg is touching off hers and I feel that familiar anger rising in me and burning my face.

"No one to confess today, eh?" she says and I feel she is mocking him.

"Nope," he says. "I might get Part Two of your life though."

Aishling laughs and rolls her head back. "Nothing else to tell, Father," she smiles. "No further sins committed."

I can see Steve looking up at me. He knows I am watching them. He knows everything.

"You never met anyone here then?"

Aishling shrugs and makes a strange shape with her lips. "Wasn't really interested. I . . . guess I didn't want it. I'm happy here. I try to keep my life simple. I work, I sleep and that's about it really."

"You plan to stay here forever? To cut yourself off from possibilities? Now, that's living like Father Hayes."

"I don't really think that far ahead. I . . . I guess I don't want to get hurt . . . or . . . to hurt anyone else. I like it here. Emma and Andy are good to me."

Steve nods and looks like he is thinking about this.

"Tell me about Christopher," he says.

I jump back from the window but I can see him looking up and I know he is teasing me. I want to open the window and tell Aishling to tell him nothing but I am frozen to the spot. He has no right.

Aishling lowers her eyebrows at him and seems taken by surprise. "What has Emma told you?" she asks, anxious not to betray her employer and friend's confidence.

"Not much. She just seems – well – sad – that's all."

Aishling sighs heavily as she tries to decide where to begin.

"I was working here before Christopher was born, you know. He was such a cute baby but as he got older, well . . . he . . . he always seemed to know more than he should. He was always listening . . . or should I say watching. It unnerved some of the staff. They've all left now. I think Kora and I are the only long-term staff left. We all thought Emma and Andy exposed him to too much, you know, when patients were dying and that. At five, he could read anything. I mean it – any book. So smart."

She is shaking her head now and I am hoping that she is not going to tell the bad stuff. I cross my fingers behind my back and pray.

"It was such a pity about his hearing. When he was a baby he had a lot of ear infections. Emma thought it was just the usual kid stuff, you know, glue ear and such – but it turned out to be something called a cholesteatoma. Emma and Andy could see that his hearing was deteriorating and organised for him to be seen by a specialist in Sydney. Before he ever got there he caught meningitis and lost what hearing he had left. He was about five then. It was so sad and . . . well . . . there's nothing much more to tell really."

I know that this is a sign that Aishling wants to change the subject but Steve ignores this.

"Does Emma blame Andy for his accident?"

"Did she say that to you?" Aishling asks, amazed.

"Not in so many words but she well – she looks so full of grief. I just thought . . ."

Aishling is uncomfortable and I take pleasure when I see her inch away from Steve.

"Steve . . . I don't think Emma and Andy's marriage is any of your business."

Steve apologies and worms his way back. "Sorry. I just want to help. That's all."

Aishling looks closely at him but doesn't smile. "Steve, it's great that you are helping the residents and you have also helped me but don't go asking Emma about Christopher. She still gets upset, even after all these years. She blames herself if you ask me, because she didn't stand up to Andy and send Christopher somewhere safer. But they are happy. So don't you go thinking anything else."

Steve knows when he is beaten and looks briefly in my direction.

I grin back at him. Loser.

I know he is trying to ask more questions but he can see by Aishling's demeanour that he will not get anywhere. He decides to change tactics and ask about my father.

"Has Andy been in Australia long?"

Aishling shrugs. "A few years before me, I think."

"He came alone?"

Aishling looks at Steve and I can see that she thinks he asks too many questions. I can see her mind working and she sees no harm in telling Steve how my father came to be in Broken Hill.

"I think he came with a friend from college. Andy's an engineer and when he graduated he got a job with an agency in Edinburgh to come here and work at the mine. He met Emma here and decided to stay but I think he misses home. He's from an island off the north coast of Scotland, not so far from my part of the world. I know how he feels. It's beautiful here and I would never want to leave Australia but a person with two homes is never happy. What you miss about there, you can never have here and vice versa. It's like – like you're torn between both countries and whatever choice you make, you lose something."

Steve is looking into her face with interest. "Do you think he wants to go home?"

"Not now. After a while too much time passes and you really don't belong anywhere. Home becomes part of your past, your history and you really can never go back."

"Are you talking about yourself now or Andy?"

Aishling smiles. "Both. We often talk about home. Things change. I think – I think what you really miss is your youth, the time when there were other possibilities, when your life could have taken a different path."

Steve nods. "And how does he feel about Christopher?"

Aishling suddenly looks annoyed. "God, what is it with you and Christopher?"

"I'm . . . just interested. I . . ."

Once again I feel that my feet are nailed to the floor. I don't want to see what she says but I cannot move away.

Aishling shakes her head again. "He's hurt, of course. What would you expect?" she says with an angry face. "He wanted him to go to college . . . he pushed him all the way. He didn't want him to go to a special school. He had someone come here to teach him. He was determined that Christopher become an engineer. Andy had come from a working-class family and he wanted to put that behind him."

"Do you think he put too much pressure on such a young child?"

Aishling ignores Steve's question.

"Do you think he should have sent him to that school? It sounds like he'd have been better off away from here," he perseveres.

Aishling lets out a huge sigh.

"Overall, yes, but at the same time I think what would have been even better was for the community to accept him as he was so he could stay with his family . . . but he was so isolated . . ." She lowers her head. "Because Christopher didn't go to school here he only had one or two friends, kids who lived on the other side of the train line and even they would shrug him off when it suited them. When he tried to mix with others, they made fun of him. He rarely spoke because he hated the sound of his voice. When his hearing went completely, he stopped speaking altogether. The kids were cruel and I think . . . well . . . that's why things changed for him. Emma, Andy and I learnt to understand sign language but I know what the child really needed back then was friends, other kids who could understand him. He never slept well and started to cling to the adults around him." She paused, brooding.

Steve beckons for her to go on.

"He changed. I think that he was depressed. He was so bright, always reading but I think this place had a bad effect on him. When he was about seven, he became obsessed with death and souls. Emma thought he'd follow in her father's footsteps and lead a religious life but Andy thought he was unwell . . . mentally, you know. So poor Christopher – even at such a young age he was torn between keeping them both happy when in reality he was struggling to find his place in this world. I think he felt he was a disappointment even back then and when the accident occurred, well, it was the final straw for Emma and Andy. The future they had imagined was gone. I know that doesn't paint them in a good light but you'd need to know them better. I . . . just don't think they realised how hard things were for him . . . and I . . . I think they know now that they should have sent him to that school. If nothing else, he would have met other deaf children – he wouldn't have been such a loner."

"You felt sorry for him?"

"Yes," Aishling says slowly. She looks up and pushes the hair back from her eyes which are slightly glassy and I know she has been remembering me as I was, running around and making mischief, a normal child. "You really do know how to get people to talk," she says, amazed that he has got the information out of her that she was at first reluctant to give.

Steve looks smug. "I've had a lot of practice. Tomorrow I'm going to try Wilfred again."

"Now *that* I'll have to stay up for," she says with an equally looking smug expression and they leave the garden and make their way into the house.

Chapter 22

The following day, Jimmy returns home by ambulance. He looks thinner and his silvery blue eyes seem to bulge out of their sockets. The ambulance men wheel him into the Penance Room and go to the office to speak with my mother. I see him glancing at Martin who opens his mouth as if he is going to say something but decides not to. I know he is glad to have Jimmy back even though he will never say it. Even though it is very hot, Jimmy is shaking and when the blanket wrapped around him falls onto the ground, he can do nothing except look at it and shiver. I watch with interest as Martin gets up slowly and walks towards him. Jimmy moves back into his wheelchair. He is afraid that Martin is going to hit him. He is right to be worried as I have seen them fighting since I was very small. Martin walks slowly and stops right in front of Jimmy. As he bends forward, fear spreads across Jimmy's face but changes to tears as Martin lifts the blanket off the floor and throws it roughly over his old enemy. When my mother comes into the room, Jimmy is crying openly and I know that it is partly because Martin has shown him kindness and partly because he could not lift the blanket himself.

My mother hugs him. "There now, Jimmy. I'd have thought you'd be glad to get out of hospital and be back home!"

But he doesn't stop crying and Mother has to take him to his room where he can have some privacy.

When the others gather one by one, I am glad to see Victoria and Penelope sitting with Iren. They are speaking French and I am sorry that I cannot read their lips. Iren is smiling and waving her hands around. I have never seen her look so happy. It is Saturday so my father is home and is in Wilfred's room, trying to talk him into speaking with Steve but he still refuses. I feel the screen door banging and I see Wilfred walk down the road toward the pub. He doesn't often go out but today he needs an escape route. I follow Steve into the Penance Room and I can see Martin looking at him warily. I know that he is almost ready to tell his story but that there is still a small part of him that thinks he was not to blame for what happened to his family. Breakfast is over and Li is sitting in the Penance Room beside Mina and Kai. Her narrow brown eyes are moving left to right as if she is reading from a book. She stands suddenly.

"Mr Laver?"

"Yes?" Steve says with a smile.

"Is it only residents that you wish to speak to or do you want to hear my story?"

Even though Steve knows that she has a story to tell, his research is confined to the elderly. He shakes his head.

"It will help others here," she says quickly, looking at Mina.

Steve suddenly understands why Li wants to recall her past and turns his tape recorder on. He introduces her and nods for her to begin.

"I came to this country in 1943 when I was only twenty-three years old. I was born in a small village south of Shanghai and had two older brothers. We all lived in one tiny house until I married at seventeen and moved into my husband's parents' house in a neighbouring village which was not much bigger. This was the same year that Japan invaded China. The war of resistance against Japan was showing itself slowly. Everywhere we would hear that villages were burned down and we could see the war coming closer to us. China had many resources and the Japanese wanted our coal and iron. My husband and I had no money and my job was to care for my elderly mother and father-in-law. Jin worked on the tiny patch of land his parents had in the mountains. He walked there every day and grew vegetables. As the last of his siblings to live at home it was Jin's responsibility to take a wife to care for his parents. It was very hard because I was not their first choice for their son but he asked for me and so it was agreed that we should marry. I was very unhappy because nothing I did was good enough and when my work was done, I would visit my mother and cry. She would say, 'Daughter, it is your job now, so smile and be thankful for what you have.' One thing I am thankful for was that she taught me to be a good cook. When I was nineteen I had my first child, a beautiful girl. Jin was happy. It didn't matter to him that she was a girl. She slept almost all the time and we named her Ning which means tranquillity. After months of fighting, my two brothers and my father died as honourable soldiers. My mother was all alone and I would visit her and try to comfort her. She said she wanted to die. She said that every day and I begged her, saying, 'You are all of the family I have left so don't leave me!'"

Li looks around the room but then focuses on Mina. Everyone knows that her story is for her benefit.

"Before the war, Germany helped China with training of our military but when the Japanese invaded China, Hitler supported Japan so the Soviet Union became our allies. Even so, many Chinese died – everywhere people were dying. I tell you this not to hold grudges but to say how happy I am now to be here. I don't talk of these things. Not even to my children but, today, maybe this story help somebody else."

She looks at Mina and then at Kai. Everyone can see tears

forming in Li's eyes. She is usually happy and we have never seen her cry before. Kai looks embarrassed and keeps his eyes on the floor. Beside him Mina is clasping her hands tightly together and looking into her lap.

"One day, I heard that houses in my mother's village had been set alight by Japanese soldiers. I left Ning who was six months old with my mother-in-law and ran all the way there but there was nothing wrong. My mother was sitting there crying for my father and my brothers like she had been doing for a long time. She had bad feet and could not walk far without help. I needed Jin to help me carry her so I told her to stay there, that I would come back for her later . . ."

Li swallows again. Everyone can see that she is reliving something awful, something she has never given words to, until now.

"I had to leave her – I was worried because my mother-in-law was old and I didn't like to leave her looking after Ning for very long. When I tried to return home, it took me a long time to get through the rows of Japanese soldiers passing me. I knew they were on their way to my mother's village but when I looked towards home, I could see smoke blowing up into the sky. I screamed and one soldier tried to . . . I bit his hand and the others laughed at him so he let me go. I ran home without stopping and when I got to . . . when I saw . . . it was gone . . ."

Li stares off into space and we know what she is looking at: rows of burnt huts and the villagers lying dead all around her.

"The house was just embers and sparks with some roof hanging down. I ran inside and my mother and father-in-law were both dead, lying face down on the floor. I screamed, 'Ning! Ning!' But I could not hear her crying. I . . . turned them over and they . . . Ning was underneath them. They had tried to protect her from the fire and she was perfect. She looked asleep. I thought she was . . . just asleep. I lifted her and, when she didn't open her eyes, I shook her and started to scream. When I realised that she was gone I sat in the embers with her in my arms and rocked her. There was nothing else for me to do. Even when the darkness fell, I didn't move. I waited until Jin came and stood inside the door. He didn't cry. Someone had stopped him and told him – they warned him that only I was left, that his family, his parents and child were gone. Someone brought us water but we just sat there and held her in our arms with screaming and chaos around us. I asked Jin why? Why did the Japanese do this to us? What did we do? Jin buried all three of his family together in the morning light and we gathered whatever we had left and made our way to my mother's village. Only once did he say to me that I should have been there. It was shortly before our second daughter was born and he never said it again. The soldiers had not gone into my mother's village which was off the main path and not visible from the road so when we got to her she was safe. Together we walked with some of our neighbours to my aunt's house in Shanghai. I remember moving forward but my heart was left behind in the damp earth with my baby's body inside it. You could not believe the awful things that we saw on the road . . . things I . . . it is best not to remember. The Japanese soldiers were advancing westwards and we had nowhere to go. People said that they were only killing enemies of Japan but everywhere boys and young men were dying and women and girls were raped."

Iren looks up and starts to cry.

"Aron! Soldiers!" she shouts and I am brought to tears when I see Penelope rub her arm and tell her there are no more soldiers. If only Iren really believed that.

"My aunt's friend was a fisherman and he said he could get all six of us into boats and that we could get away – but where to? No one knew where was safe to go. Many people were heading westward by land but so were the Japanese. When we got to the water, only one tiny rowboat was still there, the others were burned. My aunt got in and said, 'Please, everyone squeeze in!' but there was no room for us. We would surely sink the boat if we got in. We told her to go, to leave and we would find her. We said we would reach America and find each other in San Francisco."

Li smiles sadly at the naïvety of such a pact.

"Such silly talk but we didn't know. It was best that we believed. I remember her waving with her husband and the fisherman and his wife in a tiny boat. You could see flames in the water and I remember thinking at that moment that the whole world was on fire and would never be the same again. We never saw my aunt again and we never found out what happened to her. I know she must have drowned but Jin and I for a few years after used to talk of her in a fancy apartment in America. It made us happy . . ."

Li stops again and thinks about her aunt. She looks down and for a moment we think that this is the end of her story, that this is as much as she can tell us.

Steve moves into her line of vision and she looks intently at him for a moment before returning to her story.

Wilfred comes in and sits at the far end of the room, safe in the knowledge that someone else is telling their story and he will be left alone for at least another day. He smells of beer and I see my mother looking at him with her tight mouth. Li looks pleased that he is here as if part of her story will make him happy but I don't see how. She continues.

"Jin, my mother and I made our way on foot with the crowds of refugees. People were fleeing to Yunnan on the border with Vietnam and Laos. Mother's feet were not good so a man with a rickshaw took her some of the way and left her in a village to wait for us with another old woman. My mother was exhausted and, four weeks into our journey, she died. We had walked all day with little food or drink and when we hid for the night in some scrub, we went to sleep quickly. I lay beside her to keep her warm and Jin slept beside the men who took turns guarding us through the night. When we woke, I didn't even have to look at her to know she was dead. Each morning, I could feel her breathing heavily and coughing but that morning she was very still. I didn't cry although I cried for her many years later. She was tired and I didn't want her to suffer any more. I knew that worse things were to come and I was happy in my heart that she was with my father and my brothers and that she could now care for my daughter until I met them again. Jin and the other men buried her by the roadside. I could not remember where even if you brought me there now so I have nowhere to visit her except in my mind.

"We made it to Kunming where we lived for many months. A group of foreigners, including an American who had been running a Christian school, helped Jin and me and gave us shelter and some work when we were stronger. We joined the church and became Christians. One of the foreigners was from Germany and it was well known that he was a Nazi. I have often thought of him and thought that there you might think is a cruel man but he had a heart and he tried to do the right thing, even when such awful things were happening around him."

Wilfred doesn't look up but I can see his face turn bright red and that familiar cough begin to choke him. He puts his hand to his mouth to smother it and pretends to read the newspaper. Even when people are reaching out to him, even when people are telling him good things, he rejects them because he doesn't think he is worthy of any happiness.

"My husband had been a proud soldier fighting with my father and brothers so it was not safe for us to remain in China. Our new friends helped us to travel to Malaysia to some British friends of theirs but things were not much better there. This couple ran a school which was now banned. They too were no longer safe. They taught Jin and me as well as some other refugees to speak English. Some months later, they helped us to board a ship to Australia. If you could understand – we didn't even know where Australia was and the only stories we had heard in China was that this place was full of gold where many of our villagers went and never returned. Most of the people on the ship were British people living in Malay which was their colony then. They were fleeing Japanese occupation and as Australia was part of the Commonwealth, it was the safest and nearest place to go at that time. But it was a dangerous journey because the war was still in full force.

"When we reached Perth I was only twenty-three years old. I remember Jin and me standing at that port with nothing that was our own. There was a camp for us to go to until we found a home and, while most people inside this camp were nice, when we left it we had problems. Some Australians thought we were communists but we said, 'No, we are Christians.' For years we went from place to place and I said to Jin, 'Some day we will have to accept that whatever town we choose, we have to make it our home and accept that it will not be perfect. *Always*, there will be people who don't understand that we are looking for a better life, not to take anything away from anyone, not to do any harm.'

"We came to Sydney where there were many other Chinese people but, at this stage, many of these people were born here and were not so interested in newcomers. They just wanted to be Australians. So did we. Eventually Jin got a job as a gardener growing vegetables on a farm outside Broken Hill. I was pregnant with our daughter then but I did not become hopeful that she would come as I believed I would lose her just as I lost Ning. But four months after we settled in Broken Hill, our beautiful daughter was born. We named her Zhenzhen which means 'precious' but as she grew she didn't like her name and insisted we call her Susan. She wanted so much to fit in when she was a young girl. She didn't like being different. Thirteen years later, Kai was born. Jin and I had an Australian neighbour whose child was called Kai and we thought it was an Australian name but when our son Kai was two, I bought a book and found the word had many meanings. In Hawaiian it means 'ocean'. In Welsh, it means the 'keeper of the keys'. My favourite meaning is the New Zealand Maori one which says that Kai means 'food' as ever since he was a little boy he was always hungry, always wanting me to cook and, look, now he wants to be a baker! I think it must have been because I was so hungry for so many years during the war."

Li looks at Mina and keeps her gaze there for a few seconds. Mina nods as if she understands, as if she finally knows that Li is not her enemy but someone who has suffered just as much as she has.

"Susan is now twenty-nine years old and she lives in America. She was only nine when she said she wanted to be a doctor and to work in poor countries. I knew my daughter well and I knew that this would come true. So I cleaned houses and offices and cooked food for people's parties to pay for her education and, the day she graduated from university in Sydney, I didn't think about China or the Japanese, or even of my first born, Ning. I thought of how happy life turned out for Jin and me. I thought how lucky I was, that nothing more could ever hurt me. I had everything. Susan applied for jobs in Africa, volunteer work. She loved it. When she came home, she told me that she had met an American boy there, another doctor, and when she was accepted to do paediatric training in New York, she said yes, she would go there. Jin and I were upset but we were so proud of her. We wanted what was best for our daughter so we let her go and hoped this romance would not last. Two years later, she sent us the fare to America. She said she was getting married. Married to a boy that we had never met and whose family we didn't know. 'You'll meet him, Mum,' she said. 'Robert is nice. You'll like him.' Looking back, I knew she was being secretive. I said, 'Come home. Let us meet this man and your father will decide if it is right for you.' Jin and I, we tried to be Australian parents and let her make her own decisions but to let her marry a man we didn't know! We could not do it. But she would not come so Jin and I boarded a flight to New York to try to talk to her.

"When we got there, I could see why she kept Robert a secret from us. I can still see Jin's face at that airport when we saw a young Japanese boy smiling at us, standing, holding hands with our beautiful Zhenzhen. He put out his hand and in a strong American accent said, 'Hi, I'm Robert.' Jin didn't speak at all while I mumbled something. I cannot remember what I said. I was in shock. I remember looking at Susan but she could not look her parents in the eye. Later, I thought that it was our fault that she could not tell us. Jin and I thought that we had not affected our children with our feelings. We didn't speak of the war and not often did we tell them stories of how we had to come to Australia for a new life. But somehow, our daughter knew that we would judge Robert before we had a chance to meet him. Somehow our prejudice seeped into our girl's heart, without us wanting this to happen. It was wise of our daughter to take that action but still we thought that she would never marry a Japanese boy out of respect for her parents and for her dead family. Then we went to Robert's parents' home. I don't know how we got there. Jin and I held hands in a fast-moving car. I could feel the sweat on his hand. Robert's parents and grandparents had been born in America. But this didn't matter to us at that moment. We were sitting in the lounge room with Japanese people who raped and murdered our family and our friends, with people who were responsible for murdering my innocent baby girl, Susan's sister.

"That evening in Susan's apartment, we fought. We pleaded. She said, 'Mum, the war is over,' and I said, 'Yes, it is, but not in my heart,' and that's when I said to myself, 'Why is it not over in my heart and when will this be so?' The following morning, Robert's parents brought Jin and me around the city and, although it was a difficult day, we tried hard to cope. They were very nice ordinary people, people like us who had lost a lot. We had things in common: people being racist because of the colour of our skin, pride at having a child who is now a doctor, being a minority in the country you call home, lots of things that should bring us together. On our last day there, Robert's mother said to me, 'Isn't it amazing that such beautiful people should find each other on the other side of the world?' and I had to agree. It was amazing. The whole world is amazing and you have to see the good in difficult situations."

Li looks at Mina and stands. She opens a small silver locket around her neck and moves around the room, showing everybody the photos inside.

"My twin granddaughters," she says proudly. "Hua and Hana. Their names mean 'flower' in Chinese and Japanese. Susan and Robert spent weeks looking through books before deciding on what to call them. And you know what? During their search they found another meaning for Kai, something I didn't know before I named my son. In Japanese, Kai is a girl's name and it means 'forgiveness'."

Li moves towards the door. We can all see that she is overcome with emotion, with sadness and joy for telling her story, a story of loss and of forgiveness. As she passes Mina, the old woman puts her hand forward and touches Li's arm. Li stops and acknowledges her. She stands for a moment and there is a silent exchange between the women, an exchange that says that Mina also needs to forgive and forget.

"You coming to work?" Li asks.

Mina smiles, stands up and slowly moves her walking frame toward the door. She looks back into the room where everybody remains silent.

"Come on, Kai. We have work to do."

Chapter 23

The following morning, Steve arrives early but fails to talk Wilfred into telling his story. My mother decides it is best not to press it and I am disappointed that I will not get to hear about the sad life Wilfred has had. It is his birthday today and Steve is due to leave tomorrow after his party. Wilfred seems to be in bad humour and even Greta gets annoyed with him when he shouts at Iren to stop calling for Aron.

Jimmy is sitting in the corner of the room in a wheelchair and Martin is looking at him in an odd way. Kora is here and telling everyone that Jeff will be home from the hospital soon. She is smiling broadly which is not like Kora and I think there is something different about her that I cannot describe.

The door of the room is open and outside I see my mother hand Aishling a letter. My heart races. "Please let it be from her family!" I pray but I can see her peer at the postmark and she does not look surprised so I know it is not from her family. I move out to the hall and, as my mother and Aishling read the letter together, I peer over their shoulders. Aishling puts one hand over her mouth but I can see the huge smile that has erupted beneath her red-painted fingernails.

Dear Aishling

Oh, it was so nice to hear from you and to hear that Aiden is alive and well. Well, you know from my niece that Aiden and I were childhood sweethearts. We had promised to get married but of course you know all of that. I am getting on myself but I am still able to live in my house. My daughter lives with me and I go to a lot of Irish get-togethers here in Brooklyn. I never went back to Ireland. I couldn't bear to visit home after Aiden went into the priesthood. The last time I was there in my home town was when my brother met me off the train to tell me that Aiden was gone. I came to America immediately after my training finished and I've been here since. My brothers have visited which was nice but I just didn't ever want to go back.

Even though I had a happy marriage, I thought of Aiden often. I hated to think that he was alone in this world. Even now, after all these years, I can feel myself welling up thinking about him. I know they say that everything happens for a reason but I still feel bitter about losing Aiden to the Church. I hope he was happy but I doubt it. It is amazing that now after all these years I found where Aiden is, especially as I have a son in Australia. He lives in Sydney which he tells me is a long way away from where Aiden is but I am coming to visit him and his wife in a couple of months. I have a new grandson that I have not yet met. We should have asked Aiden to do the baptism. Now wouldn't that be something?

My daughter is flying with me. She isn't married. She's not interested in men, if you know what I mean. Never heard of it in my day. I walk with a stick now so I need her to help me but, although she thinks this is foolishness at my age, she has agreed to accompany me to Broken Hill and says we could easily get a train from Sydney and stay in a hotel in town for a couple of days, so if it is all right with you, that's what we'll do.

I've put my phone number on top of the letter and also my son's contact details in Sydney. Oh, I can't believe that I am going to see Aiden! I can't believe that we'll get a chance to see each other again, even if we are both old and grey now. Please tell him that I am looking forward to seeing him again and thank you so much for your kindness in reuniting us. I look forward to meeting you.

Yours sincerely
Deirdre Mahon (Née McGonigle)

My mother and Aishling look teary and are smiling at the same time. If my father was here he would raise his eyes up to heaven and say "Women!" and I am never sure what this means. Aishling goes straight into the lounge room to tell Father Francis and I watch him smile and clasp his hands tightly together as she tells him. When she leaves, his smile fades and is replaced with tears which he tries to hide. I feel a lump in my throat as he puts his bony hand into his jacket pocket and takes out his rosary beads to pray.

"I hope this Deirdre is not expecting him to be the man she knew," my mother says to Steve who is busy setting up his tape recorder for the day.

Martin is sitting beside Father Francis and raises his hand as if he is in school.

"Yes, Martin?" Steve says.

"I'll tell ya. I'll talk into the machine if ya like?"

Steve raises an eyebrow. "You sure? You didn't seem keen before."

Martin points at Jimmy who is dozing off. "If he can do it, I can. Fair's fair."

Steve smiles and nods and Martin moves forward to take the chair near the recording machine. Martin clears his throat and begins.

"I've heard you all say that no matter what happened to you,

223

you don't hold a grudge and you are thankful for whatever you've got. Well, I'm not bloody thankful and I've a few things to say about how my people were treated when they came to this country."

"Your people?" Steve asks.

"Yeah!" Martin barks back. "My father arrived here from Ireland in 1892. He was only about twenty or a little more and he came with his wife, my mother. She was about two years younger than him. They were free settlers, mind. No convicts on my side. Well, I had a grand-uncle sent out here long before that for stealing but the poor old sod did nothing more than try steal a sheep to feed his kids. It was shortly before the famine. My daughter looked into it and found out that he died in prison out here. His family never heard from him again. They were never even told he was dead. But that's the pommies for ya, greed and evil through and through. Wanting everything except what they are entitled to."

Steve interrupts him. "Martin, are you going to tell us *your* story?"

"I'm getting to it!"

I know he is shouting as he breaks into one of his coughing-fits caused by smoking and years of inhaling dust in the mine.

"One generation affects the next," he says when he recovers, more to himself than to his audience. "When they came here, my parents had nothing. Their own parents had been thrown off their small farms by English landlords and left to wander the road with small ones in tow. My mother told me that her mother had eleven siblings and only three of them survived the famine. Whole families wiped out by starvation."

Martin gives Penelope and Victoria an evil look but they don't notice and, even if they did, they would not understand its meaning. Oddly he doesn't direct this at Jimmy Young as he would have done before. Perhaps it is because he now knows that Jimmy's own ancestors were transported to Australia as convicts and were not from the English ruling classes that kept Martin's people down.

"When they got here though, they found that they were not going to get the fresh start they had hoped for. In many towns, there were signs saying 'No Irish Need Apply' or 'No Dogs, No Irish'. The kind of immigrants they wanted were Protestant, not Irish Catholics. If it wasn't for the Church help they got when they arrived here, they'd have starved. Might have been better to starve on Irish soil than come all this way and die anyway."

"But they didn't die?" Steve asks.

Martin raises an eye at Steve. The two men don't seem to like each other and I have never noticed this before. I wonder briefly what it is about.

"My father wasn't the type of man who'd let others beat him. He came here for a new life and by Christ he was going to get it. My mother, she was even tougher than him. God, she worked hard, all hours, washing clothes by hand, scrubbing other people's houses. When I think back, this land must have seemed so foreign to them with the heat, the dust. They were determined to give their kids a better life. They did all they could for us."

Martin's chin begins to quiver. Steve notices it.

"Did you do all you could for them?"

I can see the anger rising in Martin's face. He leans forward as if he is about to jump at Steve but suddenly thinks the better of it and leans back, as if in defeat. I gloat a little to myself that I know more about Martin's story than Steve but there is still work to do. He has a long way to go yet.

"My father eventually got into the mines and he straightened himself out. No drinking. Double shifts whenever he could get them. He wanted to buy a small patch of land. Just enough for some livestock for ourselves and to grow vegetables. He always said you were nothing if you didn't own a piece of this earth. He had this thing for the Aboriginals. Great respect for them. He said they were the nearest thing to brothers that the Irish had here. That they had endured the same history – eviction, starvation, murder. He had this one friend, can't remember his name, he lived on a small settlement around here. He was nice. We didn't get along, the father and me. I used to say to him 'Well, if you love the natives so much what are you doing buying their land from the whites that took it from them?' He never had an answer to that but to hit me. I used to get such beatings. I was the eldest, me and my twin, Tom. He was sickly and, well, that's another story. What I'm trying to say is that while our parents had most of the trouble, it leaves a bad taste in your mouth. It affects ya. Makes you angry from the start, before you even have a chance to see how lucky you are to be here. So that's it. That's my story. That's what I mean."

Martin stops talking and looks around the room. No one quite knows what to say as his story is so unlike anyone else's that it doesn't really seem like a story at all. Martin only seems comfortable telling us about the beginning but skims over the middle and leaves out the ending. Steve is thinking the same thing.

"What happened in your life, Martin?" he asks.

"Can't you see that's what I'm bloody trying to tell you? There is no life. It poisons ya, hatred and injustice. Before you get a chance to breathe, your lungs are so black with the world's worries there's no way for you to see things clearly. Everybody is against ya. You can't trust no one. I fought against the Japs for this country but ya think back then they saw me as one of their own? Ya don't belong anywhere. Fresh starts in a new country, my arse!"

Martin starts to cough. Kora makes her way across the room to him.

"Ya all right, mate?"

Martin puts out his hand and nods. "Bloody lungs."

Steve is not going to let him away lightly. "So, you blame everything that happened to you on your parents and on discrimination?"

"Not on my parents, well, a bit – but you're young, you don't know anything about it."

"Well, enlighten me," Steve says.

I don't like the way he is treating Martin. I know he is an angry man but I feel there is hope for him and annoying him will get Steve nowhere.

"Tell me how it was for you," says Steve. "Tell me what happened to you."

Martin cracks his jaw sideways and glares at Steve but he quietens and looks suddenly sad.

"I tried to make them proud but it was as if there was no room for me. As if I was invisible from the start. My brother, they had to take more care of him. He needed medicine and rest. I worked harder and got nothing for it. I was just looking for someone to notice me."

"And how did you eventually get noticed?" Steve asks.

Martin ignores him and jumps forward about ten years.

"When I married it was the same. My wife ignored me. Didn't appreciate me. Took me a while but I figured out she needed a firm hand. Lazy she was and stupid. I'd come home some days and find her staring into the stove. Not a thing done around the place."

"What did you do?"

"I did what any man should do. Showed her who the boss was."

"How would you do that?"

Martin knows Steve is baiting him but it is too late. He is trapped.

"I'd smack her and she'd smarten up. For a while anyway."

"Didn't you just say that you hated when your father beat you?"

"Yes, but this was different. She was useless."

"Martin, did your mother tell you that you were useless?"

Martin's chin starts to tremble. His hand shakes and he places

227

it on his bony knee to steady himself. "How'd ya know that? Yeah . . . she said that a lot."

"Did you tell your children that they were useless?"

Martin raises his red face closer to Steve. "Only when they bloody well were useless!" he shouts. He flings his arm forward, pointing angrily at Steve, and knocks a glass of water onto the floor.

"You took your revenge on those least able to defend themselves," says Steve. "You carried on your father's behaviour with your own family. Maybe your children are doing the same as we speak."

Martin looks to his right and I know that he is thinking of the frightened Ellen, the somewhat aggressive Una and his two other daughters, Nora and Bridget, who visit once a week and sit quietly as they stare at the clock and wait for the punishing hour to pass.

"But he . . . he hated me . . . I was never good enough!"

"Then you should have proved him wrong," Steve says slowly. "You should have shown him the man you could have been."

No one knows what to say and there is a silence in the room that even I am aware of. When Li calls everyone to lunch, the relief in the room is palpable. Martin stands and, as he makes his way towards the door, Jimmy gestures for him to come over to him. Amazingly, Martin obeys. As he gets closer, Jimmy tries to speak but I don't know what he is trying to say. He moves his stiff arm forward and rolls out three middle fingers, as if he is trying to shake Martin's hand. Martin understands the gesture but looks confused. He takes the fingers and shakes them.

"My fad – my – fad . . ."

Martin nods. "Your father was the same. I know, Jimmy," he says and as he walks away I can see his eyes moisten. It is the first time he has ever called Jimmy by his first name. He walks past the dining room and climbs the stairs slowly to his room. I know now that he will never tell Steve his full story, the real story of why his life turned out the way it did. I think about following him but I know that right now he would prefer to be alone. I enter the dining room and, as people are getting seated, Greta is standing at my mother's piano and tinkling on the keys. I stand and watch as she runs her fingers back and forth on the ivory. She is watching Penelope in the corner of her eye and I know she is planning something.

"Stop it!" Penelope shouts, disturbing the others from their lunch. "You can't play!"

"I know," Greta says, smiling. "Wish I could but I'll keep trying here. Maybe you could teach me. Always wanted to learn."

Penelope's expression changes and I think she is aware that Greta is playing her. She decides to ignore her and starts chopping her meat up into tiny pieces. Victoria stands up and takes her plate to another table. She senses a storm brewing and is running for cover. Greta starts running her fingers back and forth over the keys. Some of the residents place their fingers in their ears so I know the sound must be awful. Iren has stopped shouting for Aron and is saying what looks like "*No, no, no!*" over and over, though I know she is not speaking English – I guess it is "no" in French.

"Okay!" Penelope screams with a red face and throat. "Okay, I'll play. Just stop – please stop that awful racket!"

Greta apologises and thanks Penelope. She hands her some music and Penelope sits down to play. Greta relaxes but Penelope stands again abruptly without having played a single note.

"Could we turn the piano around?"

"Why?" Greta asks.

"So my back is to the wall. It's – it's safer. I can see everyone . . . I know where everyone is."

Greta smiles sadly at Penelope. We can only imagine what this means and what her father did to her when she was forced to play for him each evening.

"Sure. Wilfred, will you help?"

Wilfred and Greta turn the piano around and Penelope sits down to play. As soon as she begins I can see the pleased surprise on the residents' faces. Even Wilfred, who is a trained musician, is smiling appreciatively.

When she finishes, Greta reaches forward and pats her lightly on the shoulder but Penelope tenses and moves her shoulders towards her ears as she pulls the cover down.

Greta looks a little sad and I can see she feels even worse when Wilfred, who rarely speaks, says, "Such talent! What a pity she hates so much to play."

I can feel the door open and Henry is standing in the hall, looking for my mother. I follow them to the office and look in at their conversation from the doorway. He has two roughly folded pieces of paper in his hand and seems to be out of breath.

"Sorry, I'm just passing by and thought I show you these. Found them in my father's things. Look, it says my grandfather died of pneumonia. I think my aunts' confession might be wishful thinking on their part."

My mother nods but I can see that she is not convinced.

Henry continues. "It got me thinking about my grandmother. I know nothing about her. I decided to get her death certificate and got the shock of my life . . . well, look . . . see for yourself." He shoves a large piece of paper in my mother's direction.

My mother reads it and looks up at Henry in horror. Her face is full of questions.

"Syphilis? Your grandmother died of syphilis?"

"Yes. Syphilis. She must have caught it from Grandfather."

My mother closes the door, blocking my view. I move outside quickly and look in the window. Henry is facing my direction but I can only see three-quarters of my mother's mouth. I hope I can understand her words.

"Maybe . . . or he could have contracted it later on, after the children were all born . . . but it doesn't make sense . . . if he had it for all that time he'd have passed it onto Penelope when . . ."

My mother looks to the ground. I know what she was going to say. She turns slightly away from Henry and I can see her mouth better.

"I know," Henry said quickly. He doesn't want her to say any more.

"Unless . . ." Mother offers hesitantly.

"What?" Henry asks.

"I heard Penelope say that her mother was popular with men and they all loved her. I wonder if she was . . . seeing someone else when your grandfather was overseas. After the children were all born?"

Henry frowns. "Surely that wouldn't have happened back then?"

"Why not? Perhaps she was lonely? Perhaps she married the wrong man?"

Henry wrinkles his forehead and bites his lip. I can see that he doesn't want to think that his grandmother was unfaithful in her marriage.

"My God, he was punishing the women for their mother's actions!" my mother says. "What was it that Victoria said? That he was trying to cleanse them?"

"Was there no treatment back then?"

"Some but not like there is now and the treatment wasn't particularly effective. You had to get it early. Maybe she didn't know until it was too late? Or maybe she couldn't get the treatment she needed because your grandfather didn't want anyone to know? We'll never know."

Henry folded the piece of paper and shoved it into his pocket. A moment passes between the two, neither knowing what to say.

"You coming later to Wilfred's party?" Mother finally asks. "Penelope is actually going to play the piano."

"Sorry, I can't. I'm due back on the base now but I'll be by again soon. Tell them I said have a good night."

My mother walks Henry to the door and looks around the garden. I slip down the side and look in the kitchen window. I can smell freshly baked apple pie and my mouth waters. Li is sitting at the table with Mina and Kai and they are leafing through recipe books, planning tonight's party food.

"Well, Kai," Mina says, "I think it's time we gave you some wings."

"Wings?"

Mina laughs. "That's what my husband said to me the first time he let me bake without his help. Now, what would you like to make?"

Kai opens another book on the table. "What about a Peace Cake?" he says, smiling shyly and pointing to a large white frosted cake at the back of the book.

Mina and Li look at him and start to laugh.

"I think perhaps it is too soon for this type of cake," Mina says. "One step at a time!"

I come inside again and wander down to the Penance Room. I am about to sit in my favourite seat when I see Maria walking quickly up the wooden steps onto the porch. I can feel my heart lift and know that I am falling in love with her but my happiness is short-lived when I see that she is crying and has only come to see me because something is wrong. I open the door but she doesn't come in and walks back down the steps and towards her grandfather's house. I instinctively follow her but she walks ahead for the whole journey and doesn't make allowances for my limp. When we get to the house I instantly see what has upset her. The "For Sale" sign outside her grandfather's shop has been covered up with a large red "SOLD" sign. She starts to sob and I try to put my arm around her.

"When?" I sign.

"Today. He didn't say anything. A man just pulled up and hammered this up. I don't want to go!"

I try to think of something clever to sign but as usual I come up empty.

I take out my notebook and write.

"Maybe your grandfather will get a one-storey house? You know, with no stairs so he can manage his wheelchair?"

Maria's face turns bright red and I can see both rows of her perfectly formed teeth snarl at me.

"Are you saying it's my fault? That he is in a wheelchair because of me?" she spits.

I am suddenly afraid. If I am to be honest, it is not the first time Maria has frightened me but I am drawn to her as much as she is drawn to me.

"No," I sign.

"You are!" she screams. I can feel the vibrations of her voice against my chest and right now I am as afraid of her as I am of the night train.

I turn to walk away but she follows me.

"It's not my fault. It wasn't my fault!" she rages into my face but I keep walking away from her.

I am not unlike my mother. I don't like confrontation. I keep walking towards my house until I can no longer feel her behind me. When I get to the corner of Menindee road, I turn and am both relieved and disappointed that she is gone.

I climb the steps to my house and immediately go to my room. I lie down on my bed and try not to think about Maria. The sun is making strange shapes on my ceiling and I can see a mosquito at the foot of my bed. I reach up to pull the mossie net around me but I notice that it is gone and I wonder if Tina has taken it away to wash it. I try to have a nap but it is too hot so I go back downstairs to watch the preparations for Wilfred's party.

Kora is off today as she is picking Jeff up from the hospital and driving him home. It will be a long time before he can manage the farm alone so one of his nephews is coming to help him. Greta is blowing up balloons with Penelope and Victoria. I laugh when they jump at the sound of a burst balloon. I was the last to laugh because I didn't hear the noise it made. Being deaf is sometimes like living in a silent bubble world. You are protected from many experiences but denied so many others. Wilfred is of course in his room. He doesn't want any fuss for his birthday. He doesn't think he deserves it and he will not come out of his room until my father makes him.

I wander over to Jimmy who is staring into space with his mouth open. I think that he looks dead until he wiggles his nose at a fly that is annoying him. I wave my arms but the fly doesn't move.

I sit beside Iren who is watching the action with an amused look on her face. She looks at me and says, "*Jacob!*", then puts out her hand to touch my cheek.

My mother is staring at her and shaking her head. "Has Iren had her medication today?" she asks Tina.

I don't mind if she is confused. What is the harm if she thinks I am her son? I am making her happy and that is one of my jobs around here, that and helping my mother.

At eight o'clock the party starts and Martin is trying to get as much whiskey as he can. Poor Jimmy cannot have a drink and he looks on sadly in the corner. Father Hayes, or Aiden as many of the staff are now calling him, is sitting quietly in the corner, reading. Penelope and Victoria enter the room with Greta and everyone smiles when they see Victoria wearing her new red dress and Penelope entering with her music sheets and a tight smile. It is a night for firsts.

Penelope sits herself behind the piano that has been moved from the dining room for the occasion. It has been pushed up close to the wall so there is just enough room for Penelope to squeeze herself onto the stool and no room whatsoever for people to come behind her and remind her of the past. My father's friend Bill is here as usual to play his guitar. He has a quick word with her and together they play a slow melody that I know is not to Bill's liking. My father is already in a happy mood and I can see a large Scotch whisky in his hand. My mother will not complain.

He puts down his drink and goes to Wilfred's room to fetch the Birthday Boy. I follow of course and when we enter Wilfred is already dressed and obviously waiting on my father to come and get him. He is dressed in a black suit that almost looks like what you would wear playing in an orchestra. He rises without protest and follows my father to the lounge room. His face is red with embarrassment but he has obviously decided to go along with it. He sits himself away from the crowd and taps his foot gently to the tune Penelope is still playing. She closes her eyes tightly and seems to lose herself in the music. When she finishes, my father walks quickly over to congratulate her but she jumps up and starts to shout. Father stands back and Greta moves in.

"Sorry, Penelope," my father says. "I just wanted to say how beautifully you play."

"Penelope knows that, don't you, love?" Greta says, smiling nervously. I can see her gold tooth shining.

Penelope nods. "Em . . . yes . . . thank you," she says before returning to the safety of her seat.

My father takes up his fiddle and says, "Let's liven things up, shall we?"

Aishling is sitting in the corner and jumps up when she hears the fast tune my father is playing. She grabs Martin up to dance. Even though his lungs are very bad, he loves to dance to Irish music and says it reminds him of when he was very young. When he tires, Aishling sits him down and takes Aiden by the hand. He moves a lot slower but you can see by the expression on his face that he is having a good time. My mother is sitting beside Mina who is reading a letter from Hope. I saw her reading her letter earlier and wonder why she is reading it again. There are tears in her eyes and my mother thinks it is bad news. She leans towards Mina.

"Everything all right, Mina?"

Mina looks up and through her tears I can see a smile.

"Yes, Emma," she says, thrusting a small photo at my mother. "Hope had a baby girl last month, her first child. She named her Mina. I'm – I'm so – happ–"

My mother touches her arm. "There, love. That's wonderful."

"Hope said she'd tell her all about me when she's older and why she is named for me. She says she'll tell little Mina that without me she'd never have survived."

"It's true, Mina. You did a wonderful thing."

Mina nods and smiles.

"Let's celebrate then, eh?" my mother says and Mina laughs.

"Look at this photo," she tells Victoria who is more interested in her new red dress.

When Steve arrives, we are all surprised to see him. Tomorrow, after he talks to Wilfred, he leaves for another town. I watch as Aishling brings him a drink and gives him a romantic smile. I try not to be annoyed. She needs this little bit of happiness.

Catherine has not been wheeled up from the babies' room. She has an infection in her chest that is making her tired and cranky. Tina leaves the room every few minutes to check on her and the other babies but rushes back as soon as she can to enjoy the celebration.

Wilfred gives in to my father's constant requests for him to play. He lifts his violin and turns to face my father.

"*Beethoven Romance Number 2*," he announces and raises his violin to play.

I look around the room and watch the faces of the residents as they stare at Wilfred. He sways gently as his bow moves over the violin. His eyes are closed tightly and I can see his mouth moving with the bow as though he is speaking the music he is playing, as though the beauty of the music is running through him. The bow moves quicker and then he stops and sways, imagining his backing orchestra behind him. The expression on his face is so – so content – so happy. It is a pity that he can see no reason to wear this expression when he puts his violin away. He starts again, the smile on his face moving and changing as his bow moves smoothly back and forth. I look at Iren who is enraptured by the music. Her face is alight and she is sitting forward, fully awake, drinking in the beauty coming from Wilfred's violin. When he finishes, he lowers his bow and sits quickly in the corner out of view. "Bravo!" Iren says as she claps.

My father has tears in his eyes. He stands and moves towards his friend.

"That was beautiful, Wilfred. Truly beautiful!"

"Encore!" Iren shouts but Wilfred doesn't look at her as he retreats further into his pew. He doesn't enjoy attention and prefers to stay out of the limelight.

Bill picks up his guitar and starts to play again. I can see Wilfred wipe the sweat off his forehead. I watch him with interest as he glances quickly at Iren but she is looking away now, lost in the music.

My father hands Wilfred a large whiskey and he drinks it in one large gulp. I see Father sneak Martin a small one. He already has an empty glass in his hand and his eyes are glassy. I smile as he empties half his drink into the spare glass and puts it up to Jimmy's lips. Jimmy takes a large gulp but starts to cough loudly. He recovers and smiles appreciatively at his former enemy. I am glad that Martin is being kind to Jimmy and hope it will be the same tomorrow.

Penelope plays along to as many of Bill's tunes as she knows but I can see that she is happier accompanying Wilfred. His music is more to her liking. Greta bides her time and watches Penelope become more relaxed before suggesting she play one of her jazz tunes. She refuses but when everybody cheers she surrenders to their request and begins to play. As her tune nears the end, her nervousness eases only slightly. Greta is watching

Penelope's every move. I know what she is thinking. It will take time.

Victoria is enjoying the attention she is receiving and happily accepts compliments on her dress. I know that she is glad that Penelope is otherwise occupied on the other side of the room, even if her sister is anxious and not at all enjoying herself.

When Li brings in the cake Kai and Mina made, Wilfred pulls at the tie around his neck and quickly finishes another large whiskey.

As everyone sings "Happy Birthday" Mina tugs at Li's dress and shows her the photo of little Mina.

"She's beautiful, Mina. You know, we are both grandmothers now."

This makes Mina smile once again at the photo of the red-faced baby looking back at her.

When the cake is cut and distributed, the atmosphere relaxes and once again Bill pours something a little stronger into my mother's home-made punch. I know I should tell as some of the residents are not supposed to drink but I say nothing because I know that soon everybody will be happy. My father starts to sing and Martin sings along with him. Jimmy says something through the corner of his mouth and Martin pours more whiskey into his glass. My mother sees this and moves Jimmy beside her and away from Martin. He mutters something else and we don't have to understand him to know it is rude. Steve asks Aishling for a dance and I stand quickly and pretend to look out of the window. It is dark and I can see the shadow of a person standing outside our picket fence. I move closer and put my hand on the glass to shield out the light of the room. My heart misses a beat when I see it is Maria, standing there alone, her pretty face lit up by the street-light. I beckon for her to come in but she shakes her head. I go outside and she looks away from me. I take her by the hand and bring her up the steps. I open the fly-screen and she follows me inside. Sometimes words are not necessary. I sit her down and together we watch Aishling and Steve jive to one of Bill's songs. It doesn't hurt as much with Maria beside me.

Another hour passes and I finally gather the courage and ask Maria to dance. I don't mind the fact that the adults are crashing into us and stepping on our toes. It is a lovely dance and, although she doesn't smile, I sense that she is happy. I realise that I have never seen her smile and I think that I might never find out why.

When the song finishes, Bill, who is now quite drunk, salutes Wilfred and shouts for him to speak. Wilfred declines shyly and stands to open a beer from the bucket of ice in the corner of the Penance Room. He stumbles and pours some of the beer onto Martin's trousers. Martin starts cursing at him and I think, please no, don't spoil the night. Sometimes I think that even though I am the child in this house, I am the most sensible. Wilfred apologies and makes his way shakily to his chair. I can see his voice has got Iren's attention. She looks up at him as if she has never seen him before. I can see my mother purse her lips. She sniffs the punch but it is whiskey that has made Wilfred clumsy. Father tries to placate her and she softens a little. Tina takes the punch away but the damage is done. Even Iren has had too much and is talking to herself and shaking her head as if she is arguing with someone. When she suddenly starts to cry, my mother sits beside her and tries to quieten her with more food but she begins to shout for Aron and there is a collective sigh in the room. My mother tries all the usual strategies but none of them work. Tina tries to bring Iren out of the room but she will not leave. She is shouting now and I can see her false teeth move back and forward as though at any moment they will fly across the room. Bill tries to intervene and asks Iren to dance. Everyone is shocked when she slaps him across the face.

"Aron! Aron" she screams, looking around the room. Her eyes are frantic and she looks like a frightened hare. Iren has never done anything like this before and nobody knows what has provoked her. My mother apologises but Bill is not annoyed. He shrugs it off and sits beside my father who looks sadly on from his chair.

Greta tries next. She has a good way about her but Iren is shouting at everyone. My mother, Greta and Tina stand back from her. There is nothing else to do but give her medication to calm her down. Iren then turns her attention to Wilfred. She walks quicker than anyone has ever seen her move and stands in front of him.

"What you do? What you do with Aron?"

Wilfred's face reddens but instead of rushing from the room which he would usually do when confronted, he jumps from his usual hiding place and grabs Iren by her bony shoulders. He starts shaking her.

"He's dead, you foolish woman! They are all dead! Why can you not remember that? Everyone is dead!"

My father jumps up quickly and prises Wilfred's large hands off Iren's skinny frame. Wilfred looks at my father as if he doesn't know what has just happened. His mouth drops open and his face goes white.

"What di–? I'm – I – so . . ."

He runs from the room and pulls the screen door with such force that the bottom hinge comes undone. My father chases after him and Bill follows quickly. Steve offers to go too but my mother puts her hand up to signal for him to stay. Greta tries to calm Iren down but she is screaming now.

"*Aron dead? Aron dead?*" she cries as if she has completely forgotten. She falls into Aishling's arms and together she and my mother take her to her room.

Tina calls Doctor Alder and when he arrives he gives Iren an injection.

"Delayed shock," he tells us and explains that Iren is only now realising that Aron is gone forever but I cannot believe that she is this confused. Something else has caused her outburst, something in Wilfred's voice that I cannot hear. Slowly, everybody goes to bed.

I sit with Maria on the doorstep and explain that not every party ends this way, that sometimes we have happy parties. I offer to walk her home. I know young girls should not walk home alone at night. She laughs at me as if I am mad.

"Who do you think will harm me?" she says and I don't know what to say to that.

I walk inside and wander into the kitchen where Steve, Greta and my mother are talking. Tina is helping Aishling put the less able residents to bed. I feel restless and wander back into the darkened Penance Room and sit down on the pew under the stained-glass window. I have a feeling that something is going to happen, yet I don't know what. I feel tired so I stretch out on the pew under the window and wait for my father to return.

Chapter 24

I wake suddenly to the vibrations on the porch. For a moment I think it is the night train passing through my mind and I brace myself for those few seconds of fear but I soon realise that the vibration is of moving feet. I stand quickly and look out. My father and Wilfred are passing by the window. I watch as they sit down together in the side garden. Wilfred looks a little calmer as he pats my mother's pup who is jumping around excitedly. The dog never reacts this way when he sees me and I feel a little annoyed by this. I follow them outside and sit at a little distance in deep shadow. I look at my watch and see it is almost one o'clock and I wonder where they have been all this time.

I see my father hiccupping and I realise that they have been drinking in town. Wilfred looks upset. He is apologising to my father for ruining the party.

Father is shaking his red face and saying, "No, no, it's fine, Wilfred. It's fine."

"It is not fine," Wilfred says with a sad face. "I don't deserve your kindness. If you only knew. If you knew . . ."

"Then tell me," Father says. "Tell me and I promise you, I will still be your friend."

Wilfred raises his head and looks directly ahead. He doesn't look at my father who is seated beside him on the old wooden bench. Like Victoria, he looks as though he is watching a movie play in front of his eyes, a movie of his life that neither my father nor I can see.

He begins to speak.

"My father was an architect in Berlin and we were a comfortable family. I had only one sister, Elisabeth. She was seven years younger than me and we were very close. We had a happy life and lived in a nice home with our parents and my Uncle Wilfred, my mother's younger brother."

"Oh, you were named after him?" my father asks but Wilfred doesn't answer.

"He was only fifteen years older than me," he goes on, "and he was an invalid – you know, he lived in a wheelchair."

"He couldn't walk?" my father asks.

Wilfred nods. "He caught polio when he was seven and when my grandparents died, he came to live with us. He loved to wheel his chair out onto our street and take photos of children playing, of flowers in our back garden and of the birds that he used to feed. He said to me that he loved photos of beauty because there was so much ugliness in the world. If I remember him in my mind, he has that huge camera around his neck and is smiling. He was so nice to my sister and me and . . . we . . . loved him . . ."

Wilfred's eyes moisten but he continues. "Even though my father had no formal training, he was a talented pianist and taught my sister and me to play, but later I took lessons and finally went to learn to be a professional musician like my maternal grandfather. Uncle Wilfred played violin and he too taught me. Our house was always filled with music. In the evenings we would play and my mother would sing. She had a beautiful voice. My father wanted to be a musician but his father forbade it and insisted he study architecture. My father always reminded my sister and me that we were privileged and that we should be thankful for this and use what we had to benefit others. Often he worked for free, advising charitable organisations on buildings. He believed in equality, that all people were the same."

Wilfred hangs his head but I can see the expression of guilt and shame spreading across his face. It is an expression I am familiar with.

"I wish I had been half the man my father was." He sighs and continues.

"In 1936, it became compulsory to join the Hitler-Jugend. This means the Hitler Youth. I was seventeen then. For some years the Hitler-Jugend was often discussed in our home over mealtimes. My father was worried. He was concerned about what Hitler stood for and was not in favour of his plan for Germany. Some of my father's clients had been Jewish. You would think that someone like me . . . would come from a home where – where hatred was bred but this was not the truth. What I didn't tell my father was that I had been to many Hitler-Jugend meetings even before it was compulsory to do so. I think I first went just after my fourteenth birthday. Many of my friends were members and I didn't want to be different. My friend Klaus, his father paid my fees, and I used to hide my uniform at their house. I went there and I was listening. I remember one meeting when the leader said, 'Don't pay attention to what your parents say. If they don't embrace our belief and plan for Germany, they are not true Germans. They don't love Germany. They don't believe in a Germany for Germans.' The leader was just a few years older than me. He said that Jews and other minorities were taking from us. They were taking resources that should be for

Germans. He said there might not be enough to go around and that we would be called upon to stand up for our country and put things right. The uniform was really nice and I liked to wear it. I just wanted to be like my friends."

Wilfred looks away and stares at the house. I follow his eyes to see what he is seeing. The house looks ominous in the darkness with only a spill of light throwing the shape of the gum tree onto the side view of the building. Despite the gentle breeze, the air is clammy and the smell of the daytime heat hangs around like one of Wilfred's terrible memories.

"What did your father say about you attending the meetings?"

"As I've said, he only really knew that I went when it was compulsory and I was seventeen by then and already at college. Occasionally, I would challenge him and tell him what I was learning. I was beginning to think my father might be wrong. I was worried that the Jews were taking everything. Unemployment was high. Many Germans had no work and Hitler was going to put this right, you see. We were taught that Germany had been wronged in the First World War and that we were the most important race in the world. This is what we were told. You need to understand this."

Wilfred turns to look directly at my father. There is a look of pleading in his eyes.

"My father was sad at the change in me. Once, after a bad argument, he stopped talking to me. He said, 'I have lost you and not to a higher purpose. I have lost you to a poisonous mind.' From this point I moved onto the university campus. When I was leaving Uncle Wilfred caught me by the arm and said 'Remember me.' I didn't know what he meant and I remember standing in the sunlight watching him wheel his chair away from me.

I still visited home but only when my father was at work. My sister also was not so welcoming but my mother would hug me

245

and ask if I was eating properly. She never asked me why I believed in this new political movement and now I am fifty-four years old and I cannot explain it. I was a teenager who was involved in something that at first felt powerful and exciting. I was a fool. Not much more than a child. I believed, you see . . . in what I was told."

Wilfred stops speaking.

My father coughs. I know he is trying to think of the right thing to say. "You were young . . . and vulnerable. You didn't know."

"Perhaps, at least not at first," Wilfred says slowly, "but later, when I realised . . .Yes, I later understood and by then it was too late." He sighs deeply and then continues.

"When war broke out in September, I was twenty-one and I had never fully made up with my father. I had just finished my studies and was looking for a position as a violinist. I had hoped that being a member of the Naz– of the party would assist me to further my career. I had of course stopped going to meetings at my age and I managed to avoid conscription until I finished my studies. But my dream of a life in music was not to be. I was drafted and sent to Poland. It was then that the seeds of doubt were sown. I began to think, perhaps this is not all right. Perhaps we are wrong."

"You couldn't have avoided being drafted, Wilfred."

"No. I would still have had to be a solider but I could have been a reluctant one, a solider who held onto the principles taught to me by my Lutheran parents."

My father sighs and looks sadly at Wilfred. "What happened then?"

"I was wounded and was sent home. A bullet shattered my leg and I was no use for serving. I also lost some sight in my left eye – some shrapnel."

"I didn't know that," my father says.

"It was the least that could have happened to me. It was the least I deserved. I arrived back at my home and I was welcomed back by my parents who were just glad to see I was alive. I was shocked to see how ill my father looked. Soldiers had started to take Jews from their homes – some of them were my father's clients and some had been friends. I said to him, 'Father, they are just taking them to fight for Germany or perhaps to return to their own countries. Hitler is planning a new life for us all.' Despite what I had seen at war, I was still naïve – still an idiot boy. I remember my father reaching out across the table and grabbing me by my shirt. His eyes looked like they were going to jump from their sockets with rage. He said 'You stupid, stupid boy! They are going to kill them. What have they done to your brain? Why can you not see this?'"

Wilfred looks down at his shoes and runs them back and forth on the sand.

He pulls his mouth into a sharp straight line like a zip and it looks like he has finished talking.

"Can I have another drink, please?" he asks my father.

My father nods and moves slowly across the garden and into the house.

Wilfred stands and walks with heavy legs towards the white picket fence. I know he is thinking of running and I move from the shadows, ready to bang the gate to get my father's attention but he stops short and hangs his head down before returning to the bench. My father returns with two beers, unaware that Wilfred has been planning to run before he told my father the worst part of his story. He takes the cold beer from my father and drinks half the bottle before continuing.

"When I was able to walk I was sent to work in a factory in Oranienburg, many miles away from my parents' home. I had accommodation there and all day worked in a factory making ammunition. I remember thinking that this was a long way from a life in a celebrated orchestra. This is the life you will receive when you choose war over peace. I never played during those awful years. Not until I was made to play."

"Made to play?" Father asks.

"By this stage it was 1941 and I was sent to serve at Sachsenhausen. I was told that it was a work camp for political enemies but when I arrived there, I saw Jewish people, some of whom I knew, some of whom were schoolfriends that I had not even known were Jewish and people that I knew were good, law-abiding people, good Germans. I asked other soldiers what had they done? And they said, 'They are Jewish.' There were also homosexuals there and they were made to wear pink triangles. Everyone wore something to identify why they were there. The Jews of course had two yellow triangles, the Star of David. I was relieved when I was working only as a guard for political prisoners, people who were resisting Hitler's regime. The officer in charge of this section was nice to me. He knew I had been injured in Warsaw and boasted about me to his fellow officers. I still had a limp but this was much improved. Like me, he loved music although he could not play. One evening he asked me if I would play for him and sent a soldier on a long walk to the town to obtain a violin. I remember he said to him, 'I don't care where you get it or who you take it from, just get me a damn violin!' Of course I played even though I didn't want to. Music didn't sound right there. I would watch the officer's face soften and he would close his eyes as I played and occasionally I would see tears there although I pretended not to notice. I realised that he was as sad as me, as sad as everybody else there and so I thought, how is it that all of these people are doing things they don't want to do? How can this be? Of course there were evil men there, men who truly believed in all that the Führer said but I was realising that I was not among them. But even so . . . what I saw . . . awful things. Made me ashamed . . .

but still I said nothing . . . I did nothing . . . I just did as I was told."

Wilfred stops again and I can see his chin tremble. My father puts his hand on his friend's arm and the two sit in silence for a moment.

"What could you have done?" my father asks.

"I could have been a political prisoner. I could have stood up for what was right, but I didn't. I chose to be safe and I chose to keep quiet. I chose the side that was wrong.

"Numbers of prisoners were often removed from the camp. I saw many things that you could never believe. Such cruelty. Not soldier behaviour. In April of that year it was still very cold. I heard officers talking about the Soviets, that they were coming. One day, I was among those chosen to move the prisoners north and we had to walk a long way. Someone said we were putting the prisoners on boats to be freed and I remember thanking God that this war was almost at an end. A few soldiers remained behind with prisoners too sick and weak to walk.

"Some days into the journey, the officer shouted that we needed to shoot prisoners who were slowing the march down. I thought we were not far from the sea. I was sure I could smell the ocean but now I think I may have just imagined this.

"I said, 'Sir, we are not far from the ocean where boats will take them to freedom. There is no need to shoot them.' My leg hurt where I had been shot and my limp got a little worse from the low temperature so I said, 'I can walk with these prisoners. I can fall back.'

"He stood close to me and this man who loved music said: 'There are no boats you idiot! Do you think we are wasting our boats on them? We will shoot them and then drown them. You are a fool. Open your eyes. Nobody wants them. Better we put an end to their misery – so shoot them!'

"I said, 'No, I cannot. I cannot!'

"He grabbed my gun and started shooting.

"I watched as they fell, old men, women, children, defenceless people. Some of them were screaming, some trying to run into the woods, I . . . don't know what possessed me but I grabbed my gun back and I . . ."

"What did you do?" my father asks.

"I raised my rifle and I . . ."

Wilfred stops again. I can see the shame spreading across his face as he tries to replay the next scene.

"I shot the officer. The one who cried when I played for him. I shot him in the heart and he died staring at me."

My father's eyes open wide and I know he is lost for words. He doesn't have to ask Wilfred to finish the story as he wets his lips and goes on.

"I was taken to the back of the line and two soldiers were ordered to watch me until another officer decided what to do with me. I hoped they would shoot me. I wanted to die but I didn't have the courage to do this myself. They took my gun and tied my hands behind my back. As I lay on the ground I could hear them shooting some more prisoners and I wept with my face in the dirt. I wept because, you see, I believed that they were almost free and I could not understand why the officer was killing them.

"We camped in woods and two soldiers were ordered to strip me of my uniform. It was cold and I lay on the ground with prisoners with only my underwear on. That night a fellow soldier, Ralf, crept up and gave me some shoes that did not fit and some clothes. I had known him at school. The clothes were filthy and smelt and I realised he had taken them off a dead prisoner. The following morning, an officer came to me. He demanded to know who had given me the clothes. I could see Ralf's eyes imploring me not to tell so I refused to answer and he beat me. He pinned a Star of David on me and said, 'You don't

deserve a soldier's death so do not think I will not shoot you.'
He turned to the crowd of soldiers and said, 'Let the Jew-lover
see what it feels like to be one of them.' I was put in line with
the other prisoners and we started to march again. I looked
around those faces, people who thought they were on the road
to liberation and not walking towards their deaths. Over the
next few days, some of the SS abandoned us, especially those
who had actually been German criminals in Sachsenhausen and
had been conscripted to march the other prisoners northwards.
I knew something was happening because fewer and fewer
soldiers were walking with us. Before we reached Schwerin,
about thirty kilometres south of the Baltic, we were rescued by
soldiers from the Belorussian front. They thought I was a Jew
and I was freed. As I was taken to the Red Cross hospital, I saw
Gunther and Klaus, two childhood friends of mine, being led
away by Soviet soldiers. I remember them looking at me with
open mouths and I tensed but they didn't tell who I was and I
think later they must have been shot because I heard firing as I
walked with other prisoners. So you see, I have guilt for the
prisoners and guilt for my friends. I was suddenly on both sides
and on none.

"There were hundreds of prisoners at the hospital there so it
was easy to blend in and go unnoticed but the shame of not
owning up to who I really was remained with me. When they
asked, I gave my name as Wilfred Richter which was my uncle's
name and when I was well enough I returned to Berlin."

"You are not Wilfred Richter?" my father asks, amazed.

"No," Wilfred responds.

"You are not even Wilfred?"

"No," he answers, looking at the ground. "I am sorry to have
lied to you."

He takes a deep breath and resumes his story.

"When I returned to my street, even in the distance I could see that my house had been bombed. There was no roof on one side and upstairs the wall facing out onto the street was just rubble. I remember standing looking at it from a distance and wondering what exactly I had expected to find. Berlin had been heavily bombed and everywhere there were houses without roofs or walls. And yet with all this chaos there were children playing on the streets, tiny children for whom this sight would now be normal. I walked slowly towards my house which was about halfway down the curved street. Our red front door lay on its side and water was pouring from a drain onto the street. I stepped over the water and called out but there was no answer.

"In the hallway, Uncle Wilfred's wheelchair lay on its side but he was not there. I remember my heart beating faster. Wilfred could not walk at all so he could not leave without this chair but I willed my mind to ignore this and to believe that perhaps he was injured and at a hospital. Yes, I thought, an ambulance took him away and he is injured simply and I will go and collect him there. I went to my father's study and plans for new buildings were thrown around the floor, all burned or damaged by smoke, my father's precious work, now useless. I walked to the kitchen hoping someone would be there, waiting for me. My mother's kitchen table was still set with plates so I realised that they left in a hurry. I moved towards the stairs and stupidly called out even though there was hardly any roof left above the bedrooms so who could be up there? I walked around the debris on the floors and called out again, expecting them to be hiding. I sat for a while amongst the rubble and reasoned that they had fled when a bomb hit the house and that they were in a safe place. As I sat there with my head in my hands, I tried to think of all the places they might go until I heard a voice above me.

"'Carl?'

"I looked up to find Mr Esaias, my father's solicitor who was Jewish, standing over me. He looked older and his beard was now white. He put his hand out to help me up and I reached for it but in that moment, I pulled back and curled my arms about me. I could not take his hand. I . . . couldn't. I had an urge to cry but I bit inside my cheek and only when it hurt could I speak.

"'You're alive?' I said.

"'Yes, because of your father,' he replied.

"I remember opening my eyes wide and focusing on him. He offered his hand again and I took it. For a brief while I was vulnerable. I had nowhere else to go. He led me down the street towards his house but I stopped at the door and refused to enter. I thought to myself, please have some respect and don't accept his kindness. Even if my father had saved his life, I didn't deserve any repayment. He understood and gave me a look that said he knew where I had been, that he knew what I was but yet he was offering his hand to me.

"He said, 'For your father, please take shelter in my home,' and I began to cry – right there on the street. I just cried.

"He brought me in and led me to a chair. An old woman and a young boy sat in the room and watched me.

"'Homeless also with no family left,' Mr Esaias said sadly to explain who they were.

"A cup of hot soup and hard bread was put in front of me. As I drank and ate quickly I looked around the sparse room that had once been well furnished. I noticed Mr Esaias's clothes were worn and tattered.

"'I lost everything I owned in the war," he said quietly "but nothing more valuable than my family.'

"The shame I felt sitting at their table and eating the little they had was much worse than the shame I felt as a soldier. It is difficult to explain. You cannot perhaps understand. When I finished eating, Mr Esaias told me that my father had hidden him and some of his family in our house and at his office and that because of that, six of his family survived. I asked about his son Ely who I remembered playing with when we were young and our fathers were discussing business. Mr Esaias shook his head and the grief in his face cut into me. Although I felt ashamed, I asked him about my family. Mr Esaias said my father had died two years previously trying to save people who were injured in the street, even though his own house was on fire. He said that he and his son Abram buried him in the darkness. Then he told me that on the day the house was bombed, my father sent my mother and sister to stay with relatives in the country. Mr Esaias never saw them again.

"I remember swallowing some more hot soup quickly. 'They could be safe,' I said but he shook his head. He said he didn't think they could ever have got out of Berlin.

"When I asked about Uncle Wilfred, he said that he was in the house when the bomb hit and that he was taken to hospital. My father was dead so a friend went to the hospital to enquire about him but they said he was not there. Mr Esaias knew what they were doing to disabled people and in normal circumstances he would have made enquiries as my father's legal counsel but, as a Jew, he could not be seen. He arranged for another lawyer to go to the hospital but they insisted that they had never heard of Wilfred Richter.

"'I think we can also guess what became of your uncle,' Mr Esaias said.

"I remember standing up and walking towards the door. He stood in my way and asked where I was going.

"'To the hospital,' I said but he stopped me.

"'You'll be taken. It is not safe,' he said to me and sat me gently down.

"I asked him if he knew where I had been. He nodded and looked away from me. I could see an awful expression on his face and knew that helping me was a struggle for him. He asked me to stay with them. He . . ."

Wilfred's chin trembles as he quickly wipes unwelcome tears from his eyes.

"He offered me shelter. In his home. Even though he knew what I was and what I had stood for, he offered me shelter. I begged him to leave me alone. I told him that there was nothing for me now. I left and Mr Esaias followed me onto the street. 'Come back, Carl!' he shouted but I kept walking back to my house. For nine days I slept at my house among the debris. I found Uncle Wilfred's camera and slept on the floor of my father's study with it in my hands. Each day food would be left just inside the door. For the first couple of days, Mr Esaias would call out to me but I would not answer. Seeing what I had seen, I could not now bear kindness from a Jew and later I found it hard to accept kindness from anyone. When I was sure he was gone I would make my way to the front of the house and eat the food quickly.

"Over the next few days I ventured outside and took photos of war, photos of burnt-out crumbling buildings and old people lifting heavy bags that their dead children should have been carrying for them. I found some clothes in a wardrobe at the back of the house belonging to Uncle Wilfred. My own clothes were in rags so I started to wear his. One day while in my father's study, I remembered his safe. He kept it under the floorboards beneath his desk. I found the key and when I opened it I saw all of my mother's jewellery inside. There was also some money that my father kept hidden for emergencies, advice I remembered Mr Esaias giving him one evening when I was younger. Under the cash was my father and Uncle Wilfred's passports. I remember that they only used them once when they travelled by train to Prague to see a musician friend of my father's in concert. They didn't need passports I am sure but my mother was worried and insisted they take proper identification. They were only gone for three nights and my mother fretted the whole time. Uncle Wilfred talked about that trip for years. I think it was the first time he had seen a live orchestra. The wheelchair held him back from so many opportunities.

"It was when I was looking at his passport that the idea came to me. I was standing over my mother's sideboard which had a large mirror on top of it. A bird flew past the window and I looked up quickly, nervous of the sudden movement. I saw my reflection in the mirror, with Uncle's shirt on and I looked just like him. I know it will seem silly but I felt Uncle Wilfred had sent that bird past at that exact moment to show me what to do. In the days I had been in that house I never heard a single bird so I was convinced he was telling me to be his wings, to be his legs and to find my mother and sister. I knew I could not travel as myself. It would be too risky to do so but I could travel as Wilfred Richter and it didn't feel shameful to do this even though I knew it should. That night I left half of my mother's jewellery and some of the cash at Mr Esaias's door. I knocked gently and was halfway up his street by the time he cautiously opened his door. He stood on the street and I turned. I remember that in the light from his hall I could see him nodding at me. He knew that he would never see me again and that the money and gold was a peace offering, a way of trying to ease my conscience, a way of saying this might help us both to start new lives. The only things I took with me were Uncle's violin, his camera and some of the beautiful photographs that he had taken.

"My father was from Berlin but my mother was born in the countryside of Vogelsberg where she still had cousins. They were the only relatives I could think of so I began to walk the entire journey to their farm. I had only been there once as a boy and I remembered my father joking that my mother had to travel such a long way to Berlin for true love. Most nights I walked and bought my food quickly in markets along the way. Sometimes I ate only what I could find on the land and sometimes strangers would offer me a lift or shelter and food until I was rested and able to move on and all the time I took photos of my surroundings, photos of beautiful countryside and kind faces and beautiful flowers, the photos that Uncle Wilfred could have taken if he'd had use of his legs, if he'd lived. Often I wondered if that day when he asked me not to forget him, he knew this was all coming and if he was asking me to look for beauty when all you can see is despair. A few asked me who I was and where I was going and I was relieved on those occasions about how good a liar I had become and how easily the name Wilfred Richter rolled off my snake tongue.

"I lost count of the days but I think I travelled for over three weeks until I found Ida's home. She was living alone with her three teenage daughters, waiting for her husband Otto to return from the war. At first she thought I was there to give her bad news but she soon realised that I had expected to find my mother and sister there. Ida had not seen or heard from my mother and didn't even know that she had left Berlin for Vogelsberg more than two years before. So now I knew for sure that they never made it but still I believed that they were safe somewhere. I just had to keep going until I found them. When I was at Ida's home I began to dream that I would never sleep properly again until I found out where they were and brought them to safety – and this came true.

"In some ways it was nice to be with Ida. She looked a lot like my mother and I found some peace there but at night when her daughters slept she would talk about the Jews as if she was a party member and I could not stand her naïvety, just as my father could not stand it when I was a fool. Ida said that if her husband never came home she would blame all Jews for all eternity. I tried to tell her that the Jews had nothing to do with the war but that it was started by us by invading Poland but she didn't believe this of course. She believed the story that Poland attacked first. Like me, she had her brain made to believe these things from propaganda.

Ida said that if there were no Jews there would be no war and her husband would not be missing in Poland. After two weeks the atmosphere between us was not good so I left. Ida said that mother and she had another cousin in Argentina and that she heard many Germans were going there to avoid Soviet persecution."

Wilfred falls silent.

"So you went to South America?" my father prompts.

Wilfred nods.

"When I arrived in Genoa in Italy, I wrote to this cousin. From Genoa, it was easy to travel to Argentina from the port of La Spezia. On my ship, there were members of the Nazi party, people of importance that were avoiding trial. I kept to myself and with my limp people took me for a wounded soldier looking for a new life. It didn't take people long to know that I didn't want to answer questions and soon no one tried to sit at my table for meals. I didn't want to lie any more than I had to. When I arrived in Buenos Aires, my mother's cousin Alvin came to meet me even though he lived a long way away so I found out that it was a wasted journey the same day that I got off that ship. My mother had not arrived there and he had never had any contact with her. Alvin had lived in South America since before my parents were married and he had not seen my mother since she was a little girl. He was not at all racist and was married to a beautiful Argentinian woman named Estella. She was an artist as was her father. Each day I went out and took more photographs and she brought me to a friend to learn how to develop them. I remember sitting in my room looking at photos of my ruined house, of the countryside of Vogelsberg and of my cousin's daughters and it seemed clear to me that my photos represented each stage of my search for my family. Estella encouraged me to take photographs and when I began to run out of money, she organised an exhibition although I stayed far behind the scenes as she and her father sold my photographs.

After a couple of months there I had enough money to move on. Alvin knew someone who could get me a new passport so I could get to New York but I declined. I had become used to the name Wilfred and didn't want to change it. Deep down I knew Alvin didn't agree with my membership of the Nazi party but he never once asked me about the war, which I was grateful for. While Nazis were welcome and protected in South America, this was not the case in the US. I spent four years in New York and kept to myself. I sold my photographs directly to newspapers and magazines. Many of them paid me by cheque in the mail so never even met me. For those that did ask about my past, I told them that I was against Hitler's regime and had been imprisoned until freed by the Soviets in 1945, some of which was true. Once, an editor wanted to print a story, to say that I was a hero. The day he telephoned me I left my apartment, closed my bank account and took a bus to Ontario. Even with a new name, I felt someone would recognise my face, that somewhere out there were survivors from Sachsenhausen. It was not imprisonment I feared or even death, but that if I was captured I would never find my mother and sister, that I would never be able to put things right for my family."

He pauses again.

"Why did you leave Canada for Australia?" my father asks.

"It was a chance meeting on a street corner in Toronto. I was coming out of a supermarket near where I lived and I heard a voice shout 'Carl! Carl Erlichmann!' I froze on the spot. The accent was German and I thought this is it. I am found. I turned and almost put my hands in the air – then I saw Bert Fleischer, a man I grew up with and whom I had fought alongside in Poland standing on the street corner. I could smell drink off of him even though it was only lunch-time. He looked a little dirty and I found out that he was living only two blocks from my apartment. I asked how he managed to get free and he said "Ssh! This is a secret. I could ask the same of you but I won't!" so I never found out how he escaped. Bert brought me to his apartment. He was a night worker in a meat factory and was not married so he had little else to do during the day except have some beers. We talked for a few hours and I was actually pleased to see him. It was nice to have someone to speak in Deutsch to. I remembered that he didn't want to fight in the war. When I was about three hours at his place he said that he heard that my family had escaped to Australia. I dropped my drink – I was so happy! I asked him 'Where? Where are they?' Bert told me that he had contact with his mother who was still alive in Berlin and she said Mrs Erlichmann had made it to relatives in Perth with her daughter. I told him we had no relatives in Perth but he said, yes, yes, he was sure of it."

"So you came to Australia?"

"Yes, fourteen years ago now and they were not here. I found four families in Perth by the name Richter which was of course my mother's maiden name and none of them were any relation to my mother. More cautiously I looked for Erlichmanns but again, I didn't find anyone related to my family. I worked again selling my photographs and when I could I searched telephone books and local records but I never found them. In this country, I sometimes won prizes for my work from people who had no idea who I was. Each place I came to work, I looked again for Richters or Erlichmanns and then of course, I moved on to take more photos for the magazine. Then, I came to Sydney and I became ill. My . . . I had a nervous complaint."

My father raises his eyes, obviously looking for more information.

"I . . . was beginning to give up . . . I found it hard to go on. I was depressed and I . . . I tried to kill myself. I was put in a hospital for many weeks. When I was discharged I returned to my flat and realised how alone in the world I was. I took one last job. For this, I had to come to Broken Hill to take photographs of the dying mining industry for a magazine. I remember that all of the hotels were full and I came here looking for a room but something happened . . . I became so tired and I found I could not go any further. I was finished. I had enough money . . . enough to live for a long while so I just stayed. This was now eight years ago and still I am here. All that searching and, Andy, I never found them."

Wilfred starts crying, the pain of telling his story finally overcoming him. My father puts his arm around his shoulder and together they sit on the bench and stare out into the darkness.

"You tried, Wilfred. You did the best you could do."

"Not enough, Andy. It was not enough."

"What could you have done differently?" Father asks.

"I should have listened to my parents. I should have stuck to what they taught me and opposed the Nazis – I too could have been a political prisoner like those I saw in Sachsenhausen. At the very least, if I lacked the courage for that and had to join the Hitler Youth and the army, I could have stood there and thought this is not right. But for the Jews who were in that prison, I think I know . . . I have thought about it . . . for many years it has kept me awake . . . trying to see what other way there could be and I think I am only one man but if every man had said no, this is wrong, who then would the SS have to do their evil? We would have been shot but we would have died honourably. I know that I could not have saved the prisoners' lives but I could have refused to become part of their persecution. That I think was all that I could have done differently."

"But you did make the right choice in the end, Wilfred," said my father.

"It was too late, Andy. It was much too late."

My father doesn't know what to say to this. He can see that

261

Wilfred has suffered terribly and that his mind is so tortured that he can no longer think straight. He sighs and puts out his hand to Wilfred and after a few seconds, Wilfred shyly takes it.

"You are the first person I have ever told this to and I am no longer afraid," said Wilfred. "Tell who I am if you wish. I cannot be hurt more than I have hurt others."

"You realise your mother and sister are dead, Wilfred?" my father asks.

Wilfred doesn't answer but simply nods, his face lowered toward the ground.

"I am not going to tell anyone, Wilfred. I think you have suffered enough and what good will it do?"

Wilfred stops and turns to my father. I move quickly to see his words.

"Do you . . . think . . ." but he cannot finish his question.

My father shakes his head and puts his hand on Wilfred's shoulder. "I will always be your friend, Wilfred. You did terrible things in desperate times. I know that faced with the same situation now, you would do the right thing."

As my father and Wilfred walk slowly into the house, I can see that Wilfred is thinking about Father's words.

Wilfred eases the screen door open to avoid waking anyone up. The house is still in darkness but when I see my father run upstairs two steps at a time, I know something is wrong. I follow next and Wilfred is directly behind me. When he realises that it is Iren who is shouting, he lurks in his own doorway and watches my mother and father talking outside her room.

"Where have you been?" my mother asks. She looks tired and angry. "Iren's been calling for Aron for most of the night. Her row with Wilfred seems to have reminded her of the past."

I leave my father to explain and go into Iren's room. She is more distressed than I have ever seen her. She is speaking French with some English in between and then some other words I don't understand but I understand enough to know that she is asking to die. I leave quickly and watch my parents talking.

"I wish God would take the poor woman out of her misery," my mother says. She looks like she is about to cry and my father takes her in his arms.

"There is no God. There is only us," Wilfred says as he eases the rest of his large frame into his room and closes his door.

My mother gives Iren another tablet and I sit with her as Iren's breathing eases and her eyes gently close. My mother smooths her hair as she drifts off.

When I finally get to bed, I dream of Wilfred marching toward Iren's room in his soldier's uniform. When he gets to her door, he looks around to see if anyone is watching. In my dream I have a voice and I shout "No, Wilfred! I am the guardian of souls and you shall not kill!" I shout again in my dream and try to wake myself up but I am tired and I don't open my eyes until the sunlight has streaked across my ceiling telling me that it is at least ten o'clock. When I come out of my room I immediately sense the strange atmosphere. I walk down the hallway to where my mother and Greta are talking and realise that Iren is dead and Wilfred is gone.

Chapter 25

Later that morning, I watch as Doctor Alder tells my mother that poor Iren's heart finally gave up fighting. I go back up to her room and look at her purple skin and blue lips. Doctor Alder signs the death certificate and sympathises with Mr Berman who looks even more lost than he did when Aron died. When Mr Berman leaves to organise Iren's funeral, my mother comes into the office and sits wearily beside my father who has been on the phone all morning frantically searching for Wilfred. She strokes Father's wild hair and he calms slightly.

"You don't think Wilfred did anything to Iren?" he asks nervously.

Mother shakes her head. "Of course not. He wouldn't do that, Andy."

I have nothing to add. I keep telling myself it was only a dream, just a dream.

Father leans forward and places his chin in his freckled hands. "It's just that he said something last night. He told me everything and at the end . . . he said he should have put the Jews out of their misery by shooting them to save them from cruel deaths.

When we came in last night, you said you wished God would take Iren to put her out of her misery. It just seems . . . strange that she would then die."

My mother stares hard at my father. "She was dying, Andy. She had a heart condition. When my father was a minister I saw lots of sick people asking to die. Sometimes God answers them and takes them on their journey."

Father jumps up quickly.

"Where are you going?" Mother asks.

"To the train station."

I run alongside Father as quickly as my bad foot will allow and climb into his truck as he starts the engine. For the entire journey, he taps the steering wheel nervously and twice shouts at motorists who don't move quickly enough when the traffic lights change. We pass Maria's house and she is standing on the corner in the same white dress. I wave and she waves back at me. Her mouth is open in an O shape as though she never expected to see me driving by. She looks up at the orange lights on top of my father's truck and begins to chase after us, waving her hands frantically. Sometimes I worry that Maria is mad but as I have no other friends, especially kids who don't care about my deafness or my foot, I try my best to ignore her strange behaviour. As we turn the corner I sign to her that I will see her later but she just stares back with an open mouth and sad expression.

When my father gets into the station I have trouble catching up with him. He doesn't lock the truck but runs straight in to the ticket desk to ask if Wilfred has been there. The young girl shrugs her shoulders and tells him lots of people bought train tickets and that she only has names of people who paid by credit card. My father's shoulders slump. He doesn't think Wilfred would have a credit card as he keeps a large amount of cash in his room – he doubts that he even had a bank account. I follow my father on foot to the bus station but it is the same story there.

Lastly, we check the car rental service. My father knows the manager and asks if a German man hired a car that morning. Mr Palin laughs and says, "I'd remember a Kraut hiring a car for sure," but my father ignores his racist comment and smiles weakly at him as he leafs through the paperwork. He knows that Mr Palin doesn't mean any malice and sees no harm in using these terms.

"Moll?" Mr Palin then shouts inside to a woman who is making coffee in the back. "You hire a car to a German?"

Moll comes out wiping her hands. She smiles at my father and throws a sharp glance at her husband.

"No, dear, but I did hire a car to a lovely Polish man. A tourist."

"Did he say he was Polish?" father asks.

"No but he sounded Polish."

My father raises his eyebrows at her and she laughs nervously.

"Well, they all sound the same, don't they?" she says earnestly.

"What did he look like?" father asks impatiently.

"Em . . . he was . . . middle-aged . . . very tall . . . a good-looking sort. Hired it for a week to do some sightseeing. His name was . . . it should be here somewhere . . ." She leafs through the same pile of papers as her husband. "There – Carl – Carl Erlichmann. Has – has he done something wrong?"

Father flushes. I know that he is thinking it is a bad sign that Wilfred has used his real name.

"No! Em . . . no . . . he was staying with us at the boarding house and he forgot something . . . that's all. Did he say what way he was heading? Maybe I could catch up with him?"

Moll shakes her head, her light brown ringlets making her look like a little girl. My father begins to sweat. He knows that Wilfred could have gone in any direction so there would be no point following him into the broad expanse of the outback.

"When he brings the car back will you tell him I really need to see him?"

"No problem, I love your accent," Moll says, smiling at my father the same way my mother does.

When we leave the rental office, my father and I walk slowly back to the truck in silence. Father thumps the steering wheel.

"What has he done?" he asks as he turns the truck around. I am relieved when he takes a different route home as I don't want to see the sad expression on Maria's face again.

When we arrive back at the house, Steve has arrived and is dismayed that Wilfred has gone and disappointed that he will not hear his story.

"You mean his confession?" my father says and I know he is being sarcastic.

Steve is not put out and replies, "Whatever way you want to see it," and walks away.

A few moments later Father follows Steve out onto the porch and I watch through the window of the Penance Room as he apologises to Steve who shakes his hand warmly. Mother invites them inside but Steve stays a while longer on the porch with Aishling. He hands her a letter and, although I strain my neck, I cannot see what is written in it. I think it must be good news as Aishling reads it and smiles warmly at Steve.

"You went to all that trouble for me?" she asks.

"It was no trouble. Being an ex-member I was in a position to call in a few favours," he jokes. "You said he went to South America so I started there. I wrote to the bishop telling him your story. I – I didn't think you'd mind?"

Aishling shook her head.

"It seems you didn't do him any harm after all. Father Kearns went on to establish three orphanages in the poorest parts of Columbia. He's a bit of a national hero there. Maybe if he hadn't been blamed for . . . well, they wouldn't have shipped him off there and he'd be freezing in some old presbytery on some windswept island off the coast of Ireland!"

Aishling laughs and I have never seen her look so genuinely

happy. "A true priest," she says, more to herself than to Steve as she reads the letter quickly again.

"There's an address on the top, should you ever wish to make contact." Then he adds, "He said there are no hard feelings."

Aishling shakes her head slowly. She doesn't need to contact him. Peter Kearns has forgiven her and that was all she needed and she has forgiven her parents for turning their backs on her. She has even come to understand, if not agree with, their actions. Steve has brought a feeling of peace to her life and to the lives of some of the residents also. She puts the letter back into its envelope and smiles shyly at him. I know she hates goodbyes. I saw her telling my mother once that from as far back as she could remember, she cried when visiting aunts and uncles were returning to America or England, even the ones she hardly knew.

"So, where are you going to next?" she asks. Her eyes are beginning to water and she doesn't want him to see her cry. Inside she is still a vulnerable girl and I can see that my mother is right. Aishling gets hurt easily.

"Back to Bourke first, then Dubbo. I've a lot of interviews set up there so that'll take a few weeks. I . . . I might come back to Broken Hill then for a bit before I finish the study. I was hoping I could see you . . . if you were interested?"

Aishling's eyes light up but at the same time she bites down on her lower lip. I wonder if she is thinking of what her parents would say about her seeing an ex-Catholic priest. Steve, like me, seems to know what people are thinking, sometimes even before they do.

"I'm not a priest any more," he said, his expression turning more serious.

Aishling swallows. "Doctor Alder said that when we get old, we are least in a position to do anything about our regrets," she says suddenly.

Steve nods. "He's right."

"Then I'd love to see you when you come back."

Steve leans in and kisses her on the cheek. I know she is disappointed. I know she is hoping for the type of kiss you see in movies. He laughs and kisses her again, this time more like how my parents kiss after a party.

"Are you going to answer the phone?" Steve asks Aishling.

Aishling nods but I know she wishes someone else would answer it.

She runs inside, leaving Steve alone on the porch. He looks in the window at me as if he knew I was there all along and I tense, hoping he is not going to tease me about being in love with Aishling.

"Christopher," he says, making sure he has my full attention. "When I come back, you and I need to have a little talk."

I jump back from the window and go to my room. I am not accustomed to people talking directly to me and because I already know what Steve wants to talk to me about, I feel cold and shaky and not at all in the humour for his farewell party. I stay in my room for hours until I feel the screen door slam. Hoping it is Steve leaving I sneak downstairs but see it is Kora standing in the hallway smiling at my mother. I run down as quickly as my foot will allow as I have not seen much of my aunt since Jeff's accident and I miss her.

I move swiftly down the hallway as my mother hugs her adopted sister. It is an unusual sight as Kora doesn't really like affection.

"Married! When? Oh Kora. I'm so happy!" my mother says before bursting into tears.

"Why wait? I'm not getting any younger. I thought I'd marry on Father's anniversary," Kora says, straightening out her smile a little and returning to her somewhat stiff way.

"But – that's – well – only – less than a month away!"

"There's hardly much planning. There aren't many to invite. I think it would be too far for Jeff's sisters to come. I was thinking of marrying here, in the lounge room. That way Jimmy can attend and, well . . . I'll feel nearer to Father with his pews here and all."

Mother smiles and starts to cry again. "Oh, Kora, he would have loved to have given you away! He'd be so proud!"

My mother tries to hug Kora again but the moment has passed and she is once again her sullen, abrasive self. I can see that there is something on her mind.

"I wish . . . I wish my mother could have seen me get married. It would have been nice. Don't mean to hurt you, Emma. You've been a good sister to me, I know that, but somewhere out there I might have a mother who loves me and who could be looking for me."

My mother bites her lip. Kora and her father had well and truly exhausted all avenues looking for her mother. She doesn't know what to say so instead asks the question both she and I are dying to ask.

"How do you think Jimmy will take the news?"

I watch as Kora tenses up. She shrugs then to pretend she doesn't care how her future father-in-law will react.

"I don't really care any more. He can get used to it. I'm through letting other people make decisions for me."

Now it my mother's turn to tense but she decides not to be drawn into Kora's anger towards their parents.

"Well, whatever kind of wedding you want, I'm happy for you," my mother says, smiling through watery eyes.

"Well, what have I missed?" Kora asks, keen to change the subject. "Is everybody okay?"

My mother decides not to tell Kora about Iren or Wilfred just yet and grabs her sister by the hand, leading her into the dining room where the residents, who are as yet unaware of what happened last night, are saying their goodbyes to Steve. Kai and Mina have made a cake for the occasion. Everybody crowds around Kora and wishes her well and she smiles awkwardly. My father kisses her and she tells him off for not shaving. He would normally laugh at Kora's cranky ways but there is a faraway look in his eye. I know he is worried about Wilfred and will not rest easy until he is back with us. I walk out the front door and bang the screen door. I am not often angry but I feel threatened by something in Steve's words. I feel as if he doesn't want me here and I find myself thinking back to his conversation with Aishling out in the garden. I remember him saying that I would be better off away from here and I am suddenly worried that he is planning to send me away. I decide to tell Maria about it and make my way to her house but before I reach her corner, she jumps out on me and scratches my face.

"Why did you not stop with your fire engine?" she cries. Spit from her mouth lands on my face and I can feel it, hot and wet.

I sign to her, "What fire engine?" and she understands.

"You went by in a fire engine when I needed it. You didn't come. I was waiting. I waited and waited for someone to put out the fire!" She bursts into tears and then straightens herself up suddenly. I look over at Maria's grandfather's house and see no evidence that there has been a fire.

"It's not a fire engine," I sign but she is not convinced.

I take out my notepad and write her a note. *"The lights on top of the truck are there because father works in the mine. They're warning lights."*

"Liar!" she says, unconvinced.

"No!" I sign. *"No, Maria. It is not a fire engine. There is no fire."*

But she turns and runs away from me. I follow her and find her sitting outside her old house, crying. I put my arm around her and try to comfort her but she pulls away. I raise her face up with my hand until she looks at my mouth and I use words that I cannot hear. She is almost the only person I will do this for.

"I am your friend and, Maria, there is no fire. Why do you think this? Is – is there something wrong with you? You can tell me anything. I will not be shocked. I promise."

271

Maria looks at me as if I am the one who is mad. "You don't get it, do you, Christopher? Don't you understand what's going on?"

I sign "No. I don't."

I am unwilling to degrade myself with my terrible deaf voice for her a second time. I get up and stand over her.

"I think Steve doesn't want me at the house. I think he prefers for me to go to a special school," I sign and she laughs out loud.

"School? You're an idiot. What's the point in you going to school?"

"Maria, please listen to me. I don't want things to change."

"Welcome to my world," she says before disappearing into her grandfather's house.

As I walk towards home, I feel sudden tears welling in my eyes and hope that I have not lost her. I raise my hand and feel the long narrow scratch along my right cheek. The cost of being Maria's friend is rising and, while I am unsure if I will be able to afford it much longer, the cost of loneliness is much higher.

When I arrive home, Father is talking to Bill in the office about Wilfred because he is a policeman and might know how to find Wilfred before he hurts himself. His wife is working in the local hospital so he has his naughty son with him that I don't want to see. I briefly look into the room and sneak out again.

I go into the Penance Room and find everybody subdued. Mother has just told them about Iren, and Victoria and Penelope are sniffing into white pressed handkerchiefs. Mina also looks sad and Martin is saying, "Poor soul, God bless her" now and then, even though he was usually the one who shouted at her the loudest when she started screaming for Aron. Jimmy's head is down and Father Hayes is smiling into thin air and talking to himself. When Jeff arrives to talk to his father about his marriage to Kora, Mother decides that everybody needs cheering up and asks Tina to help her move everyone into the dining room for leftover cake and Li's fresh coffee. As we sit around the table, I can see my mother is dying to know how Jimmy is taking the news of his son's impending marriage but she continues to make small talk with the residents about the weather and of course, the arrangements for Iren's funeral tomorrow. Bill has offered to drive as many of the residents to the funeral as he can and anyone else who wants to go can take a lift in my mother's small car or Tina's Ford Falcon. When my mother hears the Penance Room door closing, she jumps up and meets Jeff coming out the door all red-faced. She fears the worst and I see her swallow hard.

"Well?"

Jeff shakes his head. I can see the long red scar on his forehead from the accident and a deep indent in his cheek.

"I don't know what to make of it. He went real quiet. I was expecting him to go on a rant but he didn't. He just sat there and said nothing. Not sure I'd understand his speech now anyway but it's strange. I – I don't know if it's a good or bad sign."

"Let's take it as a good sign. He could see how much Kora cared for you during your recovery so maybe he's come around?"

Jeff looks doubtful as he opens the front door with his good arm.

"Looks like rain," he says, looking towards the thundery red sky and sniffing the hot air.

"Been listening to that for weeks now, mate!" my mother says laughing. "And not a drop. Think it'll never happen. It's been a strange summer, hasn't it? Nowhere near as many storms really."

Jeff agrees and puts his hat squarely on his large head.

"Jeff, I'm really glad you're marrying my sister. It'll be nice to be family. I know you'll be good to her."

Jeff smiles shyly. "I'll certainly try to make her happy, Emma," he says as he makes his way down the wooden steps of the porch.

Bill comes out of the office and briefly fills my mother in on the plans he has for finding Wilfred.

"I'm going to phone my mates at the nearest stations and ask 'em to look out for him. Look, I know he's a seasoned outback traveller, but he's got to stop somewhere for supplies, so sooner or later someone will see him. Don't worry."

My mother closes the door on Bill and his unwelcome son, and goes about turning off all of the lights to prepare for bed. Aishling comes bounding down the stairs smiling and ready for work. My mother laughs.

"Oh, young love!" she jokes as she helps Aishling get the residents to bed.

When Martin is settled in his room I go inside and sit on the hard wooden chair beside his window, ready for the nightmares to begin.

Chapter 26

Just as Jeff predicted, at about one in the morning it begins to rain heavily. Fork lightning lights up my room and I wake in my own bed wondering how I got here. The last thing I remember is sitting in Martin's room watching him doze off. I get out of bed and rub my foot which is throbbing. I wonder if the rain is causing this as I stretch and pull at the stump, trying to ease the discomfort. I briefly wish that I had woken after three when my train has passed through my mind and I can return to my dreams. I feel the walls of the house shake from the thunder and I know it will be useless to try to return to sleep so I get up and walk past Aishling's desk. She is not there so I creep along the dark hallway trying to find her. I look in Iren's room. She is laid out on her bed and Mr Berman is sitting quietly beside her. His wife is with him. I have never met her before but I notice that she has a kind face with deep lines around her brown eyes that tell me she has laughed a lot. Aishling is also there although it doesn't look like there is any work for her to do. She is sitting by the end of the bed, staring into space. I look at Iren and she looks younger and untroubled. Her face doesn't look as thin and the heavy lines that made her look so old appear to have faded. There is a faint smile on her lips and I wonder if she died thinking of something good, something like Aron and the love they had for each other that lasted a lifetime. I have not seen her spirit around so I hope she is with him now and will not hang around here looking for him or for food which is the second thing she used to ask for. I go back out into the hallway and make my way to Martin's room. On my way, I check Wilfred's room hoping that he has returned and is safe but the room is the same way he left it. His beautiful photographs still adorn the walls and the album of sad photographs is most likely still hidden under his bed. On the wall above the bed there is a large photo of Uluru at sunset. The rock looks like it is on fire with deep red and orange hues dancing above it. On the far wall, photographs of thundering waterfalls and never-ending desert are hung on either side of a black and white photograph of Wilfred's mother and sister with old-fashioned hairstyles and pretty floral dresses. Sometimes, when Wilfred is out, I go in and take his sad album out. The black and white photographs are mostly of post-war Berlin with dirty children and blown-up houses. They are stark and it is impossible to avoid the sadness that rises up from the pages. I feel a need to look at those photos again and place my hand under the bed but find that it is gone. I immediately understand what this means. Wilfred has given up on finding beauty and has taken only his bad memories with him.

I walk slowly and sadly to Martin's room. I am not surprised to find him awake and cowering in the corner, silently, lest he annoy the spirits that only he can see. I sit on his bed and he looks at me.

"Where'd ya go?" he asks. There is a long crease in his forehead so I know he is annoyed with me.

I have no answer for him so I shrug which my mother says is

rude. I am afraid to ask him who is there. I know he will get annoyed if I cannot see his tormentors.

"Ya afraid of lightning, boy?" he asks.

I shake my head. I am afraid of very little. Just angry ghosts and dogs.

"We had a nag when I was young. Good worker but Christ, she was afraid of lightning storms. She'd manage to get free and run off out into the storm. Stupid horse!"

Martin stops talking but I can see his tongue moving back and forth in his mouth.

I take out my notebook.

"Is that the horse that died in the fire?" I write.

Martin reddens and starts to cough. I notice that he always coughs when he is nervous. He nods but doesn't answer. He doesn't want to talk about it.

I pull back his covers and signal for him to get back into bed. The rain has made the house feel cold and I don't want him to become ill. He still has work to do.

"You'll stay?" he asks.

I sign "Yes."

I sit on the hard wooden chair and watch him sleep for the second time that night and when I doze off I dream of speeding trains, frightened horses and fires that I cannot put out. In my dream I am driving a fire engine and suddenly Maria is there waving at me and begging me to save her. I see her grandfather running towards me and saying "Hurry, hurry!" When I wake he is gone and so is Maria. I decide that I will find her tomorrow and make my peace with her.

I shiver and decide to take a blanket from Martin's wardrobe. The noise wakes him and he looks up, an expression of fear spreading across his grey face. I sign that it is okay and he lies back down. I watch his breathing ease as his chest rises and falls gently under his thin blue pyjamas. I throw the blanket on the floor and lie down beneath his window watching the beautiful lightning. I try to imagine Wilfred sleeping in a car or a roadhouse and I say in my mind, "Look up, Wilfred, look at this thing of beauty" but he shuts his eyes tight and turns his back to me as though he no longer believes in beauty any more. When I fall asleep I see him walking through the desert. The sun is beating down on him. His lips are chapped and he is lost and alone. I look up at the position of sun and notice that he is walking away from home. I try to tell him and I even use my voice, saying "Turn around, Wilfred. Come back to us!" but he doesn't seem to hear me and keeps walking further into the desert.

The following morning, the residents eat in silence as we prepare for Iren's funeral. All of the more mobile residents want to go and we fill three cars with Jimmy, Martin, Penelope, Victoria and Mina. Aishling stays behind and agrees to watch the babies until Greta returns to take over. Mr Berman will conduct the ceremony like he did at Aron's funeral.

The rain has not stopped so Jimmy remains in the car with Martin. Neither of the men can afford to get wet but Jeff has parked the car as close to the ceremony as possible so that they get to say their goodbyes. As Mr Berman chants words that I cannot follow, I turn my eyes towards Jeff's car and can see Martin and Jimmy talking. It is hard to know how much of Jimmy's speech Martin can understand but he is nodding and answering and it is good to see them getting along. I start to laugh when I see Martin lift something awkwardly from his pocket. It is a small bottle of whiskey that his daughter must have brought in for him, despite my mother asking her not to. Martin takes a big gulp and then holds the bottle up to Jimmy's lips. Jimmy drinks, they both cough and my mother turns to check on them. Greta makes her way toward the car to make sure that they are all right and there is panic between the two men as they try to hide the bottle in time. But Greta sees it and half smiles.

"Maybe leave that for later," she winks.

Jimmy's expression changes and I see him staring to his far left and away from the Jewish section of the cemetery. I follow his eyes and see that he is looking at his wife's headstone. I walk around to the high grey stone and read her name: "*Laura Young, beloved wife of James.*"

He mouths something to Martin who squints at his old nemesis, as if this will help him understand what he is saying.

"You didn't get along? That what you said?"

Jimmy nods. There are tears in his eyes.

"Christ, join the club. Didn't get along with mine either. Bloody women. Can't please them," Martin says, trying to lighten the atmosphere.

I follow Jimmy's eyes back to the group, who are shivering in the heavy rain. He watches as Jeff takes his heavy jacket off and throws it around Kora's shoulders to keep her warm. She tries to refuse it but when he insists she holds her umbrella up higher to cover his head and back. Jimmy stares at this mutual act of love and I can see it is something he is not accustomed to. He moves his leathery tongue around his mouth and mutters something that even Martin doesn't catch. The funeral ends and everyone slowly goes back to the cars for the drive home.

When we get home, Li has an early lunch ready and we all sit down to eat. My father sneaks into the office to phone Bill. This is Wilfred's second day away from home and I know my father is thinking the worst. When he comes in and takes his seat, he looks disappointed so I know there is no news. As lunch finishes, Mr Berman asks my mother if he can speak to her and my father in private. They return to the office and sit down. I move out to the porch and sneak a look in the window.

Mr Berman looks sad. "You know, it's like losing my mother," he says.

My mother nods and touches his arm. "I know, David. She felt the same way about you."

Mr Berman coughs and shifts on his seat. "Anyway, it is business I wish to discuss," he says. He is slightly embarrassed and is trying to avoid their sympathy. "You remember Mrs Levi?"

"Yes," my mother and father said simultaneously.

"She wasn't with us long," my mother continues. "About a year or so. It must be well, fifteen years ago, more? We hadn't been open very long."

"She was a widow with no family," Mr Berman reminded my mother. "She came to Broken Hill to find her brother but she did not know he had been ill and had already died."

My mother is nodding. Mrs Levi's story is slowly coming back to her.

"When she became frail, you took her in. She had no money but this didn't worry you. The local Jewish group asked Aron and Iren to visit her."

"Yes." My mother is smiling now. "That's when I first met them," she replies. "But the state did pay some of her costs," she adds. My mother was raised to be humble and she doesn't like to be praised.

"Even so, it didn't cover her care. Iren and Aron were so impressed with your kindness that they asked me to ensure they came to live here if they ever needed nursing care."

Tears form in my mother's eyes. "They used to buy all of Mrs Levi's clothes, I remember. She was a sweet lady. I'm glad they felt that they would be well cared for here."

"So, the reason I ask to speak with you and Andy is for the Kleins' will. As you know, I was also their solicitor as well as their friend. I don't have the paperwork with me today and tomorrow I have to travel to Sydney for business but I thought you should know that Aron and Iren remembered you very well in their will."

"They did?" my father asks surprised. "We certainly didn't expect that."

"Nor want that," my mother adds.

"Nevertheless, they were aware that your building required some work and so they instructed me that when their smaller bequeaths were settled, the rest of their assets should go to you."

"The rest of their assets?" Father asks.

"Yes, it is a rough figure but I think it will be approximately $120,000."

Mother looks at Father and their eyes open wide. I know my mother fleetingly thinks of en suite bathrooms and a lift for Jimmy who since his last stroke has had to move into the babies' room downstairs, but she shakes her head to dispel these thoughts.

"We can't take it, David. We're so – so very grateful that they were so happy here but we just cannot. It's too much. What – what about you? You were the closest person to them. Aren't you disappointed?"

"Not at all. I have known their wishes for many years now. They left me their house in the town which I have many happy memories of, and of course Aron and Iren paid for me to go to university. My uncle would not have had such money. They gave me a start in life that I would not otherwise have had. My work has made me a wealthy man. I don't need more than this. They taught me to know what was important: my family and my community. What they wanted was to ensure this house lived on and that there was somewhere the people in this town could come when they needed help most, all people, from any country and any religion. Those were their words."

My father looks out the window and I know he is thinking of Wilfred.

"I ask that you please accept their gift. It would mean that at least one of their dreams came true," Mr Berman says, rising from his chair.

"We'll talk about it," my father says quickly, opening the door and letting Mr Berman out.

As his wife joins him in the hallway, Mr Berman shakes hands with my mother and father. He appears nervous. His mouth is dry and he licks his lips several times to moisten them. He walks into the Penance Room and begins to shake hands with all of the residents. He wishes each one health and happiness and turns to my mother. There is an expression on his face that I cannot yet read. It is as if there is something that he needs to do, something he is not looking forward to.

"The German man. He is not here?"

My father moves forward and stands in front of my mother, anxious to prevent her from telling David what has happened.

"Wilfred's gone away for a while. We expect him back soon," he says.

I can see my mother's forehead crease behind him and know she is annoyed that Father is lying.

Mr Berman looks both relieved and disappointed. He nods and moves to the door. He starts to say something but changes his mind. My father thinks that Mr Berman is looking for Wilfred. I watch as he moves his mouth, trying to form his words before he says it out loud. There is something that he has to ask.

"David, what camp were you at?"

Mr Berman freezes at the mention of the word "camp". He licks his lips again, takes a deep breath and drops his head.

"I was at Sachsenhausen."

"So you knew Wilfred there. You saw him there?" he asks.

"Yes," he says through tightly closed teeth.

"And you didn't say anything? You've been coming here for years and you kept silent?"

"As I said, I learnt much from Aron and Iren. I remember him. He was not a bad man. Just young. Very young. And I was just a boy." He opens the door and ushers his wife out in front of him. He closes the door quickly to prevent my mother or father asking him more questions about a time in his life that he has worked hard to forget.

I watch him from the Penance Room window as he stands on our porch and places his black hat on his head. His wife touches his face gently. I can see his chin quivering as he takes her arm and walks slowly out our gate and onto the street. He turns left and I can no longer see his face. He quickens his step and they climb the street until they are almost at the top of the hill. I watch him stop abruptly. His wife turns to him and places her hands on his shoulders. He leans on a fence and she moves her arms around him. I know by the movement of his shoulders that he is crying and that the loss of Aron and Iren is for him like losing his parents all over again. I move back from the window and I know that it will be too painful for him ever to come back here and that I will never see him again.

I sit down on a pew and watch the remaining residents. The rain stops suddenly and the sun throws brilliant rays of light through the stained glass. I watch as it shimmers across the wooden floor. Penelope is reading her music sheets although she has not touched the piano since the party. Victoria is reading a romance novel and Mina is rereading the letter Hope sent her. I notice that each time she finishes reading the letter, she looks closely at the photo of Hope's daughter Mina and then reads the letter again. Kai comes in and asks for her help making some pastry and she rises happily. I watch as he moves her frame around to help her. She smiles appreciatively.

My mother says, "Good boy. Kai, you're a real gentleman," and I feel slightly jealous at the attention she is giving him.

Father Hayes is praying again and I realise that it will only be a few weeks before his old love arrives from America. Martin is reading a newspaper. He is seated beside Jimmy and everybody has noticed how close the two are becoming. Kora is standing at the door with Jeff. They are going for a walk before Kora starts her evening shift with my mother. Jimmy murmurs something and Jeff looks in but he doesn't understand what his father said.

"Christ," Martin says, annoyed, "don't know why you don't bloody understand him. It's plain as day, mate. He said, 'Bye, Kora'."

My mother looks crossly at Martin. She doesn't like people taking God's name in vain. Jeff smiles and tips his hat at his father. Jimmy nods. It is the best he can do for now.

Martin laughs and says, "Good on ya, mate! Ya made that boy of yours smile, sour puss that he is an' all!" which finally makes Jimmy laugh also. Later, I watch my mother telling Greta about Jimmy's attempts to be polite to Kora. Greta laughs and throws her head back, revealing even more gold teeth than I had previously noticed. They are sitting together in the dining room having a coffee. The babies are either asleep or staring into space and the other residents are as usual sitting in the Penance Room.

"How'd you ever come to be sisters? I assume one of you is adopted" Greta asks, laughing.

I can see why Penelope and Victoria get on so well with her. Greta makes a joke out of everything which puts the other person at ease. My mother sighs and runs her finger around the top of her coffee cup.

"My father was working as a minister at the orphanage Kora was in. She was one of the thousands of mixed race and full-blood Aboriginals taken from their parents at that time. Anyway, all Father found out about Kora was that her father was a white drifter from England and there was no information about her mother. No name, no address. Kora was only about three when she was taken there so she had no memory of where she lived or what her mother's name was. When I was around eight, Father got another transfer and he decided to take Kora with us. We had become good friends and he wanted to give her a normal life. She – she resents this. She doesn't say much but I know she didn't want to go, that she thought she was being taken just as a playmate for me, but that wasn't true. My mother couldn't have any more children after I was born so I was an only child, but it wasn't that. My parents really did love Kora. I don't blame her thinking that though. She asked me once how I would feel walking around with blackfella parents and a black sister. I never saw it that way. I never saw her skin colour. She was just my sister. She said that she wished we had left her there where there were other Aboriginal kids. She felt she belonged with them, that they were her people and that at least her mother would know where to find her.

"When she was a teenager, Father and Kora spent hours writing to government departments all over New South Wales trying to find out who she was but they never came up with anything. My father died regretting his work with the Aboriginal community. It took him years to realise that what they were doing was so wrong. Some of the kids were being neglected by their parents. That happens in any race so of course those kids needed to be taken into care but, for the majority of them, the reason for taking them was to make them like the rest of us and when my father was old, this haunted him and in his mind undid all the good he had done. I think it quickened his end. He saw Kora suffering so much. As a teenager she was defiant and yet at the same time lacked confidence. She was bright but wouldn't go on further at school. She backed off as soon as anyone said anything bad to her.

"Well, you know she liked Jeff since they were teenagers but as soon as Jimmy put his foot down, Jeff crumbled and Kora ran for cover and that's where she stayed. Till now, that is. I'm so glad she's marrying Jeff. I just wish she could have been reunited with her mother. I doubt she's still alive now. We have no idea how old she was when she had Kora, but believe me, we searched everywhere we could think of." My mother takes another sip of her coffee and stares sadly across the dining table.

Greta looks up. "Maybe you weren't looking in the right places?"

"What do you mean?"

"Well, you said your father and Kora wrote to government departments. Doesn't sound like the sort of place someone like Kora's mother would go for help. She'd have no reason to trust them. Not when it was them that took 'er daughter away."

"Well, where else is there to go?" my mother asks, confused.

"What about the newspapers or local radio? You could put an ad in all the local papers – or, even better, in the national ones."

My mother lets out an embarrassed laugh and puts her hands up to her cheeks. "Saying what – is this your long lost daughter? No – it seems – well, undignified. Kora would kill me. She's very proud and . . . can be cranky . . ." My mother doesn't like to say anything bad about people, especially her sister.

"It wouldn't have to be like that. It could be small. Maybe you could give them a photo of Kora as a little girl. If you found Kora's mother, wouldn't it be worth her getting angry with you?"

My mother shakes her head. She thinks this conversation has gone too far.

Greta gets the message and changes the subject. She rises from the table and washes both cups, anxious not to annoy Mina who still hasn't quite worked out that she is not in charge. As my mother goes about her duties, I can see she is thinking about what Greta has said. Later, I see her watching her sister through the window of the Penance Room. Kora has brought

Aiden into the garden for some air. Kora smiles at the old priest as she lifts my mother's pup up and places him in his lap. She sits beside him on the bench holding the other pup. She has started to bring her dog with her to work each day, leaving me to contend with not one but two dogs that are never happy to see me. When the pup squirms to get down, Kora's smile fades. She glances at her engagement ring in the bright sunlight and that faraway look returns to her deep brown eyes. My mother opens the window.

"You coming in for dinner?" she asks.

Kora snaps back. "I'll be there when I'm good and ready."

My mother sighs as she closes the window. I move toward my mother to hug her. I don't like to see anyone hurting her but she moves quickly from the window and goes into the kitchen to help Li.

I open the screen door just as Kora is coming in. The two dogs are chasing after her as she tries to help Aiden raise his foot over the threshold. The dogs stop in their tracks and start to growl at me. Kora shouts to quieten them and they sit down obediently, their long pink tongues hanging loosely over large teeth. I tense and inch by them towards the fence, opening the gate quickly and slamming it behind me. Kora looks away and the dogs come running to the gate, growling and barking until I am out of view.

I decide to take the route along the train line. It has been a while since I faced it and I am anxious to have something good to tell Maria. I cross the main line quickly and wipe the sweat from my forehead as I turn and make my way towards her grandfather's house.

When I get there, I find Maria sitting on the back steps. She is playing with an old torn doll and even though I think she is far too old for such things, I say nothing and sit quietly beside her.

"I'm sorry about your face," she says.

I instinctively put my hand to my face and feel along the scratch.

"It's okay," I sign.

"I like your voice," she says but I don't answer.

I feel she must be lying. I wonder whether to talk about my father's truck and how it is not a fire engine but I decide to let sleeping dogs lie and hope we can have some fun together. It has been a hard day and I am not in the mood for arguing.

"Granddad was packing things and look!" she says, showing me the doll which I now notice has only one eye. "She was mine when I was really little and I loved her. Her name is Natalia. That was my grandmother's name."

I remain silent, anxious not to spoil her good mood.

"Do you want to see my other old toys?" she asks.

I agree and together we look through a box of toys and games. On one side of the box, someone has written in large black pen: *"Maria's toys. Don't throw out."*

I point at it with my questioning face.

"My mother's writing," she says, smiling.

In the bottom of the box is another smaller box. Maria takes a deep breath in as though she never expected to see this. She opens it and gently lifts out white paper that appears to have something inside. She slowly unwraps it and reveals a crown of diamonds on a comb and I have no idea what it is.

"My First Holy Communion Crown," she says. She looks at me and notices the confused expression on my face. "You're not Catholic?"

I sign "No."

"This is very important. I wore it on my Communion Day," she says but her eyes look so sad that I am glad that I cannot hear her voice.

"It's beautiful," I write and she smiles through watery eyes.

"Thank you," she signs back even though I can lip-read.

"*You're beautiful,*" I finally write even though my heart is beating with fear.

"Sign it," she asks, so I sign and she smiles again, a beautiful smile. She leans forward and kisses me on the mouth. My heart misses a beat. I put my arm around her and she leans against me as we sit together on the steps. After a while her grandfather wheels his wheelchair out. I feel the vibrations of his wheelchair above me although he cannot see us.

"Is he calling you?" I gesture.

"No. He's calling the cat!" she replies, laughing. "Christopher, it must be awful to be deaf."

"*I don't remember hearing,*" I write and she leans back into me to think about this.

The light above goes on and she stands suddenly. It is getting dark.

"Oh oh, that's my cue to come in," she says so I stand and kiss her gently before making my way back to my house.

When I arrive home, my father is back having finished a late shift at the mine. He looks tired and I know he is not sleeping because he is worried about Wilfred. My mother is sitting in her office and when I sneak up behind her I see that she has already written five letters to regional newspapers. In each unsealed envelope she has placed a small photo of Kora in short dark plaits or pig-tails but each photo looks to have been taken when Kora was eight or nine so I am worried that her mother will not recognise her five or six years after she last saw her. When she finishes the last letter and seals them all, my mother stands but suddenly bends over and leans against the chair she has been sitting on. Her face goes red and she puts her hand over her mouth. "Andy!" she says.

I run from her office to get my father but he has heard her and almost stands on my bad foot as he rushes to help her. He sits her down and gets her a glass of water.

"I feel sick," she says so he leads her to the bathroom at the end of the hall. It is the only bathroom on this floor.

"An en suite would come in handy now," he jokes but I can see that he is worried. My mother is never sick.

When she has finished vomiting into the bowl, my father pulls back her hair and helps her into bed.

He half closes the door, leaving me outside. I move sideways and watch them through the small opening.

"I'm okay," she says as he fusses about her.

"I'm getting Doctor Alder," he says but she laughs and asks him to sit down.

"I don't need a doctor," she says. "I wasn't going to tell you until after we found Wilfred, but I'm pregnant."

My father's mouth opens wide but not as wide as mine. A myriad of emotions surge through me and I now know how Maria feels about her mother's expected baby.

"I've known a few days but there was never the right moment. What with Iren's death and Kora's announcement. I decided to wait for a while to say anything."

"When?" father asks, smiling. There is something about his face that makes him look like a little boy.

"You figure it out, Birthday Boy!" she teases him and I feel my face redden with embarrassment. There are some conversations that I just should not see.

"Oh!" Father says, remembering his party. He kisses my mother passionately and she pushes him away.

"I've just been sick!" she laughs.

"I don't care. You're beautiful!"

"So you're happy?" she asks but I can see the sudden sadness creep onto both their faces.

"Yes," he says "and this time we'll make sure you get all the rest you need. We don't want you mis–"

Father stops talking. I know he is referring to the two miscarriages my mother had when I was still a toddler.

"It's all right, love. I'm happy too. Our luck has to change sometime, doesn't it?" Mother says.

I move back from the open doorway and go to my room. Deep down I am happy too. I am not completely like Maria. I am not angry. There will be room for me, even if it is a boy. So I sit at the side of my bed and I pray for a new son for my parents and more than anything else, I pray that he will not be deaf.

Chapter 27

Two weeks pass and my mother has not received any response to her advertisement looking for Kora's mother and neither has my father heard anything from Wilfred. Bill called twice to say that he was doing everything he could and warned father that at this stage he should not expect Wilfred to be alive. Both my mother and father try to hide their disappointment by talking about the baby that my mother says will be born in less than seven months. She didn't tell her sister or any of the staff the news as she doesn't want to take any attention away from Kora's wedding. Even though the atmosphere in the house is not as sad as normal, I spend my time walking through the park with Maria talking about our future which seems to makes her laugh.

"Christopher, you're a funny boy!" she says whenever I tell her about my plans.

Even though we are getting on better, I know that there is something strange about Maria that I have not yet figured out.

She is smiling though and I think this because her grandfather has decided to stay in Broken Hill and has told his son and daughter-in-law that he will definitely not move to Sydney when the new owner arrives. I ask Maria if her mother has had her baby and she says, "Yes. A boy," and adds nothing further but there is a smile on her face that tells me she is happy it was not a girl. I tell her my hopes for a brother who can hear and she looks at me with a look of disapproval. "Christopher, you are too kind," she says and walks ahead of me. Before I leave, I ask her to be my date at my aunt's wedding and she says "I'll think about it" which I know means "Don't ask me again – if I am going, I'll just show up."

When I arrive home shortly before lunch, Aishling is talking on the phone.

"Tomorrow? No, that's grand. It doesn't matter. You'll fly in? Ah yes, that's better. Train is awful long. Grand. He'll be delighted to see you earlier than expected. Yes, he'll understand. Well, you'll see when you get here. Good days and bad days . . . yes . . . oh yes . . . grand so . . . grand . . ."

I know Aishling is speaking to someone Irish because she keeps saying "grand" which she once told me means "that's fine".

When she puts down the phone I stand in front of her, anxious to know who it was and to see her repeat the other half of the conversation to my mother.

"That was Deirdre. She's coming a day early."

There is a crease on her brow that tells me that something is suddenly worrying her, something she hadn't really thought of before or, in her enthusiasm to reunite the couple, had pushed to the back of her mind.

"I . . . I hope he recognises her," she says, biting down on her lower lip and looking at my mother expectantly.

"You did tell her how he is, didn't you?" Mother asks.

"A . . . little. I didn't want to spoil it"

My mother frowns at Aishling but says nothing.

Aishling shrugs her shoulders, trying to unload her sudden doubt and goes into the Penance Room to tell Father Hayes but he is asleep on the chair with the sun in his face so she leaves him and goes about her duties.

After my mother organises Father Hayes's clothes for tomorrow, she drives over to Kora's house to try on wedding outfits. Mother is Kora's bridesmaid and is wearing a long green dress that matches her eyes. Even Jimmy seems to be looking forward to the wedding. Yesterday, I watched as my mother helped him try on a dark-blue suit. He grumbled as she pulled the jacket around him but, when she left to get sewing pins, I watched him smile at his reflection in the mirror. When she came back, he tried to tell her something but she didn't understand. I watched his face turn red with frustration as he repeated the words twice. I know how he feels. I want to tell him that it is best to stay quiet, that it is useless to try to communicate with most people.

The following afternoon, a taxi pulls up and we all watch out the Penance Room window as a tall, slightly overweight woman slowly raises herself onto a walking stick and waves her arms about at the taxi driver who is lifting two huge suitcases from the boot. Another equally tall woman gets out the other side and helps her onto the path. The women have the same dark-red hair and only Deirdre has a tell-tale narrow silver streak running along her parting. My mother opens the door and welcomes them. Aishling is directly behind her and speaks to Deirdre in Gaelic.

Deirdre breaks into a huge smile. "Oh, thank you . . . it's so long since I heard anyone speaking Irish. Music to my ears!"

My mother looks a little put out. I can see the crease appearing on her forehead. It is the same frown she wears when my father is speaking Gaelic to Aishling which they only do when they have been drinking and are reminiscing about their homes.

Aishling picks up on my mother's discomfort and quickly says, "You've developed a slight American drawl, Deirdre."

"So my brothers tell me," Deirdre replies cheerfully. "Forty years in America. Guess it rubs off after a while."

"This is Emma Monroe. She's the owner of the nursing home," Aishling says.

Deirdre introduces her daughter who has been standing behind her mother, trying to keep both suitcases upright.

"She's cranky because we didn't go to the hotel first but I just couldn't wait another moment to see Aiden," Deirdre says as her daughter frowns and thrusts her large bony hand towards my mother.

"I'm Megan," she says as she moves closer. I can see she has the same large green eyes as her mother.

The pair come inside and my mother quickly introduces them to the residents. I can see Deirdre scanning the room for Aiden and she looks deflated when he is not there.

"Greta, one of our nurses, is helping him get ready," Mother explains.

I can almost feel the skip in Deirdre's heart as she puts her hand to her chest and takes a breath. I know that only now has she truly realised that she will see her first love again.

"I – I can't believe it," she says with tears in her eyes.

"Mum!" Megan says, slightly embarrassed.

"Why don't you come into the dining room and have a cold drink while you are waiting," Mother offers but before they move Aiden appears at the end of the hallway with Greta by his side.

I see Aishling and Mother's jaw drop at how different he looks in his suit and tie. His face is freshly shaved and his grey hair is slicked back with oil. Greta makes herself scarce and my mother goes into the dining room, leaving only Aishling to reintroduce the pair.

Aiden makes his way slowly down the long hallway towards them with the help of his old cane.

Deirdre begins to cry. I can see her chin tremble. "He looks –

so helpless," she says. Her daughter moves closer and takes her hand.

"He's fine," Aishling reassures her.

"I – I'd – hardly know him," Deirdre sobs but Megan squeezes her hand tighter and moves her mother towards him.

Aiden stands still and looks at Deirdre and then at Megan. His eyes light up.

"You found me," he says in English.

"I did," Deirdre says.

He moves closer, his weak eyes trying to focus clearly on the women. He stops a few inches from them and holds out both his arms. His legs buckle a little and Aishling moves forward to steady him. Deirdre gulps at his frailty but her expression changes when she sees Aiden reach forward and put his arms gently around the young American.

"I've waited so long, Deirdre! You still look so beautiful," he says.

Megan tenses and moves back a little. "I'm Megan," she says with a voice that bounces off the floor. I know she must have said this rudely as Aishling gives her a sharp look.

Aiden looks confused as he moves his gaze from one woman to the other. He then looks at Aishling and an expression of complete bewilderment spreads over his lined face.

Aishling, unable to bear his pain, says, "Aiden, this is Deirdre," pointing at the older woman and moving him towards her.

Deirdre's chin wobbles again and she quickly wipes tears from her eyes. She reaches forward and wraps both her arms around him then stands back, taking in his face, his eyes, his smile.

"It is you, Aiden. It's really you!" she says through her tears. She begins to laugh and only then does Aiden realise who she is.

"Deirdre! *A stór!*"

The two stand wrapped around each other, unable to believe

that they have been reunited, if only for a while. Aishling opens the dining-room door and beckons for Deirdre to go inside. She helps Aiden in and leaves the two alone to talk. Li places cold drinks and cakes on the table and excuses herself. Aishling then takes Megan into Mother's office and offers her some refreshments there. I stand outside the partly closed door of the dining room and watch but I can only see Aiden's face. I push the door open a little wider but when Deirdre looks up I shrink back and decide to watch them talk through the window.

I move out onto the porch and down the side of the house. I climb on top of the three bricks I have left there for snooping purposes and find that I have an excellent view of their lips. Aiden reaches out his left hand across the table and Deirdre takes it. They begin to speak in Gaelic and I sigh. I remain there in case they revert to English and watch the conversation flow easily between the two as if they had never been parted.

At last Deirdre throws some English words into her conversation and Aiden's eyebrows move upwards.

"I'm rusty," she explains in English, "and there are so many new words that I never knew in Irish. You know, microwaves and things like that. There were none of these things when I left Ireland so I have no word for them."

Aiden smiles but I don't think he understands what she means. He looks as though he is lost in his youth and is smiling at the girl Deirdre once was.

"Microwaves," he says slowly.

I watch Deirdre tell Aiden that she was married to a kind man who unfortunately died some years back and that even though she had a good marriage she never stopped thinking about her first love. I watch her tell him that she went to America to get as far away from her memories as possible and that she has never returned to Ireland since but that she thinks that, now they have seen each other again, she might make that trip. During her entire story, Aiden nods and smiles. Sometimes his face looks sad and sometimes happy as she recalls the life she went on to have without him. She tells him that she never stopped wondering what might have been and that most important to her, then and now, was that he was content with his life as a priest. She said that that would have been the only thing to make their parting worth it.

"So . . ." she asks. "Were you happy, Aiden?"

Father Hayes looks at her and reaches into his pocket. I can see his right hand fumbling for his rosary beads. He presses the hard beads into his hand and his mouth turns downward.

"Yes. I was," he replies.

Deirdre smiles weakly but leans further over the table and grips his hand tighter. Something in his face has told her he is lying.

"Really?" she asks again.

"Yes," he says.

Deirdre leans back and stares at him. I watch her tap her flat brown shoes on the linoleum as she decides whether or not to take this conversation further.

"How long have you been here?" she says.

"Oh a good few years now. I don't know exactly. I get . . . a little confused at times."

"Don't we all?" she says, squeezing his hand tighter. "But, Aiden, why aren't you living in a priest's house? Isn't that the norm?"

Aiden looks away from her and stares out the window. I duck and laugh at my silliness as I know he cannot see that far. I know he is not trying to delay his answer but that he is genuinely trying to remember the sequence of events that resulted in him coming here.

"Aiden, were you really happy?" she asks again but he doesn't answer.

"I got sick," he says, answering her previous question as to why he was not living in a house for clergy.

"Sick?"

"I . . . became . . . I became sad."

Deirdre swallows. I feel she knows that at some point during this reunion she will find out exactly how Aiden's life has gone but she wonders if she is ready to hear it.

Then out of the blue, as if Aiden knows this, he goes on. "Every day of my life I imagined myself meeting you off that train. I remember the past more clearly these days. Other memories are not so clear. But I remember the beautiful sunset that evening and how I looked out my kitchen window knowing you were waiting for me but I knew . . . I knew if I went to meet you that I could not have gone through with it. I'd have had to let my mother down. I knew that for you there would be another love. You were so beautiful. Any man would have been lucky . . . but Francis was dead and my mother now had only one son. All her hopes were on me and I couldn't let her down, Deirdre. I had to choose but you had children and grandchildren . . . you were all right . . ."

Deirdre interrupted him. "I wanted these things with you, Aiden."

He lowers his head and she regrets her words.

"But I understand. Aiden, we were both robbed of our life together. We both suffered but you suffered far more than me. I am not angry with you. I am sad for you and for me . . . for what we could have had together."

Aiden looks up and tears fall freely down his face.

"I should have gone to the train," he says, sobbing.

Deirdre fights hard to hold back her tears.

"It took me a lifetime to see that I made the wrong choice," he goes on. "I was a terrible priest because it wasn't what I wanted. It wasn't for me. I don't tell people. I stay quiet and pray. I was reluctant in my duties. As I reached middle age things changed. I remember that now. I became nervous and anxious over things. They – they asked me to leave when I got sick so the sacrifice I made for my mother was for nothing. In the end I let everybody down."

"I'm sure you were not a terrible priest," she says, squeezing his hand. "You were a kind man, so loving to me. They were lucky to have you."

Deirdre looked more intently at him, reading his face, trying to reach out to the lost man in front of her, to tell him that all was not lost.

"So much time has passed, Aiden. Is there any point in wondering what might have been? It doesn't change anything. I lost my first baby when he was a few weeks old and, you know, I spent years wondering what he'd look like, what I'd dress him in the day he started school, what colour his Communion suit would be. I even thought about these things when I had my second-born and third. There came a day when I said, what do these thoughts change? They don't change a thing. They just make you miserable."

Aiden nods and his eyes glaze over. He looks like he is returning to his inner world. Deirdre notices this and reaches forward to bring him back to her.

"You can never go back," he says as his mouth narrows and turns downward as though he is trying not to cry.

"You know . . . I'm an old widow now on a stick but would you like to kiss me?" she asks, smiling shyly.

Aiden looks at her as though she has woken him from a dream. He reddens a little but leans forward and kisses her lightly on the cheek. She laughs.

"Like how you used to kiss me!" she says, rubbing his thin hand.

Aiden smiles like a schoolboy and stands shakily. She moves toward him. He puts his hands on her shoulders and gazes at her face.

"You're so beautiful," he says and she laughs which makes him smile.

"And you are still a charmer," she says. "So are you going to kiss me or not?"

Aiden steps closer and kisses her so gently that you would think she could not feel it but she moves her heels off the ground and inches even closer to him. He kisses her in the same sweet gentle way and she puts her hand on his face and then smooths his hair.

"I remember that kiss," she says but there is a sad look in her eyes.

She knows that the man in front of her is not the Aiden that left her behind but a shell of the man, the remnants of her love beaten down by a life of missed opportunities and disappointment. She also knows that she is no longer the naïve country girl she once was and that she too has experienced many losses in her life and although they are both changed people, they have been given a chance to make their peace with each other and with those responsible for keeping them apart. She wipes small tears from her eyes and links arms with him.

"Well, will I introduce you properly to my daughter?" she asks, laughing. "Now, Aiden, if you thought I was wild, this one will shock you!" She laughs as she leads him out of the dining-room door and up the hallway.

He stops suddenly and digs his cane into the floor. There is something he has to ask.

"Deirdre . . . do you forgive me?"

"For loving me? Aiden, the only person we need to forgive is your mother. I can do that. The thing is, can you?"

Aiden looks down and I know that he is struggling with this question. Now that he has made his peace with Deirdre, he knows that his deep-rooted grudge against his mother is the one thing that is preventing his mind from finding peace.

They move forward and my mother meets them at the door of the Penance Room. Deirdre tries to help Aiden across the room even though she is also walking with a stick.

301

"I had my hip done," she tells my mother. "Blasted thing is still sore."

"Will you stay for lunch?" mother asks. "Our cook has made an Irish dish especially for the occasion. Bacon and cabbage."

Deirdre accepts and thanks my mother for her hospitality. I think I am the only one who notices Deirdre grimace slightly so I know she doesn't like this dish. It reminds me of something my father says. "Why do people think I like haggis just because I'm Scottish?" My father really hates haggis.

When we all sit down to Li's lunch, I notice that Aiden has returned to his silent self and that faraway look in his eye has returned. Every once in a while he looks up from his plate and smiles but it usually immediately after Deirdre has laughed at something someone has said. I spend the hour watching him with interest as his expression continually changes from amazement to find that she is here to that faraway look that tells me he is once again waiting on a summer's evening for that train to arrive. I wonder if he will remember that she was here and that he had a chance to make his peace with the love of his life.

As Deirdre and Megan leave for their hotel, my mother decides to invite them to Kora's wedding which is now only five days away. Deirdre happily accepts while her daughter frowns in the doorway.

"Oh we'd love that! That's Saturday and we leave the following morning so it'd be a nice end to our trip. Em . . . would it be all right it I visited again tomorrow? I'd like to see Aiden as much as I can while I'm here."

Megan sighs and shrugs her large shoulders.

"You can do your own thing," Deirdre says to her daughter with a cross face. "I'll be fine getting here. I'll catch a cab."

Mother agrees and says it would be good for Aiden and that Deirdre can visit as often as she likes.

The rest of the day is spent organising the residents' clothes for the wedding ceremony. Victoria is very excited and plans to wear her red dress again but this time she also plans on wearing the red lipstick that she bought when on a recent shopping trip with Greta in town. My mother and Greta have noticed Victoria becoming more assertive since Penelope, who has reluctantly agreed to play piano, became distracted with her music sheets. When Kora asked her to play, we were all shocked that she agreed and were even more shocked when she said that it was a pity that nice German man had left as she had enjoyed playing with someone who knew about real music. Reverend Williams, who replaced my grandfather when he died, will conduct the ceremony. He is getting on in years and my mother says he will soon hand most of his duties over to a younger minister.

That evening, my mother and father sit in her office listening to music. I watch from the hallway as they talk about the changes to the residents since Steve came into their lives. Father is supposed to be working on his speech for Kora but my mother has made him cross out many of his jokes which she knows Kora will not care for.

"I think Mina has benefited most," my father offers but Mother shakes her head.

"No. It's just that she was first to tell her story. She's had more time to look forward and make changes in her life. The others will follow too. I'm sure of it. Look at Penelope, practising today for the wedding and looking proud of herself."

"Ah, but she did stop playing when I entered the room suddenly. She looked like a roo in headlights. Frightened the life out of her."

Mother sighs. "That'll change. I'm sure we don't know the half of what she went through. She'll get there."

"What about Victoria?" Father asks.

Mother laughs. "You know, she still thinks she's a young woman. You should see her outfit for Saturday. Even I wouldn't wear it!"

Father smiles and shrugs. "I guess she's trying to get back the years that were stolen from her. All those experiences she should have had that were taken from her. You reckon she's still holding a candle for the chap that died in India?"

"Yeah. I never see her without the brooch he gave her. It's sad but romantic. I don't think she'd want to find anyone else. I think a part of her wants to hold onto that innocent love she had for him. You know, I think she should write it down. She's always reading those romance books. She could easily write her own."

"Except this time with a happy ending?"

Mother nods and stretches out on her chair. "I might suggest it to her."

"Well, think about it first. It could upset her to bring it all up again."

Mother tenses and I can see her shoulders rising up under her blue blouse.

"I think it is good to get things out into the open. It does no good to harbour feelings," she says before turning her face away from him. She looks out the window so I cannot see her expression. A quietness settles between my parents until Mother finally speaks again.

"Andy?" she says and I know she wants to talk about me. I move further into the hallway. For a brief moment I fear that Steve has talked to her about sending me away.

Father seems to know instinctively what she wants to talk about. He stands suddenly. "Not tonight please, Emma," he says but he is not angry. He looks sad.

Mother relents and looks out of the window. I follow her gaze and see a long tear escape from one of her green eyes and flow down her cheek. She wipes it quickly and stands. Under her skirt I can see a tiny bulge, my brother growing inside her stomach. I see Father looking at it. His face softens and he relaxes. He moves towards her chair. He lifts my mother to her feet and they look out into the garden. It has started to rain again but this time it is not as heavy.

"Well now! No rain for months and now it never stops," Father says, looking out into the blustery evening.

He is trying to change the subject and my mother knows this. He turns to her and puts his hand on her stomach. I feel a strong vibration run through me as though someone has punched me in the ribs and an invisible pair of hands is pulling me into the darkness. I walk backwards and hide in the darkened Penance Room, watching them.

"Everything will be all right, Emma. We'll talk about Christopher, I promise, but not now, please."

I see another tear fall down her cheek. He wipes it away, flicks the light switch off and they move into the brightly lit hallway.

"Come on. Let's get you to bed. You need an early night," he says, leading her into their bedroom.

Then, just as I am about to emerge, he appears again and makes for the office. I move swiftly forward and see that he is on the phone. It is very late and I wonder who could be ringing at this time.

"My God, Bill, that's . . . When? Where?"

My heart lurches and I wish I knew what Bill was saying. I know it is about Wilfred and I feel sick and dizzy waiting to know if he is all right. My father puts down the phone and I scuttle back into the Penance Room. He hurries back to the bedroom and, before I can decide whether to stay in hiding or appear at their door, he emerges again and races upstairs.

I follow and find him in Martin's room where Aishling is trying to coax Martin out from under his bed.

Martin sees me and says, "He's the only one who believes me!"

I sign and tell him it is all right to come out. He is learning fast and now knows lots of simple signs.

He signs back saying that he wants to stay where he is and my father and Aishling look at each other in amazement.

"He knows sign language?" Father asks.

"Looks like it!" Aishling replies and I sign yes.

"Listen," my father says, "Bill phoned. They found a man matching Wilfred's description off the main road into Lightning Ridge."

"Where's that?" Aishling asks.

"Bill said it's a good ten – eleven-hour drive."

"How'd he get that far? And – where has he been all this time?"

"We're still not sure it's him. Bill said local police tipped him off. They found him wandering through scrub off the highway. His car broke down and it matches the make from the car-hire company here. He got stuck in the mud during the heavy rain. He was disorientated and dehydrated when the police picked him up. They told Bill he wasn't making much sense."

"What are you going to do?"

"Bill's picking me up in half an hour. We're going up there tonight."

"But you don't even know if it's him!" Aishling replies.

"I do. I can feel it, Aishling. I know it doesn't make any sense but I've been dreaming of him walking through the desert. It's him. I'm sure of it."

My mouth drops open when I realise that my father has had the same dream as me. Aishling says nothing. She doesn't believe in these things but she will have to get used to it if she is to become Steve's wife because Steve sees everything that I see.

"Just make sure you are back for the wedding!" she says as he leaves.

I am tempted to go with him but know I need to stay with Martin. Besides, my father probably wouldn't agree to take me.

I follow Aishling down to the medicine cabinet where she takes out another tablet to make Martin sleep.

"You're getting too used to these," she says to him while warning him to keep his ghost stories down. "They aren't working any more."

"That's because I'm not taking them!" he says after she is gone. He throws the tablet into the top drawer of his locker and laughs.

I take a blanket from his wardrobe and sit beside him. He knows what I want. He knows what I need to hear.

"I'm not ready," he says so I take my blanket and sit by the window. As I gaze out into the darkness I try to send a message to Wilfred. I say "Stay strong, Carl. Father is coming for you. He's coming to take you home."

Chapter 28

The following morning, Deirdre arrives at eleven o'clock and asks my mother if it would be all right to take Aiden into the garden. I watch her lead him outside to the old wooden bench where they eat apple pie and drink lemonade that Kai prepared for them. I saw Li tell my mother that Kai has got a place on a confectioner's course in Sydney that starts in a couple of months and that he will have to leave home. She said that although she is sad for him to leave, she knows it is what Kai wants to do. My mother agreed with her and I tensed when she said that if you really want to hold onto your children, it is better to let them go. I am becoming more afraid that Steve is whispering in her ear. Like Maria, I don't want to leave here, even if I spend most of my time with the dead and dying. It is all I have ever known.

After lunch, my mother answers the phone to my Father. I know he is speaking excitedly because each time she tries to say something; she doesn't get to finish her sentence and frowns into the telephone. I watch her shoulders rise and fall as Father informs her of Wilfred's situation and I only relax when I see the frown lines change into a half smile that tells me that Wilfred is all right. When Father finally gets off the line, my mother goes to the kitchen to tell Kora the news.

"It's definitely Wilfred. He's all right!" she says, hugging her sister tightly. Kora squirms and when they separate she looks down at my mother's stomach and raises her eyebrows quizzically at her. Mother blushes. She is normally very thin and her sister has noticed the small bulge that seems to have appeared suddenly.

"I wasn't going to say anything until after the wedding," she says.

Kora smiles. She has been in good humour lately. "You didn't need to worry. I'm so happy for you. 'Bout time you and Andy had some good luck. When is it due?"

"I'm only three months – almost three months."

"That all? Still, you're so thin, mate, that you'd see it a mile off. Sure your dates are right? Look bigger than that."

My mother frowns. She isn't sure.

"Anyway," Kora says, breaking her thoughts, "it'll be good to have a baby in the house after all this time." She eyes my mother to make sure she has not upset her.

"It's okay. It's been ten years since I had that last miscarriage. I have a good feeling this time. I'm sure this one will make it to full term."

Kora nods.

"Maybe you'll be joining me soon?" Mother asks, teasing her sister while she is in good humour.

"Maybe," Kora replies.

Deirdre comes into the kitchen with Li and puts the dirty plates and cups into the sink.

"Thanks so much for all of this," she says to my mother. "I really appreciate it. I can see that Aiden is well cared for here."

Mother moves toward her, looking sympathetically at her.

"Must be hard for you, seeing him so frail?"

Deirdre closes her mouth and thinks about this. "Yes. It's hard. You know, I still have feelings for him but, well, he can only talk to me about the past. He goes in and out of reality. Most of the time he thought we were in Donegal. It's – it's really sad."

"Maybe it's wishful thinking?" Kora offers. "Maybe he wants to pretend for as long as he can that nothing has changed. Maybe he knows only too well that you are going back to America and he is trying to take as much happiness as he can. A lifetime in a few days?"

My mother looks at Kora. It is unusual for her sister to be so insightful. Kora's usual emotion is anger. Anger and sadness.

Deirdre nods slowly, taking this in.

"I'd say that's what's happening," says Kora. "Some days he's quick as can be. Knows everything that goes on 'round him. Ask me, he runs into that shell of his when he's upset or wants to hide from reality and who could blame him? It's rare that any of us have much to look forward to." She glances at my mother. "Want my advice, go along with it. Enjoy it while it lasts." She fills herself a large glass of water and moves towards the Penance Room.

Deirdre looks at my mother. "Same time tomorrow, okay? Megan and I are taking a trip out west this afternoon. It's with a tour. Wouldn't have the courage to drive into the outback myself. Not with those killer spiders and God-awful snakes!"

When Deirdre leaves, Li leafs through a small notebook that she keeps in her pocket.

"That for the order?" Mother asks.

"No. It's my 'Mina count'."

"What?"

"Since Mina started helping in the kitchen, I keep a count of every day that she steals food. I want to know how long before she trusts that there will always be food."

"And?" mother asks.

"She hasn't stolen anything in . . . thirteen days."

Mother leans back on the kitchen counter. "Really? That's brilliant. Think she's cured?"

310

"Maybe. Either way, it's progress. She's become attached to Kai. She's come a long way from the old lady that shook with fear when she saw a young Oriental boy in her kitchen."

Mother agrees and touches Li's arm as she passes. "You've done good, Li."

When Kora takes a half-day to do some shopping for the wedding, Greta comes in to finish her shift. She follows my mother out into the garden where Penelope and Victoria are enjoying the sunshine and drops her body heavily onto a wooden bench, wiping the sweat off her brow.

"Blimey. It'll take me years to get used to the heat 'ere," she says.

My mother says nothing but I know what she is thinking. So many people come to Australia for the blue skies and sunshine but complain that the sun is too hot! My father is one of them.

"Any news on Kora's mother?"

My mother shakes her head and says nothing. I know this is a sign that she is both disappointed and embarrassed that she made Kora's personal business so public.

"Did you leave your phone number?"

Mother nods. "And the address just in case she preferred to write."

"Well," Greta says, "there's time yet. She might show up."

Mother nods again and sighs. I know she regrets sending those letters and that she is worried that Kora will find out. She opens her mouth to voice her concerns but changes her mind.

"Well, I better get to work," Greta says, lifting herself off the bench and making her way to the porch.

My mother stays in the garden and enjoys the cool breeze that has suddenly whipped up at the side of the house. She looks around the grounds that run all the way down to the train line, about an acre and a half in total. She moves her eyes across the lawn to where Martin and Jimmy are sitting quietly.

"That money would build a good extension. Completely block

out that view of the train line," she says to herself. She walks towards the two men. "You men all right? Yeah? Right, then I'll go inside. Call out if you need anything!"

My mother takes one last look at the garden and I see her look out over the train line. I know she doesn't really like sitting out here. It reminds her too much of my accident. She smooths down her skirt and sighs before walking across the scorched lawn and into the house. It is almost time for lunch.

Chapter 29

At two thirty the following morning, I feel the crash of the screen door against its frame. I jump from my bed and think how odd it is that I have again found myself in my own bed as I had settled down on a blanket in Martin's room only hours before. The only conclusion I can come to is that I moved to my own room in a half-awake state that I have no memory of afterwards. I rush downstairs and see my Father and Bill help Wilfred down the hallway. I move to one side as they push him up the stairs to his room. His face is ashen and he has bandages on his arms and legs. My father spends a few minutes talking quietly to Wilfred but he has his back to me so I cannot see his words. Wilfred looks ashamed and keeps nodding at my father but he doesn't speak. He looks thinner and his bulging eyes roam quickly around the room as though he never expected to be back here.

I leave his room as Father closes his door. My mother has come out of her room and is standing downstairs waiting for my father to tell her what happened to Wilfred. Bill has a coffee with them in the kitchen and then laughs about how much trouble he will be in at the station for disappearing for two days. Father nods and says he is in the same position but he is not laughing and knows that things are bad at the mine and that he needs to pull his weight to keep his job.

Mother looks tired and asks Father for the short story. She is interested but she wants to get back to bed before she has to turn the patients with Aishling at four thirty. Father explains how a police patrol found Wilfred's empty car about forty miles outside Lightning Ridge. It had gone off the road in the heavy rain and had become stuck in the sand. There were empty bottles of water and an empty esky in the boot so they feared whoever was on foot had little or no water. When they searched the immediate area, they came up empty so they organised a wider search. When two rescuers found Wilfred in some scrub, he had been without food or water for at least two days. His skin was badly sunburnt and his arms and legs were cut from the scrub that he tried to shelter in. He had insect bites which were infected and needed treatment but when they tried to take him to safety, he refused to go. He told them that he was looking for the ocean, that he wanted to save the drowning people and that if he couldn't save them, he was going to drown himself. The police knew nothing of his past and they just thought he was "gone troppo" so they manhandled him into the car and told him he was about as far away from the sea as could be.

My mother listens with interest and sighs and shakes her head as my father recounts the story of how Wilfred would not tell hospital staff his name. He refused food or drink and told them he wanted to die. Once they had rehydrated him, they began the process of transferring him to the nearest psychiatric hospital. When the local police informed them that there was a missing person's report from Broken Hill station on a man matching his description, they contacted Bill straightaway.

When Father arrived in the ward, Wilfred would not look at him.

Mother becomes upset when Father tells her that Wilfred

begged him to leave him, that he wanted to die, that he was so very tired of living – and that he had not said one word for the whole journey home.

When there is nothing left to say, Mother goes back to bed but I can tell that she will not sleep.

Father climbs the stairs to Wilfred's room and knocks. He opens the door and finds Wilfred sitting on his bed. I hide in the hallway as Father looks into the room. Wilfred has taken down all of the beautiful photos off his wall, including the one of his mother and sister. Father notices this but says nothing. He sits down beside him.

"Wilfred, I know that things are bad for you but you put Emma and me and everyone here through a lot of worry. We care about you. This is your home. I just wanted you to know that."

Wilfred doesn't answer but stares at the empty wall in front of him. I can see the skin peeling off his face and the small bite-marks running along his eye sockets.

"There is something I need to ask you and I really need you to be honest with me," Father says.

Wilfred looks up and narrows his eyes. He has told Father everything there is to know about him. There is nothing left to say.

Father swallows hard. He has built up a strong friendship with Wilfred and I know he is worried that his question might destroy what is now left of that bond.

"Did you . . . did you do anything to Iren?"

"Who?" Wilfred asks. It is the first word he has said since father helped him up the stairs.

"Iren," Father says. I can tell his tone is sharp.

I can see Wilfred straighten up and then slump down as though father has taken the air out of him.

"No! Why do you ask me this?"

"Because she's dead, Wilfred – or Carl. Iren is dead."

Wilfred leans forward on his bed and stares at the ground. "Good. I am glad this lady is dead. She is with her husband and boy now. But I didn't harm her. I only wish I had courage to make her at peace."

"I'm sorry then. I am sorry to have asked you but you understand, don't you? The night you disappeared she was upset and you said . . . about those prisoners . . ." Father tries to explain why he thought Wilfred had harmed Iren but he can't find the words and neither can he cope with Wilfred's staring eyes. Father sighs again and rubs his hands slowly together. I know this sign. There is something else on his mind, another question he must ask.

"Then why . . . why did you run away?"

Wilfred exhales and runs his hand over a large dressing on his forearm and then clasps his hands together on his lap.

"I was ashamed. When we finished talking, I sat on my bed and thought what have I done? I had too much to drink. I never told anyone before . . . I never had a friend like you to talk to. Later, I regretted my words and I decided that I could not face you again. I decided to leave and hoped you didn't think I am an evil man."

"I don't think you are an evil man, Wilfred. I think you are an ordinary man who was caught up in an extraordinary situation. Have you thought of the thousands of other German soldiers out there who also survived? There must be other soldiers like you, thousands of men who are feeling the same way. Soldiers who followed orders even though they didn't agree with them. You are not alone in this, Wilfred."

Wilfred doesn't answer.

"Wilfred, you are sorry for what you did but there is nothing you can do now to change things. You will have to try to forgive yourself."

"Never!" Wilfred says, becoming suddenly annoyed.

"Then do something to make amends. Do something to help

yourself find some peace. You are still a young man, Wilfred, and you waste your days hiding here and going over things that you can never change. There is a reason you survived. There is a reason you are home safely with us. Find out what it is."

Wilfred looks up for the first time since Father entered the room. Father's words have got his attention.

"Andy? When I was in the desert, I heard your son calling to me. I heard his voice. He was telling me to come home. I must have slept because I saw him walking towards me and his foot – it was fine and he could hear. I answered him. I remember it so clearly."

Father stares at him and it looks as though he is about to break down from exhaustion. He leans against the now empty wall. I can see his chin shake.

"Perhaps it was dehydration," Wilfred offers when he sees my father's face sadden.

"No. Christopher always had special abilities but . . . there was a time that I didn't believe . . . that I didn't believe in him . . . I couldn't face up to what was wrong with him . . . I should have been looking at what was right with him, the things he could do. I let him down, Wilfred. I gave up on him but I won't give up on you."

He gets up and goes to the door. I slink back into the darkened hallway and try to stifle the sobs that have risen in my throat. Father's legs appear to shake as he negotiates his way down the narrow stairwell. He passes his bedroom where my mother is sleeping and sits in the Penance Room alone. I creep down and watch him from the door. He sits down on my favourite seat and stares sadly out the bay window into the night. I wish my mother could see this. I wish she knew how sorry he is and that together they can move forward and, like Wilfred, make the best of what is left.

I leave Father there and return to my room to sleep. I look briefly into Martin's room as I pass. He is awake but calm.

"Christopher? I want to visit my brother."

I sign "Good" and make my way past Aishling's empty desk. I ease my tired body into bed and for the first time I dream that everything is all right in my home. Everybody is happy, even Kora. I can see her standing in the Penance Room in her cream wedding dress, laughing and crying at the same time as though her whole world has changed in an instant. I hope it comes true.

Chapter 30

The following morning, Tina makes a call to Martin's brother asking if it would be all right to visit him. I watch as she writes the date in the diary *"Tuesday at 10.00 a.m."*

Martin seems pleased and tells Jimmy all about his plans to make up with his brother before he dies. Jimmy nods and mumbles a response but his thoughts are on his son's wedding to Kora in two days' time. Deirdre has arrived without her daughter and is once again sitting in the garden with Father Hayes. She has brought old photos with her and is showing them to him. Greta and Tina, who are watching through the window, are thrilled at how happy he looks but say that they worry how he will react when Deirdre leaves. When she comes inside for more water, Tina makes small conversation with her even though she is worried for Aiden.

"He looks happy."

Deirdre nods. "Oh, we're having a lovely time. We've been going over old photos of home. He remembers everyone in them. Names and all. He's got a better memory for the past than I do!"

Tina bites her lip. She doesn't want to spoil their happiness by mentioning her concern for Aiden when Deirdre is gone.

"Your daughter's not with you?" she asks, changing the subject.

"No. She's met someone at the hotel named Charlie who is giving her a tour of the area on a motorbike today. Never seen her look so happy."

Tina nods and opens the door for Deirdre as she goes back into the garden. She shrugs at Greta.

"A little happiness is better than none at all," Greta says, smiling her broad smile and revealing her gold teeth.

My mother is phoning people who have been on the waiting list for a room. Aron and Iren's room is empty as is Jimmy's since he moved downstairs. She is discussing this with my father who slept in and has phoned work asking for some holidays. It has been a rough few days on my father and he has dark circles under his red eyes but I know that more than anything he is thinking about what Wilfred told him last night.

Father didn't always believe in my abilities. He once asked a doctor in town to talk to me about the dead people I spoke to. Doctor McCabe said that he shouldn't worry, that I was a lonely child and would grow out of it. I didn't. Father is sitting on a chair in Mother's office, distracting her from her telephone calls. He rereads a letter that came a few days ago from Mr Berman informing my parents that the Kleins' bequest amounted to $126,000 and asking them to inform him of their decision as soon as possible.

"You know," he says, running his freckled finger over the letter, "we could do an awful lot to the house with that money. We could build on so people would not be on a waiting list. We could have ramps outside and a special bus to take residents out. Oh, a lift or even a ramp inside would mean Jimmy could have his room back. He's been miserable since he's had to go into the ward. He hates it –"

Mother raises her hand to stop him but he laughs and goes on. "– and we could even offer some residents that just need a little security a small unit of their own. We could build four of five of them for people like Mina and Wilfred, people capable of living independently. It'd give them their dignity for as long as they are able to live out there and, then, when the time comes, they could move inside."

I can see he has got my mother's attention but she frowns. "I think you're getting carried away, Andy. I don't think the money would stretch that far! Look, aren't you supposed to be working on your speech? The wedding is in two days!"

Father ignores her. "If we at least build onto the house and take in more residents, we could afford more staff. You wouldn't have to do as many hours. You'll need time when the baby comes."

Mother is looking more intently at Father now but I know that if she accepts the Kleins' gift, she'd rather it was for the residents' benefit and not hers.

"Air-conditioning!" Father says. "You said yourself that the bed-ridden residents are baking in the long ward. At the very least we could get some proper patio doors and throw them open in summer."

Mother turns her face away from Father and I see her say: "Catherine."

"What?" Father asks.

"Catherine. She's always so hot." She bites her lip the way she always does when faced with a decision. She shakes her head a couple of times and I know that in her mind she is arguing with herself.

"All right. We'll accept the Kleins' kindness," she says at last, "but let's take things slowly. We'll start with some bathrooms for existing rooms and get a quote for air-conditioning. We can see how much we've got left after that. Now, will you let me get some work done here?"

Father laughs and hugs her. He is still thinking of me and I know he needs something cheerful to look forward to. He leaves her and goes to check on Wilfred.

I sit with my mother as she works her way through a pile of paperwork.

About half an hour later I see Father and Wilfred passing by the window. They open the gate and walk together in the direction of the town. My mother runs to the door but they are already out of earshot. She goes into the Penance Room where Tina is helping Deirdre to sit Father Hayes in his favourite seat.

"Did Andy say where he was going with Wilfred?" she asks.

"Em . . . something to do with the community centre," Tina absentmindedly replies.

"The community centre?"

Tina nods but barely looks up. "Yeah, you know. The one Aron and Iren set up."

My mother frowns. She can think of no reason for Wilfred or my father to go there.

"Better not be going to the pub!" my mother mutters with her back turned to Tina.

I follow my mother into her office. She begins to make calls to people on the waiting list. I watch her strike off those who have found a place and put a note beside those who want to come and see the vacant rooms. I watch the times and dates she writes in to see who might be coming to live with us. "*Joe, Wednesday, 2 p.m. Olivia, Friday 10.00 a.m.*"

I return to the seat under the window and daydream of the type of people Joe and Olivia might be and what secrets they will bring with them. I wonder if Steve will help me when he returns or if his intention is to take Aishling to live in Sydney with him. I dream of a plaque being placed in the garden in my honour for all the souls I have helped and I can see myself making my acceptance speech through sign language with Maria, my wife to be, interpreting for me. When my mother suddenly stands and rushes to the window, almost knocking me off my seat, I reluctantly leave my dream and look out the window to see what is troubling her.

A large muddy pick-up has pulled up right outside our gate. The door is open and a large woman is trying to free her foot to get out onto the pavement. When she turns to face the house I can see that she is a young Aboriginal woman. She is followed by another woman. They look just alike and I think they must be sisters. Together they help a woman who is sitting in the back out of the pick-up. She seems to be having trouble and they pull at her until she has managed to put her two swollen feet on the pavement. She fixes her skirt and mops her brow. The three women face the house and look nervously at its white façade. My mother gasps and puts her hand to her neck. She opens her office door and runs to the kitchen to Li.

"Is Kora here?" she asks.

Li shakes her head. "She'll be here in about an hour. What's wrong?"

My mother is trying to think on her feet. She decides not to tell Li and races to greet her visitors at the door. When she opens it, the two younger women have only managed to get the older lady up two of our five wooden steps. She is panting in the heat but her eyes are fixed on my mother who is smiling nervously. Mother seems a bit tongue-tied and stumbles over her words.

"I'm Em – Emma" she says. "Did you come about . . . about the newspaper article? Sorry, come in, come in, please!"

Mother steps out of the way as the women enter and then she leads them into her office. She leaves them for a moment to ask Li to bring some cold water.

I watch them while they sit and look around the room. They seem as nervous as my mother who eventually returns and sits facing them. She takes a deep breath, unsure where to start. One of the young women opens a newspaper and thrusts it toward my mother. It is open on the page where Mother's article is. Mother cringes slightly at the sight of an eight-year-old Kora beaming into the camera. The caption says *Lost daughter desperate to find family*" and Mother's face reddens with the indignity of it. She looks at the woman's face and knows she is far too young to be Kora's mother. She looks at the other young woman and comes to the same conclusion. She focuses finally on the older woman who looks like she is in poor health.

The woman with the newspaper finally speaks.

"This is our mother, Burilda Hill. This is Lurnea and I am Nadda. We've come a long way. A relative of my husband told us about your article and posted it to us. Said it might be our own Kora."

Nadda looks at her mother who is running a tissue between her hands.

"You want me to tell the rest of the story?"

The older woman waves to her daughter and nods her head. Her chin wobbles and I know she is too upset to speak.

"Mother lived on a cattle station eastwards. Good long way. The owner made her pregnant when she was only nineteen. Threw her and her brother Jirra off the station. Jirra was eighteen. He's gone now. Mother was responsible for him. Her father Natan was killed in town when she was only one and her brother just born. When Natan was killed, her mother threw herself in the river, didn't want to live without him. There were no other family alive in those parts so they were just taken care of by the other Aboriginal women working at the station. Owner of the station was Tom Hill. He was married, old enough to be her father with a wife that was more in charge than he was, so he threw her off before anyone figured out about the pregnancy. But Burilda knew that if her father had been alive Hill would not have touched her. She had no one to protect her."

My mother looks out the window. She has heard the name Natan before. Her eyes move right to left as she tries to recall. When she opens her eyes wide and puts her hand to her throat, I know that she has remembered that Natan was the name of the Aboriginal man Jimmy's father murdered. She pulls her lips into a tight line and shakes her head. I know that she is hoping that this is a coincidence but in her heart she knows and I can see her shrink down under the weight of this knowledge. My mother doesn't believe in keeping secrets but she is sure that this one should remain unspoken. She tries to compose herself and asks a question.

"Hill wasn't a drifter?"

Nadda shakes her head, unsure why Mother asked this question.

"How come your name is Hill if you weren't married to him?" she asks Burilda.

"Blackfellas took the name of the station owner in those times. We were all named Hill," she says somewhat shyly.

My mother takes a deep breath. She tries to say something but changes her mind.

"Mother and my uncle made their way to the station at Grenfell but it wasn't a proper reserve. No teacher there. Just police came to keep eye on men drinking. She had her baby on that station and named her Kora. She had no money and had to keep watch on her brother at this station. Nothing to do there and no work going. Just a few tin-roofed huts and dust. She said Jirra was angry with her for getting them thrown off Mr Hill's land but it wasn't her fault. He wouldn't leave her alone. Uncle would not do what she asked and hung around the station all day with the older men. She got some work in a house few miles out, washing and cleaning clothes with a little farm work and a woman watched Kora on the reserve till she got back. It was a good job and the people were kind. Burilda hoped they might get some living space there but that didn't happen. Each day she would walk a long way to that house and a long way back in the heat. Some days Uncle would steal her wages for drink and disappear off the reserve for days. The woman who looked after Kora got sick and Mother said Uncle should watch Kora and for a while he did and he understood they needed to get off that reserve and into a proper one where Kora could get taught. But soon he was back to his ways and Mother would get mad and shout. He didn't take proper care of Kora. A few days she carried her with her to the farm but the owner's wife hadn't been able to have children and didn't want reminders of what she was missing so she told Burilda not to bring Kora there any more. Couple years later, things were the same. Burilda still walked to that farm each day and some days she would come back and find other women trying to look out for Kora and no sign of Uncle.

"One day she arrived home late. She had to work extra hours at the farm. Everyone was crying and she thought someone must have died. Lots of people on the reserve were sick and there was no doctor.

"A woman screamed when she saw her coming: 'Kora's gone, Kora's gone!'"

Nadda stops talking and all three women well up. Burilda looks out of the window, the pain of the memory still haunting her after almost thirty-five years. "They told her that the police came and found Kora wandering around, half dressed and thirsty. They took other children too. Six altogether and all of them half-whites. The woman said a man wrote all of the children's names down and pinned their names to the smaller ones' clothes.

Burilda, here, she started walking right away. She asked which way and followed the tracks of the trucks for hours until she fell down into the scrub with exhaustion. In the morning, she walked again. She got to the town and the police wouldn't tell her anything. They said awful things to her, that she shouldn't have her daughter back, that her daughter needed proper family, proper care but Burilda loved Kora more than anything and she was working to get them out of the reserve and into a proper place to live. She remembers crying outside the police hut and then a woman, a white woman, said go to the Mission Home. She said it was a long way southwards. A big place where they took Aboriginal children. So Burilda walked there. It took her four days in the heat. She had very little money and took water at any station along the way. We told her many years later that she had walked over one hundred kilometres but she doesn't understand how far this is. When she got to the mission, they would not let her in. It was run by religious people, people who were supposed to be good."

Nadda grits her teeth but Burilda touches her daughter's hand firmly. I understand her look. She is saying don't be angry, it does no good. But Burilda is sad. I can see a lifetime of hardship and despair in her large bloodshot brown eyes. Nadda accepts her mother's direction and returns to her story.

"Four, five days Burilda stayed in the town and in the daytime she stood outside the mission and waited to see her daughter. Every day, children came out to play and Burilda would wait to see if Kora was among them. She said she was three then and was more white than black but there were lots of children like Kora and each time she tried to take a closer look staff would chase her off. They told her 'You are in the wrong place, your daughter is not here,' but Burilda didn't believe them. She said she could feel her. She said she knew her flesh and blood was inside those walls. One day the staff called the police and two men pulled her inside the big house. There were stairs that looked like they went up into the sky and she had never seen anything like them. The police dragged her from room to room. There were so many children in cots and bigger ones running around. She tried to look at all their faces but they dragged her so quickly from room to room that she could not be sure. She kept saying 'Wait! Let me look!' but they didn't listen. When they had taken her through all of the rooms, Burilda cried because Kora was not in any of them. They said 'Now are you satisfied? Your daughter is not here. Now you make it easier on her. Wherever she is, forget about her – let her have a normal life.' She hit out at the men and spat at one of them. He thumped her in the face but she was not afraid. She screamed 'I cannot forget my baby! I will never forget her! I'll keep looking!'"

Burilda cannot keep her tears in any longer and cries openly. My mother leans forward to soothe her but she pulls back and reaches for her silent daughter's hand. Nadda is now fighting to hold back her tears but she keeps going. She has an angry face.

"Then they put her in a truck and drove her for miles. She remembered seeing the sun lowering in the sky to her right and she tried to remember the direction she was going so she could come back. It got dark and the truck stopped. The same two men pulled her from the truck and one of them looked like he felt sorry now. He said: 'Your girl is not there, woman. Now go and find work and know that wherever she is she is safer than on that reserve.'

"Burilda broke down and as she found shelter for the night she knew the man was right, that Kora was safer wherever she was than on that reserve, but she also knew that no one could love her as much as she did and that this was more important than anything that whites could give her. The next day she walked to the nearest town and when there was no work there, she walked to the next and the next until she found another station looking for labour. She saved her money up and when she had enough to move on, she went back to the reserve looking for her brother but the men said Uncle was dead, that he got sick with drink and died. He was only twenty-three. It left a hole in Mother's heart." Nadda put her arm around the old woman's shoulders.

"Burilda found work at a mission. It was run by Catholic nuns. She stayed there for two years and these nuns tried to help her find Kora. Burilda could not read or write then so they taught her a little and also put her in contact with people that might help but everywhere doors closed in her face. No one wanted to help a blackfella get a half-white child back. One woman said that the report on Kora's removal was bad and that no court would give her back to Burilda. Burilda left the mission and moved onto another cattle station. She met our father there. A year later, I was born and two years later, Lurnea came.

328

Burilda made sure we went to school and now that she had a husband earning a little money, she could stay at home and look after us but she was always nervous. She lived in fear that we would be taken from her. She worried about everything. If we got dirt on our clothes, she'd wash them straight away. Even if we were sick she sent us to school, but we knew about Kora so we understood. She never gave up looking for her. Sometimes if we were angry, Lurnea and I would say 'You prefer Kora to us!' and she would cry. She would say there was love in her heart for all her daughters but that she never felt she could rest until she saw her first-born's face again. On my tenth birthday, my mother found out where Kora had been taken that day. It was the same mission she had stood outside for five days, the same one in which two men dragged her from room to room, telling her that her daughter was not there when all the time they must have hidden her. But it was too late. Kora was no longer there. She would have been about fifteen then and had been adopted by a family years before who moved westwards.

"That was my parents," Mother says. Her face is bright red and I know that even though her parents gave Kora a good home, she is feeling deeply ashamed because her sister's real mother and real sisters were out there looking for her.

Nadda says nothing but her expression is disdainful. Burilda looks out of the window again and Lurnea has not stopped looking at her shoes since she came into the house.

"The trail went cold and Burilda gave up. She said she would never see her daughter's face again. She was always sad. It took up her thoughts and took her away from us." Nadda squeezes her mother's hand.

Burilda nods and wipes hot heavy tears from her face. She decides to speak.

"That was until Nadda's husband's family saw the paper and sent it to her. She didn't know her sister's face but recognised my eyes in the photo. Kora looked just like me when I was a young girl. And I knew – I knew it was my girl and we wanted to get here quickly – I wanted to see her as soon as I could –" She sobs, finding herself unable to speak.

Lurnea hushes her mother but still keeps her eyes focused on the ground.

My mother tells the three women the story of how her father took Kora from the orphanage and brought her here to Broken Hill. She tells them something of their life as a minister's children and how they had a happy home but that Kora never gave up hope of finding out who she really was. She tells them of Kora's impending to marriage to Jeff Young but doesn't mention her suspicions that Jeff's grandfather was the man responsible for Burilda's father's death.

When she finishes Burilda, who seems to be barely listening, says, "Can I see her? Can I see my baby?"

"I'm here," a voice says from the doorway.

Kora has come in the back door and made her way to the front of the house. None of us know how long she has been there and I am surprised that I have not noticed her standing in the shadows. Burilda's mouth drops open and she tries to stand. Lurnea helps her mother up as both sisters rise and stare at Kora.

"Kora?" Burilda says. "Kora, Kora!" Heavy tears fall down her face as she moves to embrace her daughter.

Kora simply stands and stares at Emma as the large black woman hugs her so tightly that it almost hurts. She puts her arms loosely around the stranger and looks at the faces of the two other women who are still staring at her. I watch as they scan her from head to toe and know they are thinking about how much lighter her skin is and how much taller she is than them but, more than anything else, how much she looks like their mother, more so than either of them.

When Burilda loosens her grip on Kora, the two younger women move forward.

"I'm Nadda and this is Lurnea. We're your sisters."

Kora nods but says nothing. I can see that she is in shock and that she is feeling awkward. Burilda steps back further but never takes her eyes off her lost child. My mother moves to Kora's side but doesn't look directly at her. Kora decides she had better say something.

"This is my . . . sister, Emma," she says, obviously realising how strange this situation is.

Everyone nods politely but nobody speaks. My mother decides to break the silence.

"Kora, would you like me to show your . . . sis–"

The word "sisters" is choking my mother. I know what she is thinking. She had wanted Kora to find her mother but she didn't bank on her sister having siblings, real siblings who might take her place.

"Would you like me to show Nadda and Lurnea around?"

Kora nods but gives my mother a strange look, an expression that almost looks like empathy. Mother takes the two women out and brings them to the dining room for coffee. As she busies herself at the kettle, I know she is pondering how Natan's death resulted in Kora's birth as Burilda had no father to protect her from Hill and how that same murder resulted in Jimmy's mother's arrival in Broken Hill and a life of hardship for Jimmy from a stepfather who never wanted him. And here they were now, two generations on, neither having any idea of their connections which I know my mother thinks is best for everyone. She knows that Kora and Jeff's marriage will bring their families together and try to mend the past, even if they don't truly know what that past entailed. She knows that the truth is likely to emerge with time but she is hoping that by then the new bonds between the two families will be unbreakable.

As they sit around the table, my mother makes polite but strained conversation. I know she hates these situations. I know she would like to explain her family's part in this saga and that now is as good a time as any to do this.

"I . . . I am sure that you feel resentment towards me . . . and towards my family but I would like to explain. You see, my father was a good man. He spent many years working on the missions. He helped a lot of Aborigines but when he was older and he saw how much Kora suffered for not knowing who she really was . . . he knew that . . . he felt that it was not right, that wherever possible children should stay with their families. The orphanage told him that Kora had been living in deplorable conditions, that she was – neglected and undernourished and there was no record of her mother anywhere. He tried. He and Kora spent hours writing to the government looking for her family and, like you both did, I can say now that I felt a little neglected by all the attention she got. In her teens she was really angry and our parents spent a lot of time talking to her and trying to help her.

"I've never told anybody this before, but she ran away once – she ran away a lot actually but this one time it was for days and both my parents drove out looking for her. My mother could not drive and she was the only one Kora would listen to so they had to go together and it was best to leave me behind. While they were gone, our house was broken into in the middle of the night and I hid in a cupboard until the burglar had taken whatever he wanted. He shot my dog and I had to bury her myself. It was two days before they came back. They found her on a nearby mission looking for her mother. I was only thirteen and I didn't speak to Kora for weeks afterwards. I felt that her anger and her moods took up all our parents' energy. But it wasn't her fault. It wasn't my father's and it wasn't mine. It was just how it was.

"I want you to know that I love Kora. She is my sister. I want her to be happy – as happy as she can be considering all that she has lost so don't hate me or my family. My father thought he was saving her from a dreadful life.

"I want to assure you that my father didn't know that Kora's mother was looking for her and if he was alive now he would tell you how sorry he is but it wouldn't change anything. It wouldn't bring a three-year-old child back to her mother – it wouldn't give me parents who were not distracted by Kora's needs and it wouldn't give you a mother who could hug you without you seeing the pain in her eyes. The most any of us can hope for is to get along and try to look forward together."

Mother stops speaking and looks shyly from one sister to the other. Nadda turns her head and looks out the window. Lurnea looks up and finally speaks.

"Reckon Kora was lucky to have a sister like you," she says. Nadda cuts Lurnea a look.

I smile to myself. They are so like my mother and Kora – one is resentful while the other is trying to make peace.

"You've been good to her so that makes us happy," Lurnea adds.

Nadda flushes and I wonder If Lurnea's words have made her feel ashamed of her behaviour.

"I understand how you feel," my mother says, "or at least I am trying to . . . could that be enough for now? Kora and your mother have been the most hurt. Maybe we need to try to get along for them."

Nadda nods and looks away again. "That'd be all right," she says reluctantly.

The kitchen door opens and Kora is standing on the other side. Mother stands and the two sisters follow her out to the hallway. Burilda is standing at the door and my mother scans her face to see if the reunion has gone well. Her eyes are red and her face is swollen from crying. Mother looks at Kora who also looks tearful but her mouth is tight and she cannot tell if her sister is happy. Kora's face is hard to read and I have seen my mother say that she keeps her cards close to her chest.

"Burilda is staying in town for a few days," says Kora. "They live a long way off. I asked her if she wanted to stay with me, at Father's house." She doesn't look at my mother while she speaks.

"Hotel won't take us," Burilda says.

My mother doesn't know how to respond to this. She frowns at how accepting Burilda is of the prejudice her people sometimes endure.

"The cottage would be better anyway. More private," Mother says but she cringes. I know she is worrying that Burilda will think she prefers that no one sees them anyway. Nothing could be further from the truth but Burilda will learn this when she gets to know my mother and all that she stands for. Mother hangs around. I know she is dying to ask if Kora has asked her family to her wedding but one step at a time, Mother is thinking.

"You need me this evening?" Kora asks.

Mother shakes her head. "No. I'll see you tomorrow."

Kora walks behind her siblings as they help their mother back to the truck. My mother goes inside and watches from the Penance Room. As Kora closes the gate, she looks up and stares in through the window. My mother tenses and is about to step back, anxious that Kora not be annoyed at her for snooping, when Kora gives her a half-nervous smile and waves. Mother touches the locket around her neck and simply nods as Kora gets into her car and signals for the women to follow her.

When they disappear from view, my mother sits down and stares into space. I sit beside her and watch her face change from joy to sadness and I know what is worrying her. She thinks she has lost her sister to her real family and that, while doing something good, she has robbed herself of her only sibling. After a while she stands and looks out into the garden at the pup running around.

"Well, sister, at least you remembered to get me another dog," she says to herself as she returns to her work.

Chapter 31

The morning of the wedding arrives and everybody in the house is rushing around, trying to make the perfect day for Kora. When she arrived at the house yesterday, my mother and father were anxious to find out how she had got along with her family but found she had returned to her distant, uncommunicative self. My mother has told Father all about their meeting, even about how Jimmy's father was responsible for Kora's grandfather's death but she has sworn him to secrecy. Although my parents are disappointed that Kora will not tell them about her reunion, my mother has asked Father not to pry. She understands that this is private for Kora, that this is something she has waited on for a long time and she may never be willing to share those memories with them.

Li has organised a huge buffet and Mina and Kai got to make their Peace Cake after all, a two-tiered iced wedding cake decorated with tiny flowers. Aishling is happy because Steve is here for two days in between his research in other towns. Everybody laughs as he tells them that nowhere has he encountered such interesting stories as in Broken Hill Nursing Home.

Jeff has had a strong word in his father's ear about being polite to Kora's new-found family and everyone is amazed when he shakes their hands and tells them he thinks a lot of Kora and that she was very good to his son during a recent accident. As he shakes hands with Burilda, my mother and father exchange glances and I know they are grateful that Jimmy and Burilda have no idea at this point about their families' shared history.

Martin is on hand to interpret for Jimmy and is continuing to enjoy his new role. I watch as he puts his hand to his head from time to time and grimaces and I worry that the clot on his brain will move before he has had a chance to speak with his brother on Tuesday. He is coughing more also and my mother says his lung condition is worsening but this doesn't stop him having a large whiskey, compliments of Bill who has been drafted in to liven the music up when people have tired of Penelope and Wilfred's classical tunes. Kora's mother and sisters are seated on one of my grandfather's pews which have been moved into the centre of the room.

Deirdre is here and is sitting with Father Hayes. He has a red rose in his buttonhole. Deirdre has become used to Aiden's confused ways and no longer becomes upset when he moves in and out of reality. When he tips her arm and says, "This is what I would have worn," she turns her head sideways, waiting for another memory to resurface but he puts his cane to the floor and moves his body until he is facing her. "If I'd been lucky enough to marry you," he adds.

Deirdre gulps and her daughter, who has reluctantly come along, pats her mother's back gently.

Victoria is, true to her word, dressed in her bright red dress and matching lipstick and has managed to ignore her sister's early-morning scolding. She has taken my mother's advice and has started to write her own novel, a love story between an innocent girl and her handsome Australian officer. Greta helped her to buy an old typewriter which she is slowly learning to use.

Victoria tells my mother that while this one will not have a happy ending, her next novel will. Catherine, who is now feeling better, was due to be wheeled up for the occasion but has started to shout "Clowns! Caution, clowns!" so mother has decided to leave her where she is.

Then, as Penelope wedges herself behind the piano and Wilfred tunes his violin, I notice Mother ask Father where he and Wilfred went the other day.

"You'll see," Father says with a twinkle in his eye.

Mother shakes her head in an annoyed manner, thinking she knows very well where they went but she is wrong. Wilfred has a plan, a lovely plan to make his life worthwhile again.

When the music starts to play Father goes in to collect Kora from their bedroom but she asks him to send my mother in. When Mother rushes in, afraid that Kora is about to change her mind, Kora closes the door after her and sits on the bed in her beautiful cream dress. Her brown eyes are filled with tears.

"I just want to thank you for being my sister," she says. "I need to talk to you. There are a lot of things I want to say, a lot I have to apologise for." Kora swallows hard. I have never seen her upset like this. Usually she is just angry but there is something different about her.

"Stop! Ssh!" my mother says, taking her hand. "There's nothing to say, Kora."

"You found my mother," Kora says, becoming uncharacteristically emotional.

My mother nods.

The sisters hug and Mother dries Kora's tears with a tissue.

"You'll ruin your make-up," she says.

"Stop telling me what to do," Kora says sharply but laughs when my mother tenses. "I'm just kidding," she adds.

My father comes in to collect the bride. He looks smart in a deep-brown suit and cream shirt.

"Is all the mushy stuff over?" Father asks.

As he takes Kora's arm he whispers into her ear and only I see his words.

"I'm glad you didn't have a brother. I wouldn't have missed giving my beautiful sister-in-law away for the world."

She squeezes his arm and whispers back. "Andy, even if I'd had a brother, I'd still have chosen you."

My father looks astonished at Kora's sentiment but tries not to show it. As he leads her down the hallway, I slip inside and sit on my favourite pew under the window. Jeff is standing nervously at the front of the room. He is wearing a navy suit and it is the first time I have seen him without his akubra. His father, who is best man, is sitting beside him.

When he sees Kora enter the room Jimmy's mouth drops open. "Beauty," he says to his son and Jeff understands.

I look around and find that I am sitting directly opposite Aishling and Steve who are smiling at each other in a silly childish manner. I am moving sideways on my pew to block my view of them when I see her, my beautiful Maria, standing on the front steps in a pretty white dress and sandals. My heart beats faster and I go to meet her but she beckons for me to stay and she walks up the steps slowly as though she is walking down the aisle. She is carrying a small bunch of wild flowers and I redden, hoping no one has noticed our silliness. We are both very young and a long way off getting married. I quickly glance around the room and find only Steve has noticed us. He tips a pretend hat towards me and watches as Maria takes a seat by my side.

The music starts and Kora enters the room.

I lean towards Maria and use my voice. "This," I tell her, "is going to be a happy party."

The minister asks Kora if she takes Jeff as her loving husband and everyone cheers when she says "I do" and they repeat this for the shy groom who looks acutely embarrassed. My mother and Li throw confetti over the couple and as it falls slowly down I sneak a kiss from Maria who looks happier than I have ever seen her. I don't even mind Steve's eyes on me. He has not yet had the talk with me that he threatened but today I don't care what he will say to me. Today I just want to enjoy being here with the people that I love.

The party starts and Bill has been warned off coming within five feet of my mother's punch. Kai has been put on guard even though I see him looking longingly at the bucket of cold beers and bottle opener that someone has foolishly left beside Martin. Martin lifts two beers out of the ice, one for himself and one for Jimmy. He clinks his bottle against Jimmy's and then helps him to put it to his lips. My mother quietly tells Martin that while she won't interfere in them having a few drinks today, she doesn't want Jimmy getting drunk and perhaps saying something to upset Kora or her family. Mother squirms when she says "or her family". It is going to take her a long time to get used to this fact.

Penelope sits behind the piano and seems less nervous than she normally does. She has been practising with Wilfred and looks pleased with herself.

Wilfred, acting in the role of conductor as well as violinist, stands to attention and tips his bow twice as a cue for Penelope to begin. He proudly says: *"Busoni – 'Violin Sonata 1' – Allegro Deciso* followed by *'Wiener Tanzweisen'."*

Martin growls. "How 'bout some Banjo Paterson? 'Man from Snowy River' or 'Waltzing Matilda', anything, just make it cheerful, please!"

Bill waves to him. "I'll play them later, mate. They're my speciality. Now let Wilfred here do his thing."

When Wilfred and Penelope begin, the group are surprised at the upbeat tunes they are playing, even Martin who taps his toe. "Not bad," he says "but it's not Banjo!"

Bill laughs and the party takes off. The group ask for one more and Wilfred shyly looks at my father. He smiles, which is something we rarely see him do.

"For Andy," he says.

He breaks into a solo piece. I see his bow move rapidly back and forth and the expression of surprise on my father's face. Everyone taps their toes so I know it must be one of my father's favourite Scottish tunes that the residents have become familiar with over the years.

"'The Flowers of Edinburgh'," Wilfred says proudly.

My father has tears in his eyes. The tune is cheerful but it reminds my father of the home he misses. Wilfred takes a break and Bill takes over. He looks at Burilda and her daughters sitting quietly.

"Burilda, you and your girls are guests of honour here today. This one's for you. It's an outback song. It's not written by an Aboriginal, unfortunately, but I think you'll like it."

"Who wrote it?" Martin shouts.

"I did," Bill replies, reddening slightly.

I watch Burilda and her daughters as Bill plays and they seem to enjoy the music. Like Wilfred, Burilda is shy and I know that she would prefer if she wasn't mentioned. When he finishes everyone claps and Bill moves straight into the Banjo Paterson tunes that Martin and Jimmy have been waiting for. When Bill takes a break, Wilfred takes over so everyone gets to listen to the music they like.

Li serves the food and everybody sits down in the dining room. There are not enough chairs so my mother has to bring some in from the garden. The meal is lovely and my father is in charge of the speeches. When it is Jeff's turn he quickly tells the group that after over twenty years of waiting, he is lucky to have finally made Kora his wife. Jimmy stiffens and I know that he is thinking that his son could have found happiness a lot sooner if he hadn't interfered. Steve leans towards him and says, "Better late than never" and Jimmy stares at him, wondering how he knew what he was thinking. Steve smiles at me then, a smile that is saying "I can help you too. I can give words to the things that you see."

Kai and Mina wheel their Peace Cake in together and show it

off before Father takes photos of Kora and Jeff cutting it. He takes a lovely photo of Aiden and Deirdre which he promises to send to her. She is due to leave early tomorrow morning and I wonder if Aiden has remembered this. When the meal is finished, the music starts up again and soon people are feeling drunk enough to dance. I watch Nadda and Lurnea compliment Kora's dress as they stand with her in the Penance Room. All three look uncomfortable and I know it will take time – it will take time for them to feel like a real family.

Martin is also watching them and as he sits down beside Jimmy he says, "Well, least Kora's not as dark as them," and I am delighted when Jimmy grumbles something at him.

"All right, keep your shirt on," Martin replies, unsure why Jimmy has turned on him.

Jimmy continues to stare at Kora talking to her sisters. Jeff comes to her side and asks her to dance but only because my father has badgered him into it. His father watches as the pair dance together self-consciously and rush from the floor when Penelope finishes her solo piano tune and even with his sideways face I can see that he looks happy.

When the evening draws to an end, my mother calls a taxi for Deirdre. Her daughter leaves her to say her goodbyes to Aiden in the hallway. He stands facing her with his old cane keeping him upright. Aishling is standing behind him but is looking away, embarrassed to be present during such an intimate conversation. Deirdre doesn't look as sad as I expected her to. She has come to terms with the fact that Aiden is a changed man and that distance, both mental and geographical, would prevent them from being any more than old friends temporarily reunited. She hugs him and stands back.

"Aiden, these few days have meant so much to me, seeing you again and knowing that you are all right, having a chance to make amends although I realise now that I was never really angry with you. I was just sad for what we lost. I feel that I can rest easy now, that I can live what is left of my life knowing we had a chance to see each other again."

Aiden looks miles away and Deirdre doesn't think that he has heard much of what she said.

I suddenly realise that Kora is right. Aiden is beginning to withdraw into his shell again, withdrawing to prevent himself from feeling her loss all over again. He shifts from foot to foot, trying to find a comfortable position and looks outside through the open front door.

"It's dry today," he says for no apparent reason.

Deirdre looks at Aishling and I can see she is disappointed that he has not responded to her goodbye.

Aishling smiles sadly at her and mouths, "He'll be okay."

Deirdre hugs him one last time but he grabs her tightly and kisses her passionately on the lips, embarrassing Aishling and causing me to look at my feet.

Deirdre laughs. "Wow! Now I *don't* remember kisses like that, Aiden Hayes!" she says and he smiles.

"Looks like he is saying goodbye after all," Aishling says.

Deirdre lifts her bag and moves to the door to her daughter who looks sullen. Deirdre rolls her eyes up to heaven. She moves closer to Aishling. "She's in foul humour. Turns out this Charlie that she met is actually Charlene and she's broken-hearted to leave her. Love hurts." She moves her eyes back to Aiden. "I know exactly how she feels." She turns back to Aiden. "I'll write, Aiden, I promise," she says as she moves down the steps towards the gate. Aiden nods and waves as he walks onto the porch, with Aishling still by his side. He is smiling and nobody can tell what he is really thinking, not even me. As the car pulls away, Aishling moves to take Aiden back into the party. He stops suddenly and beckons for her to wait a moment. Aishling stands still and as Deirdre's car climbs the hill and disappears from view, his chin wobbles and his eyes fill with tears.

"Now I'm ready," he says.

As the door closes and he returns to his chair, I watch as he takes his rosary beads from his pocket and begins to move the wooden beads swiftly through his fingers. I don't know if he is thanking God for giving him a chance to see Deirdre again or praying that he will see her again, if not in this life, then in the next.

Kora leaves the party to take her wedding dress off and when she returns she is wearing a lovely green dress and matching high heels. She looks beautiful and when Jeff glances her way I can see that he thinks he is the luckiest man on earth.

I look at Maria and she is also watching the scene. She comes toward me.

"Thank you for inviting me," she says.

I sign thank you and she knows that I am pleased that she came even though she didn't spend that much time in the Penance Room and spent a long time walking around the home, looking in rooms. I also saw her staring at my mother although I have no idea why. She opens the door and disappears quickly down the steps without the goodnight kiss I was hoping for. For a moment I am disappointed but I am becoming used to her unusual ways and I realise that I will just have to accept her as she is. As Greta says, a little happiness is better than none at all.

When the newly weds are preparing to leave for their honeymoon, Kora tells the group her plans for her two weeks off. First, she and Jeff are going to Sydney and staying at a hotel on the seafront. Kora is more excited than Jeff who has already been to Sydney and didn't take to the busy city but Kora tells everyone that she has never seen the ocean and that this is what she is most looking forward to. She then shyly tells the group that she is travelling to her mother's town to spend time with her and her sisters. I see her looking at my mother. My mother looks away and I know that Kora feels sorry for her adoptive sister. She finishes by telling everyone that she will be looking forward to coming back home then and that while she has a lot to find out about herself, Broken Hill is her home and is where she plans to spend the rest of her life. My mother knows that this reassurance is directed at her and I see her wipe a quiet tear in the background. Kora turns her back and the women all huddle to catch the bouquet. Bill encourages Penelope and Victoria to stand alongside Kora's sisters who are already married. I can see one of Penelope's hot flushes spreading up her neck and face and I know she doesn't want to catch the flowers. She doesn't want anything to do with men. Even though Victoria's heart will always belong to James, she is more enthusiastic and is pushing her way through the women and giggling like a teenager. I am sorry that Maria didn't stay for this fun. I would have liked her to catch Kora's posy so that I could have dreamt about it later. When the flowers are finally thrown, Aishling who is already a head and shoulders over everyone leaps forward and catches the bunch as it flies through the air. She waves it about and my mother and Kora laugh. She makes her way over to Steve who is laughing heartily.

"Make an honest woman of her!" Martin shouts and Steve reddens. I have never seen him embarrassed before. It is usually he who puts others on the spot.

Everybody cheers and I try to pretend to share their feeling but my heart is sinking. Even though I know I am being selfish, I don't want Steve to take Aishling away.

Aishling comes to her senses and laughs. "Hold your horses! I expect to be courted properly."

She throws the bouquet in Victoria's direction but Wilfred instinctively reaches out and catches it. He flushes and stammers before handing it to Victoria who misinterprets the gesture and tells him that she appreciates his gift but that her heart is spoken for. My father laughs as Wilfred turns bright red and moves quickly away from Victoria. My mother invites Steve to stay in Iren's old room. He is only here until Wednesday and didn't manage to book a hotel. Slowly everybody drifts off to bed.

I am as usual last to climb the stairs and do my usual check on the residents. I look in on Martin and he is asleep with a smile on his face so I go to my room. As I open my door I see Steve slip into Aishling's room. She has the night off and Tina is on guard outside my bedroom. I am not too young to understand what they will be doing and I know my mother would not approve but Greta's words keep sounding in my ears. Take any little bit of happiness you can. I know she is right and I know that there is more joy here since Steve arrived. I hope that when I drift off to sleep happiness will reign over fear and drown out the vibrations of the dreaded night train.

Chapter 32

On Tuesday morning Martin is standing at the front door with Tina, ready for his visit to his brother who lives a few miles outside town. His daughter Una offered to take him but my mother declined and suggested that the brothers might speak more freely if left alone. My mother has asked Tina to drive him there. She is discreet and will wait outside while Martin tries to make peace with his brother. I would like to go with him but I know that it is best to let the brothers talk and I hope that Martin will tell me how it went.

My father is still on holiday from the mine and is talking with my mother in the office about the plans to renovate the house. Together they look through rough plans and I think how happy they look. The expected baby and the money from the Kleins have given them something to look forward to. Together they discuss building a new house and how this would be cheaper in the long run. I smile as they shake their heads in unison. Even though that is the most sensible option, they love this house and it holds treasured memories for them.

As my mother's morning sickness causes her to run off for the third time this morning, Father takes a phone call for Wilfred. By the time Wilfred comes to the office to take his call, my mother has returned and listens in with interest.

"Yes. Of course. Yes. I can do this. Yes." When he puts the phone down he tells my father that he has a meeting at the community centre at two o'clock. My mother looks from one to the other and waits for them to tell her what is going on. Father lets Wilfred give his news.

"I am going to teach violin to the children at the centre. Already eleven children want me to teach them," he says proudly.

My mother opens her mouth but for a moment nothing comes out. "Wilfred, that's a wonderful idea. How did you think of that?"

Wilfred shyly tells her that it was Father's idea, that the night he returned from Lightning Ridge Father told him to look for a reason he survived, to see how he could give something back.

I can see my mother blush and Father knows what she is thinking.

"Yes, go on, you thought we were at the pub."

"I did," she laughs. "I'm sorry. Oh Wilfred, it's a marvellous thing you are doing!"

Wilfred nods. "My father would be glad that I put training to use for good purpose. And I think the centre will like also for Penelope to teach piano. I asked and they said yes."

My mother is a little more worried about this.

"It's all right," Father says, raising his hands up. "Greta will go with her until she feels more comfortable."

A huge smile spreads across Father's face. I know he is going to make one of his jokes. I cringe and wonder why he always seems to joke with people who have no sense of humour.

"Hey, Wilfred, that might get you in. You know, including Penelope like that, it might get Victoria to notice you more!"

"I have no interest in Victoria. Yesterday she looked

embarrassed when I came into room. I tell her to stop. I only like to hear Penelope play. This is all."

Mother and father laugh but Wilfred stands with his mouth in a tight line.

That night, my mother works a double shift with Greta and Father helps Li in the kitchen. We are all thinking of Kora and Jeff and hope they are enjoying their honeymoon. My father told Jimmy about our plans to put a lift in so that he can have his old room back which cheered him up a little. My mother has noticed him becoming quieter and more thoughtful and says she saw him express concern for Martin's worsening headaches by stretching his arm out as far as possible and patting Martin on the back while he waited on Tina to get some painkillers for him.

As the residents move off slowly to their rooms, I visit Martin and wait to hear how he got along with his brother. He has been very quiet since he returned and my mother has not asked him how it went. I sit beside him and watch him lie in his bed, his blue striped pyjamas moving quickly over his troubled lungs. He coughs and spits a black tarry substance onto a tissue.

"Being doing that all day," he says. "You going to stop with me?"

I nod and write him a note, asking him to tell me about Danny.

He sighs and closes his eyes tightly as if he is trying to block out something painful. My heart speeds up. I am frightened that it was not a happy meeting.

"When I got there, his son was there. Brian. Nice lad. Don't know him though. Don't know any of my nieces and nephews. Never invited to anything, weddings, nothing."

Martin coughs and when he wipes his mouth with a tissue, he raises it to his eyes to dry the small tears that he hopes I cannot see. He sits up, hoping it will ease his laboured breathing.

"Tina stayed a few minutes. She knew I felt – uneasy there. I don't know why I went there. It just came to me one night. Tom asked me. With that awful raspy voice he had. Clear as day he said 'Go see Danny' so I did."

"Are you glad you did?" I write but he doesn't answer.

He looks away from me and his breathing quickens. He coughs again and his shoulders shake with the exertion.

"Danny's the same. All cough and only skin and bone behind it. Bloody mine! He was a big man once, like me. And now . . . we're just two old men . . . wasted."

Martin rubs his hands together and thinks a while. He knows what I am waiting on and he is stringing it out because he knows . . . he knows . . .

He takes a deep breath and looks at the empty wall in front of him. I move my chair to get a good view of his words.

He sighs again and opens his mouth, revealing only a few yellow teeth.

"We talked. He almost seemed like he'd expected to see me. I mean . . . long before the arrangements were made. He looked relaxed and . . . resigned to seeing me. I wondered if Tom had come to him too . . . or Liam . . . I wondered if they were haunting him but then I thought why should they? What did he ever do wrong? What did Tom or Liam ever do wrong? It was just me. I have to tell you that. I know you've been waiting so I should tell you."

I sit completely still. He continues.

"My mother . . . he told me this . . . she was broken-hearted when Tom died. She fell to pieces. My strong mother with her sharp tongue and her – her – vengeful ways . . . she was hurt . . . when my father died, that was the end of her. Danny said she sat and poked an empty fire and lamented their passing. She wouldn't allow any singing in the house – nor dancing – nothing like that. And she used to love that . . . music and stuff. She loved stuff from the old country. Only one that she'd talk to was my father's good friend – the Aboriginal fellow. She told Danny that he was the only one who understood her loss. He said it was a mercy that she died before Liam was lost in the war. Even when Danny married and his children were born, she didn't come back to the living. He lived with her there and he said most days he thought she was almost dead, that her mind was gone and only her heart was beating. But he told me – that she missed me – she asked for me when she was dying. It was the second time . . ."

Martin started to cry and he put his fist to his mouth to try and stop the gush, the waterfall of tears that was waiting finally to be set free. He shook the tears from his face and continued.

"Good job Jimmy's not around," he joked through his shiny eyes. "He'd have me guts for garters."

I ignore his attempt to lighten the atmosphere, anxious to hear the rest of the story.

"It was the second time she asked. Danny said . . . when father died . . . she asked Liam to go to town and tell me. Danny didn't know about this until years later when Liam and he were organising her funeral. Liam . . ." he says his name through gritted teeth, "he didn't come for me. He didn't want me there. He had grown up knowing that I – I . . . the others poisoned him against me so he told her that he went to my house but that I wouldn't come. Liam told Danny that years later because he was eaten up with guilt. He told him because when my mother died, she asked Danny to fetch me and he didn't. She asked him to make sure that I was at her funeral, that she wanted as many of her sons as possible to carry her coffin. When Liam heard this he told Danny about the mistake he had made and how sorry he was for that. He pleaded with him to contact me but Danny wouldn't do it. He said I had ruined his life and that he would never forgive me. Liam died in the war and Danny kept what he knew to himself. He said that when I asked to see him, he knew it was time to tell the truth."

"How did you feel?" I write.

"How the bloody hell do you think I feel? I feel bloody

cheated. She asked for me. She wanted me there and they – both of them – they didn't tell me." Then he broke down and turned on his side, his sobs slowly turning to a whimper.

"My head hurts so badly!" he cries.

"I know, Martin, but do you forgive them?" I write.

He tries to pull himself back up on his elbows and I can see every muscle in his body slack. He looks deflated and there is an air of exhaustion about him. He looks at me through half-closed lids and nods.

"I – I'm tired" he says. He takes a deep breath and lies completely still and for a moment I am afraid that he is dead. I poke him and he opens his eyes angrily at me.

"What?" he screams.

I feel the strength of his word bouncing off the wall. I move back and he softens again.

I shove my note towards his face and his expression changes from anger to resignation.

"I do!" he cried. "I do. They shouldn't have done that but I do. I forgive them."

"They need to forgive you. You need to tell me what you did," I write.

Martin opens his eyes wider. I can see him shake slightly. He lowers his chin and braces himself. He knows he has no choice. I will not give in.

I watch him as he remembers the fire that swept through the barn when he was only seventeen. I watch his thickened tongue move back and forth under his cheeks. His eyes are darting from left to right, trying to find some way out of the situation he is in but there is none. I am waiting. He lowers his head and starts to speak.

"I tried to get her out but she was tied into the back of the barn. I ran in twice but the flames threw me back. There was smoke everywhere. The hay was on fire. God, the hay, I remember thinking what would we feed her with if the hay burned but she was burning. She was screaming. I never saw her so afraid before and she was a stupid horse – useless – I tried to get to her but I couldn't – after I realised – after I thought – what have I done? Why did I do that? Why? It was – why – I don't know – I was jealous – I felt left out – I wanted – I wanted to be the same as him – as Tom – to be treated the same. But she was burning and Tom . . . he went in further . . . and my father . . . and then . . . everything was lost . . . too late . . . I could not turn it back – take it away. Tom was dead and my father . . . not that long after him. It was me . . . I . . . caused all that to happen . . ."

And he finally breaks down . . . finally admitting . . . finally acknowledging the truth about that day he changed the course of his life, the day he decided to blame everyone else and take no responsibility for his actions. I know how he is hurting. I have similar things to confess . . . things only Steve knows . . . things that will have to come out soon.

"You started that fire," I say. It is a statement, not a question, because I have always known.

"Yes," he says, "and I'm sorry. I'm sorry to Tom . . . and Liam. I'm sorry to my mother and father . . . and to Danny. I am sorry for them all. I didn't mean to hurt anyone but that day, it started me on that road where I was always angry and I could never figure out how to get off it, how to turn around."

"They forgive you," I say but he is not finished.

"And my wife. I carried what I'd done with me. I was cruel. My children . . . I was as cruel to them as my father was to me. I did the same . . . beatings. Steve was right. I just couldn't face up to it."

"They all know," I say.

"Can I have your notebook?" he asks weakly.

I watch as he writes a letter to his children. On top he lists all of their names, four daughters and two sons. I know he is hoping that his letter will explain his actions but I also know that it will be up to his children to decide if it is enough or if they too will carry their father's regrets into the next generation. He asks me to make sure the letter will get to them. I promise and he lies down. I watch his breathing soften and quiet, his cough ease and his headache disappear. For a while he seems to be asleep and when he opens his eyes I watch as he looks around the room. He is smiling and reaching out for spirits only he can see. I leave him to his vision and make my way to my room. There is no more that I can do for him. As I move to the door he turns his head and looks at me.

"Can you see them, Christopher?" he asks.

I sign "Yes" and he smiles and looks away.

I make my way down the hallway and once again meet Mrs Bianchi looking for her wedding ring. I feel sorry for her because she is one of the ghosts that stay behind. These are the ones I cannot make happy. I conduct the usual ritual of searching the floor until I once again pretend to find it. She smiles and thanks me and disappears but she will be back again because it will never be her ring.

I lie on my bed and when I hear Tina's chair scratch against the floor and the gush of wind from opening doors I know that Martin is dead and that he is finally at peace. I drift off and try to dream of my own peace. I know it is coming. I know it is not far away.

The following morning, the air has saddened once again at the passing of Martin. My mother stands in the hallway with Ellen and hands her the letter he left for his children. She reads it quickly but her heart is not sad. Martin didn't put any joy there so there is no loss for her to mourn. Una is busy in the office making telephone calls with military precision. I watch her tell her brother that their father has passed away. She finishes the call quickly and phones the next sibling. I don't need to be able to hear to know that none of them are upset at their father's passing.

When Una and Ellen leave to make their arrangements, my

mother checks her schedule for the day. She is meeting with prospective residents and I look over her shoulder and remind myself that Joe will be here at ten. I sit in the Penance Room waiting and my heart leaps when I see it is Maria's grandfather being pushed up our pathway by his son. He shakes as the chair is pulled up each step and I suddenly see Maria standing in front of the wheelchair, holding his chest in case he falls. I try to stand but I feel weak. I pull myself off the pew and make my way on shaky legs to my mother's office. She gives Mr Moretti a glass of water and tells his son that she would like to speak with Mr Moretti alone. Frank Moretti leaves but Maria stands firmly behind her grandfather's wheelchair and doesn't budge. She doesn't speak to me so I sit on the window-seat and watch my mother talk to Mr Moretti.

"Welcome, Mr Moretti. It's been a long time since I last saw you."

I am shocked as I didn't know my mother knew Maria's grandfather well.

Joe Moretti smiles and shakes her hand. He waves his right arm around.

"I know. I remember your father well. Good customer," he says. "And you, since you were a little girl I know you. So sweet. Yes."

Maria is looking anxiously on. I realise now that when she came to Kora's wedding she must have known that her grandfather had chosen to move here and that's why she was looking around the house and watching my mother. What I don't know is why she didn't tell me this.

"So you are sure about this. About moving here?" my mother asks.

"Ah yes. I think my son is unhappy but I no want to leave this town. Is difficult for me now to manage. I need more help so this is fine. This is good place. You know, this will be a surprise for you but this is the first place I live when I come to Broken Hill."

My mother raises her eyebrows. "Really?"

"Yes. I was a young man – fresh from Italy. I stay here for four months and I work to rent a house and then I buy my shop. I live there too. It is like I am back to where I begin."

"You were very successful. I remember your shop."

His eyes glaze over. "Yes. It was very good. I have very happy life. One son of course die in the war. I was very sad. My Natalia, she is now passed also but my son he live in Sydney now. He too sad to stay here. You remember of course."

My mother nods. "I do. It was terrible. She was beautiful."

Joe's eyes moisten and he dabs them with an old dirty handkerchief. "My Maria. My sweet girl. Her Communion Day!"

My mother moves and puts her arm on his shoulder. "I'm sorry, Mr Moretti. I didn't mean to upset you."

He waves her away and gathers himself together. Maria stares at me and I am rooted to my window-seat. My heart quickens as I try to understand why my mother is talking about my friend in the past tense. She is standing in front of me and she is still beautiful. I look at Maria and huge tears well in her brown eyes. I can see her heart breaking for me.

"Is okay. I try. I know I try save her," Joe continues. "We have party and she get annoyed when her mama say take off her veil. The comb come loose and need fixing. She no want to take it off. So she go upstairs and she cry. Soon, she fall asleep and my daughter-in-law take the veil across to my shop to mend it. I say, I come too and we fix together so my son and his wife and I go across to my shop which has air-conditioning. They are tired and they enjoy the cool of my house so soon they fall asleep on the armchairs. I sit in my shop and look across at the house in case Maria wake and wonder where we are gone but soon I doze on my chair. A fire . . ." his chin trembles again and hot heavy tears cloud his vision. "A fire break out. I wake and see black smoke upstairs. I shout for my son to wake and I run across the road to

Maria. A neighbour telephone for fire brigade but lots of bushfires that day so no one can come soon. People run from their houses and try to throw water. I run upstairs and I try see her but there is too much smoke and I call, I choke, I call 'Maria!' but there is no sound. I put my body on the ground and I move on the floor. I feel on her bed and she is asleep. I say, how can this be? How can she no hear the shouting for her? I lift her and she almost fall from my arms. She was so still. I didn't understand. I move to the stairs but the floor was old. It was on fire and when I try to cross it break and I fall downstairs a long way. I still hold her. I don't let her fall and when I reach the bottom I cannot move. Her father take her from my arms. I say, 'Is she all right? Is she all right?' But she was not sleeping. My Maria was dead. She . . . the smoke . . . she die and I . . . can no longer walk."

He sobs and I watch Maria pat his shoulder and soothe him but it is me she is looking at. I should have known. Why did I not know? I cannot believe that she is not really here with me. That we are not going to have the future I had imagined together. Heavy tears fall from my eyes. I bend forward and begin to sob.

"But . . ." he says, wiping his eyes, "you also have had such tragedy. I shouldn't cry. I am old . . . you . . . I feel so sorry for your loss."

My mother swallows and touches the locket around her neck. "They were around the same age. I remember. A few months apart. Andy and I had struggled so much with his deafness and we – we did our best. It wasn't the right choice but at the time . . . when he was hit by . . . that train . . . I knew as I held him . . ."

I gasp and turn away from my mother, unable to breathe. I cannot bear to see her say it. I don't want to see her say those words. But a small hand suddenly takes mine and sound explodes in the room like shattered glass: my mother's words. I can hear her. I can hear but I do not want to.

"I told you that you don't need sign language any more, Christopher," Maria says and I hear her.

I am weakened and I kneel down on the wooden floor. Maria stays with me and I can feel her tiny cold hand in mine.

"Listen," she says. "Listen to your mother."

My breathing quickens and I don't look around but I can hear her words. I can hear my mother tell the sorrowful story of the day I ruined her life.

"I remember saying 'Stay with me, Christopher, stay with me' but I knew. I needed him to keep his eyes open so he could see my words but he closed them so slowly. I ran to the house. Aishling and Kora were screaming. I can still see it. The ambulance. The doctors trying to stop the bleeding. The waiting . . . and yet he slipped away from me. I kept praying . . . I said 'Stay with me, stay with me.' It was 3 a.m. when he died. Andy and I sat in that room and watched him drift away from us. Our only son."

I gasp and kick out at Maria.

"*I am not dead!*" I scream but she soothes me and shakes her head sadly at me. I jump from the window and move toward my mother. I scream again into her face. "Mother, I am here, please, Mother! Look at me!" but she stares blankly ahead and wipes tears quickly from her face.

I kneel on the ground in front of my mother and collapse into a heap at her feet, sobbing loudly. Maria kneels beside me and dries my tears with her tiny hands.

"She cannot hear you, Christopher. We are both gone. Only our sadness remains. Sadness for what we caused – for the damage we have done."

My mother touches the locket around her neck, her favourite photo of me. Not a photo of me when I was younger as I like to believe but the last one taken – taken days before the accident.

"But I always feel him near me. I sometimes think that this is what he remembered as he died. Me calling him, begging him not to leave me and I – I have often felt him here. I know he guides me. I know he somehow makes things happen . . . I just hope . . . that I have not stopped him from moving on to where he is supposed to be . . . from finding peace . . ."

My mother starts to cry and moves her hands to her face. Joe Moretti looks at his shoes that he will never walk in again.

"I feel her too. Maria . . . all of the time. Sometimes I hear her playing in the garden. I can sense her. My son, he say I spend too much time alone and that I am imagining it but I know is true. She is watching over me but I am fine now and I want her to go to God. I want her to go to a happier place. I want her to know that I will be all right."

My mother looks at Joe Moretti as if she too should feel this way but I know she needs me and she knows this to. Maria stands and tugs my hand as she looks toward the window. She wants me to go with her but I shake my head. She smiles to tell me that she understands. I look down at her white dress and her shiny hair, full of pretty ringlets. She kisses me on the cheek and lets go of my hand as she disappears from my sight and my mind.

I am alone now and I move from my kneeling position and look around the window, anxious to see her, the only person I can communicate with. But it is Steve I can see looking in at me. Without feeling myself moving through the house as normal I find myself on the steps with him. He is sitting beside me, his eyes imploring me to do something, something I cannot agree to.

"You knew?" I ask.

"Yes," he replies.

I can hear his voice and wonder how this can be.

"You must have known," he tells me. "Did you not notice people ignoring you?"

"People have always ignored me," I sign.

He frowns so I speak. I repeat, "People have always ignored me."

"But your mother, your father, people who love you?"

I lower my head to the ground and nod. I knew . . . a long time ago I knew but I tried to forget.

"Do you want to tell me what happened on the train line that morning? I mean what *really* happened?"

I nod and clear my voice anxiously. I know now what this felt like for the residents. My heart beats faster and I flush with the shame that I have been telling you about because what happened to me was not all my parents' fault.

Steve nods but this time there is no tape recorder. I open my mouth and I am amazed that I am no longer self-conscious about my voice. I can hear each word and I am mesmerised by the clear sound coming from me.

"Simon was my best friend. He didn't mind that I was deaf but when he started school he had new friends. He still came around here sometimes but his new friends were not interested in playing with me so he called to the house less. My mother was worried that I was lonely and sometimes I'd go red in the face when she'd phone Simon's mother and ask that she send him over to play with me. I hated when she did that because I needed someone who wanted to spend time with me. Someone who wanted to be my friend.

"On the day of the accident, I was alone throwing stones into a water hole on the opposite side of the railway line. I saw Simon coming up the track with his friends Jude and Philip. I didn't like them much and I knew that they made fun of my voice. I watched them from the distance playing 'chicken' on the line. Each time the train approached, they'd jump on the line and jump off quickly when it got near. They took turns and dared one another to stay longer on the track, laughing and slapping each other's backs with every success. I thought if I could do that, they might think I was okay and would let me hang around with them so I went against my mother and father's rule that I stay far away from the train line. I walked up to them and asked if I could join in. I could see Simon looking nervously at me.

'Careful!' he warned as I took a turn. He was nervous the whole time I was there and I knew he felt responsible for me. I . . . well, all I wanted was to be like every other boy. I didn't want anyone thinking they had to watch out for me. Anyway, I could feel the rumble of the train before any of them could hear it so I was even better at the game than they were. After about a half hour, they got tired of playing chicken and said they were going home for their lunch. I was enjoying their company and I realised just how lonely I was as I pleaded with them to stay, offering them some of my toys if they stayed a while longer. When Jude and Philip walked off, Simon stood in front of me and told me to go home. 'It's dangerous here,' he said. 'I'd feel better if you went home now, Christopher.' I remember thinking that – that he was talking to me as if I was stupid. I wanted to prove to him that I was just like any other boy.

"When he walked away, I quickly tied my shoelace to the joining bolt on the line and called for him to look back. I stood on the edge of the line and tried to keep my balance. I waved at Simon and I was happy when Jude and Philip turned to watch me. They were a good distance from me but I could see by the expression on their faces that they thought I was brave. Simon started to walk back towards me. I could see his jaw drop but I thought it was because he was impressed at my courage. He started waving his hands frantically. He kept pointing for me to look behind me. I thought he was joking as I knew the train timetables by heart and it wasn't until that moment that I felt the vibrations moving up my feet. I – I tried to run but I fell backwards onto the long strip of grass that ran along the side of the train line. I panicked and tried to untie my lace but it was stuck in the bolt. I tried to pull my shoe off but the lace was caught so tightly that there was no room for me to get my shoe off. I – I was frightened. I could see the train moving quickly towards me on my right while on my left Simon was still running toward me, shouting. In the distance Jude and Philip stood and didn't move to help me. I kept pulling at my shoe but I didn't look at the train. I looked at Simon and when he stopped running I knew. I knew that it was too late and that the train was going to hit me.

"The next thing I remember was my being lifted up in my mother's arms and being carried to the house. I felt very cold and my mother kept telling me to look at her, to stay with her. I could not stop myself from closing my eyes but as I drifted off, I knew that I could do this one thing she asked me. I could stay with her and this is what I have done ever since."

Steve sighs and I know that my story has made him sad.

"You cannot stay here, Christopher. What is left of you must move on," he says and I nod.

"There is one more thing I am waiting on," I tell him. "One more thing."

LIMERICK
COUNTY LIBRARY

Epilogue

Ten months later

I sit and coo at my brother, using my real voice. He came two months earlier than expected and confirmed my mother's suspicions that she was further on in her pregnancy than Doctor Alder thought. I am relieved that he can hear me as he laughs at the faces I pull and the silly sounds I make. He can see me but all babies can see ghosts. After a while most people lose this ability, except people like Steve and me. My mother looks up from her book but Father beats her to it and lifts young Andy Christopher and bounces him on his knee. Mother smiles and her watery eyes are not due to sadness but happiness. One night shortly before my brother was born I sat in the Penance Room and listened to my parents having the conversation that they should have had about me a long time ago. Father told my mother that every day since my death he regretted his decision not to send me away. Mother told him that she was angry with him and that she was sorry she did stand up to him. They both cried and I watched from the window in the darkness as they made their peace with the past and with me. There is a part of me that is glad they kept me here where my special abilities went to good use with the dead and the dying.

I move outside and look at the renovations on the house that are now complete. Downstairs Mina is sitting in the extended kitchen with Li looking through the most recent photographs of her grandchildren and talking about how Kai is the top student in his confectioner's course in Sydney. Father Hayes died but he received several letters from Deirdre after her visit and when her daughter wrote to tell us that she died the day after him, we were not surprised. Upstairs, Victoria and Penelope have been given separate rooms and although Penelope has not yet moved into hers, she stops at the door every day and smiles in at the pink décor and new piano that her nephew bought for her. Victoria is sitting in her room and is dressed in a flamboyant orange dress tapping away on her typewriter. A publisher rejected her novel because it didn't have a happy ending. I watch as she tells her sister that her new novel is about a pianist who falls in love with a much younger violinist. Penelope tut-tuts at such nonsense and gathers up her music sheets for her lesson plans with Wilfred which is her favourite part of the day. Together they now run a small music school, as well as the voluntary work they continue to do at the renamed Klein Community Centre, which has given them both a nice wage. As Penelope makes her way across the lawn to one of the self-contained units where Wilfred now lives, I visit with Jimmy who is also living here until the lift is installed in the main house.

Jeff and Kora are there with their new son. I smile as she tells him that they have decided to call the baby Nathan after Jimmy's real father. Jimmy's eyes water as he holds the tiny sallow-skinned baby in his arms. "He looks like him," he says through his tears. I listen to Kora tell him that the baby must look like both sides as her mother swears he looks just like her brother who died as a young man. Kora and Jeff understand most of what he says but he still misses Martin interpreting for him. Kora spent a couple of days with her mother and sister after her honeymoon and while she enjoyed hearing about her past and her ancestors, I heard her tell my mother that it is too late to form strong bonds with her family and that she found herself to be very different from them and more like my mother than she would previously have admitted and that while she will always mourn this loss, there is nothing she can do to change it, so she has accepted it and is trying to move on with her life. She never found out when her birthday was. Burilda could only tell her that she was born one bright starry night in January. She visits her mother and sisters regularly and is glad to have found out who they are.

Kora no longer works at the home. We have new staff now and a lot of new residents. Greta is still here as is Tina but Aishling moved to Sydney to be with Steve. On the table in mother's office there is an invitation to their wedding. Three weeks after she left, a letter finally arrived for her from her family. My mother posted it to her but no one knows if she read it and, if she did, if she replied. I go back inside and sit down on my favourite pew in the Penance Room and I can hear them all, the voices of those that passed through here, Aron and Iren, Father Hayes and Martin and all of the other souls who I hope are now happy and at peace. I got my wish about the plaque. A week after the renovations were finished, my father planted a gum tree in my honour. Following Steve's suggestion, he nailed a little silver plaque on its trunk saying: "*Christopher Monroe. Died 1967 Age 8 years but lived a special life. Sadly missed by his parents and all of the people he helped at Broken Hill Nursing Home.*"

I look out of the stained-glassed window and I know that it is time for me to go. As I drift away, I can see Maria waiting for me. I can see my grandfather and grandmother and all of the past residents and as I look down I can see my father place his arm around my mother as she holds my brother in her arms. I don't need to be afraid. They are going to be okay.

The End

An Interview with

CAROL COFFEY

1. The theme of migration plays a big part in this book. Have you had personal experience of living abroad?

I lived in Australia for over ten years and this experience gave me an understanding of the losses and gains people experience by leaving their home: the loneliness and longing for familiar surroundings and yet the independence and opportunity that migrating to a great country such as Australia provides. For most of the characters in this book, the experience was even more difficult. Due to the long distance and the cost involved, many of Australia's earlier migrants never saw their families again and many experienced more prejudice than later migrants who were welcomed and who could afford to return home for holidays.

2. Did you do a lot of historical research when writing the book? Was it interesting/time-consuming?

Yes, even though I love history, a lot of research was necessary for this book. It was time-consuming but very interesting and worthwhile. I learnt a lot about Chinese history post Japanese invasion, something I had no prior knowledge of and the fate of many surviving Jewish people post holocaust. Of particular interest to me was the fate of German soldiers who fought for Hitler, either willingly or unwillingly. Not a lot has been written about these people and I feel this would have been useful to help the outside world understand the mindset of German people at that time. I feel that there must have been a lot of reluctant soldiers during this period of Germany's history and that they were to some degree also victims of this terrible tragedy.

3. Do you have a favourite character in The Penance Room?

Overall, Christopher is my favourite character because despite all that he has lost out on, he remains a good person who has everyone's best interests at heart. However, almost everyone in the book endured great hardship, so I feel sympathy for them all. Aron and Iren's kindness to those around them despite such hardship was admirable as was Penelope and Victoria's gentle disposition despite the violence they had endured. Mina's strength in such adversity and Wilfred's quest to find his family to make up for his wrongdoings are equally inspiring. Martin Kelly and Jimmy Young's belief that they were victims despite their own wrongdoings and their eventual embrace of the truth was also emotive. In short, everyone in the book suffered either from their own doing or by others, but in the end made efforts to make peace with their past.

Wilfred is the character I feel most sorry for. Mina had her husband and brother to face her post-war years with. Aron and Iren had each other and their community for support, but Wilfred had no one to confide in and this isolation prevented him from facing his demons and trying to make a success of his life after such a dark past.

4. *What character/scene was the most difficult/interesting to write?*

Two characters stand out for me. Writing about Kora's experience, while uplifting in many ways, was also very emotional and upsetting. I think writing about Wilfred in his youth was difficult but what I wanted to portray was that everyone has their story. Everybody has a reason why they took a particular road in life and thirty or forty years later it can be difficult to reconcile those decisions with the person they have become in later life. This is often where great personal suffering and regret can occur and the penance phase of life begins.

5. *Redemption is also another focus in the book – forgiving yourself and dealing with and facing up to the past. Most characters in this book struggle with their past. Why is that, do you think?*

Someone once said to me that we are forced to face our pasts when we are least in a position to deal with them, for example when we are old and perhaps unable to make amends to those we have wronged. This theme interested me and I decided to create a cast of characters that are forced into a situation where they have to face up to the wrong they did and forgive the wrong that was done to them. Peace of mind is a less obvious theme in the book but failing to face up to your failings and refusing to accept what you cannot change makes peace almost impossible to obtain. Also interwoven throughout the book are the themes of racial, class and religious prejudice.

6. *Australia and the Aboriginal people are an integral part of everyday life in the nursing home. However, Jimmy's prejudice*

affects Jeff and Kora's relationship. What are your views on this issue?

My view would obviously be that wrongs were done to the Aboriginal people but I also feel that in recent times the Australian government has done a lot of work to redress the wrongs of the past. This perhaps doesn't help the thousands of children taken from their families, but I think my overall point is that what is important now is to try to move forward in a way that values the rights of all people and that harbouring feelings of bitterness does no one any good, least of all the victims. It is certainly my experience that Australia is now one of the most accepting and welcoming multi-cultural countries on the world.

7. *Where did the title* The Penance Room *come from? What is its multilayered meaning for you?*

Each character in the book has some sort of regret or resentment that they are harbouring as they while away their remaining days in a room occupied by other people whose race, religion or class they are intolerant of or with people who are intolerant of them. I worked in nursing homes in Australia and noticed that residents often ended up sitting side by side with people whose countries they once fought against or whose religion or race they hated. I witnessed personally the difficulties this can cause for people as they near the end of their lives and this had a big impact on me at that time. I deliberately cast Emma's father as a minister in order to create the church-like feel of the "Penance Room" with pews from his church and stained-glass windows, which are actually a regular feature of many of Australia's older federation-style houses. The placing of these people together in such a room created the atmosphere of people waiting in limbo for a confession which would lead to an opportunity to change long-standing resentments and prejudice and offer an opportunity for reconciliation and redemption.

8. Who are your favourite authors and why (worldwide and Irish based authors)?

Unfortunately, I don't get much time to read at the moment but I like Irish writers such as Sebastian Barry (*The Secret Scripture* was brilliant), John Banville, Alice Taylor and Joseph O'Connor. I enjoy reading the American authors Anne Tyler and Annie Proulx. I prefer books about the struggles of troubled or colourful characters. I also enjoy the classics such as novels by the Brontë sisters, George Elliot and F Scott Fitzgerald and I'm happy to reread these from time to time. In contrast, I like the darkness and twists and turns of Lee Child thrillers. I like a book with a fast pace and an unexpected ending!

9. Was Christopher your starting point for writing The Penance Room or did he develop out of the material as you explored the book's setting and themes?

Christopher was my starting point for the book but I began to develop the rest of the characters soon after. I liked the fact that although Christopher was a very young boy who was also deaf, he was in fact more grown up than the adults in his life and took charge of the work he felt needed to be done in the nursing home. The presence of a young, innocent boy with an idealised view of the world was important against the backdrop of so many characters whose lives revolved around harbouring old grudges and feeding off the wrong that was done to them at some point in their lives.

10. How important is the Australian setting for this book? Could you have written it using another country as a background or is Australia integral to the book?

Australia as a setting for this book was very important and I don't believe that I could have set the book elsewhere with such conviction. Firstly, I wanted to set the nursing home in a dry, arid environment which I hoped would reflect the parched souls living in the nursing home. Also a nursing home set in damp, dark Ireland wouldn't have seemed so attractive to read about! I also chose Australia because of its long history of immigration and resultant multicultural identity, which was necessary to tell the stories of the characters. Finally, my time in Australia meant I could write with knowledge about the beautiful landscape and the people.

11. Thinking of your previous book The Butterfly State *and this one, you seem to have a particular insight into the thought processes of people with disabilities. Have you always has this interest /insight?*

I have worked in the field of disability for over twenty years as a special needs teacher, manager of group homes for people with challenging behaviour and in various institutions and government organisations and I feel privileged to have got to know so many people with special needs, some of whom later became my friends in adulthood. I was lucky that I knew from early on that working with people with special needs was what I was interested in although I don't know where this interest stemmed from.

Yes. I think that I always had an insight into the needs/thoughts of people with disabilities and that this empathy and understanding helped me in my everyday working life. I hope that by incorporating this knowledge and perception into my writing, I can bring the issues of people with disabilities into the minds and hearts of others too.

12. Do you find it very illuminating to understand the world of the disabled? How does the theme of disability relate to this book?

Yes, I do and as I've said above, I feel very lucky. In this book, Christopher has lost his hearing due to a pre-existing condition which was worsened by meningitis. This is particularly unfortunate and sad, as losing a sense that a person once had I feel is worse perhaps than being born deaf. The isolation that people with hearing impairment experience, particularly those who are deaf from childhood, is often overlooked and in a young child can affect social development, peer acceptance and as is the case with Christopher, lead to social exclusion and loneliness.

13. Would it be correct to say the book suggests that secrecy in itself can be the most soul-destroying thing of all?

Yes. Many of the characters in the book are harbouring secrets that are gnawing away at their very souls. For some, the secrets were too shameful to admit to those close to them. For others, keeping silent about their pasts kept them from falling apart, or so they thought. For people like Wilfred, having no one to confide in and the fear of being judged prevented him from revealing his dark past. What they all have in common is that these secrets are in themselves a prison, binding the soul in torture and preventing the characters from finding peace. Only when they reveal their sins can they free themselves from the chains of their transgressions and, in hearing each other's confessions, realise that they have more in common with each other than they would previously have thought.

14. *Do you think the era spanned by the character's lifetimes (roughly early to mid twentieth century) was one particularly destructive to the human spirit?*

Many previous generations have seen wars, famine, emigration and unnecessary hardship, but I believe that the generation of the characters in this book lived through a time of particular worldwide unrest. Some of the characters lived through two world wars while others endured forced economic migration to a country whose language they could not speak, often simultaneously having to cope with the fact that they were unwanted in the country they had hoped to call home. These were also the generation that saw the most change from a technological viewpoint and as they aged the world must have seemed like a frightening place that had passed them by and no longer had any use for them or their memories. They also lived through a time when respect for the older generation was not what it had been in their parents' time, so all in all, yes, I believe that this was a time of radical change that was difficult for these particular people to deal with.

15. *Was the writing very demanding technically, considering the book itself (like its characters) has a secret that it must protect until the end?*

Yes, it was difficult to maintain but it was necessary for the pace of the book and I hope made it more intimate. Difficulties set aside, I enjoyed writing this book immensely and I fell in love with Christopher and all of the tragic characters he was trying to help.

16. Tell us a bit about your next book – have you started writing it?

My third book is about the cycle of dysfunction in generations of families. The main characters are two dysfunctional sisters whose own traumatic and disrupted upbringing inadvertently results in emotional difficulties in their children. Only by addressing the wounded children in themselves can they become the mothers their sons really need. The book's theme of the long-term damage of poor parenting and the difficulty in repairing the lost child runs throughout the novel.

If you enjoyed *The Penance Room* by Carol Coffey,

why not try

The Butterfly State also published by Poolbeg?

Here's a sneak preview of Chapter One

The Butterfly State

CAROL COFFEY

POOLBEG

Chapter 1

1981

Tess Byrne had thought it would be a sleepless night until she awoke to the sound of the cleaners mopping the long corridor outside her room. It was a comforting sound that she had become used to over the ten years she had spent at the institution. She placed her bare feet onto the cold tiled floor and walked gingerly across her room to look out into the bright, frosty February morning. This was the first thing she did each day. Tess enjoyed the ritual of seeing the same things: traffic passing by on the road, cyclists taking a short-cut through the grounds on their way to work, nurses arriving in taxis or on foot. However, this morning was different because this was the last morning she would ever see these things, this was the last day she would ever spend in this place. Today she was going home.

Tess dressed slowly and methodically, carefully unfolding each item of clothing separately. She took her small suitcase from beneath her bed and packed in silence. She did not have much to pack, mostly her drawings and coloured pencils along with a few clothes. When she finished she sat on the bed and stared around the sparsely decorated room. Apart from her bed and locker, the only other piece of furniture was an old wooden wardrobe that smelt of mothballs. The walls of the tiny room were painted white, which made the quiet room appear colder than it was. Apart from a few of her own drawings that she had decided to leave behind, there was nothing on the walls except for a round white plastic clock and a large wooden crucifix that she had taken a long time to get used to. What she liked most about her room was the large shuttered window, which had a deep windowsill in which she often sat and painted.

Tess settled down to wait to be called for breakfast which was more than half an hour away. She took a small notebook from her suitcase and opened the first page. Written there in large red letters was a list with the word "Apologise" written neatly above.

Apologise
Seán
Kate
Ben

Dr Cosgrove had asked her many times what the list meant but she would not tell him. It was her secret and you had to keep secrets. She put her list back into the suitcase and took a deep satisfying breath. Today was the first day of her new life. She was going home and she had work to do.

Dr Martin Cosgrove lowered his large body into the black leather chair in his stuffy office overlooking the institution's exercise yard. He leant forward, his thin blond hair falling over his dark-rimmed glasses, and watched as rows of children played under the watchful eyes of two orderlies. He sighed as he thought of the responsibilities of his job and knew that he could not say with any certainty that he had helped any of the hundreds of disturbed children who had passed through this institution's doors.

And Tess Byrne was no different. Looking through her file, he found it hard to believe that she could ever have hurt anyone. There had been a few small incidents in the early years which resulted in her being placed in a room on her own. Later, when her behaviour improved, none of the other children wanted to share with her, saying she was odd and stared at them. He had spent years trying to talk to the selective mute, with some success, yet in almost ten years he could count the number of times he had heard her speak at any length. Cosgrove exhaled loudly. Tess's family, who were farming in a remote part of County Wicklow, would collect her today and for all he knew she would spend the rest of her life cut off from people, but there was nothing he could do about it.

She was twenty-one years old and, apart from her detached personality and occasional loss of emotional control, she showed no signs of mental illness. He understood a little about her condition, autism, and knew that she had a younger brother with a more severe form of it, but he could never claim to have understood her. All of the children who passed through his office had behaviour problems, most of them due to mental illness, but he felt that Tess had never really belonged here. This saddened the weary psychiatrist and made him wish he could have done more for her over the years.

It worried him that he had never met Tess's siblings. This had spurred him to contact the local GP, who informed him that while Tess's older brother had a drink problem, her sister was a strong, capable woman who would take good care of Tess. Cosgrove wanted to talk to Tess's siblings in person so he phoned. He found Kate Byrne to be a soft-spoken woman whose voice gave the impression of a mildly depressed person and not the strong woman Dr Doyle described her to be and this concerned him a little. This was a big move for Tess and he had to be sure he was doing the best for her. Cosgrove decided to organise for the local community nurse to check in on Tess when she arrived home. That way he would have a pair of eyes within the house to be absolutely sure that she was okay.

When he had told Tess the news, the young woman had stared back at him, absorbing the information and fidgeting with her jumper. Tess had turned into a beautiful woman with porcelain skin framed by thick black hair, her expressionless face making her seem almost doll-like.

"Are you pleased, Tess?" he had asked, smiling at the girl, whose expression had not changed and who continued to stand staring as usual over his shoulder. She did not answer but simply nodded and walked away.

Cosgrove raised his body slowly from his chair and stood there, holding Tess's file tightly in both hands, lost in thought until awakened by the sharp shrill of the exercise yard's bell. He lowered the file slowly into the tall metal filing cabinet. He gently shut the drawer, picked up files on the two new children who had arrived today from his desk and prepared for his rounds.

Dermot Lynch was a serious man who at age thirty had found himself not only landless but also homeless following a dispute between him and his headstrong, domineering father. Despite being long past retirement, Dan Lynch had still been interfering in how his eldest son ran the farm and Dermot had finally had enough.

Dermot thought of going to London or New York or even as far as Sydney. He had family in all those places, but he knew he was not cut out for the building game and definitely not cut out to be cooped up in a factory. Instead he had come here to Wicklow, where he worked in his aunt and uncle's pub and also worked part-time as a farmhand for the Byrne family. That farm would never be his but at least it kept him in the work he loved.

Like his own family farm in Galway, it was a livestock farm. The climate was milder over here in the east with much less rain. He liked it, worked hard, and generally kept out of the way of his employers – not that they bothered him much. The brother, Seán, had a drink problem as far as he could see and rarely helped out. The sister Kate wasn't a bad-looking woman and ran the house, caring for a younger brother, Ben, who never spoke and rocked and hummed to imaginary music. The silence in the house was always palpable and Dermot usually kept his visits to a minimum, eating whatever meal was put in front of him and trying to ignore the boy's staring eyes before darting back out to his work. He couldn't actually say he minded the strange atmosphere at the farm. No one asked him any questions, which suited him fine. The last thing he needed was small-town gossip about how he lost his own farm to a younger brother. It may have been 1981 but things changed slowly in Ireland and he had no wish to be the focus of gossip in the small County Wicklow community that he now called home.

Dermot spent each day in the same way, tending to the livestock, cleaning out barns and going to marts with Seán Byrne whenever he was sober enough to go. This morning, however, was different. Dermot thought it strange that the family did not drive to Dublin themselves to pick up their sister who a little local gossip had informed him "was not all there". He felt uneasy about this task and uncharacteristically wished one of the Byrnes would accompany him. Why weren't they collecting her themselves? Why was she living in an institution? Would she be some kind of nutcase that might attack him on the way back to the farm?

All these questions clouded Dermot's usually calm mind until he arrived at the institution with a throbbing headache and sick stomach. His father would be laughing his head off if he knew what he was doing this morning and the thought of this made Dermot angry.

In the waiting area of the hospital, he shifted uneasily from foot to foot. Eventually a large official-looking man approached him with a smile that looked more nervous than happy.

"Hello, I'm Dr Cosgrove," the man said, shaking Dermot's hand a little too enthusiastically. "I'm a psychiatrist. You must be Seán, Tess's brother?"

Dermot could feel himself turning bright red. He was not used to speaking to educated men like this psychiatrist and the man seemed to be expecting his employer instead.

"Eh, no, I'm – I mean – I work for the Byrnes – they sent me to collect her – Tess, I mean." Dermot recognised the look of shock on the doctor's face and had no idea what else to say.

Eventually, after what seemed like hours, the doctor spoke. "Are they ill, the family – is something wrong?"

"No," Dermot replied, not knowing what answer would cast his employers in a kind light when he himself thought it downright bad manners not to have come here themselves. "They just asked me to come. I'm Dermot Lynch, I work at the farm . . ." His voice trailed off as he could see the look of disbelief deepening on the doctor's face.

"She does know you though, she's seen you before?" the doctor asked.

"No, sir, eh, Doctor – I just started on the farm a few months back. Do ya want to call them? I mean, check who I am and all that?"

Dr Cosgrove stared incredulously at the young man. He could not believe that Tess's family, knowing her condition, would send a complete stranger to collect her. He suddenly had grave misgivings about releasing her into their care but knew that there was nothing he could do. She was, after all, an adult now and could no longer stay in this section of the institution. She was supposed to be moved into the adult wing once she turned eighteen and he had done everything in his power to prevent this, citing that her disability would make the adult ward unsuitable for her. There were times during her early years when he thought she would end up there and would remain in care for the rest of her life, but she had eventually settled in and he had seen no reason not to release her into the care of her family. Until now. He was aware that the family had not visited over the years and the fact disturbed him though he knew Tess's siblings were under pressure caring for their younger brother and running the farm and that their parents were dead. In reality, Tess could have been returned to her family some years back but they hadn't responded to his requests to attend progress meetings. The older sister sent Tess a present on each birthday and at Christmas but he had often wondered why they couldn't visit even a couple of times a year. But to do this! She needed to see a familiar face, not the face of a stranger he knew she would be afraid of. The doctor ran his fingers through his hair and turned slightly to look around the large foyer, as if an answer lay in one cold corner or another, and then he saw her, packed, waiting, watching.

"Tess! Em, this is Mr, em, I'm sorry, what did you say your name was?"

"Dermot, Dermot Lynch."

"Mr Lynch. He has come to take you home today. How did you get downstairs?"

This was an afterthought. He was always meeting Tess on stairs she shouldn't be on, in rooms she had no access to, staff never knowing how she got there. After many incidents he stopped investigating her whereabouts as she never once went outside the grounds and did not seem to be doing anything wrong. So everyone got used to seeing her anywhere she wasn't meant to be and not finding her where she was expected.

"I'm sorry, Tess. I was expecting your brother or sister to come. I'm not sure what's happened but I will telephone immediately and ask that they come on another day to collect you."

Tess shook her head at the doctor and walked slowly towards the shy young man.

Dermot felt as though he was on one of those television programmes where a joke was pulled on you and everyone watched you look like a complete idiot.

Dr Cosgrove thought that she didn't understand. "Tess, this is not your brother but I will telephone him to sort this out. I'm sorry, Tess." He knew she had been looking forward to this day.

"I'll go," Tess said flatly.

Dr Cosgrove was taken aback but recovered quickly. "I'm sorry, Tess," he said again and knew that he was not apologising for this mix-up but for the years he had failed her. "Goodbye and keep in touch. If there's anything you need or . . ."

But she was already walking out of the building, sailing past nurses and orderlies who had been part of her life for so many years. She did not look right or left but carried on straight with her suitcase. With ease she climbed up into the truck, pausing only to look for her window from a different angle, from the outside. She had promised herself she would do that although she didn't know why and she pondered this as the truck started up and headed for home.

Árd Glen was a small farming community in the south west of Wicklow county. Although a beautiful scenic place, surrounded by mountains and lakes, its population count of about three hundred people remained generally unchanged over the years. There was little to do here, most families having small livestock farms, the land too hilly for crops. Spring was busy with new lambs to tend to. Summer brought the usual snippets of tourists, mostly Americans looking for their great-grandfathers' or grandmothers' graves, but in autumn and winter a heavy grey sky descended on the village, confining all within to their memories, good or bad.

It was these memories that made Seán Byrne pace the kitchen floor of the modest house in which his family had lived since he was a baby. The house had a long dark T-shaped hallway. The room to the left of the hall, once a bedroom, was now a sitting room that they rarely used. To the right was Seán and Ben's room. Kate and Tess's room was around the corner to the right at the end of the hallway and faced the small bathroom which Seán had built on to the back of the house, his father being too mean to allow the family such "luxuries" in his lifetime. The kitchen was at the end of the hallway to the left. It was dominated by a large old-fashioned range that had blackened the once whitewashed walls. A small sink stood underneath the window that faced out onto the back yard and was flanked either side by two cupboards, their doors peeling and flaking. An old-fashioned wooden kitchen table and four worn upholstered chairs sat in the middle of the kitchen, using up the limited space.

Seán was proud of the changes he had made to the house and farm as a young man. Preferring farming to school work, he had left the books for the fields at thirteen. His family didn't have the best of reputations in the village and he had worked hard to change this during the late 1960s. But it had all been for nothing. He had spent his youth trying to develop a farm and a reputation that was destroyed faster than a fire spreads through a barn of hay. It was hard to imagine himself now – young, fit and full of hope – but he had been that man. Now he spent his days trying to hide his drinking from the nag his sister had turned into and from the farmhand who, although he said nothing, could see that his employer was an alcoholic. Over the past ten years they had managed to maintain some semblance of normality within the house: Seán working the farm as best he could, if only to keep some money coming in; Kate, resentfully running the house and caring for Ben who would never be a man and who would need to be cared for long after they were both gone. Somehow they had managed. Now, when they seemed to be getting on and putting the past behind them, it had reared its ugly head in the form of their younger sister. Old memories would be stirred up in the village and people would begin talking about it again. Seán could feel his face redden. If only they didn't have to have her back. If only the institution could have kept her there. If only she was fit enough to have lived out her life in Dublin on her own or in one of those residential homes. He had tried to put the nosy psychiatrist off, ignoring letters regarding her wellbeing, not visiting. You'd have thought they'd have got the message. But no. He couldn't very well have said "We don't want her back." It wouldn't have seemed right, would have got people talking just the same.

He could feel the blood rising in his face, not sure himself if it was in anger or shame, when Kate interrupted his thoughts.

"No point dwelling on it, we have to make the best of it. Maybe she'll have changed, mellowed a bit. She was just a child, remember. She might be a good help with the lad. God knows she might understand him better than me."

Kate always knew exactly what he was thinking and even feeling. Kate, always one step ahead of him, cool and calculating, smarter than her older brother by far. Seán looked at his sister who he felt was just like their mother had been, calm and beautiful. He was always conscious of how different he looked to his siblings and parents. He was the only redhead in a raven-haired family. He had green eyes and freckled skin whereas his siblings had blue eyes and clear white skin that neither burned nor tanned. He stared at Kate, envious of her composure. His sister had even more reason to resent Tess's return than he as she was engaged when the "accident", as they liked to refer to it, happened. Kate was a different woman then, popular and about to be married to the eldest Moore son who would eventually inherit a large farm and money with it. But it wasn't just that. She was in love with Noel Moore. His family hadn't been the happiest about it in the beginning but Kate soon won them over, even Noel's mother who had thought there would never be anyone good enough for her eldest son. Her future looked bright and happy but Tess had been waiting in the wings to destroy it all.

Dermot sat uneasily into the driver seat of the battered truck and shot a nervous smile in Tess's direction. She didn't look dangerous. She was small and like her older sister was not bad-looking. Dermot thought that she looked like a younger Kate, with long hair that was so black it made her white skin look even paler than it was. He noticed she did not look at him when he spoke and that her dark blue eyes looked neither happy nor sad. He hadn't realised that he had thought so much about how she would react both to leaving this place and going home but she didn't seem to care much one way or the other and spent the journey staring out of the truck's muddy window.

The silence was making Dermot uneasy.

"Shouldn't take us too long to get back at this time, not much traffic."

No reply.

"You must be looking forward to seeing your family again – it's been a long time."

Silence.

"Do ya not answer someone when they ask you a question?"

"Yes, I do."

"Well, why don't you answer my questions?"

"You didn't ask me a question. 'Shouldn't take us too long to get back at this time, not much traffic' and 'You must be looking forward to seeing your family again, it's been a long time' are not questions."

Dermot stared back at the strange girl, amazed that she had repeated word for word what he had just said and a little annoyed that she was right: he hadn't asked her a question.

"Sorry," he said. "You're right, they weren't questions."

"I know," Tess said coolly and turned her head towards the window.

She didn't want to talk to this man who she had never met before. She wanted to savour every minute of this drive, hoping to get through noisy Dublin city quickly and arrive at the edge of Wicklow with its cool mountains and lakes, hoping they would be as she remembered them. Dermot, sensing this, focused on driving as fast as the law allowed. He wasn't great with people at the best of times and this one was different, impossible to talk to. He couldn't wait to get this job done and get back to what he loved best, tending to animals.

If you enjoyed this chapter from

The Butterfly State by Carol Coffey

why not order the full book online
@ www.poolbeg.com

*See website for details

POOLBEG WISHES TO

THANK YOU

for buying a Poolbeg book.

If you enjoyed this why not
visit our website:

www.poolbeg.com

and get another book delivered straight to
your home or to a friend's home!

All books despatched within 24 hours.

POOLBEG

WHY NOT JOIN OUR MAILING LIST
@ www.poolbeg.com and get some
fantastic offers on Poolbeg books